BENE

Beneath These Wings
Cover by Crimson Phoenix Creations

1

Prologue

Tresa had never wanted to celebrate her birthday during an alien invasion. But life didn't care about what she wanted or didn't want, and her birthday had come anyway. Her dad, Jefferson, had somehow managed to make a cake and even found candles, which was mind-blowing given that it was impossible to get to a grocery store and even if he had, there probably wouldn't be anything left on the shelves.

Still, he'd done it.

She had no idea how.

Her two sisters even managed to make it home in time. Tresa wasn't surprised to see Phoenyx. If Phoenyx said she'd be there, she'd be there.

Unless the Garce stopped her.

She was surprised to see Cherish. Cherish was the oldest and their mom's favorite. Her little sisters weren't high on her priority list.

Yet, they were together as a family, and for a few minutes there, Tresa could block out the aliens outside, the Garce that devoured half their neighborhood already, the dark, shadowy monsters that looked like giant dog demons with red, glowing eyes. It was hard to forget them, but she managed.

For a blissful fifteen minutes, at least, they were just a family and she was just a girl, turning fifteen, surrounded by her family and friends.

"Make a wish," Phoenyx said, leaning her head against Jeff's shoulder and watching Tresa with sparkling eyes. The world hadn't broken her yet like it had so many others. Phoenyx was still strong, still smiling. Still unwilling to give up. That's how Tresa knew everything would be okay.

"I wish..." Tresa closed her eyes. "*I wish I was strong enough to kill the Garce.*"

All hell broke loose.

Before she could open her eyes, glass shattered. Before she could open her eyes, screaming tore through the room. Before she could open her eyes, Phoenyx was yelling at them all to get to the roof and her dad had gone for his gun.

Tresa didn't want to open her eyes.

But Phoenyx was shoving her, pulling her, doing everything humanly possible to get her to move, and Tresa knew if she didn't open her eyes, they would both die. Phoenyx wouldn't leave her.

Tresa's eyes flew open, but her body wasn't as quick to respond. Garce had found them. The shadowy aliens were already tearing through the windows with claws and teeth. They should have boarded them up weeks ago, but her mom had wanted the view. She'd said the Garce couldn't get through windows. They had reinforced glass.

Reinforced glass wasn't stopping them now.

"Tresa, *run!*" Phoenyx screeched, shoving her again, harder this time and Tresa stumbled out of her trance and ran for the stairs at the back of the house.

The Garce were already there.

"*No,*" Phoenyx half-moaned. She spun in a circle, but there was no way out. Tresa stood frozen. Her mom and Cherish were gone, hopefully up to the roof, leaving Phoenyx and Tresa alone to make a stand in the kitchen.

She felt her sister tense beside her, and a horrible foreboding coiled in Tresa's stomach. Before she could object—she didn't even know what *to* yet—Phoenyx lunged.

Straight for the Garce.

She dove right between them and they whirled toward her, snapping and snarling. Phoenyx sprang to her feet in one fluid motion and ran for the door. "Tresa! Get to the roof!" she screamed over her shoulder.

The Garce followed her out the door and into the night and Tresa, sobbing, realized she would never see her sister again.

From the living room, the roar of a fifty caliber rifle shook the house. Jeff had gotten his biggest, most powerful gun. Tresa wanted to run. She wanted to make it to the roof. She wanted to do what Phoenyx said but she also couldn't leave her out there alone. Phoenyx was fast—she'd been a track star before the world ended—but she wasn't as fast as the Garce. Nothing was. Her sister had just sacrificed herself for Tresa.

"*Don't make it be in vain, Tres.*" Phoenyx's voice echoed in her head, and finally, *finally,* Tresa got her feet to move.

It was too late. More Garce, either the ones Phoenyx had tried to lead away or new ones, Tresa couldn't tell, stood between her and the stairs.

One lunged and she tried to move, tried to dodge out of the way or dive between them like Phoenyx had done, but she wasn't fast enough. She felt the teeth clamp around her upper thigh, felt its saliva burning away at her skin and she screamed.

She screamed and screamed and clawed and fought but there was no moving, no escaping. The pain made her weak, made her crazy, made her long for the sweet blackness of death. But she kept hearing Phoenyx's voice in her head, and something in her—something she hadn't known she had, some hidden strength—kept fighting.

The roar of the rifle shook the cabinet doors and she felt the bullet hit the Garce. Saw the black blood splatter, felt it burn her face, but the pain didn't lessen, the powerful jaws didn't release. Again and again, her dad fought for her, but the Garce were stronger than his bullets.

Not much stronger, though. She felt it weaken the monster holding her, but it was unwilling to give up its meal.

Instead, the Garce turned and ran. "Tresa! Tresa, keep fighting!" She heard her dad yell. "I'm coming!"

She was dragged out the door and into the night, the Garce limping and bleeding but not dying because they were un-killable; moving slower than usual but not slow enough. Tresa just caught sight of her mother and sister, safe on the roof and watching in disbelief.

They didn't move.

Every loping step was agony as the teeth were driven deeper and deeper into the bone. She fought blackness, refused to give up, refused to die, and between one breath and the next, she heard the rev of an engine.

Her dad was coming for her.

Every time the wounded Garce slowed or tried to stop, Jeff caught it. He shot it, attacked it, fought it, but it wouldn't free Tresa. It would only sprint away, faster than Jeff's motorcycle, and he'd be forced to chase them again. She'd never heard of anyone escaping once they were in the jaws of the beast. She tried to tell her dad that, but the words wouldn't form. Her mouth wouldn't cooperate.

She realized two or so days in that she was paralyzed.

Phoenyx had given her life for nothing. Tresa was going to die anyway.

SHE caught glimpses of the ship between bouts of semi-consciousness. Before the world had ended and TV had gone off the air, the news reports said the ships were impenetrable. Bombs did nothing against them. The government had attacked with a nuke over New York.

It had backfired horrifically.

The ship was black as night, like the Garce, and seemed to suck the very life and light from everything around it. The door slid open unprovoked as they approached and though Tresa wanted to fight —because she wasn't stupid enough to think that once she was inside she would ever make it out — she couldn't. Her limbs had long since stopped responding. She couldn't even feel pain now, but oh, she would have gladly taken that pain if it meant the ability to move again. Helplessly, she could only watch as the world beyond was shut behind a black, black door.

In the distance, the roar of a motorcycle engine faded.

Run, Dad. There are too many here for you to fight.

Please run.

He wouldn't run. She knew that. But she kept praying for it anyway.

"Oh my," the voice purred, soft and sweet. She'd never heard the Garce do anything but hiss and snarl and snap, and instinctively, she knew this voice did not come from them. There was something else here. Something far more terrifying. "What did you bring me?"

Chapter One

Three years later.

Tresa scooted closer to the rocky precipice, and then just a bit further so she could curl her toes around the edge. The wind howled and jerked at her hair but she ignored it, staring down into the abyss, judging the shadows. It was so far she couldn't see the bottom in the darkness, but then, the moon didn't give her much light tonight.

Just like she liked it.

She spread her arms wide, embracing the emptiness, and tumbled forward.

She fell so fast that the mountainside blurred around her and the scream of the wind in her ears almost, *almost,* drowned out the roar of adrenaline. The ground raced up to meet her, seemingly hungry for her blood, aching for her death.

Not today.

She grabbed a shadow, thrusting her tattooed hand into its inky depths. She slid through the darkness before zipping, as she had come to call it, to the shadow below her, and then to the ones on the ground.

"Much faster than hiking down," she murmured.

Although, if Jeff saw her, he'd probably kill her dead. He hated it when she did that and always launched into a lecture about

8

how it wasn't safe, and one day she might miss the shadows and fall clear to the ground and many other things kind, loving parents were supposed to say. But zipping from shadow to shadow was the fastest way down and she had to make sure the area was safe for the rest of her tribe. Jeff protected them while she was gone, but if she heard the roar of his gun, she'd have to make it back up fast.

Thank goodness for shadows.

Tonight, though, the only sound was her breathing. Zipping, her word for running through the shadows because it was super fast, took a lot of energy and despite her freakish strength, it exhausted her to do it that quickly. She bent, hands on her knees, for several seconds before she finally straightened and sucked in a breath. The city of Scottsdale spread below her, scraggly sagebrush and red sand burying what once had been the plush golf courses the city was famous for. What was still visible had been baked by the summer sun into nothing but scraggly wisps of grass.

She was super strong and super fast and pretty damn indestructible. But unlike the Garce, she was smarter than a mindless zombie. She could use their skills to her advantage in ways they would never figure out.

She was grateful for that at least. She'd only had to trade her soul and her humanity. No big deal.

Said no one, ever.

Her black, twining tattoos sparkled in the darkness, but she did her best not to notice them as she zipped from shadow to shadow, moving across the valley systematically looking for threats. Eighteen years old and hunting un-killable aliens.

Not where she'd thought her life would go, but whatever.

"Hey sis. Been a long time since we've been to Scottsdale, huh? Remember how Uncle Dan used to live there?"

Phoenyx didn't respond. She never did, which was good because if she had, that meant Tresa was hearing ghosts and that might just push her tenuous grasp on sanity over the edge.

Still, it gave Tresa comfort to talk to her dead sister while she was alone in the moonlight.

Which wasn't morbid at all.

Phoenyx was her guardian angel. She'd always been Tresa's protector, big sister, best friend. She'd never missed Tresa's softball games or her plays. Not once.

"You finally got your wings," Tresa murmured and as always, she had to fight tears. Phoenyx had sacrificed herself almost three years ago and it still hurt every. Single. Day.

Brushing the tears from her cheek with her tattooed right hand, she skimmed through the shadows, searching, searching. Watching the skies for wings and the ground for red, glowing eyes.

Her brothers, as it were.

Thankfully, of all the traits the Empyrean witch had forced into Tresa, the red glowing eyes weren't one of them. Hers were more black, but still with a hint of her old brown struggling to be seen. Bonus.

The shadow skipping, the sparkling tattoos, the freakish strength and speed, those wouldn't have been so bad. The constant cravings for meat in a world where meat just didn't exist anymore, that she could have done without.

Eating humans wasn't even an option. She protected them. She was the only one who could.

Sure, she scared most people at first, with the tattoos similar to the Empyreans, or Pys as the humans called them. But theirs were sparkling blue and they shot fire-riddled blood balls from their hands. And they had wings and blue skin. She had none of those things and her tattoos were black, but they did sparkle. Under all that Garce shadow-fur, they were tattooed just like the Pys. Who knew.

Well, she did, now.

She felt the eyes before she saw them. Felt their confusion. She was one of them, but she didn't *look* like them and the Garce weren't smart. Not even a little. She froze, turning in a slow circle.

The eyes were across what had once been a parking lot, next to a movie store. What with Netflix and Redbox, Tresa hadn't even known brick and mortar rental places existed before the world had ended.

"Hello, brother," she murmured, baring her teeth. They were sharp, but not vampirish, thank the heavens. That would have been super weird and probably wouldn't have helped with the not-being-a-scary-alien part of her life.

The Garce launched itself from the shadows and raced across the cracked parking lot toward her, hissing and snarling. From above, where Tresa had jumped, she could feel Jeff's worry. She could feel his emotions because Garce preyed on fear. But she also knew that he had his gun trained and was ready to back her up if she needed.

She wouldn't need, though. Garce were nothing to her. Not when she could use their own tricks against them. Not when she had just enough Py blood in her to take them down. She couldn't throw blood balls, but the blood lit under her fingernails, curving her fingers into sharp claws, sparking as she leaped back into the shadow and zipped to one closer to the Garce. Since it was night and the sliver of the moon cast shadows everywhere, she came out nearly right on top of it.

There was more than one, which she hadn't realized, and she slashed with her right hand at the first one. It screamed as the fire slid through its skin, tearing the shadows, and cauterized its heart. Before it fell, she was spinning, twirling on feet far lighter than they should have been, so light she felt like maybe, *maybe* she had the Py gift of flight, and then she was slicing with her claws, jamming her fingers up through the top of the second Garce's jaw as its teeth clamped down on her arm.

From somewhere beyond the pain, the roar of a rifle echoed through the night and the Garce shrieked as a bullet slammed into its side, knocking it over. Her blood ate through it, stopping its heart and ending its life and Tresa stood next to it, breathing heavily. It took a lot of energy to pull the fire through her. The Py had given her so little to begin with.

Speaking of Pys...Tresa scanned the sky. Where there were Garce, there were usually Pys. But also, where there were Garce...

There were people.

That meant maybe a wanderer here. A lost warrior. Someone who needed help. Tresa had to find them. No one deserved to be out here alone.

No one.

Chapter Two

Roman slammed one last nail into the plywood that covered the windows. They kept the Garce out, sort of, and the Pys couldn't peek in when they flew by. It wasn't foolproof and it wouldn't keep either alien species out by any means, but every little bit helped.

He couldn't believe this building didn't have boards up already, actually. Maybe the attack had hit too quickly in this part of Arizona and there hadn't been a chance.

It was a horrific thought.

Scottsdale had once been one of the most affluent cities in the country. Now it was empty. Roman had picked up a few wanders in the last week who had been roaming alone and miraculously survived, bringing his band to over twenty. There was strength in numbers, or so they say.

Except against the Pys.

The Empyreans, had come in the third wave. First, two waves of Garce. The Empyreans had followed them, promising to defeat the Garce for the humans. Promising salvation, eternal life and beauty. They'd feasted on the shadowy aliens and took what was left of the human population, either killing them or...who knew what happened if someone were unlucky enough to be pulled into their ship.

All women. The Pys didn't want men.

There were rumors. Rumors of ten who had escaped, but no one could confirm or deny. No one had ever seen them.

In Roman's opinion, they were a myth. Millions of women had been taken onto those ships, and he'd never seen even one make her way out. The only ones to escape those ships were Pys themselves.

Pys, who were supposed to save them from the Garce. They only came out at night, looked like fairies, sang like sirens and attacked like vampires. Winged, beautiful, and fast as lightning.

"Never trust beautiful things," he muttered, dropping the hammer to the floor. "Angel, Ben! Get back to work. You want Garce in here by nightfall?"

Most days he felt like a babysitter. Yelling at them to pick up after themselves, do their jobs, sleep when they were supposed to. He was keeping them alive but some of them did their best to make that difficult.

Very difficult.

"I don't see you doing anything," Angel said under her breath, but Roman heard her. He debated yelling again, of telling her he'd done a whole room while she'd done one board, but he was tired. Tired of trying to keep ungrateful people alive.

"Fine. Die tonight in your sleep. See if I give a damn. For those of you who do care if you live to see morning, get your boards up."

Not the best way to handle things probably, but he didn't care. He didn't sign on to be their babysitter. He signed on to keep his sisters alive, and those two liked to gather roamers like they were lost kittens. Michelle and Kylie had kind hearts. They were the reason his group was more than the three of them, and also probably the reason he hadn't killed any of them himself.

"You need a break." Kylie, his littlest sister, appeared from the darkness of her already boarded up room. "They're getting to you again."

They were also the reason he was still alive.

He muttered under his breath, hoping she missed all the swearing. By the raised eyebrow, she did not. "Going for a walk," he finally got out, curse-word free.

"Are you sure that's safe?" Michelle asked. His middle-little sister. He hadn't even heard her show up but there she was, watching him like a silent ninja.

"Safer than being here," he growled.

Kylie smirked. "For them or for you?"

He scowled at her and turned on his heel, snatching his gun that leaned next to the door. It wouldn't stop the Garce, but it would slow them down. Give him time to run. That was all he needed.

If a Py showed up, though, he'd be screwed.

Except that Kylie and Michelle both fell into step next to him, guns at their sides and already loaded. It was death to leave the compound alone. The Garce were heavy here, which is why he set up camp where he had. They literally couldn't leave. They were trapped and he wasn't sure how long they would last but he'd do everything he could to keep them alive.

"Just so we're clear," Kylie said. "We're not going outside, are we?"

He glanced at her out of the corner of his eye. "You're the one who told me to go for a walk."

"We're in a massive office building. There are plenty of places to stroll without even touching a door." Michelle grinned angelically.

"Mom told us to protect you. So here we are, protecting," Kylie said in response to Roman's annoyed sigh.

"Mom told me to protect you. I'm the big brother."

"We're supposed to protect each other. And we're doing a good job so far." Michelle lifted her gun as they went around the corner, looking for Garce, ready to run. Always ready to run.

The Garce had killed their parents. Long before the Pys had shown up with their plan to take all the women away and not give them back, the Garce had taken everything from them. It was the reason so many in his band were teenagers. Their parents died to save them.

"Wait." Kylie held up a hand, forcing Roman and Michelle to stumble to a stop. "Listen."

It wasn't the noise that Roman caught first, but the smell. The smell of Garce was unmistakable. Indescribable. Like rot and decay and death. He immediately raised his gun but there were no Garce in the hallway in front of them.

He turned, too slowly, too slowly. In horror, he saw the red, glowing eyes seconds before the Garce sprang at him. His sisters fired, he raised his gun as they fell back, further into the darkness and away from the rest of their band. Drawing the Garce with them.

Bullets embedded themselves in the shadowy flesh but the Garce didn't slow. There was just one, but they almost never traveled alone. So unless its partner had been killed...

Michelle gasped and spun, firing in the opposite direction. There it was.

They passed what had once been a doorway, but it was badly boarded up now and would take them too long to fight their way out of it. By the time he pulled that board down, they'd be dead—

What in the world...?

A face on the other side distracted him, and distraction meant death. A human face, a girl's face, eyes huge against her pale skin. That was all he saw before the Garce lunged, tired of playing with its prey, and he was grateful the girl was on the outside looking in and not the other way around.

He threw himself backward, firing two more rounds into its throat, but the Garce barely noticed, too frenzied at the thought of a fresh meal.

The girl sprang from the shadows, barreled into the Garce, slicing across its throat with her fiery fingertips. The Garce shrieked an evil, horrific sound that he would hear in his nightmares for the rest of his life, and it fell lifeless onto Roman's legs. Had she not...done whatever she'd done, it would be alive and devouring him by now.

But she was gone, moving, sliding through his sisters, dodging the bullets, seeming to disappear into the shadows before she reemerged further down the hall. She lunged, too quickly for his eyes to follow, and caught the Garce as it tried to leap past her. Again, her hand shot out and sliced through its throat, her fingertips glowing and sparking like—

Like the Pys blood balls.

The Garce squealed and fell, black, acidic blood pooling at her feet as she turned back toward them, breathing hard. "Are you okay?"

Michelle and Kylie both stared at her, mouths open. Roman shoved himself to his feet, reloading his gun. "What are you?"

"I'm a...I'm a Tresa." She smiled. "Are you okay?"

"Yes," Kylie said. "Yes." As if answering both times Tresa had asked at once. "How did you—I saw you outside. How'd you get in?"

"She jumped through the shadows," Michelle whispered. "Like they do."

Tresa's smile died a little, became more forced, as she wiped the alien blood from her hands. Hands that were tattooed like the Pys. Tattoos that swirled around her eyes. "I could have broken through the board but it would have taken me longer and you didn't have that much time. Plus," she continued with a brightness that didn't make it to her eyes, "you would have had to re-board the window, and that takes time and resources."

"What are you?" Roman asked again, raising his gun and training it on her forehead. She was beautiful, mind-numbingly so. Flawless skin, huge dark eyes and a body he would throw himself in front of a Garce for. The Pys were beautiful, too, ethereal like she was.

The Pys had taken out more than half the world's population.

"I'm a friend," she whispered. "I was taken. By the Garce. They changed me—"

"The Garce changed you?" Roman scoffed. "The Garce don't even know they can't swim until they drown themselves."

"The Py controlling the Garce." Tresa tipped her head, watching him with bright, slightly glowing eyes. They almost sparked, like they were lit by an inner fire. "They're her pets. She wanted to see what would happen if she crossed a human's DNA with their alien one. I happened."

"You're telling me you were taken by the Garce and escaped? There are so many plot holes in that story I can't even—"Michelle started.

"I didn't escape," Tresa interrupted. "My dad saved me."

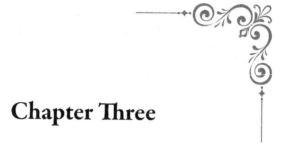

Chapter Three

It probably hadn't been Tresa's best idea to introduce herself by attacking the Garce, but these people would have died. And how did they thank her? By pointing a gun at her head.

Awesome.

"Your dad saved you? From an alien spaceship?" The boy, one who couldn't have been much older than Tresa, didn't lower his weapon.

She stifled her annoyance, very aware of how terrifying she could be to someone who was just attacked by an alien. "From a Garce ship. They're not as hard to trick as the Pys. That's all I'm saying. I don't owe you an explanation. You owe me a thank you, though. I just saved your lives."

The memories hurt. She still woke screaming from the night-mares on a regular basis. It had been almost three years, but it didn't matter. The nightmares were as vivid now as they'd ever been.

"Thank you," the younger girl said quickly. "I'm sorry for our hesitation, you just seem an awful lot like the Pys." She winced. "No offense."

"None taken," Tresa sighed. "But I'm going to go. My tribe can't be alone with this many Garce around. My dad is tough, but a gun can't do much against a whole pack."

"Your tribe?" Kylie asked. "There are more of you?" She risked a glance at Roman, and Tresa could see the distrust in her eyes.

"No." Tresa edged toward the shadows. "They're humans. Like you. Not hybrids. As far as I know, I'm the only one of my kind."

"You—you have a pack of humans?" the boy shifted his weight, the muscles in his arm straining against his t-shirt.

"Tribe," she insisted. "Not a pack. We're not Garce. We're family. And I need to get back to them."

The younger girl glanced at the boy again, read his gaze and seemed to disregard it as she rushed forward, reaching out a hand to Tresa. "I'm Kylie. Do you have shelter? The Garce—I mean, I don't know how fast you can move, you took care of these pretty quickly, but they're bad out there—"

"Kylie," the boy hissed. "Stay away from her."

But Kylie slid past him. "She saved our lives. With one hand! Tresa, right? You should bring your tribe here. We can protect each other."

The older girl leaned against the wall and crossed her arms, trying to hide a smile. "I don't think she needs protection, Kylie."

"Well, she can't fight continuously, can she? Look how tired she already is."

It was true, Tresa's hands were shaking and the fire was gone, slowly replenishing, but she didn't realize it was so obvious. She'd fought more than two Garce before, but not after jumping through shadows like she had earlier. That had been stupid.

"She can't stay here. We don't know what she is," the boy snarled.

Tresa tried to pretend his words didn't hurt. The Garce and the Pys both had taken so much from so many, and she didn't blame him. "I'm going to go." To Kylie, she said, "But thank you so much for your offer. That was very kind of you."

Kylie sent an infuriated glare over her shoulder at her brother. "We've scoured this whole area. It nearly killed us. There isn't anywhere safe here and if you've got a whole group of you, I won't sentence you to death because of fear. Get your tribe. I'll have the board off before you get back."

"No, it's fine. Really. We've survived this long—"

Kylie shrugged, plastering on a too-bright and slightly mischievous smile. "Fine. But I'm taking the board down anyway, so..."

"What?" the boy asked flatly. Tresa's eyes returned to him, trying her best not to notice how hot he was.

Because holy crap.

He was taller than all three of them, probably as tall as Cole, Phoenyx's boyfriend, had been. Broad shoulders, muscled chest and arms, narrow waist. His hair, light brown, fell across his forehead and his unreadable brown eyes didn't move from her face. The gun in his hand didn't waver.

"Why don't I come with you? I'll make sure you get back here safe," Kylie said brightly, already reloading her gun.

"What?" It was Michelle's turn to exclaim.

"No, Kylie. You're not leaving without us and not with someone we don't even know." The boy glowered at his sister, but Kylie didn't seem phased at all.

"Oh, Tresa. This is my big sister, Michelle, and my bigger brother, Roman. He thinks he's in charge."

"I—what? I am in charge!"

Kylie grinned at him.

"Look, I didn't want to cause problems. I was just trying to help. I'm going to go." Tresa backed closer to the shadows, trying to calculate how much energy it would take to get back up the cliff face. She could go around and climb back up but that would add several hours.

Kylie's hand shot out and caught her arm before Tresa could zip away. "Look, we've lost some of our own lately because the Garce are running rampant. You could help us fight them. We could all protect each other. Please come back."

Tresa glanced at Roman to see how he would handle his sister's idea. His jaw clenched and his hand tightened on the gun until his knuckles were white.

"There could be more Garce in this building. We've shut ourselves in. There's a whole group of us, too. I mean, I'm just saying..." Kylie deliberately trailed off, somehow already knowing Tresa's weakness. She couldn't leave them there to die.

"I—"

Roman sighed. "Just watch the skies. If there are Garce out there, there are Pys. I don't want them to see anyone coming or leaving this building. Understand?"

When Tresa still hesitated, he lowered the gun, clicking on the safety. It echoed through the empty hallway and bounced around her soul. "Look, I've been trying to save as many people as I can for over a year now. I'm not going to turn you away. Don't get us all killed."

And he turned and walked off.

Tresa glanced uncertainly at Kylie, who beamed at her. Michelle smiled encouragingly. "Okay. I'll—I'll be back."

She slid into the shadows, confused and conflicted. She didn't need their shelter. She could survive in a valley full of Garce with no problem. But her dad, her friends, they couldn't. They couldn't escape from shadow to shadow. They couldn't kill when they had to. They had no defense.

They have me. I'm their defense.

But they also needed shelter. Somewhere safe to sleep, if only for a couple of days while they recovered. Luckily, it was winter in Arizona or the sun would bake them alive, which was the whole reason they'd come south instead of north, toward home. Winter in Arizona would be a lot easier to survive than winter in Utah.

Plus, there was nothing for them in Utah. Tresa refused to go back, back to a mother who had watched her be dragged away in the jaws of a monster, and a sister who hadn't even bothered to look horrified when it happened.

Relieved, that was all.

That her baby sister had been caught and not her.

And Tresa had no desire to walk into that kitchen, to see the last place Phoenyx had stood. What if she ran into Cole or Enika, Phoenyx's best friend? How would she explain her sister's death?

She zipped up through the shadows to the top of the cliff they'd arrived on. Her dad waited with his gun, watching like a silent sentry while everyone else huddled together, waiting for the next attack.

"I found shelter. Someplace safe. We can recover there, rest up. Sound okay?"

Jeff's eyes swept the area again. "Lots of Garce down there."

They'd been attacked just a couple days ago. Tresa had fought them off, but her little tribe still lost one in the process. Everyone was scared now. If only she didn't get so tired so quickly...

"Can you get us there?"

She nodded, brushing her black hair over her shoulder. "I think so."

"Okay. And you think this place is safe?"

"I'll do a more thorough sweep when I get back but yes, I think so. There's already a group there. They seem well equipped to handle trouble."

"Do we trust this group?"

The saddest part of the invasion wasn't what the aliens had done to their world, but what the humans had done to each other because of it. There were riots, murders, unspeakable crimes because the world was falling apart and there were no police, no government, no military to control it. Everyone was on their own, and the aliens weren't even always the predator.

Tresa had heard rumors about humans betraying other humans to the aliens. For what, she would never understand. It was horrific and she hoped never to meet someone like that, because if something like that caught something like her...she could only imagine the reward if she was given to the Pys or the Garce for more experiments.

Horrific flashbacks nearly drowned her.

"I've made humans into Empyrean before, but never a human into one of my pets. I wonder what you will become."

"I think I'm losing her. Do I save her with my own DNA or watch as yours devours her?"

"There, my pretty pet. You're going to do amazing things when you wake up."

"She's not strong enough to be one of us. Get her out of my sight."

"Tresa," Jeff shook her gently, pulling her out of the flashbacks, just like he'd pulled her out of that ship. She tried her best not to think about it but sometimes...

Sometimes she lost.

It had taken her months to recover. Months just to walk again. Months to figure out how to eat again. Almost a year before she could run. Another year before she realized she could hunt. That she could kill them. The zipping through the shadows thing, that had been a new development she'd discovered only a few months ago.

And her favorite.

"We're going down the mountain into the valley." She spoke to her tribe, who all looked as exhausted as she felt. But right now, she couldn't be tired. She had to be tough.

"Phoenyx, help me be strong."

"I'll protect you, but you have to be fast. You can't hesitate, you can't take a leisurely stroll through the streets of Scottsdale and marvel at the massive houses. Do you understand? I can only do so much."

They were on their feet immediately. There were ten of them, twelve counting her and her father. *There were thirteen of us two days ago.*

When she'd failed to save them all.

"Ready?" she took a deep breath and met Jeff's eyes. He nodded, winking because he could see the fear no one else could. "Let's go."

She led them down the side of the mountain, grateful these weren't like the huge, rocky cliffs in Utah. They slid through the red dirt, dodged sagebrush, avoided cacti and kept a careful watch on the ground. Tresa hadn't seen any wildlife at all for over a year, but now would be a bad time to find out rattlesnakes or scorpions had survived the Armageddon.

Luckily, the only sound she heard was the snarls and hissing of the Garce in the distance.

It woke something in her blood, something that didn't belong to her. Something that fought for control.

Something that would never win.

"Faster. Faster. Move it, guys." She prowled restlessly around the shadows, trying to zip as little as possible to save her energy. In case she needed to fight. She could see the building in the distance, but it was too far. If they didn't move faster, they wouldn't make it.

They moved faster.

That was the amazing thing about her tribe. They knew she had her limits and they fought with her, not behind her. Their ragged breathing drowned out the Garce, almost, and she could smell their fear and their sweat.

If she could smell it, the Garce could, too.

But thank the heavens the Pys weren't in the skies. Maybe they hadn't discovered this huge pack of Garce yet and didn't know the humans lived here as well. It was unlikely but it would explain why the pack had grown unchecked.

It wouldn't last, though. The Pys knew everything. And Tresa could fight them, but they were faster than her. They could throw their attacks and hers were limited to her fingers. Pys were not her friend.

"Almost there," she murmured. The closer they got to the building, the tenser she became. The Garce closed in and the fire in her blood hadn't replenished yet.

She jogged along next to them, circling them, sprinting ahead and falling behind, trying to be everywhere at once. Jeff led, carrying more packs than he should have. He was stronger. Bigger than everyone else. He had military training and the majority of her tribe were just kids.

Kids like her.

But she wasn't a kid, not anymore. Maybe none of them were.

The first Garce spotted them when they had maybe a hundred yards to go. She felt it the instant it caught their scent. Fear was powerful. It carried much further than it should have. "Run!" she screamed, and although she had nothing left and she could feel her tribe's exhaustion as if it were her own, they ran. They sprinted as hard as they could go, stumbling over weeds and torn metal, breathing through sobs of fear and memories too fresh.

Tresa zipped. She dove through one shadow and out another, coming up in front of the Garce. Too close. Its jaws closed around her arm, her shoulder, and clamped down. The flashbacks hit her again, of being dragged for days on end, pulled broken and paralyzed into a ship.

If not for that DNA change, she would have stayed paralyzed. She owed the very fact that she was walking on the thing that had caused that pain in the first place.

I wish I was strong enough to fight the Garce.

She'd gotten her wish and she willed the fire to her hands, felt the claws light up under her fingers and she slashed across the Garce's snout. But her fire was too weak. It would take too long to kill the Garce. That monster would kill her first.

Out of the corner of her eye, she saw Jeff hesitate. Torn between the need to fight for her and the ten people following him to safety. He couldn't save them both. It was her or them.

"Dad, run!" she screamed.

Please choose them.

He ran. He sprinted, leading her tribe to the building. Fast enough that they struggled to keep up and she realized instantly what he was doing, trying to get them to safety and come back for her before she was lost. But Tresa could see the building now. Could see the board still up. The other group—Kylie, she hadn't taken it down.

They were all going to die.

Fight, Tresa!

It was Phoenyx's voice in her head, bellowing with so much fury it seemed to spread through Tresa's whole body, lending fire to her exhausted resources. With her other hand, she attacked, slicing again and again at the Garce. With every strike, its jaws weakened as the poison spread through its blood.

She hit it hard, punched it in the face and she felt the bones crunch under her fist. The teeth retracted and it fell backward with a screech that nearly split her eardrums. She couldn't zip to her tribe now, couldn't get to the building before they did. She had nothing left but anger— red-hot anger.

That girl had said she'd be ready for them. She'd lied and now they were all fighting to survive.

She ran. She'd never been a runner like her sister. Phoenyx had been freakishly fast, had won state championships, had actually run just because she loved it.

Tresa hadn't, but when her whole tribe, her family, everything she had left, were facing death so bravely, she found her speed, rocketing across the cracked asphalt. She launched herself through the air, tackled the Garce that was four times her size, and they tumbled end over end into the building.

She heard a scream, many screams, maybe some of her own, she didn't know. She couldn't fight it. She had nothing yet. Not yet. If she could just hold it off...

The crack of a gun, many guns, and the heat of bullets too close to her skin drew her out of her own head. Before she could say goodbye to her father. Before she could ask Phoenyx to meet her wherever souls went next. The Garce screeched and fought her off, hurt and bleeding black, all-consuming blood. But the noise would draw more Garce. She had to get away, get her tribe somewhere safe—

"Come on!" a boy voice roared, and she was plucked unceremoniously off the Garce's back and hauled to her feet. "It's not going to stay down forever!"

"What—what are you doing! Let me go!"

The door was still boarded up, but her tribe was gone. She whirled, still fighting his grasp, panic making her weak and senseless.

A window. High above, wide enough to fit them through. Jeff stood in its frame, firing shots at the Garce still trying to escape.

"You—you let us in?" she gasped.

"You're going to bleed to death. Come on." Roman dragged her up the ladder before she could tell him it was impossible, she couldn't bleed to death and that only Py blood could kill her.

She climbed as best she could with only one arm, and he caught her when she fell. Pulled her the last few rungs up into the window. Through the window.

To safety.

"Pull the ladder and get this boarded up," he snapped and several she didn't recognize leaped to do his bidding.

Her tribe was being ushered up a stairwell. She caught their footsteps and their scent. They were terrified, relieved, safe. Worried.

Worried for her.

"Get the med kit," Roman snarled, but Kylie was already coming around the corner with it. "This is going to take everything we've got left."

He wasn't happy about that, she could tell.

"I'm fine. But we can't—it will know we're here. I have to finish him—"

"No offense," Kylie said gently, kneeling next to her, "But with what? Your sparkly stuff is pretty dull right now."

"I'll follow it—"

"There are more already trying to fight their way in downstairs. If they could figure out how to climb that ladder, they would have. You go out there, you're dead and I'm not going to save you." Roman leaned against the wall, casually reloading the rifle in his hand.

"I don't need saving," she snarled back at him.

"My sister trying to stop you from bleeding to death says you do."

She glared at him. "I've killed three tonight. How many have you killed in the last year or so?"

Kylie snorted, her eyes flying open as her hand flew to her mouth. "I mean...you know. She saved your life, Ro. You saved hers."

"I wasn't dying," Tresa snarled, but it lacked vehemence when it was aimed at Kylie.

"Okay. But you were losing. Sorry to point that out. Let's just all call you two even, okay? Michelle and I will still do our best to repay you though."

Tresa sank against the wall. "You let my family in. That's payment enough."

Chapter Four

The size of their band had now almost doubled. Roman watched them silently, his eyes never straying from the beautiful monster in their midst. She'd saved them. She'd risked her life, knowing she had nothing left to fight with, to save these humans.

He had no idea what she was and he didn't trust her at all, but her little tribe, as she called it, they adored her. They fawned over her and took care of her and protected her from his group.

All of whom were rightfully suspicious.

And she had saved them all.

"This is double the amount of mouths to feed," Roman muttered.

Michelle glanced up, raising an eyebrow. "Double the amount of hands to help."

He glowered at her. Michelle was eighteen and far too wise for her age. The invasion had done that. It had done that to them all. Kylie had just turned seventeen and he would be twenty in a few months, but fighting through three years of alien invasions made him feel closer to fifty.

"I'll take first watch. You guys get some sleep," he finally announced. It was safer to sleep during the day so they were prepared if the Pys showed up. Although it didn't help.

"I can take first watch." Tresa appeared at his side like a wraith, small and dark. "I don't sleep."

"You—what? Ever?"

She shook her head.

"That's not even plausible."

She shrugged, meeting his eyes with her fiery black ones. He could see a hint of brown in them and wondered if they'd been that color before she'd been changed. The darkness nearly drowned it out, though. "Everything I am isn't plausible."

"Well, no offense but you're part alien. I'm not leaving the safety of my band in your hands."

She wrinkled her nose. "Offense taken. You're an evil human and I'm not leaving the safety of my *tribe* in your hands. Where do you watch from?"

He hadn't expected that and gaped at her for several seconds. "What—I—we left small holes in the windows on either side of the building."

"Perfect. You take one and I'll take one."

"Right. So the Garce can sneak up on your side and you'll let them in?"

She called him on it before he could even wince at how stupid that sounded. "Yeah, because I let one chew me up just so I could get into your building and let them all in later. Makes brilliant sense."

"She can keep watch here," Kylie said. "Where the rest of us are. We can keep an eye on her." And Kylie winked.

At the alien.

He couldn't even—his sister was seriously taking Tresa's side? He looked to Michelle, but Michelle shrugged. "I think we can handle that."

"Then who keeps an eye on him?" Tresa crossed her arms over her chest. "How do I know he's not going to sell us out to the Pys?"

"Why would I do that?" he exclaimed. "It would take down my own band with it!"

"Sounds stupid, doesn't it?" She smirked.

"I'll go with him." Tresa's shoulders immediately tensed and she spun on her dad, who stood behind her with his ever-present rifle. That thing was huge and Roman didn't know where he could have found ammo for it. It wasn't a gun he'd ever seen in his life.

"Dad, I don't think—"

"What's he going to do? Attack me?"

"Well yes, that's exactly what I'm afraid he's going to do."

Roman threw up his arms. "Holy shi—this is insane. I'm not the enemy. I let you in here!"

Kylie glanced at Tresa, back to Roman and then to Tresa again. "I'll go with them." When Tresa looked like she was going to argue, Kylie spoke again. "Do you trust me?"

That was stupid. They'd just met. Tresa was obviously the type that didn't trust easily—

"Yes," Tresa said quietly. Her voice had the lyrical quality of the Pys, and it sent chills spider crawling across his spine.

"What?" Roman snapped. "Why her and not me? I saved your life!"

"She can feel it. Like the Garce can." Kylie bent to retrieve her pack and gun. "Let's go."

"How did you know that?" Tresa asked, frozen in what appeared to be shock.

Kylie shrugged. "I have gifts of my own. Ready, Ro? Jefferson?"

"Jeff," the man said with a smile. "Ready."

"Wait," Roman said as he grabbed his own pack and followed his sister. "She trusts you and not me? I saved her life. I went out and pulled her off a Garce's back."

Kylie glanced over her shoulder at him as she led the way down a dark, dark hall. His people would spread out into these halls eventually if the Pys didn't find them first. They would make this into a home. But for now, he was leaving the majority of them behind in the care of an alien monster. And his sister, who was pretty damn formidable. "I think the only thing she feels from you is hate and anger. Not exactly trust inspiring."

He hesitated. At one time, before the world ended, he would have thrown himself at Tresa's feet. She was that gorgeous. She probably would have run the school, and he would have fought his way through a whole pack of guys to even catch her attention. Sure, he'd been a baseball player and thought he was a hotshot, but none of that mattered now. He would have judged her on her appearance then, same as he was now, but it would have been a completely different outcome. "She looks like them."

"Like the Garce? Are you serious?" Kylie scoffed. "She doesn't have five inch long canines. She's not made of shadows. She certainly doesn't resemble a giant dog."

"She sucks the light from around her. She jumps from the shadows..."

"Then she has some of their traits. That isn't the same as looking like them."

"I meant the Pys," he said quietly. "Same tattoos. Same weird glow. Same lilt to her voice."

"She was changed from both their DNA before I could get inside. She's made up of both of them."

Shit. Roman had forgotten Jeff was even there. He walked as silently as his daughter. "I'm—I'm sorry. That was—"He didn't even know how to recover from that. "I didn't know you were behind me."

They walked the rest of the way in silence. Roman was used to feeling like a jerk. He had to, to keep them all alive. But this was a whole new level he hadn't wanted to reach.

"I'll take first watch. Or don't you sleep either?" he asked Jeff when they finally got to the lookout. It had been an office once. One of the few he'd scouted that didn't have blood spatters or teeth marks and horrific remains.

"I sleep. She's the only one who was changed against her will." Roman sunk lower.

"Well, you've had a long day. I'll go first."

Although he doubted very much that Jeff would sleep at all. How could a father sleep, after watching his daughter go through what Tresa had that night? Or since she'd been taken, from the sound of it.

"Can you—can you tell us what happened?" Kylie asked, settling next to Jeff on the floor, pistol within easy reach. Always, within reach.

"We were attacked. On her birthday. Lost my other daughter that night. I shot the Garce that had Tresa in its mouth, but it wouldn't drop her. I followed it, but couldn't get into their ship for several days."

"How'd you get in?" Roman interrupted.

Kylie shot him an annoyed glare.

"With the Garce. Then I found Tresa and got the hell out of there."

"They just left her unattended? Convenient." Roman didn't look at them, scanning the skies for Pys as he was.

"Yeah. Because there was one Py on that ship and Tresa was paralyzed and mostly dead. She'd been tossed aside after the Py got tired of trying to save her."

"Wait, what?" Kylie sat forward and even Roman dragged his gaze from the slit in the wood. "There was a Py on that ship? Full of Garce?"

Jeff nodded, staring at the ceiling. "They're her pets. She controls them all."

"What? That can't be. How would she control the ones on the other continents?" Roman went back to staring out the slot, but his mind was spinning. A Py controlled the Garce? How? The Garce craved the Pys. They were like a drug, with the killer side effects and all. Which was probably how Tresa killed them. She had the Py blood, too. Wouldn't that mean, though, that her Py blood was killing her Garce blood?

It all made his head hurt. Complicated didn't work for him. It didn't keep people alive.

"She created them. She continues to create them but she's trying to make a race that isn't easily killed by the Pys. The Garce's downfall is their stupidity. They know how to zip through the shadows but they don't use it to get to their meal on the roof. She's trying to mix DNA with humans and use their intelligence with the Garce's lethal abilities. Unfortunately, the Garce usually eat the humans instead of bringing them back to her." Jeff's voice was grim and full of pain and it made Roman ache for him. Compassion. Something he tried never to feel.

Compassion didn't keep him alive.

"Why did they keep Tresa alive?" Kylie asked softly. Michelle had followed them and sat next to Jeff on the other side, both hanging on his every word. Roman wanted to point out that she was supposed to be watching the alien in the other room, but couldn't make himself interrupt Jeff's story.

"I kept shooting. Every time it would stop, I would shoot. I was hoping to hurt it enough that it would drop her."

"Instead you had to watch it take her inside their ship. That's so awful," Michelle whispered.

"And your other daughter?" Kylie whispered. "Did you just have the two?"

"There was one more. Not mine, but I raised her. She survived, as far as I know. My real daughter, Phoenyx, she tried to lure the Garce away from Tresa. She...didn't make it back." His voice broke and despite his best efforts, Roman hurt with him. He'd watched the Garce tear his parents apart right in front of him. He knew how awful it was. Hell, he was still plagued by nightmares when he was able to sleep. This man had lost two daughters.

And was given back a monster.

He didn't seem to mind, though. His voice still shook with pride when he talked about Tresa, about how she'd fought to survive, fought to learn to walk again, fought to teach herself how to use this horrible curse and make it into a gift. She didn't ask for any of it, but she was making the best of it.

Roman wasn't so sure. The way she'd moved, the way her eyes had lit when she'd sliced through the Garce's throat. Too fast, too bright. Like the Garce and the Py, his two greatest fears, all mixed into one small, beautiful and very deadly creature. The only thing worse would be if she had wings.

Thank goodness it hadn't come to that.

"Have you, in your travels, heard rumors of any others like her?" Michelle asked.

Roman tensed, terror chasing its way down his spine. If there were more...if that Py got her wish and created a human/Garce hybrid race, they were all doomed.

"No. We've heard whisperings about Py hybrids. Known as The Nine, but no one has actually seen them. They fly around and fight the Garce and the Pys. We've been all over Colorado and Arizona, even New Mexico. Never seen a thing. No one we've talked to has, either. Just friend of a friend type thing." Jeff shook his head. "I can't even imagine how dangerous something like that would be."

"So you admit they're dangerous." Roman pounced. "And yet—"

Jeff cut him off. "Yes. Dangerous to the other side. Look, son. I know you don't trust her, but remember you're speaking about my daughter and show some respect. She's doing more than any of us ever could."

No one had spoken to Roman like that in over a year. Not since his parents had died. His dad had used those exact words when Roman had talked back to his mother. *"Show some respect."*

He dropped his head against the board, felt the rough wood dig into his forehead, and blew out a breath. "I'm sorry."

"We all are. We...it's been rough," Michelle said.

"Rough on all of us," Jeff agreed. "Let's make it as kind as we can, huh?"

"Michelle, Kylie, get some sleep. You'll take second watch," Roman said by way of answer. Kindness didn't belong in this world. Not anymore.

His sisters, for once, did what he asked and both settled onto their mats. They were tough, so strong it blew his mind on a daily basis. The things they could do, the things they could endure. They were the only bright spots in a dark, dark world with no hope and no chance of long-term survival. He kept this band alive but he wouldn't have done it without them. He wouldn't have fought for his own life, let alone anyone else's. They were the heart he lacked. And the brains he sometimes failed to use. He made the hard decisions, he yelled enough to keep people in line. They did the rest.

"What will you do now?" Jeff asked, his voice quiet in the darkness. "How will you survive here?"

Roman glanced at him. "We have seeds. We have plants. We saved as much of our garden as we could from our last compound. Tomorrow we'll start building a new garden. Everyone helps. They don't help, they don't eat."

Jeff didn't respond. He wasn't asleep because Roman could feel his gaze. Watching him in the darkness with sad, sad eyes. It was almost an hour later when he finally said, "They broke you, didn't they?"

Broken. Yeah. That was an understatement.

Chapter Five

Tresa hadn't stayed in one place for longer than a day in over a year. They were always moving, always looking for the next source of food and water, the next safe place. It never lasted, though, and they were on to the next one.

When Roman barreled into the main room the next afternoon like an angry bull and demanded everyone get to work, she was confused, to say the least. His people went to the roof, which seemed random and slightly unsafe given the flying aliens. But at least the aliens could only come out at night. She followed out of curiosity and also because Roman bellowed that whoever didn't work, didn't eat. It was an interesting threat.

She, due to her unique DNA, only ate meat. And in a world where there seemed to be no animal-life whatsoever, that left her only one source of food.

The aliens that created her.

It was at least sixty degrees outside when they finally emerged from the darkness of the boarded-up building. In a few months, it would be almost too hot to breathe, but right then, it was perfect. Beautiful. The reason her uncle Dan had lived there year round. She tipped her head up to the sky and let the sun warm her face. *"Pretty, isn't it, Phoenyx?"*

Except it wasn't, not beyond the roof. For as far as she could see, there was no life. Buildings crumbled, asphalt cracked and broke. Nothing moved, except the Garce roaming the city. Cars sat abandoned, some with doors open and bodies strewn through them. Or, what had been bodies. There wasn't anything left now but sun bleached bones. She was glad her tribe couldn't see that far. Grateful that it was only her that had to know the horror these people had gone through. She made a mental note to avoid the freeway on their way out and turned back toward the roof.

Roman's band was pulling plants out of their packs, plants and packs of seeds and dirt, of all things. "When people started looting and stealing food, for some reason no one was interested in potting soil. It's one of the few readily available things still left on the shelves." Kylie hefted a small bag from her pack. "It keeps us alive now."

Because there were still bugs to pollinate everything. With no animals to eat them, bugs were...plentiful. Except that many bugs fed on animals, and the whole circle of life thing was knocked askew. "What can I do to help?" she asked, kneeling next to Kylie.

"Well, we've got the adult plants that just need water and sunlight. But we need to get a fresh crop coming in. Grab a pot for me, will you?"

"You really think you can build a garden big enough to feed all these people?" Tresa asked. She juggled the pot with one hand, since her other hand was useless still. It hurt more than she would like to admit, and she clenched her teeth to keep from whimpering whenever it moved. Super impressive.

Of course, the pot slipped from her fingers, too big to hold one-handed.

"Here." Roman caught it and passed it to Kylie. "She can't carry it."

"I'm so sorry. I didn't even think—"Kylie winced. "Sorry. That was stupid."

Tresa shrugged. "It's okay. I would have made it."

"You dropped it," Roman felt inclined to point out. "It would have cracked and not held water."

"It's plastic," Tresa shot back.

"And old. It would have cracked."

"Roman, go bellow at someone else. We've got this." Kylie shooed him away, tucking a seed into her pot.

Roman looked mildly offended before he found someone else to snap at and wandered away. The guy seemed to have zero patience, and why he was leading a bunch of exhausted teenagers was beyond Tresa. He seemed the least qualified to deal with them emotionally.

"He keeps us alive," Kylie said, following Tresa's gaze. "I mean, he's a jerk for sure. He hasn't smiled in years. Not since my parents died in front of us, actually. All he cares about is surviving and not letting anyone else die."

"That's not going to happen. People die. It's an invasion. No matter what you do or how hard you fight."

Kylie winced. "You lost someone."

Tresa nodded, pounding the dirt a little too enthusiastically. "A few days ago."

"I'm so sorry. You take it as hard as he does, don't you?"

"Seeing as he doesn't seem to have a heart, I think I probably take it harder." She grabbed the next pot and started again.

"He does. He's just got these giant walls up because if he cares, it will tear him apart."

"Dammit, Kevin! That's a meal we won't ever get to eat. Are you happy? Do you want us to starve?" Roman snapped from across the roof. The kid at his feet was frantically picking up seeds spilled all over the concrete.

"Right," Tresa nodded. "Walls. That's gotta be it."

Kylie smiled and went back to potting.

Tresa kept her eye on Roman because he was volatile and made her nervous. She didn't like him. Not even a little. But he'd kept these people alive. He'd had the presence of mind to save their garden when everyone else was fleeing for their lives. And he'd saved her the day before.

Although she hadn't needed saving.

It had absolutely nothing to do with the fact that he was gorgeous beyond anything Tresa had ever seen before.

Nothing at all.

She didn't even like him.

He finally stopped prowling and settled on his knees in front of his own plot, working quietly. It was then that Tresa saw it. The anger in his eyes died a little, the always-tense set of his jaw loosened and he seemed to almost not seethe with hatred. She had to wade through the many emotions to get to his, and it certainly wasn't peace she found. It was suspicion, anger, hatred, but maybe not directed toward her. Hopefully not directed at her. Everyone else seemed to more or less accept her presence there. They were suspicious for sure, but she didn't get a lot of hate from them. Maybe because they'd seen what she'd done the day before and maybe because a half-breed alien just wasn't worth the energy it took to hate her.

Except Roman. He seemed to have plenty of that energy.

At that moment, though, he was content. Yes, that was it. Not at peace. Tresa wasn't sure he'd know what to do with peace. If he would recognize it when it faced him. But content, yes. His fingers worked in the dirt and he did his best to save that little plant.

Like he was doing with everyone in his little band.

She almost felt sorry for him.

Almost, but not quite.

She did it, too, and she didn't try to rip everyone's head off on an hourly basis.

They worked until sundown, when they brought every single plant inside and Tresa understood why they had everything in pots. So the Pys couldn't see them. Roman was strict. He snarled and snapped a lot and it was true what Kylie said. He never smiled. Not once.

"We have enough rations for my band until our garden starts producing. We'll have to scavenge for more food to feed your *tribe*." Roman fell into step beside her, sighing when she almost dropped her pot before he juggled his to one arm and took hers, as well.

"My tribe can feed itself. And I can carry my own pot." She snatched it back, balancing it like he had. She healed faster than the non-hybrid human, but an injury like that wasn't going to make itself better in a day.

He smirked at her. "Right. With what garden?"

"With what garden can I carry my pot? Gardens don't have arms, Roman."

He raised an eyebrow and she smiled sweetly before she continued. "We have our own rations. Did you somehow think we weren't eating at all until we showed up here at your mercy? We were surviving just fine."

He stalled in the hallway and she let him fall behind. Seconds later his long strides caught up to her. "Where do you get your food from?"

"Warehouses. Stores that haven't been completely looted. People's pantries. The Garce came so quickly very few people made it through their food storage. Everybody looted everything but didn't get a chance to eat the loot."

"We were scouring the area but were driven in here by the Garce. Our rations are low. If the garden doesn't work out..." He didn't seem to realize he was talking to her like she was a real person. Worry apparently did that to a guy.

"I'll get you more before I leave. I can get places others can't." She set the pot next to the others. "I'm going to search the building for more Garce. Will you not kill any of my tribe while I'm gone?"

Roman's mouth opened and closed like a giant, very hot fish before he found his voice. "I was going to do that. And what do you mean you'll get us more? And before you leave. You're not staying?"

She glanced at her little group. "It's not safe to stay in one place."

"We've managed."

She frowned, looking back at him. "You literally just got here."

"Yeah, but before that, we stayed in the same place for almost a year."

She wanted to ask how many he'd lost when the Pys had found them. How hard it had been to move on. But she could see those answers in his dark eyes, written in the pain there. "I see," she said instead and started down the hall, leaving him standing alone in the shadows with no one to snarl at.

It was best to start from the top down. The building had eight floors and lots of windows, but Roman had boarded up many of them. He'd made camp on the sixth floor, putting them not too close to the top, which was smart, and not near the ground. Also smart. The Pys might search the first flew floors but they had a short attention span. They couldn't sense the humans like the Garce could and instead just looked for traces of them. The Garce couldn't look for traces but they could sense them. It was like being trapped between two sides of the same coin.

A coin that wanted to either enslave them or eat them.

The Garce could easily go up the floors, knock through the boards and walls and whatever stopped them, but they were stupid. They wouldn't knock through the boards and walls unless they saw some reason to. Their intelligence was often what saved the humans who fled from them.

Well, the lack thereof.

They zipped through shadows like Tresa did, but only the shadows in front of them. They didn't use that advantage to jump off cliffs or get to the roof or through metal doors. Which was why the Py in their ship had been trying to use humans with Garce DNA to make a more intelligent species.

"I said I'd go." Roman fell into step beside her.

"Oh. Right. And what will you do if you find one? Shoot at it and run away?" Tresa rolled her eyes, sending light bouncing off the dark walls. She was her own miniature flashlight.

At least it wasn't glowing red light.

"What will you do?" He shot back. "Jump on its back and go for a ride?"

"My flames are back. I'll kill it." She left him behind, jumping into the shadow and zipping away, further down the hall where all he'd be able to see of her was the sparks from her tattoos.

She heard his frustrated sigh but she didn't wait for him. Instead, she ran and knew he couldn't keep up, even with his long legs. No one could keep up with her, except the aliens.

She enjoyed that.

She flew through the floor, checking in each office, each bathroom, each closet. Making sure everything was empty and clear. She couldn't sense anything else, but she couldn't be too careful. Not when so many lives were at stake.

She cleared the eighth through fourth floor and was just starting on the third when she ran into Roman and nearly clawed his throat out. "What the heck! You scared the crap out of me!"

"Heck? What are you, four?" He raised his flashlight, nearly blinding her.

"What are you doing down here alone?" she zipped backward, into another shadow and out of his light's reach.

"Sweeping the floors. For Garce. Not, like, with a broom."

She almost heard a...not quite a teasing note in his voice, but whatever was close to that but still locked behind his walls.

"I told you it wasn't safe yet. You have no way to defend yourself against them." She glowered, letting the full force of the fire in her blood light her eyes and shine back at him, rivaling his flashlight.

"I'm not sure how you didn't realize," he paced closer, "but we have miraculously survived this long without you and I'm the reason why."

Tresa smirked, leaning against the wall. "Really. You alone? And not your badass sisters up there holding everything together?"

He shrugged, the light jiggling in his hand. "They helped."

"It's a team effort. If you don't realize that, you're not a real leader." She turned her back on him and started prowling through the halls. "How many floors have you done?"

He hesitated. "Just this one. And I didn't ask to be their leader. When my mom died *in my arms* because of a Garce attack, one that moved just like you do, she told us to protect each other. I'm protecting. All these other people just showed up."

"So I did four floors in the time it took you to do a half of one. Interesting." She dropped her hand to her hip and tapped her chin. "And I hate to be the one to tell you this, but you're leading those people. And you care about them, whether you'll admit it or not."

She didn't mention his comparison to the Garce. She wasn't what she moved like. That didn't define her. Her actions with those special talents did.

Even still, his stupid words hurt.

Jerk.

"I don't care about them. They're here. I—"

"I can feel it, Roman. Argue all you want. Scream at them, yell at them, whatever. I can feel what you can't say." She smiled brightly.

Hopefully she'd blind him with her teeth.

He ran a hand through his dark hair. "You're a pain in the ass."

Her smile grew.

Chapter Six

They swept the remainder of the floors in silence, and though he hated to admit it, Roman felt a hell of a lot safer with the tiny demon creature at his side. He was well over six feet tall and she probably didn't even hit 5'6" but she felt like a giant force field between him and whatever evil stood on the other side.

A force field he hadn't asked for.

He didn't need saving. He didn't need her protection or her zipping or whatever else she was capable of. And he sure as *hell* didn't need her feeling what he felt. Things he wouldn't admit to.

He didn't care about those people on the floors above him. If he cared, he wouldn't treat them the way he did. He was only there for his sisters. That was all.

"My sisters need me," he finally snapped.

"Right." She glanced sideways at him. "They sure do."

"They do need me. We need each other."

"They hit that Garce more often than you did."

That Garce. Yeah, and never mind the one behind them that would have torn them to shreds if Tresa hadn't zipped into the hallway. It would have killed them. He would have failed.

If not for her.

"What's it like, killing your own?" he snarled because he didn't want to deal with her logic. Let her feel his anger if she was going to go prodding through his emotions.

She tensed next to him. "They are not my own."

And she was gone. Literally stepped into a shadow his flashlight created and disappeared. It was damn creepy but at least she was gone and he was free to climb the six flights of stairs alone with no one reading his emotions or telling him his sisters would be fine without him.

He already knew that. His mother had told them to protect each other. She hadn't told him to protect them alone. They had each other's backs. They were all he had left in this world, his reason for living. Without them...

There would be no reason to keep fighting.

She was already in the common room when he got there, which infuriated him to no end. She looked tired, though. Like she hadn't slept in—

Oh. Right. She hadn't slept. She didn't sleep. But she did look more tired than she had on the floors below. She was with her own little group, taking stock of their supplies. Kylie sat next to her, the little traitor.

"Is the building clean?" Michelle asked, looking up from whatever conversation she'd been having with Jeff. Jeff nodded at him before walking back to his own group. Tresa was the protector of her tribe, but Jeff led them. Like Michelle did for his own band.

The similarities weren't lost on him.

"Yeah. It's clean. She must have gotten the only Garce in the building yesterday. Besides herself, of course."

Michelle raised herself to her full height, which wasn't even close to his. "Knock it off, Roman. Don't make me kick your ass in front of all these new people. And you know Kylie would happily jump in on that."

"I'm sorry." Roman held his hands up, snarling more than he meant to. "She gets in my head. It...pisses me off."

"Well stop it. She's done nothing but be helpful. Kylie adores her."

"Kylie's just happy to have someone her own age—"

"Half our band is Kylie's age. You're the third oldest one here." Michelle raised an eyebrow. "She saved us, Roman. That was one little fight we weren't going to make it out of."

"We've made it out of worse."

"We haven't. We were surrounded. There was no way around them and nowhere to run."

"What about that time there were four of them and we were stuck in the middle? We outran them."

"Barely, and you almost lost an arm, remember?"

"But we survived," he pointed out triumphantly. "Plus, I saved her, too."

"She jumped on its back, Ro. She didn't fall on it. She knew exactly what she was doing." Michelle gave him a look, crossing her arms over her chest like she didn't believe he was triumphant after all.

"Yeah, to sacrifice herself so the others could escape. She didn't expect to survive."

Michelle smiled. "Exactly."

He'd walked right into her little trap.

Traitors, both his sisters.

He swung away. There was work to be done. He didn't have time for this crap.

Tresa found him two hours later. "We have enough rations to support us for two days, maybe three. I need to go scavenging. Will you be able to hold down the fort for the day tomorrow?"

It was so dark with all the windows boarded up, he had no idea if it was day or night. He checked periodically with whoever was on lookout so they could take their plants back outside but it was late evening as far as he could tell. "Tomorrow? As in a few hours from now?"

She pursed her lips, regarding him for several seconds before she nodded. "That's usually what tomorrow means."

The dark eyes flashed, sparked, unsettled him and he moved away. "Fine. I told you, I don't need you here."

"Well then we can just not share our food and you can all go hungry until your sad little garden decides to grow. How's the pollination coming with that?"

"If you paid attention, you'd notice there are still bees out there. Lots of them. That's why we're here and not somewhere cold. We have enough food for *us* for several weeks."

Which would be stretching it and they would go hungry often, but he wasn't telling her that. They'd survived it before. They would survive it again.

"So that's how it is. Every tribe for itself. I see."

She walked away.

He stared after her, wondering when he'd put his pride above feeding his people. She'd offered to feed them with her own rations. And he'd thrown it in her face.

His mother would be so proud.

"No," Kylie came around the corner, looking angrily from Roman to Tresa before she cut in where she clearly didn't belong. "That's not how it is. We'll all share. We'll all survive. And I'll help you scavenge. What can I do?"

Tresa paused next to his sister. "Thank you. But I think it's time we go."

"You can't!" Kylie sounded downright panicked and Roman studied her, wondering when this little alien hybrid had become so important to his sister. They'd literally been there not even a day. "There are too many Garce and you're still injured."

Tresa tipped her head to the side, eyes lit from some internal fire. He'd come to realize quickly that meant something bad was about to come out of her mouth. "Then I'll go hunting."

"Tresa," Jeff started, but Tresa smiled at him and the fire died.

It was a sweet smile; she adored her father, and Roman was reminded painfully of when Kylie and Michelle had smiled like that. They didn't. Not anymore. "It's okay, Dad. I'll take one at a time."

"No," Kylie said. "Not yet. Heal. You said your arm will be better in a few days. Go hunting then."

"We don't have enough food to wait until I'm healed." Tresa nodded toward their packs on their side of the room.

"But *we* do," Kylie said, motioning between herself and Tresa. "My brother's an idiot, but I'm not. We can feed each other until you're healed. Then you can go look for food and if you absolutely *must* kill something, you can do it then."

Tresa blinked owlishly at her for several seconds before she burst out laughing.

No one laughed anymore. The sound was so foreign in Roman's ears it took him several seconds to comprehend what, exactly, was happening. Plus, he'd just been called an idiot. By his own sister.

"Deal?" Kylie asked hopefully. She had huge brown eyes. It was impossible to say no when she pulled the puppy dog bit. How many times had he fallen for it in the last year? In his life?

"Roman, please let me play. I won't get in the way."

"You'll strike out, Kylie. We'll lose. You're too little to play comp ball. And everyone else on our team is a guy. You'd be the only girl."

"Your secret weapon. Please?" And the eyes. Kylie had been a miracle baby. He'd prayed so hard for her to survive. They all had. He would have traded his soul for hers given the chance. When he'd met her in the hospital for the first time, through the glass of an incubator, she'd looked at him with those same eyes, and he'd been wrapped around her finger ever since. How could he possibly say no?

"Fine. But you have to practice with me. Every night. Deal?"

She grinned, throwing her arms around his neck. "Deal."

He hadn't played baseball in so long. It was another life, and he never thought about it anymore. Until now. It hit him hard how much he missed it. How much he missed that other life. There was no room for fun here. Only survival.

"Deal," Tresa smiled faintly. "But you don't get to come. You stay here, where it's safe."

"I'll be your lookout. You come back to my shadow and I'll tell you where they are." Kylie looked positively giddy and Roman could only stand there, wondering what on earth had just happened.

For the next couple of days, Tresa avoided him. She took her spot at the slot to watch the skies and he went to the opposite side of the building to do the same. Michelle spelled him just before the sun came up, and they had the same argument every time. "You should get some sleep."

He pulled away from the window, completely exhausted. "I'm not tired."

Which was an outright lie.

"You're trying to compete with her, and you'll lose, Roman. Stop competing and collaborate instead. You guys would make a pretty awesome team."

"I won't lose," he said stubbornly, and then shook his head. "I'm not trying to compete."

"So you've been up all night because—?"

"Because I lost track of time." Which was true. He'd lost himself in memories he hadn't allowed himself to think about for over a year. His childhood. His parents. Their death.

Honestly, he didn't want to hate Tresa. It was possible she wasn't totally evil, despite being amazingly annoying. He'd seen her risk much—everything—to save those people she called her tribe. But he couldn't get past it. Her alien traits were too much and who knew when they would take over and she'd turn on them all. If she could kill a Garce with one swipe of her hand, imagine what she could do to a human.

"Any signs of Pys?" Michelle pushed him aside, peering through the slot in the board. The sun had risen, so there certainly wouldn't be any signs of Pys *now*. The sun was their only weakness, and it burned them alive. Well, the sun and the Garce. But thankfully, he hadn't seen any during the night, either.

"Not yet," he said grimly. Because they came. They always came. Where there were Garce, there were Pys. Lots of them.

Michelle blew out a breath. "Well, we can move the garden now. Which doesn't require your supervision. Go get some sleep."

Roman rubbed a hand over his face. "I'm okay."

"Yeah? And if we're attacked and you're sleep deprived? Then what?"

He thought it over, raising an eyebrow. "Adrenaline will get me through."

Michelle snorted and returned to the darkness. "Get some sleep. I've got this."

Roman sighed. "I don't even remember where my bedroll is."

"It's in the common room with all the rest of your stuff. Seriously, Ro. Duh."

"No one says duh anymore, Michelle."

She grinned sideways at him, her white teeth barely visible in the darkness. "I still say duh."

He hesitated before he left the shadows for the relative twilight of the common room. "Keep an eye on her, okay? We don't know when she could turn on us. We need to be prepared."

"Yeah, because I'm sure it could happen at any second." Michelle rolled her eyes.

"Exactly." Realizing he sounded paranoid and slightly insane, he tried one more time. "Please. Just—just keep an eye on her."

"That will be hard," Kylie interrupted from just beyond the doorway. "Because she went out hunting as soon as the sun came up."

"What?" Need for sleep forgotten, Roman spun toward his sister. "She was supposed to heal first. They'll tear her apart."

Kylie shrugged. "She went while I slept. Left Angie, one of her leads, in charge of her tribe while her dad keeps lookout from the roof. Apparently, she can't jump to any random shadow. She has to be able to see it."

"When did she leave?" Roman's heart pounded in his chest. He wasn't clear on why that was since he couldn't stand her and didn't trust her. "I didn't okay this."

Kylie laughed, one short, worried bark of laughter, passing him on her way toward the stairs leading to the roof. "I don't think anyone told her you're in charge."

The rest of their group, his and hers both, were moving the garden into the sunlight above, and he had to shove his way through them to get to Jeff. Tresa's father stood on the ledge of the roof, watching through the scope of his gun.

"How's she doing?" Roman asked, which surprised him because he meant to ask who the hell gave her permission to leave.

"She's moving too fast. Needs to slow it down some or she'll get too tired. I think the sheer number of Garce out there makes her too nervous for her own good."

Roman motioned to John, who brought his binoculars and Roman raised them to his eyes. He'd watched Tresa in action before when she'd shown up unexpectedly in the hall and potentially saved them from the two Garce, but it hadn't been like this.

She moved less like a Garce than he'd initially thought.

And more like a Py.

Chapter Seven

T resa jumped from shadow to shadow, trying to control her breathing and save her strength. She understood why the Garce did it so infrequently. It took so much energy — energy she needed for fighting. For killing.

She'd counted the Garce earlier. There were over fifty in this small city block, surrounding the building her tribe was in because they could smell the humans and they were hungry. They'd depleted their food source, were all starving and the scent of humans, so close yet so unattainable, was driving them all insane.

She had to cut their numbers down quickly or the Pys would show up. And with this big of a pack, it would draw more Pys than she could fight. So she moved from shadow to shadow, running when she could and zipping when she couldn't, until she was close enough to several of them at once. Since the sun was still rising over the abandoned freeway in the distance, there were plenty of shadows to disappear into.

She hesitated at the last second, hiding in the darkness. It was safe here. The Garce could sense her but as always, her presence confused them. She could go back. Back to the rooftop and they could stay hidden and pray the Pys wouldn't come or if they did, they wouldn't find the humans hidden carefully away.

But Kylie had told her stories the night before while she kept them company.

The Pys always found them.

At one time, Roman's band had over fifty people in it. While the Garce had picked off three or four every few months, when the Pys found them...well, they lost a lot more than three or four.

She had no choice. Fear couldn't hold her back. It couldn't keep her in the shadows. She had to fight. Even if she got hurt, it would be worth it.

She just couldn't die. That wouldn't help anyone.

She tightened her ponytail and raised her chin. "Be with me, Phoenyx."

She jumped. Springing from the shadows, Tresa hit the first Garce and let the flames in her light her nails and curve her fingers into claws. She drove her hand deep into the shadowy flesh, let the flames escape her fingers and pulled away before she could feel the tremors of death overtake it. Moving, moving, on to the next Garce as others from across the city came running, the noise and the smell of death drawing them too quickly. She had to move faster.

She slashed out with the sharp, fiery claws, tearing at whatever she could catch. The Garce hadn't yet realized she was an enemy and so hadn't started to fight back. But it was coming. She could feel the mounting confusion turn to panic and then rage.

Her job just got infinitely harder.

Dodging teeth now and claws that were not hers, she willed the fire to grow and at that moment, would have given anything to be able to throw her weapons like the Pys did instead of fighting up close and within biting range. She dove backward, zipping from one shadow to another, out of the center of the pack to the outskirts. The fire was dying, she had to get back. Two Garce were down and she'd wanted to kill five before she fled.

Three to go.

While everything in her screamed to run, that she was getting too tired, that she couldn't do it, she kept fighting. She dodged their claws, zipped out of the way of their teeth, and kept fighting. Over and over, she slashed out with her own talons and brought two more down.

To let one get behind her was death, she knew that. But trying to keep track of them all — she couldn't. There were too many. More had come from the surrounding city blocks. More that she hadn't counted.

It was the sun that saved her, Romans yell and the rifle firing. Tresa raised her head at the sound and just caught sight of the Garce's shadow as it sprang from behind her. She dove to the side, rolling across the ground as the Garce flew over her head. She felt the claws slash across her face and neck, felt the blood gush to the surface, and as it whirled around, turning on her, snapping and snarling, that very blood splashed onto its face and into its mouth.

One more down. She scrambled backward on her hands and feet, trying to get to its shadow before it fell, just caught her finger in the darkness as several others attacked.

And was gone.

Zipping through the darkness, letting the cool safety heal her. She didn't want to come out, didn't want to keep fighting. Fear nearly devoured her, but they could follow her here, if they were smart enough. She couldn't always count on their lack of intelligence to save her. She had to keep moving.

She leaped from the shadow as far away from them as she could get, close to the building but not inside, and felt the last of the fire flicker out. She was on her own.

So she ran.

The Garce were behind her, but she was just as fast as they were. She dodged bodies, thinking she could maybe make it around the building and find a way in without them following. Phoenyx would have been so proud of her, running so fast.

But she tired quickly. Stupid alien DNAs trying to kill each other inside her.

She wasn't going to make it.

She whirled again, slicing at the Garce closest to her and she saw that just enough of her blood slid through its shadowy skin to slow it down. Eventually, the blood would kill it, but not soon enough.

"Tresa!"

Roman's voice echoed and bounced through her head and she risked a glance up, a dangerous move when one false footstep could cause her to fall and falling meant certain death.

A rope ladder tumbled down from the third floor.

She threw everything she had left into making it to that ladder. She willed her feet to run faster, for her lungs to not burn, for her body to keep fighting.

"Run, Tresa."

It was Phoenyx's voice and Tresa had no idea if it was real or imaginary, but she found the strength. With the Garce snapping at her heels, tearing at her sweater, she dove, practically climbing up the wall. The Garce jumped for her and Roman hauled the ladder up, Tresa clinging to the rungs and scraping against the hot brick.

Teeth closed around her ankle and the ladder pulled taught between her hand and Roman's as the Garce tugged her back, hanging with its teeth lodged in her bone. She screamed and clawed at it with her free hand, but between its weight and her own, Tresa's one hand wasn't strong enough. Her fingers slipped on the rung, the rope burning her flesh.

"Tresa, hold on!" Roman bellowed.

The rifle shattered the air, the bullet lodging itself into the Garce's skull. It screeched and its jaws unlocked. Tresa gasped and tightened her grip on the ladder, watching as the Garce fell down, one horrific claw scratching at the bullet hole in pain while her blood burned it from the inside out. It crashed into the pack and they devoured it. They were starving and didn't care that it was one of their own.

Her blood from the ankle wound rained down on them. It would kill them slowly, but it *would* kill them. While Roman pulled her the rest of the way up, she shook her ankle, trying to get as much blood on the Garce as possible. It was a morbid little game and hurt like hell, but it was several more Garce she wouldn't have to kill later.

"Knock it off, Tresa. You're going to bleed to death," Roman grunted as he hauled her up. She tried to ignore the stiffness in her arm from her last adventure with the Garce and climbed as he pulled.

"You're oddly light." Roman tugged her through the window. She nearly collapsed on top of him, trying not to put any weight on her foot.

"Hybrid shadow monsters," she gasped around the pain, "Don't weigh much."

He scowled. "You almost got yourself killed. And I guess we'll be using more of our medical supplies on you, huh?"

"I didn't ask for your precious medical supplies," she snapped back.

Her dad came around the corner and swept her up into a tight hug. "That was too close, Tres."

She nodded, the weight of what she'd done crashing into her like a truck. A big truck carrying bricks. "I know. I just get so tired so fast. I can't ever tell when it's coming."

"Then you need to build your endurance," Roman said, startling her. She'd assumed he'd stalked off by then to find someone else to bellow at. "Slowly, not all at once or you won't get any better."

"Since when are you an expert on hybrid Garce behavior?" she asked, but was too tired to give it the vehemence it required.

"I'm no expert," he drawled, wrapping the rope ladder around his arm "But I played a lot of sports and endurance is key to everything. You can't just run out and play a doubleheader. You have to work up to that."

She squinted at him. "That wasn't a doubleheader."

Roman nodded toward the window before one of his guys boarded it back up. "No, I'd say that was a...five header? Maybe seven. Two look kinda wobbly."

She sensed something from him. Or maybe a lack of something.

Hate. When he spoke to her, she didn't feel it. Not anymore.

"Let's get you cleaned up, Tres. The Garce will smell the blood and be pacing the area for weeks." Jeff helped her slide to the floor as she wrenched her jacket off and shrugged out of the flannel shirt.

"Wrap it with this."

It was cold in just a tank top, and she never left that much skin exposed. Too many tattoos. She was too scary with so much of her alien self showing. Luckily, it was only Jeff and Roman in the shadowed hallway, and Roman already looked at her in fear and loathing.

"I've got the antiseptic!" Kylie barreled around the corner, waving the tube. Antiseptic was like liquid gold in this new world. She could have gotten a month's worth of food for that little bit.

"I don't get infections from Garce bites." Tresa winced as her dad bound the wound to stop the bleeding. That had been her favorite shirt, too. Such a loss. "And it will be healed in a few days anyway."

Kylie wrinkled her nose and for a second, Tresa assumed it was at her alien-ness swirling across her skin. But Kylie barely seemed to notice it. "Fine. But you could easily get an infection from something other than the Garce bite. I mean—"

"She doesn't," Jeff interrupted. "She doesn't get infections. Heaven knows, she would have died from it long ago if she could."

"That's...good?" The crease between Roman's dark brows seemed to question whether it was actually good or not.

"It's ironic, actually," Tresa said through gritted teeth. "The only thing that can kill me is the two alien DNAs they combined with mine that are trying to poison each other all the time. No big deal or anything."

"So if a Garce bites you, the Garce part of you protects you from their poison even as it's killing the Py part, and if a Py attacks..." Roman bent to examine the bite on Tresa's ankle as Jeff and Kylie worked on it. His hands on her leg were cool and did strange things to her stomach as he curiously traced the tattoos along her calf leading the bite. "They're on fire," he murmured.

"If the Pys hit me, I'm dead pretty much. Their attacks are too powerful and they easily kill the Garce and each other, if they need to. But what makes me useful is that I can kill them and you can't. So there's that."

"Why are they on fire?" Roman glanced up through thick lashes, his eyes metallic in the light.

"The Pys?" she asked stupidly. Must have been the blood loss making her brain foggy.

"The tattoos. Are they always this hot?"

Kylie touched one curiously, too, and Tresa wondered if that was what it felt like to be a specimen under a microscope. "No. Just when they're trying to heal me. They'll cool down in a few hours and by the time it's completely better, they'll be the same temperature as the rest of me."

"So this is what heals you?" Roman sat back on his haunches and regarded her. "Your arm should have been out of commission for weeks. Yet here it is, climbing ladders and stuff."

Kylie snickered. "It's not climbing ladders all by itself, genius."

Tresa saw his lips twitch. Almost, almost thinking about a smile. He would have been beautiful when he smiled, although she couldn't imagine it. His face was hard lines and perfect cheekbones and his eyes were always hard. Picturing him without the constant anger was impossible.

But he'd been so close.

"Yeah. It takes me a few days but if I lay low I heal pretty fast. If I hadn't gotten bit I would have been able to go back out tomorrow and fight more, though."

"It's too bad she didn't give you more Py powers instead of Garce ones," Kylie said. "The wings and the blood balls they throw? That would have come in handy."

"But Tresa can go out in the sun," Roman argued. "Pys can't. And the shadow jumping thing almost makes the flying thing unnecessary."

"She only gave me enough Py DNA to try to save me. Because I was dying. She didn't want me to be stronger than her," Tresa whispered. The pain from those days in the ship still came back to haunt her. It made her ache and the fire died under the fear.

"Let's get you upstairs," Kylie said briskly. "Food will help. It always makes me feel better."

Tresa should have objected because food was scarce, but she didn't have the heart. She'd have to sidestep it when she made it back to the common room. Really, all she wanted, more than anything in the world, was sleep.

And sleep was impossible.

Chapter Eight

It only took Tresa two days before she was up walking on her ankle, which Roman would have sworn was at least fractured under the force of the Garce's jaws. In that time, she managed to get around just fine with her zipping from one shadow to another. Several times he found her on the roof, ankle stretched out carefully in front of her, bent over a plot trying to coax life into the little plants.

"I can't believe this garden sustains your whole team," she murmured.

He sat down next to her because it hurt his neck to stare at the ground where she sat. "It was a lot bigger before. We grabbed what we could, but there wasn't a lot of time."

She nodded, peeking up at him through that mass of black hair sparkling in the sun. "The Pys came too quickly?"

He nodded. "Most of us escaped just because the Pys could only carry one human each and there were only two of them. But I wanted to be long gone before they came back with help."

"They're relentless," she murmured, going back to her plant, and he wondered how well she knew that. She'd said she could fight them, but had she? Judging by the tense set of her shoulders and the downturned lips, he wasn't going to push it.

Clearly, it was a subject she didn't want broached.

"I've been thinking about your freaky powers." He slid to the plot next to hers, keeping an eye on the sky. The sun was setting, but slowly. There wasn't much time before they'd all have to move below, into the compound.

"Alien DNA," she corrected him. "Freaky powers is offensive."

"Well, they're freaky," he shot back. When she raised an eyebrow but still focused on the plant, he backed off. Pushing her buttons was too easy and something angry in him wanted to see how far he could take it. But he had a prerogative and fighting with her wasn't going to get him there any faster. "You need a plan. Like, did you do sports in high school?"

"I didn't get to go to high school. Aliens invaded first."

"What?" Roman sat back on his haunches. Her face was flawless. Ageless. Like a photoshopped cover model, but she was real and not a magazine. "How old are you?"

"I turned eighteen about four months ago, I think. I lost track of time on the ship. But," she scooted herself over to the next plot. "I did play softball from kindergarten to ninth grade. High school in Utah started in tenth grade."

"Really?" His eyebrows shot up and a frizzer of excitement climbed his spine. "Ballplayer, huh? I would never have guessed."

She smirked at the dirt in front of her. "It doesn't really make any sense to carry around my mitt and bat in an alien apocalypse."

"I dunno. It might." He almost smirked back at her. Not quite a grimace, not quite a smile, appropriate for the situation and not something he'd done or even felt the need to do in months.

Years.

"A bat, maybe," she mused, unaware of the near-epiphany she'd just caused. "But the Garce would catch it when you swung and you'd get thrown off your feet and then they'd pounce."

It always went back to aliens. Which brought him neatly to his point. Well, maybe not quite so neatly, but in the general area. "My point is that when you started playing, you couldn't just go and do everything you wanted right away, right?"

She blinked at him and he could believe that yes, she probably did hit home runs before she could hold a bat and probably never had to struggle at anything in her life. But he knew that wasn't true. He'd watched her fight the Garce and nearly die.

Twice.

"I guess," she said slowly.

"So look. You have to start smaller. You go out and try to murder ten Garce and when they bite you, you use the blood to poison them instead of trying to escape—"

"Five."

"What?"

She shifted her weight, trying to get her ankle comfortable. "Five Garce. That was my goal. If I could kill five Garce a day, we'd have the city clear in twenty days, give or take a few days."

He nodded, trying not to roll his eyes. That wasn't how the Garce worked. They would either attract more Garce or run.

Or run.

That's what she'd been trying to do. Not kill them all. She'd been trying to chase them away before the Pys came after them.

He was an idiot.

"So what I'm thinking is you train yourself. Instead of starting huge, build your endurance by zipping or whatever it is you call it. A little more each day. Then you can start hunting when you're strong enough to get out there and actually fight."

Her dark, dark eyes narrowed. "I don't know what you call fighting, but I'm pretty sure I kicked ass out there."

"You're chaotic," he interrupted her before she could start yelling because heaven knows, that's what they seemed to do best together. "You don't have a plan, you have no idea what you're capable of, and you run the risk of getting out there and dying every single time because you run out of energy with no warning."

She glared, shoving herself to her feet, balancing unsteadily on the injured one. "You've seen me fight once and you think you're an expert?"

"Look, I've played a lot of sports — "

"Good for you. Sports and alien hunting are not the same thing at all. I've been doing this for over a year now — "

"Then you'd think you'd be better at it," he snapped back, which he hadn't meant to do. He'd just been trying to help, but she had such an innate ability to piss him off.

"And you've been trying to keep these people alive for how long? How's that going for you?" She whirled and half-stormed, half-limped off the roof, leaving him sitting there with half his band and half her team staring at him with angry, accusing eyes.

"I was trying to help," he snarled.

THE next time Tresa went hunting, Roman didn't watch. He stayed below, going through their ammo stock and inventorying supplies. It had to be done.

Even if he could barely concentrate the whole time. What if she got attacked, like last time? What if she didn't make it back? What if she died trying to protect them?

She's part alien, dumb ass. What do you care if she dies out there?

But he did care because she was doing it not just for her team, but his. And while she'd never complained about her foot or her torn shoulder before both had healed, he knew they hurt her.

A lot.

And what if someone needed to get her out of there quickly? Jeff had to stay up top so he could shoot and Kylie wouldn't be able to pull her up. His sister was strong, but she wasn't that strong. Michelle could help her, maybe between the two of them...

By the time he was done arguing with himself, he was halfway up the stairs to the roof and running hard.

Kylie passed him just as he made it to the door. "Where are you going in such a hurry?"

"Is she okay?" he asked more brusquely than he meant to.

Kylie grinned. "She's just fine. I think she just zipped inside."

He ground to a halt, breathing hard and wondering why on earth he cared so much. It annoyed him that she was fine even as relief swept over him. Confused and angry, he spun around and went back into the darkness to work on inventory.

They were running dangerously low. If the garden didn't start producing soon, they'd have to go out and scavenge, and their ammo wasn't stocked enough to survive a trip like that. Not with so many Garce loose.

He had to monitor how much each person in the compound took, trying to make sure everyone had enough without anyone getting more than he or she needed and it felt like it was breaking his brain.

They weren't going to make it.

"I took your advice."

He almost jumped, so engrossed was he in the worry at hand that he hadn't even heard her approach. That, or she'd zipped out of the shadow next to him. But she was usually pretty spent by the time she came back, so he'd bet she'd walked up behind him.

"What?" he half-snarled.

She didn't flinch, didn't even blink, like she just assumed that was how he spoke and didn't really hold any anger.

Maybe it didn't. He didn't even know anymore.

"I took your advice. I tried to make a plan. I mean, it—it kinda failed. But I came back before the fire was gone. I was able to zip to safety."

He leaned one shoulder against the wall and crossed his arms, raising an eyebrow. "I thought I didn't know anything."

She grinned. "You can learn things from all different useless sources."

"Useless and yet," he ran his eyes over her, from the shimmering black hair to her dusty boots, trying not to notice the seductive curves under the flannel and leggings she always wore, "here you are, not bloody and not half-dead."

She shrugged, still smiling.

He took a breath, knowing he could incur her anger. "What if we slowly build up your zipping ability? Inside, where it's safe?"

She pursed her lips, nodding. "Maybe, one day. For now, I need to focus on getting out, past the Garce and getting more food. And more ammo. I know my dad's running low."

Roman wanted to argue and tell her that plan was stupid because if she was stronger, she had a better chance of surviving the trip, but she was doing this for all of them, not just her and not just her team. "Okay. Then we make a plan first. You can't just go skipping through the shadows and hope to make it back alive."

Compromise. He hadn't realized he was capable of it.

Tresa played absently with a strand of silky hair, eyebrows drawn together in thought. "We need someone who knows the area. I mean, I've been here before but I wouldn't know where an armory or military base would be. Not even a grocery store. It's been years. A map would be handy."

"Weren't you guys coming through the area on foot?" he asked, which was stupid. Everyone was on foot now. Fuel stores had been depleted months, if not years, ago.

She nodded, her eyes running over his inventory. He had to keep it under constant guard, usually by Michelle or Kylie because there was no one else he trusted. He wasn't sure when Tresa had added her own supplies to his, especially since she had never confirmed that she was staying.

She did it like she did everything. Quietly and without fanfare.

"We don't have a lot of time. I should be up and running again by tomorrow night—"

"No. Absolutely not. The Pys come out at night."

She turned toward him and he expected her anger — which he usually got when he told her no. But he was only met with a grimness that made his heart cold. "We can't wait longer than that, Roman."

He turned back, scouring the little in front of them. "We've always made it before..."

She laid a hand on his arm and her fingers were warm against his skin and soft, so soft. "You aren't alone anymore. You're not carrying this all by yourself. I got this. No big deal."

He stared down at her, memorizing her face, studying the freckles just visible across her nose. The Py hadn't been able to erase all her humanity, then. The real Tresa was still in there. Which left him no choice. "Fine. But neither do you."

She raised an eyebrow, her hand still resting against him like she'd forgotten it was there. "What?"

"I'm going with you."

She hauled back, black eyes widening so that he could just see the brown underneath. He knew her eyes had been brown once, before that Py had changed her, but he couldn't tell how dark, or if they were more of a golden brown, honey-kissed. "No, absolutely not."

He smirked, his lips just turning up and it felt so wrong, to mock her with an almost smile. So wrong, to smile when he'd lost so much. When the world had lost so much. "I didn't ask your permission."

"How do you think you're going to keep up with me? I zip through shadows and when I don't zip I run — "

"Freakishly fast. I know. I'll manage. You're not going out there alone, Tresa." He turned away from her to stalk down the darkened halls, making sure everything was hidden, everything covered, before the Pys could show up for the night. They'd been lucky so far, but he knew better than anyone that luck didn't last.

She followed. "Roman, you'll slow me down. I can't save us both."

"You won't have to. I save myself. I'm a big, strong boy."

She rolled her eyes. "Big and strong can't fight the Garce."

"And yet it has," he said softly. "For three years now, Tresa."

She ignored him, and he could see how agitated she was by the anxiousness of her movements, the way she ran a hand through her hair and fought with the tangles. It was thick and shimmered in the darkness like it was lit by some internal Christmas light. "What could you possibly help with? You can't run as fast as me. You can't get into buildings I can get into. You can't kill the Garce. You can't —"

"I can carry what you can't. And I'll have your back." He reached over and untangled her fingers, letting the silk run across his skin. "As soon as your *fire* returns, come get me. We'll go."

He left her there, standing alone in the darkness gaping after him. He didn't have time to argue with her anymore. He had shit to do.

It hit him, really hit him, when he was just emerging onto the roof. He'd heard her, used her argument against her, but hadn't really realized what she'd said.

"You're not alone anymore. You're not carrying this all by your-self."

Chapter Nine

Tresa paced. Her dad was busy, doing his own thing and it thrilled her that he finally felt safe enough to let her out of his sight. Their whole tribe seemed to have assimilated seamlessly into Roman's band. Making them a team, instead of opposing sides. Even Roman, apparently.

Sure, the lack of constant bickering was nice. Kylie had been right when she'd said if they used their differences to work together, they'd be stronger. But she was fairly positive Kylie wasn't going to be happy with Roman's shiny new idea.

"I am a demon hunter," she told Angie, who was watching the sky for Pys. "Not him. What does he honestly think he's going to do? He can't outrun them if they attack. He can't fight them. He can't heal like I can and if he gets bit, he'll have to worry about infection like I don't. What does he think he's going to do?" she asked again, breathlessly.

"Apparently he thinks he's going to have your back. Something none of the rest of us have been able to do."

Tresa stopped pacing. "That's ridiculous. You've always had my back."

"No, we try to stay in front of you and out of your way so you have to do as little saving as possible." Angie sent her a brief smile before she went back to the skies.

Tresa grumbled but couldn't think of anything else to say. The fire in her blood, the Py DNA, whimpered for more Garce flesh, for their blood on her hands. She hadn't gotten enough earlier that day, trying to stick to her plan— which had failed.

But at least she'd had enough energy to make it back.

"Oh no," Angie whispered, jerking back from the slot in the window. "Tresa."

Tresa didn't have to make it to the slot in record time to know what would cause the tremors in Angie's voice. But she did anyway, hoping beyond hope that Angie was wrong. That there weren't the beautiful Pys streaking through the skies like overgrown fairies, looking for humans...

Calling for humans.

She could hear their voices, lilting and beautiful like a thousand lullabies. They called, begged, pleaded, searching for anyone they could steal away to their ship.

Never to be heard of again.

"Run. Tell Roman. On silent feet, Angie."

Angie whirled and was gone, disappearing into the halls before Tresa could even turn around.

Grateful that she hadn't used all her Garce energy earlier, she zipped through the shadows to the common room down the hall where everyone had gathered for the night. "Silent. Everyone. Not a sound."

She'd expected panic, fear, chaos. Instead, they moved together, extinguishing lights without a sound, plunging the room into darkness. "Whatever you do, don't listen to their voices," she whispered.

She knew they could see her eyes, glowing like the Garce's, but a gold color instead of red evil. Hopefully, it gave them comfort instead of terror. She stayed with them in that room, and she could feel their fear like it was a palpable thing. On light feet, slipping from shadow to shadow, she passed among them, judging without words whether her presence was helping or making things worse.

She'd expected that her own team would be comforted by her presence, and they were, but Roman's group didn't like her or trust her yet. She could feel it from almost all of them. Kylie was an exception, and Michelle. But the rest, while grateful for her help, still distrusted her, probably feeling as Roman did—that she could turn on them at any time. Maybe, she would always be regarded with suspicion, she didn't know. She tried not to care.

She was surprised, knowing what she did, that all she felt from them was hope.

They thought she could protect them from the Pys. The beautiful, fairy-like creatures who were far deadlier than any Garce. And these people knew what the Garce could do to her. Yet, she brought them hope.

She wanted to. More than they could ever understand, she wanted to. A small part of her craved the Garce's flesh, but a huge part of her, a nearly uncontrollable part, craved the Pys more.

It was the Garce's greatest flaw. They craved the Pys with their poison, flaming blood. Blood that ate away at the Garce from the inside out, lighting them on fire even as they devoured their prey. They could kill the Pys when no human weapon could, and Tresa didn't understand that. She did understand, though, that they died doing it.

She'd killed a few Pys, but only one at a time. She'd never taken on more than that and she knew for certain that she would die if she did. She also knew that there were three, four, maybe five hunting in the desert beyond and yet...

And yet everything in her wanted to go after them.

"Come to us, pretty ones. Let us help you. Let us feed you. Let us heal you. We're not your enemy." Their voices were lilting, beautiful, haunting. Rumors swirled through what was left of the human population that they were the fairies, the vampires, the sirens of legend. That the Pys had been there before and left in their wake horrible, beautiful tales that would persist for centuries.

"Cover your ears," Tresa whispered. She wanted to cover her own, but she didn't dare. She had to listen, to feel the emotion in their voices. It was the only way she'd know if they found this small band of humans struggling to survive.

Plus, it wasn't their words that called her.

It was their blood.

The need to attack was nearly overwhelming. She shook, her fingernails turning to sharp claws, tearing through her palms. She could smell her own blood, but it did nothing to detract from theirs.

"*Shhhh, Tresa,*" she heard Phoenyx whisper. "*You're not what they made you. You're my baby sister and you're stronger than they are.*"

Well. That was twice now that her dead sister had spoken to her. Tresa was officially losing her mind. Really, though, what did she expect? Phoenyx had always been there when Tresa needed her.

Desperate to ignore them, she started to sing the ABCs in her head like she had when she was little and scared of the dark. When that didn't distract her, she sang them backward and then moved on to *Bah Bah Black Sheep* and *Twinkle Twinkle Little Star*.

As she passed her dad, he reached up and squeezed her hand. He alone knew how hard this was for her. He alone knew of the cravings, of the bloodlust. And yet, she felt no worry from him. No fear. Only perfect faith. Always, he believed in her.

She would have been so lost without him.

She was starting on her fifth round, moving mechanically among the others, trying to keep them calm when she didn't feel calm herself, when the screaming started.

It wasn't human. It was Garce. Horrific, terrified, confused screams that echoed through her head and shattered around her heart. She wondered if they screamed like that when she killed them. She'd never noticed, but then she didn't usually torture them first.

The Pys liked to play with their food.

She could feel them, feel their pain and their fear and she almost, *almost* felt pity for them. Nothing deserved to die like that.

Nothing but the Pys.

And the Garce, who had taken so much from her. So she stuffed the pity away and went back to singing. All night long, she paced among her tribe, listening to the screaming and the singing and the chanting. A couple of times, someone would get up. Someone would try to go to the window or escape down the hall and she would chase them and drag them back and the others would hold them down until they could break the hypnosis. Most of the time, the Garce's screams drowned out the Pys' voices.

Thankfully.

When dawn approached and drove the Pys to wherever they went to hide, Tresa collapsed to the floor, more exhausted than she could remember being. Michelle pulled her to the wall so she didn't get trampled by everyone attempting to escape, and she dragged her legs up to her chest and dropped her forehead to her knees.

That sucked.

"Is everyone okay in here?" Roman's voice was hard but panic radiated from him in waves. He cared about these people, whether he admitted it or not. She didn't have the energy to raise her head, though. She felt like someone had mushed up her brain and then swirled it all around with a whisk. She'd never been so tired.

"Everyone's fine. Tresa kept us safe." Michelle was grateful, really and truly. Tresa could feel it. It wasn't much that she had done. It wasn't like the Pys attacked. But she felt tears well in her eyes and drip onto her jeans anyway.

"She did." Roman didn't sound entirely convinced and dropped his voice so only Michelle could hear him. And Tresa, because super human alien hearing and all. "Is she okay?"

"Yeah. I think she's just tired."

"She doesn't get tired."

"Well, then maybe she just doesn't want to deal with you. Who knows," Michelle shot back.

But she did get tired. So soul weary she wanted to give up. Maybe physically she didn't sleep anymore, but she would have traded her right arm for a chance to take a nap. To close her eyes and not feel them fighting against it. Of everything she'd lost when she was turned, she missed sleep the most.

Roman knelt next to her. She could see his boots and then his knees in her peripheral line of vision. "Hey."

"What?" she mumbled, the word slighty slurred.

"You alive?"

"Last time I checked."

"What's going on here?" she just caught his hand gesturing in her general direction. Apparently meaning her hot mess situation.

"I'm resting my eyes."

"Did they get to you?"

Sighing, she raised her head and let it fall back against the wall. "Roman, if you're worried that I'm going to suddenly turn Garce and eat everyone, you're a little late. It would have happened —"

He scowled, dark eyes narrowing before he tapped her on the forehead. "The Pys. They get to everyone, not just you, genius. I didn't say a damn thing about you eating anyone. Your teeth would never survive that."

She blinked at him in confusion. "Did you — did you just make a joke and insult me at the same time?"

He shook his head, rising to his full height. "The Pys get to everyone. We all hear it."

Not the way they get to me.

She didn't say that, though. She just closed her eyes and prayed for sleep that wouldn't come.

She heard his footsteps fall away and then he started barking orders. Gardens still needed to be tended, work still needed to be done. It didn't matter that they'd all spent the entire night in silent terror. Roman didn't have time for that.

And she was grateful.

Pushing herself to her feet, she followed him up to the roof.

"You need to rest," he said over his shoulder when he realized she was right behind him. She didn't know how. She walked on shadowed feet. Literally making no sound.

"I'm fine."

"You look like crap."

"As do you." He didn't really. Roman was beautiful. If the world hadn't ended, he could have been a movie star. Or a male model.

Not a chance she'd tell him that, though.

"Rough night for both of us, I guess. Can you load me up?" He hefted one pot into one arm and held the other one out and Tresa obediently handed him the heaviest pot she could, relishing the fact that his arm sank under the pressure and hers didn't.

"You have no idea," she murmured instead of gloating.

He waited until she'd grabbed her own pots and followed her up the stairs. "No. I don't. Want to talk about it?"

She smirked. "With you? No."

"What's wrong with me? I'm an excellent listener."

Tresa set her pots down, turning her back on them to go to the edge of the building. "Yeah, in between all your snarling and yelli—" her voice died in her throat as she scanned the area below them.

The Pys had fed well the night before. The city was littered with torn, bloody Garce bodies. Everywhere she looked, corpses rotted in the sun.

"Holy crap," Roman breathed next to her. "It's like those pictures of when the railroad workers killed all the buffalo."

What Garce had survived fed greedily on the bodies. They didn't kill each other, but they had no qualms eating their brothers when they were dead.

Tresa swallowed hard. Fear shook her bones and her heart clattered against her chest but she couldn't show it. If they knew how much it scared her, there would be chaos. She was their hope. She was their weapon. She couldn't break down. Not here. "Less Garce for me to kill, I guess."

She went back to her plots, going through the dirt, adding precious fertilizer and hand pollinating each new bud because she wasn't sure the bees were doing their job.

Kylie knelt next to her, taking the plot Tresa hadn't worked on yet. She hadn't noticed Roman across from her until Michelle settled on his other side. "Do you think they knew we were here?" Kylie asked, keeping her voice low enough that only they could hear. Everyone else had seen the Garce bodies, but most thought it was a great stroke of luck. Less for them to have to fight through later.

"No." Tresa shook her head. "If they had known, they would have come in. They suspect, I think."

"Because of all the Garce in the area." Roman nodded. "They think we attracted them."

Tresa frowned. "Why *are* there so many Garce here? Did you see any other humans when you moved in?" And why on earth had it had taken her so long to notice that? Clearly, she was not at the top of her game.

Roman glanced at Michelle, who shook her head. "We picked up a few people in the last couple weeks, but there were no big groups. We thought we were alone here until you popped out of the shadows."

Popped out of the shadows. It made her sound like an evil jack in the box.

"So...what were they doing here?" Kylie dug viciously at her plot, shoving the dirt around with her fingers. "They had to be feeding off something."

"Indeed," Tresa murmured. Roman raised his head and she could feel his eyes studying her.

"What are you thinking?" he finally asked when she didn't offer more. Kylie and Michelle both looked at him in surprise.

She sat back and dusted her hands off. "I'm thinking we're not the only ones in this city."

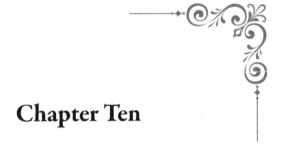

Chapter Ten

Roman followed Tresa down the stairs. She'd escaped just after her epiphany, muttering that it was time to go.

He assumed she meant it was time to go scavenging and not leaving the compound for good. "You're not ready yet," he said for the fourth time, but she didn't slow. The fact that she didn't jump into the shadows to get away from him was telling, though. She didn't have the energy.

And yet, she was going out there.

"Tresa!" he finally snarled, grabbing her arm. She stopped, facing him but her eyes were dark and dangerous.

Probably shouldn't have grabbed her like that.

"You're. Not. Ready."

"It just hit me," she said, shaking him off her. "Why there are so many Garce here. But there are no humans, right? So what's going on? And then I realized. It has to be. I can't believe I missed it. I mean, I've never seen it myself but I've heard others —"

Her babbling finally started to make sense and his blood ran cold. Something just as terrifying as the aliens. "Traders?"

She nodded, gnawing on her lip. "It has to be."

There were rumors, things he thought couldn't be true because no one could be that evil. People he'd met in passing said there were traders — humans, who kidnapped other humans and used them as bait, drawing all the Garce into one area and keeping them there by feeding them.

Feeding them other humans.

That gave the trader the ability to live wherever they were with relatively low Garce activity. And with few Garce meant few Pys.

"But — but how? How would they feed the Garce without getting themselves killed in the process?"

"They have to have cars," Tresa whispered. "And the Garce wouldn't chase a moving meal when they have an easy one right in front of them. I need to talk to my dad."

Who was on the seventh floor. They'd just walked down seven flights of stairs and she was going to turn around and go back. Which was good, when Roman thought about it. It meant she wouldn't be trying to pry the boards off the doors to escape outside because she wasn't strong enough to blink yet. "Yeah. Yeah, let's talk to your dad."

She started back up the stairs before she stopped and turned her face up toward him. She was so tiny but she seemed so formidable, so big and powerful that he forgot sometimes that she barely came to his chin. "Why would they do this, Roman? Why could anyone do this?"

There was so much pain in her eyes, like she was taking all of the hurt and betrayal that had been heaped upon the world and it was drowning her heart in torment. The black swirls across her forehead and around her eyes sparkled in the darkness as if they fed on her misery. Without thinking, without meaning to, he pulled her against his chest and wrapped his arms around her, trying to envelop her enough to protect her from all that pain. "We don't know that's the case, Tresa," he murmured against her hair. "It could just be they like the mild weather and beautiful sunsets."

She tipped her head so she could peer up at him again, scowling. "Did you just make a joke?"

"No. I was being completely serious."

She laid her head back against his chest, very still. "I like it when you forget you hate me."

"I don't hate you. I could never, even when you're at your very most annoying."

He expected her to object, deny that she was ever obnoxious and probably attempt to blame it all on him. But she shook her head, pulling away and tapping his chest where his heart beat under her finger. "I can feel it."

He blinked, dumbstruck. Before he could form an answer, she had turned away and started back up the stairs, still fighting with the pain of her own realization.

Aliens were bad. But humans could be so much worse.

He followed her up the stairs, but slower because she ran from him and he wasn't a mind reader, but he knew her well enough to know she needed space. He wanted to ask what she meant when she said she could *feel it*. Could she sense his hatred? His distrust?

Although he hadn't exactly made it a secret.

BY the time he made it to the common room, Tresa, Jeff and both his sisters were missing. Angie, her second in command, was gone, too. Once, this space had probably been a conference room of some type. Now, it was swathed in darkness and fear.

"Where'd my sisters go?" he asked Kevin, who was, as usual, doing nothing he was supposed to be.

Kevin shrugged. "Dunno."

Roman glared, crossing his arms over his chest until Kevin broke. "I think they went to an office." He motioned down one of the corridors and Roman stalked away. Before the world had ended, Kevin had been a home inspector. Roman had thought he'd be useful to the team.

Not so much.

He was lazy and sneaky and dishonest. When Roman had to post guards at the door to the storage room, he was one of the reasons why.

Voices distracted him from his own internal seething, low and rushed. He followed the sound until he was at the very end, in a corner office not yet boarded up but with a heavy door left slightly ajar. He inched into the light, thinking idly that they should probably board these windows, too. Which meant they had to find more materials...

"Took you long enough." Michelle winked at him.

"Seven flights of stairs," he responded, jerking his head back the way he'd come. Michelle smiled and Kylie rolled her eyes.

Tresa perched on a desk. It was broken, claw marks dug through the laminate, and the distinct rust-red of dried blood covered the chair behind her, but thankfully there were no bodies. By now, most had deteriorated and were just the bones, but for the first year, things had been really bad.

"I think we should tell them," Kylie said. "Give them warning that this is out there. Make sure they don't go anywhere alone."

"Tell them —" Roman pointed back toward the common room, where thirty-something people all lived blissfully unaware that they had stumbled into such a horror. "— that there are traders in our midst? They'll panic. Or worse, go try to join them."

Tresa raised an eyebrow. The sarcastic movement didn't match the pain in her eyes. "You think very highly of them."

He shrugged. "I'm not stupid."

"You're jaded. My tribe would never do that."

He crossed his arms over his chest and eyed her. "Really?"

Tresa raised her chin, the familiar spark back in her eyes, chasing away the pain. "No."

Angie sat next to her, and Jeff watched out the window but spoke over his shoulder. "We wouldn't have survived what we have if we thought that way."

"Well, we wouldn't have survived what *we* have if I didn't."

Angie spoke for the first time. Her black hair curled around her face and her voice was soft. "They've betrayed you?"

Grudgingly, he pushed away from the wall. "No. Because I didn't give them a chance."

"People are what you expect them to be," Tresa said. "You expect them to be monsters, eventually they'll have no choice but to be a monster."

"I thought you were a monster."

She nodded slowly. "Exactly."

Kylie's eyes shot open and Roman had no idea how to respond to that. Tresa never reacted the way he expected. After so many years, he thought reading people and anticipating their responses was his gift. It was how he protected himself. He couldn't protect himself from her when she didn't answer the way she was supposed to.

"But you're not a monster," Kylie said. "You're our little hybrid."

"Little?" Tresa asked in mock outrage, the pain in her eyes evaporating at Kylie's words. "I'm perfectly average."

"Yeah." Roman almost smirked. "What are you, five feet tall?"

"I'm almost 5'6", thank you." She scowled back at him. "National average is 5'5"."

"My mistake." Roman coughed. "I don't know what I was thinking."

Jeff sighed. "This is solving all our problems."

"Right." Roman shook his head. He'd been teasing her. In the middle of an alien apocalypse, while they were trying to figure out how to fight for their lives, he'd been teasing a hybrid who could turn on them at any second. "We don't tell them. Understand? This knowledge doesn't move past these walls."

Tresa pushed to her feet. "I'm sorry, but you don't get to say what I tell my own people. I trust them that they can handle the knowledge that traders are out there and not cause mass hysteria."

"What? No. It's not an option." Roman raised himself to his full height, and while he towered over her by six inches, it didn't seem like much all of a sudden. Not when her eyes flashed black and the tattoos winding across her face sparkled.

"You're afraid of me." It wasn't an accusation and it wasn't boastful. There was pain in her voice and he realized belatedly that yes, she could sense their emotions. Like an animal.

Like the Garce.

"I'm not afraid of you. I'm afraid of what you could become if you're ever angry enough." There. He'd said it. He'd said what they were all thinking.

"I see. Well, to save you all from myself, maybe it's time that we go. We've been in one place too long anyway. Good luck on your own." She stalked out. Angie glared at him for good measure as she followed Tresa.

"Awesome. That went well." Michelle paused in the doorway, as if unsure which side she wanted to be on.

"You gotta learn to compromise." Jeff finally turned from the window. "Two strong leaders can't work together without compromise."

Before Roman could think of a way to respond to that, Jeff was gone, too.

"She has no common sense," Roman growled. "Tell them? Has she even ever met these people? They'll freak out. They'll turn on each other."

"Look, Ro." Michelle rubbed the bridge of her nose. "She looks at those people as family. She'd do anything for them and I don't know if you've noticed, but they'd do the same for her, and for each other."

"She's a hybrid!" Roman bellowed. "How do they know she's not gonna turn on them?"

"This again?" Kylie groaned and thunked her head back into the wall behind her, staring at the ceiling. "If she was going to turn on us, she would have. If she was going to turn on *them*, she would have. What more do you want her to go through to prove she's one of the good guys, Roman?"

He ran a hand through his hair, staring out the window. They were right, of course. He was being an ass. Over the last few days, he'd discovered that somewhat impossibly, he appreciated having her there. Appreciated having someone to share the burden with.

And then he'd gone and opened his mouth. "When did you get so wise?"

"We've always been wise. You're just too stubborn to see it." Michelle ruffled his hair and he scowled, smoothing it back into place.

"She'll leave us, Roman. We aren't keeping her safe here. She's protecting us. Unfortunately, you don't get to talk to her like you talk to everyone else." Kylie sighed. "Remember before the world ended, and you weren't a jerk all the time? You were my hero, Roman. I thought no one could ever be as amazing as you and I wanted to be strong and funny and *kind* just like you. Where did that Roman go?" Sending him one last hurt look, she left with Michelle, leaning on her shoulder.

"How come I wasn't your hero?" he heard Michelle ask, teasing. Trying to help Kylie feel better.

"I have two heroes. Apparently, you're the good one and he's the big dumb one."

Michelle's laughter mocked him as it disappeared down the hall with her.

Alone in the room, Roman sank into the broken chair, balancing precariously before he dropped his forehead to the desk in front of him. He could feel the claw marks against his skin. Garce had attacked this place, and probably Pys, too, although he hadn't been looking for the scorched walls and burned carpets. They'd killed everything. They'd killed his parents. And he was just supposed to let that go and embrace Tresa and her Garce powers with open arms? He wasn't wrong. He'd seen the tattoos sparkle and her eyes darken dangerously. He'd seen —

He'd seen her have a temper when pushed too far. Just like any human.

So what was he going to do? Let her walk out of there, put all her people in danger?

No. He wasn't.

He'd been Kylie's hero once. Like a sharp blow to his heart, he realized he'd do anything to be that hero again.

Not the big dumb one.

He shoved himself to his feet and jogged down the hall. The common room was packed, but Tresa wasn't there. Just her team, gathering their things. "Settle down." He fought his way to the middle where they could hear him. "It's not safe to go out there. Tresa knows this —"

"If Tresa knew this, she wouldn't be taking us out there." A woman Roman didn't know said. Tresa knew everyone's names, even his team's. He barely knew his own group.

"Tresa thinks she's keeping everyone safe by doing this, but she's not. I —" he swallowed, trying to figure out how to phrase it. "— I gave her false information that led her to believe leaving would be the best idea for everyone. It isn't. And if someone will tell me where she went, we'll figure this out together."

No one spoke, exchanging glances and internally debating. Which one did they listen to? The one who had their hearts or the one who told them to stay where it was safe?

He knew, without having to be told. His team would have stayed. Hers?

They would follow her anywhere.

No one answered him, so he fought his way back out and went exploring, starting at the bottom floor, thinking she would have been looking for a safe exit or something. He searched every floor, and only found her when he made it to the roof. She stood at the far corner, silent like a guardian, her long dark hair billowing behind her in the cool breeze. Jeff and Angie stood next to her, jotting notes and speaking in low, urgent voices. He didn't exactly sneak up on them, but he also didn't make an effort to announce his presence.

"The Garce are at the west side of the valley," Jeff said, lowering his binoculars. "We can't go back the way we came."

"That's probably where they wait for the traders. The Pys killed a lot of Garce the other night, but there are still too many for me to fight through. The east is an option but without sending scouts ahead, I don't know what to expect."

"North? Back to Utah? Utah homes have a lot of food storage," Angie suggested.

"Maybe. But it's cold there now. We'd have to worry about frostbite and fires lure the Garce..." Jeff mused.

"Go away, Roman. I could turn into a raging Garce at any second." Tresa spoke without turning and although her voice was flat, he could still hear the pain in it.

"Look, I was wrong. I'm sorry. It's just — the Garce took everything from us. When you move like them and have their same weird powers, it brings back memories. Memories I've tried too hard to bury."

"Took everything from you?" Tresa turned, balanced on the corner of the wall. One false step could send her falling to her death but she moved too fluidly, blending in and out of the shadows. "Are you serious with this, Roman?"

"I—my parents—"

"Yeah. And my sister. While my mother and my other sister watched. And then they took *me*. They made me into a monster, just like you thought. Into something everyone fears, whether they try to hide it or not. So please, spare me the sob story of how they took your parents. At least you still have you."

Chapter Eleven

Jeff and Angie escaped the roof and the volatile argument threatening to shatter the stillness around them. Tresa barely noticed, breathing so hard her breath rose and fell and she could feel the Garce blood roaring in her ears. Making her more powerful. She felt like she could take on every Garce in the city.

"I'm sorry they took your sister." Roman's voice was so low she could barely hear it, would not have heard it if it weren't for her super alien hearing.

"She tried to save me. She failed." Tresa gritted her teeth and swept her eyes away from him, back out to the city and the Garce below.

"I'm sorry."

That was three times he'd said it in the space of two minutes. Probably a record of some kind for him. "I'm sorry about your parents."

"Kylie and Michelle, they lost our parents, too. But they're braver than me. They move on, they relive memories. They don't shut down and shut everyone out. And they're not afraid. I live in constant fear." He shrugged, running a hand through his hair.

He was still afraid. Maybe he always would be. Tresa didn't know how to get past that and she really wished she could shut off the emotion-sensing thing. Shut it off and be a normal human with normal feelings who had no idea what everyone else might be thinking.

But she wasn't. She never would be. She had to embrace what she was and move on, or she would lose her mind. "Everyone's lost someone. Some have lost everyone. We deal with it the best we know how and we move on. Some of us forget to smile. Some of us forget who we were."

She made to pass him, to go back downstairs and gather her things. She should have known better than to think they could stay in one place. They hadn't, in all this time. They'd been nomads and they had survived. Hungry, most of the time. Under attack constantly. But they'd made it this far.

"Don't go, Tresa." His hand shot out and caught her arm and how, she couldn't understand because she thought she'd kept adequate distance between them. "I'm sorry for what I said and I know you can feel my fear, but it's not because I'm afraid of what you are —"

"No. You're afraid of what I'll become."

"No," he snarled, his usual sharpness almost covering the vulnerability. Almost. "No. I'm not. I thought by telling you why —"

"Telling me why you're afraid of the Garce will make me feel better about why you're afraid of me? That doesn't help, Roman!" she yelled, her hands fisted, feeling the sharp claws digging into her skin. Below them, the Garce went into a frenzy.

She swallowed hard, closed her eyes and berated herself for being so stupid. If the Garce were still clawing at their building when the sun went down, the Pys would know exactly where to find them.

"I'm trying, Tresa. That's all I can give you. Rationally, I know you're a nice little human and you'd do anything for any of those people down there. But I can't always be rational. I can pretend, but you see through that. So all I can give you is that *I'm trying*. And I think if we work together, we can survive this. If we go our separate ways, I don't know."

She shoved her black hair over her shoulder, wondering when it had tugged itself out of the neat braid she'd had it in. "We'll survive just fine."

"You're going to take them out in this?" he asked. "Look at the Garce, Tresa. How are you going to get past them?"

She didn't know. She'd damned them with her yelling. The Garce knew there were humans in the building and who knew how long they'd keep trying to get in if she kept making noise. "Then I'll lead them away."

"What?" Roman's face paled imperceptibly.

She met his eyes, startled by how bright they were. He'd been afraid before but now —

He was worried about her. He feared her, he hated her, he didn't loathe her, but still feared her, and now he worried about her. "You make no freaking sense." It was her turn to snarl at him for a change.

"Tresa, you can't go out there yet. You're not strong enough. You said yesterday that you couldn't go out until tonight, and now you can't because the Pys will be back. Just lay low, they'll go away."

She listened to his speech. She really did. But she had another plan, one she had no intention of asking his permission or opinion on. "Or not," she said simply. Tresa jumped back up onto the cement wall surrounding the roof and dove.

She heard Roman yell, heard him bellow at her to get back on the roof, and she almost smiled because it felt like he thought she might listen.

She didn't.

She free fell until she got close to the ground, keeping a careful eye on the shadows even as she tumbled head over feet toward certain death. Roman's panic brought the Garce closer, and they waited at the bottom with jaws agape, hungry for her blood.

Not today.

She grabbed a shadow before she could reach them, zipping through it and coming out behind the Garce, near a patch of scraggly trees that had been planted by some long-gone company in an attempt to make their parking lot less scorched. "Hey!"

The Garce snapped their heads toward her, looking from the building she'd been falling from to her and back again. And then, like her, they zipped into the shadows.

Luckily for the human race, the Garce hadn't figured out how to use the shadows to climb yet. Or fall, as she had. But they did sort of know how to dissolve into the darkness and come out closer than they would have if they'd run.

That was not so lucky for her, but she'd been expecting it. Making as much noise as possible, she ran backward, pulling the Garce with her. Away from the building.

"Tresa! Watch your energy levels!" she heard Roman bellow.

Right. Good idea.

Much better than him just screaming orders that she would just ignore.

She ran hard in the opposite direction, watching for Garce to emerge from the shadows in front of her. If they were smart they would, and she wouldn't have time to get away.

She prayed for their continued stupidity.

They were fast, but she was faster because she had Garce *and* Py blood running through her veins. But they didn't get tired and she did. Probably also because she had Garce and Py blood running through her veins, trying to kill each other and her weak, human half.

"Faster, Tresa!" Roman yelled, and she could have cursed him because the Garce stopped and headed back toward the building.

"Hey!" she screeched, turning and waving her arms, trying to get their attention. The problem was, they weren't sure if she was one of them or something they should eat, and they *knew* that Roman was food. But they paused as she screamed, turned slowly back toward her and she sent a furious glare Roman's way before she turned and ran again, sprinting over sagebrush and red sand and cracked asphalt. *Don't trip. Don't trip.*

She could feel them breathing down her neck, feel their teeth snapping at her back and the red-hot eyes boring holes through her skull. She needed to zip away from them, give herself some space, but they were so close. Who was to say they wouldn't follow her and devour her in the shadows?

Fear propelled her forward, and then anger. Anger at Roman, anger at the Garce and anger at the Pys. It gave her strength, fueled her with hot, raging fires of hate. She pulled ahead, hit the next building's sidewalk and tore around the corner, out of sight.

Just before she dove into a shadow, just before the cool blackness passed over her and carried her away, she saw something.

Something crouching, something scared. Something with sparkling tattoos.

But no wings.

She gasped, leaping out of the shadow of the tree. It had taken a lot to get back that far, but the Garce hadn't heard her and the majority of them were still running in the opposite direction. Roman stood on the third floor with the rope ladder, and she ran for it, but her feet stumbled to a stop and she turned to squint into the shadows of the building across from theirs.

"Tresa!"

Right. Survival first. She clambered up the ladder to safety, Roman pulling her up as fast as she could climb. She took his hand and climbed to her feet, trying not to notice the heat that radiated through his skin to hers. "I saw something."

"What? The Garce nearly eating you? I saw that, too. Do you know how stupid that was? There was no plan, Tresa. No plan and you weren't fully recharged and we had no backup. Your dad's gun was two floors away and I couldn't go get him —"

"No. Not that," she said, interrupting his tirade. "I saw...a Py?"

Roman went very still. "What? In the day?"

"In that building."

"Are you sure?" He jerked the site of his gun up to his eye, searching the building but whatever Tresa had seen was gone.

"No. No, I'm not sure. I just got a glimpse before I zipped. The tattoos, the metallic eyes, but no wings. And no blue skin." She ran a hand through her hair, shaking her head. "I don't know what I saw."

Roman studied her, his dark eyes more worried than usual. "Maybe it was fear. It can do crazy things to your head."

"Maybe your head," she shot back. "My head is just fine."

Roman raised an eyebrow. "You just dove off a roof and willingly got chased by a pack of Garce. I don't think you can say anything about your head being fine."

She waved him away, but her hand shook and she didn't know if it was because of the Garce chase or whatever it was she saw. Pys were scary, after all. Especially one that saw her escape right into Roman's compound. "At least the Garce are away from the building now so we can get out of here."

He sighed, running his hand through his hair. His hand, which she noticed shook just like hers. "You're going to punish them because you're mad at me."

"I'm not punishing them. I'm keeping your people safe from a dangerous hybrid who could possibly snap at any moment."

"Well, I can't let you do that. You promised me you'd help us look for more food." He crossed his arms over his chest, positively smug. "Are you going to go back on a promise?"

"I—what?"

"You promised. We were going out tonight."

"Yeah, but the Pys, Roman. They'll be back. And I can't work with you."

He ruffled her hair, messing up what was left of her braid. "Sure you can. I'm easy to work with. Ask anyone."

She rolled her eyes. "You're impossible."

"I just watched you throw yourself off a roof, Tresa. It scared me more than I want to admit. I'm conflicted, trying to sort through feelings I've blocked out for years. Give me a chance to come to terms with them."

"I throw myself off roofs a lot."

He nodded, taking a slow breath and squinting out over the crumbling city below them. "I'll get used to it."

"Maybe you wouldn't be so ornery all the time if you actually dealt with your feelings instead of shoving them all away."

He scowled at her, turning the dark eyes back to her. "What are you, a shrink?"

"Common sense."

He ignored her. "What if we compromise? We'll tell them there's danger. We won't tell them exactly what we think it is until we're sure."

Before she could answer, Kylie bolted out of the door, waving rolled up papers. "I have a map!"

"Why?" Roman asked flatly. The little spark of personality she'd seen in him disappeared and his shoulders hunched protectively as more people followed Kylie onto the roof.

The weight of leadership pressing down on him.

Kylie stared at him as if it were obvious. "For scavenging. So you know where you're going. I found an old phone book."

Jeff had come back with her and helped spread the papers on the ground, scanning the tiny words while everyone else waited silently.

"There's a grocery store." Kylie jabbed at the paper. "And a pharmacy."

"Those would have been cleaned out long ago," Roman said.

"Maybe. Maybe not, depending on how fast the Garce moved in. We've seen areas that still had stocked shelves. No one had time to make it to the stores."

Before they were all killed.

Tresa didn't say that part.

"Several grocery stores, actually," Jeff said slowly. But that wasn't what he was looking for.

"Look, we can't go out tonight, not with the Pys. Tresa's tough but even she can't take on a whole bunch of Pys and a pack of Garce at the same time. We'll go in the morning."

"I thought we were leaving," Angie said quietly.

Tresa gnawed her lip. Decisions, making them for an entire group and not making them based on emotion, was Tresa's weakness. She thought too much with her heart. "We need to have a meeting to see what everyone else wants to do."

"There's an armory." Jeff stood, holding the map out to Tresa. "Can you make it that far?"

She scanned it, gnawing on her thumbnail. "Yeah. Yeah, I can do that."

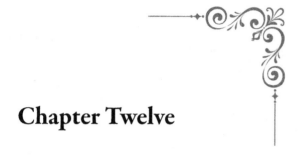

Chapter Twelve

"Angie, can you gather our group? We need to figure out what we're doing," Tresa said in a low voice, probably hoping no one could hear her but Angie.

Roman, though, was right next to her, leaning over her shoulder to scan the maps Kylie had spread all over the ground. He heard her and when Angie left to do Tresa's bidding, he followed, waiting in the back of the conference room. No one really noticed him, probably because he made people so uncomfortable they blocked him out.

Tresa appeared a few minutes later, literally materializing out of the shadows. It startled him, but her little group didn't seem to even notice. "We need to talk, guys."

He knew a few of their names, but not many. Tresa already knew all of his team's names and he wasn't quite sure how or when that had happened. She hadn't been there long. And most of them were afraid of her, as he was.

It didn't seem to matter.

"We've been here a little while now. It's weird, right? We're not used to staying in one place so long. I'm wondering what you guys are thinking. Do you like it here? Should we stay? Should we go? I'm going to be honest with you..." she hesitated, and he distinctly saw her eyes stray to the ceiling. As if she could see through the plaster and wood and nails and concrete to the roof, where he was supposed to be. "We know there's a danger in the city. We aren't sure what yet, but we're investigating."

She'd taken his compromise. Something in him warmed just a bit.

"Traders," someone said. He didn't know her name. Tresa blinked and Roman sucked in a breath as the entire room tensed.

"What makes you say that?" Tresa leaned both hands on the table in front of her. That was when her eyes found Roman and her lips twitched to the side in annoyance.

"The Garce. There's so many and no food. Unless someone is feeding them."

Slowly, Tresa nodded. "Maybe. It's a good theory, but please don't panic until we know that's what's going on."

"Why would we panic?" someone else asked. Roman leaned forward, studying her face. He really needed to learn these people's names. "Just because there are traders doesn't mean they can get to us. They're not in this building. Knowing that they're out there reminds us to be careful, but it doesn't really change anything."

Tresa pursed her lips and nodded.

"Right, but the other team...there's some I wouldn't trust with that knowledge. No offense, Roman, but there are a few people on your team that are just...well, they're kinda weird."

So he hadn't gone unnoticed. "No offense taken."

The rest of the room murmured their agreement and for the thousandth time, Roman was astounded at the difference between Tresa's little tribe and his band and he wondered why the difference existed.

"Okay, so that being said, what do you think? Should we stay or should we move on?" Tresa paced and Roman watched the movement, so graceful it was almost catlike. Had she always moved like that, or was it a Garce thing? They weren't graceful. They stalked and lumbered and moved so quickly they blurred, but he wouldn't call them graceful.

But Tresa...Tresa moved like a dancer, even when she was trapped in a tiny space and nervously fidgeted. Her dark waves tumbled behind her, thick and shimmering as if the fire that ran through her blood flowed through her hair. She was beautiful. There was no denying it. Hauntingly beautiful, with the huge black eyes and the heart-shaped face with the halo of hair cascading down her back.

"Roman?"

He jumped at the sound of his name, so caught up in watching her that he hadn't realized they were talking to him. "What?" he snarled. Yeah, that was smooth.

"Is your tribe leaving as well?"

He chose not to point out that his wasn't a tribe. Tribe seemed to imply unity and harmony and his wasn't like that. His was a band, like thieves that could turn on each other at any second. "No. We're not leaving until we're forced to."

"So we'd be going alone?"

Tresa nodded, but Angie answered for her. "It's not like we've not done it before. We've only been here with this group for a few days."

Roman frowned. It seemed like much longer.

While her little tribe spoke quietly amongst each other, he sat forward, the legs of his chair thunking down against the laminate flooring. "You told me that I wasn't alone in this anymore. That I didn't have to bear all the weight on my shoulders, and I agreed. I was just getting used to the idea and now you want to take it away and put everything back where it was before. I think distributing the weight of survival is a less hopeless plan."

Tresa met his eyes, her black ones widening as those around him agreed. Shrugging, he said quietly, "I kinda liked not being the only one in charge."

"Tresa, we'll go where you lead. But if the choice was up to me, I would stay. Make a home. A fortress. Make a stand."

Tresa tore her eyes from Roman and looked to the girl who spoke. This one, Roman knew. Jessica, he was pretty sure. Tresa called her Jessi. "Do you all feel that way?"

There were nods and murmurs. Tresa glanced at Angie and he could see the sparks traveling through the tattoos at her face, illuminating her eyes and flawless skin. "Does anyone want to go?"

No one said anything. Roman waited for several seconds and when no one did, he spoke quietly. "What do you want, Tresa?"

She raised her hand to her mouth and gnawed on a thumbnail. He'd noticed it was a nervous habit and he knew she was conflicted. She might be able to sense their emotions and feel their fear, but she wore hers very clearly across her face in the shimmering tattoos and the sparks at her fingertips. "I want them to be safe."

"We're safe wherever you are," Francheska said in the stillness. She was another who's name Roman remembered.

"Not always," Tresa whispered. Roman knew. He knew she carried the weight of them on her shoulders, but he hadn't realized how much the ones she lost hurt her until that second. How could he have known? She didn't refuse to smile. She didn't scream or yell or snap or snarl, except at him. She still laughed, made jokes, most at his expense, and actually still fought for her humanity.

And yet, there was her pain, so stark in her dark, dark eyes that it floored him. She was haunted by those deaths, by those she had failed to save as much as he was. Maybe more, because she felt like she was the only one who could kill the Garce, and therefore all death was her fault.

Roman could only stare while the conversation moved on around him, and he watched Tresa battle that pain and fight to get it under control because she wouldn't let it rule her.

Like his ruled him.

Something in him shifted, tilting his entire world off its center. Tresa had been through everything he had been through but she still had hope. She still fought to hold her heart together. She still believed in the goodness of people.

And he...

He didn't.

He stood abruptly and when Tresa raised those dark eyes toward him, he didn't know what to say or what to do. He could only stare at her.

"Roman?" Her brow creased as her gaze slid sideways to Angie, who shrugged minutely.

"I've — I've gotta go. I just —" He scrubbed a hand over his face. "Don't leave. Please. We can make this work. We can thrive here." He met her eyes for several long seconds before he turned on his heel and escaped the room.

He hadn't cried in years. He couldn't even remember the last time he'd cried and the tears were foreign. Shameful. He made it to the fourth floor where it was quiet, no people, no one watching, and he slid down to the Berber carpet and he sobbed. He sobbed over who he'd lost, yes, but also what he'd lost. Himself. He cried over what he'd become and the boy he'd been that he'd had to abandon. With his head in his hands, he mourned everything he'd had to leave behind to survive.

Kylie's hero.

"Roman." It was Michelle, her cool hand on his shoulder. He hadn't even heard her come in, which was dangerous and stupid but too late to worry about now. "What's wrong?"

He shook his head and rubbed his eyes, dropping his head back against the wall behind him. "Nothing."

"Tresa said you were upset. We've been looking for hours." He hadn't realized Kylie was there, too. That she knelt on his other side, her eyes glinting in the nonexistent light. "You made the rule, Roman. We never go anywhere alone, especially in the dark. Yet, here you are, living dangerously."

He half-laughed but it held no mirth and his lips didn't turn up in the required smile. Maybe he didn't remember how. Maybe he couldn't smile anymore.

"Tresa's team decided to stay. I don't know if you knew that and that's why you're upset or —?" Michelle swallowed. Boys didn't cry. When his team had lost in the championship, when their grandpa had died, when his dog he'd had since he was four had been hit by a car, he'd cried in his room, alone. Where no one could see him.

To be fair, that's what he'd tried to do here, too. But they'd found him. Sisters were like bloodhounds.

"I didn't know. I left before they'd decided. That's good. We need them. We need her." He scrubbed at his cheeks and stared at the ceiling.

Kylie sat next to him, her back against the wall, and stroked his hair away from his forehead. "I can't remember the last time you cried."

"Three days after Mom and Dad..." Michelle swallowed and tried again. "Right after we buried them. He hasn't cried since."

"He hasn't smiled since, either. Maybe that's coming back, too?" The hope in Kylie's voice nearly destroyed him. His darkness had hurt them. The last thing he'd wanted was to hurt them, and he'd been doing it for years. He'd pushed them away when what they needed was the comfort of a big brother.

Kylie's hero.

He'd thought he was protecting them when in reality, he was slowly tearing their souls down, day by day.

"I'm trying," he whispered, dropping his cheek against the top of Kylie's head. Michelle leaned against his shoulder and they sat in the darkness in silence. Their nearness was something he'd forgotten, the warmth of shared contact instead of being lost in the cold of a solitary existence.

"I know," Kylie whispered back, eons later. He closed his eyes, exhausted — both emotionally and physically. He'd been awake all night, then Tresa's run and the meeting and his complete emotional breakdown. He didn't have the strength to get up and go back out there. Out into the light.

Maybe he never had.

Maybe that was the difference between him and Tresa. She was strong and wore her hope as a shield. He drowned in the darkness with no hope to light his way.

She brought it with her, though. The sparkling black tattoos shimmered in the darkness like they were lit by an internal fire, and maybe they were. The Pys threw blood balls that burned and sparked. Tresa could pull flames from her fingertips when she fought the monsters outside. Maybe she *was* lit by an internal flame.

She paused by the door, probably unaware that they could see her clearly. Unless she specifically tried to hide in the shadows, she was like a beacon in the darkness.

"We found him," Kylie said needlessly.

Tresa jumped, confirming Roman's thought that she didn't realize they could see her. "Oh. Good. I—I was worried. Roman, if you—"

"I'm glad you're staying," he said, hoping she wouldn't read unnecessarily into his flat, monotone words. The emotion needed was too exhausting and he just didn't have it in him. "We probably shouldn't go out tonight, though. Not after your trip through town earlier."

She hesitated. "Okay. I'll wait."

He closed his eyes and longed for sleep. Before he could force them open again, she was already reading his weakness. "You should rest now before nightfall. It's coming and the Pys come with it. I'll take care of the garden and anything else."

Roman heaved himself to his feet, dragging his sisters up with him. "No, I'm coming. I'll help, too."

Tresa was in front of him before he had a chance to take a step toward her, either moving with that freakish speed or zipping through the blanket of shadows. She placed a hand on his chest and held him in place. "I don't sleep, Roman. I can do this. It's not all on your shoulders anymore."

Kylie squeezed his hand and left with Tresa but Michelle stayed. "It's never been all on your shoulders. We were here. You just wouldn't let us in."

"I know." He pulled her against him and rested his chin on top of her head. She came tentatively because he hadn't let anyone near him for so long. "I won't do it again. Mom said —"

"Mom said we're supposed to protect each other. I know you're the boy and you seem to have this stupid idea that boys are the protectors or something—"

He let out a short bark of laughter, and almost, *almost* felt like he could smile. "Not because I'm a boy. Mom raised me better than that, Michelle. It's because I'm the oldest. I'm supposed to be the protector."

"You're barely the oldest. And that's a stupid rule."

He nodded. "It is."

Michelle had been born just ten months after him. Kylie had waited a more considerate amount of time before making her way into the family but Michelle hadn't given Roman any time to be the only child.

He wouldn't have had it any other way.

Chapter Thirteen

Tresa heaved another pot into her arms and started toward the stairs. On a random impulse, she zipped into one of the long shadows reaching across the roof, wondering if she could pull the pot with her.

She couldn't.

It slipped out of her fingers as she escaped into the darkness and she couldn't zip out fast enough to catch it. Images of the poor, struggling plant splattered all over the concrete flashed through her mind in those horrible moments between the roof and eighth floor, and by the time she got back up, mere seconds later, she was almost in tears.

"Got it." Kylie grinned, the precious pot snuggled safely in her arms. "Apparently you've never tried to zip with anything in your hands before?"

Tresa shrugged, taking her pot so Kylie could grab another. "My clothes always come with me. Thanks for that," she said to the sky and whoever was responsible. "Otherwise...awkward."

"Yeah. Thank goodness for that. Do you ever wonder how the Pys get dressed with those massive wings? That would be a pain. What if they were forced to wear human clothes?"

"Probably muumuus and leggings," Tresa giggled. It felt good to laugh in the face of oncoming darkness. Like she was laughing in the face of the Pys themselves. "Super attractive."

"Are you kidding," Kevin, one of Roman's team, shook his head as he passed them. "The Pys could wear potato sacks and be gorgeous."

"Yes," Kylie agreed. "And bloodthirsty and murderous. But ya know. Priorities."

Tresa hid her laugh behind the plant, biting the inside of her cheek when Charles glared at her. Kylie bounded back up the stairs and she followed, grabbing more of their struggling garden before bringing it back down. "It would be so much easier if we could just put camouflage above and around the garden instead of moving it every night. I worry about the roots with the constant moving."

Kylie stopped so suddenly Tresa almost ran into the back of her. "Why don't we?"

Carefully maneuvering around Kylie and further down the stairs, Tresa answered, "Because the Pys can fly and aren't stupid birds?"

"Firstly, have you never met a crow or a raven? Birds aren't stupid." Kylie held up one finger. "Secondly, *no,* they're not stupid and yes they can fly, but they aren't familiar with our ways. We could build like a duck blind or something —"

"Something that would trick a bird but probably not a Py," Tresa pointed out, "Because they're not stupid birds."

Kylie rolled her eyes, but her hands flitted about her face in excitement. "No, we'd have to modify it, of course. But there are a lot of pollinators that only come out at night. If we could figure this out...I gotta tell Roman. Hurry up, Tresa!" she shooed Tresa playfully back up the stairs. "Get your dad. He knows stuff."

Tresa bounded back up the stairs, grabbed a pot, and went back down. "That he does."

They finished the garden while Kylie plotted and planned and went over logistics out loud and Jeff and Tresa let her ramble, only adding their input when she would stumble to a stop. Roman had been a hunter, which was fitting. Kylie had gone with him many times and knew what she was talking about, while Tresa had never hunted a day in her life and hadn't even liked killing bugs until she'd been forced to fight the Garce. Now she took some kind of sick pleasure in it.

Which was somewhat alarming.

"The issue, though, is making sure the plants still get enough sunlight. And making sure the Pys can't see right through it, of course. Plus, having it on the roof puts it right at their eye level..."

"So we'll move it to the ground." Tresa paused, brushing her hair from her head. "I'll keep the Garce away while we tend to it, and we'll hide it every night from the Pys."

"That...sounds dangerous and unlike something Roman would approve of." Kylie scrunched her nose. "But tons easier for us."

"Plus, it wouldn't be readily moveable should the need arrive."

"And I've never tried to grow a garden in Arizona before, but I would think the ground is baked of nutrients." Kylie stared over the side, gnawing on her thumbnail. "And transplanting them could kill them all. That always happened to my aunt. She was the definition of a black thumb."

"Okay. We stick to pots. But we figure out your camouflage thing so we don't have to keep moving them and risk breakage and root damage." Tresa nodded. "What do you need?"

Tresa's dad had been in the army before the world had ended. He was plenty familiar with hiding in plain sight and making use of natural resources. Between the three of them and Michelle, who had left Roman to rest, they created a detailed spec sheet of everything they would need to gather to create the garden hideout. By the time night fell, they had a definite plan for the next day.

All they had to do was survive the night.

Tresa saw Roman wandering down the hall toward the other lookout across the building. The bulk of their forces were in the common room with her, but there were a few who kept watch and he must have headed to monitor them.

Meaning, he trusted her to protect not only her tribe but his as well.

Something warmed in her chest, something that had unthawed when he'd asked her to stay earlier that day and had completely broken free of whatever ice still clung to it when she'd seen him break down with his sisters.

"Incoming," Kylie breathed. Tresa froze. She'd been so focused on Roman she hadn't felt the Pys until Kylie alerted her. She scanned the room, grateful to see her father on his sleeping bag, surrounded by several of her tribe and some of Roman's. He had a calming effect that they very much needed. Michelle wasn't there, but it was normal for her to be on the opposite side. She was Roman's second in his odd little chain of command and she stepped up when he wasn't there to fill whatever gaps needed to be filled.

"Quiet. Be still, don't listen to the Pys," Tresa murmured. They extinguished the candles and the very few flashlights they still used and settled in for the night.

Tresa swallowed hard, closed her mind to the Pys' voices and their smell, and focused everything she had on soothing the fear in the room with her very small and ineffectual presence.

Half-way through the night, while the Garce screamed outside, she met Kylie's eyes. Of everyone in that room besides Jeff, she was the calmest.

Kylie wasn't scared ever. She had literally no fear, which Tresa didn't understand. She watched the Pys through the slot in the board as if memorizing their movements. It wasn't until the moon was low in the sky that she turned and to Tresa and held up three fingers.

Three Pys.

Tresa nodded slowly. She wasn't sure if Kylie could even see her until Kylie turned back and held up all ten fingers, closed her fists, then held up five more.

Fifteen.

Fifteen Garce had been killed in the night. By three Pys.

Would they stay until the Garce were all dead? There were many in the surrounding area, and it would take the Pys quite a while to kill them all. That meant they would keep coming back, night after night until the Garce had run off or they were all killed.

But with such a big population of humans so close, it was unlikely that the Garce would go anywhere. Which meant Tresa and her little group were stuck with the Pys.

Unless they moved on. But no one seemed to think that was a good idea, and even Tresa wasn't sure they would make it alive to somewhere safer. The only alternative was to stay and wait out the storm.

And hope they didn't all die.

"I'm going, Roman. We can't wait any longer." Tresa hadn't slept. She was fairly positive Roman hadn't, either, by the circles under his eyes. Michelle had said he was resting the day before but an hour of sleep in a forty-eight-hour stretch wasn't enough to survive on.

Too bad he didn't have Garce blood, like her.

"Tresa, you zipped in and out a lot yesterday. You're not strong enough to go." Roman ran a hand through his hair but his usual vehemence was gone. He hardly snarled at all.

She grabbed his arm and dragged him away from the others. Kylie followed, of course, and Michelle wasn't far off. "We're out of food. If I don't go today before the Pys come back, they'll hear the empty bellies grumbling in hunger and they'll come crashing in to kill us all."

Roman arched an eyebrow. "I don't think their hearing is that good."

Tresa raised her chin. "Want to risk it?"

"And what if you get killed? Then what, hot shot?"

She smiled, amused at his attempt to insult her. "Then you come up with a new plan."

"Speaking of plans, Ro, we have one. We worked on it while you were out yesterday." Kylie held up their list. "For the garden."

Roman pinched the bridge of his nose. "Okay, one scheming woman at a time. Do you have a plan for *this* crazy mission?"

"We know the locations of the armory, several grocery stores and a distribution center." Jeff dropped the maps Kylie had found in front of Roman. "And two pharmacies. Within a twenty mile radius."

"Twenty miles?" Roman shook his head. "It's too far. We can't risk going that far."

"There is no we. There is me," Tresa pointed out for what could possibly have been the thousandth time. "You can't keep up, you can't zip, and you can't kill the Garce."

"And you have a hard time thinking straight and not blowing all your strength in the first two minutes," Roman shot back. "I'm going."

"If you go, it makes sense to hit them all, even if it takes two days," Kylie said slowly. "It's dangerous, but if it will keep us going for a little while longer..."

Tresa sighed. "Two days on my own is no big deal. But trying to keep Roman alive in the Garce infested waters out there for that long is impossible."

"You won't have to keep me alive, Tresa." Roman's voice was surprisingly gentle. "We'll work together. You can't carry back everything we need. You can't zip through shadows carrying stuff in your hands."

Tresa's lips twitched to the side and she glanced at Kylie who at least had the decency to wince in shame. "It seemed pertinent to the conversation," she said defensively.

"Ready?" Roman didn't look afraid. He hid it well, but Tresa could feel it rolling off him in waves. But he would face it for his sisters. For his band.

For her.

"No. We have to gather supplies. You'll need food, at the very least."

"There is no food, Tresa. I'm not taking what little is left for myself. I've got bags ready to carry what we can back. Assuming we can find anything."

So he wasn't a complete jerk all the time. The guy had a heart. She wasn't surprised, actually.

"Dad, will you be okay without me?" Tresa swallowed hard. She didn't like leaving him. What if she didn't come back? He would go looking for her.

And he wouldn't survive.

"I'll be just fine." Jeff hugged her tight and there was a strength there that Tresa wasn't sure she could exist without. "You come back to us, do you hear me? And you bring him with you."

Kylie threw her arms around Tresa, as well, as Michelle squeezed her hand. "I'll take care of your dad. He's going to help us with Kylie's camouflage shelter."

"Thank you," Tresa murmured.

"Just bring our brother back, okay? We kinda like him."

"Why does no one tell me to bring *her* back? Before we knew she existed, I was the tough one. In case you forgot." Roman hefted his bag to his shoulder and tossed Tresa hers.

"Bring her back," Jeff said quietly and it made Tresa's heart ache.

The half-smirk on Roman's face died abruptly and he nodded. "I will."

"So we're really doing this. I have to keep you alive out there for two days?" Tresa grumbled as they started down the stairs. She could blink through the shadows. He could not.

So they were forced to take the slow, human way.

"Yep," Roman said almost cheerfully. "We really are."

Maybe that was why he was so cranky all the time. He wasn't made to sit and do nothing. He was meant to move, to fight, to *live* and not just survive. And this was Roman, living.

Chapter Fourteen

Roman kept pace with her while they were in the building. But as soon as they pried the boards away from the door and escaped through...

She left him.

Dropped her bag at his feet and disappeared into the shadows. "Tresa!" he snarled, but she was gone.

Awesome.

He knew she didn't want him along, but really? To just abandon him? She must have hated him more than he thought.

He had the map, though, and unless her Garce powers included a photographic memory, she didn't know where she was going. So he stayed on the sidewalk, running lightly and focusing on his breathing like every coach he'd ever had had drilled into his head. He stayed close to the building for as long as he could, knowing Jeff watched with his giant Garce-stopping gun, and he hoped he was sorely disappointed in his daughter's total abandonment of their carefully laid plans.

And of Roman.

He was so focused on running, staying steady and reaching his next goal, which was the building across the parking lot, that he didn't realize what Tresa was doing until he ventured beyond the relative safety of his compound's walls. He sucked in a deep breath, paused at the corner, and sprinted out into the field of Garce.

But they weren't there.

Mid-way across the baked and crumbling asphalt that once was a parking lot, he realized the Garce were gone. He waited to investigate — because he wasn't stupid — until he reached the shadows of the next building. Breathing hard, he leaned against the wall and stared around him.

"Where the hell are the Garce?"

He knew the Pys had taken care of many of them. That morning he and Tresa had counted another twenty down. But that still left over a hundred in just this small corner of the city, and suddenly they were all just gone? No, that couldn't be. He'd seen them on the roof before they'd left.

It hit him too slowly, and he felt like an idiot as he peered around the corner. Tresa had led them away. To protect him.

Because of course she had. And apparently, couldn't be bothered to tell him that plan ahead of time. She'd missed completely the fact that plans were what made Roman's world go 'round. "Tresa," he muttered, "If I ever catch up to you, I might just strangle you."

"You could stop grumbling at me and stick to your plan, Roman." She bounced out of the shadows next to him, not even giving him the time to jump in alarm before she was grabbing his arm and dragging him along the sidewalk toward the opposite end of the building.

Each tower was huge, rising into the sky and taking up half a city block. Their first target was a pharmacy a mile and a half away. They'd decided to start at the closest building and work their way out in case they had to turn back before they completed the mission. At least they wouldn't turn back empty-handed. But while meds were vital to their survival and one case of a contagious infection could quickly spiral out of control, it was food he was really worried about.

He honestly wasn't sure they would even find anything. Three years after the initial invasion, he doubted there would be anything left. But they had to try.

"Can you go faster?" she hissed and he realized he'd slowed to a jog and the Garce could catch his scent at any minute. Mentally cursing, he sprinted past her.

For a second, anyway. But she moved freakishly fast and roared past him like a blurred hurricane. "Faster, Roman. We've gotta make it into that pharmacy."

And onto the roof. Until the Garce gave up and went away. That was the plan.

Stick to the plan.

He was used to running. Running kept them alive. But his lungs burned and his legs shook long before they made it the mile and a half to the pharmacy. He had no choice but to ignore it. He didn't realize Tresa was murmuring next to him until they slowed to cross the last street. "Almost there, Roman. You can do this. You got this."

The Garce were coming and he hadn't realized. His own breathing had drowned their snarling and hissing out almost completely. Tresa didn't seem to notice or care, and he really had no other option but to keep running.

So he did.

They hit the middle of the street when she started yelling and he realized she'd known the Garce were there all along and she'd been watching him, monitoring how much energy he had left.

"Come on, Roman. Everything you've got. Everything you've got, now!"

He lengthened his stride and pushed forward, drawing strength from somewhere deep where he'd forgotten it existed. He sprinted next to her and when they hit the pharmacy's entrance, he didn't even hesitate. He threw himself against the board, knocking it inward as it shattered around him. Tresa dove through the torn wood behind him. "To the roof!"

She didn't even sound winded.

He might have hated her a little right then.

Not every building had roof access, and this, unfortunately, was one of those. They raced through the store, feet skidding on the dusty laminate, trying to find any way up, or anywhere to hide.

But it was the Garce. There was no way to hide from them. They had noses like bloodhounds. On steroids.

"Well, that didn't last long," he breathed, hands on his knees. Waiting for death to find them. He'd let his sisters down. He'd let her dad down. He'd promised to bring her back.

Tresa scowled at him. "I'm not done yet."

She whirled away from him and sprinted, straight at the wall. Before she could smash right into it she leaped, arms cartwheeling through the air, and crashed through the high glass windows. He saw bright blood mixed with an inky blackness stain the shattered glass, but she didn't seem to notice. "Rope!" she bellowed.

Roman jerked it out of his bag and threw it to her just as the Garce hit the broken board at the front door. She tied the rope off and he used it to climb the wall up to where Tresa balanced precariously. She untied the rope and jumped, her claws digging into the red tiles on the roof, and inch by inch she pulled herself up until she could tie the rope to the exhaust fan at the center.

Below, the Garce were leaping desperately after him and he froze in morbid fascination. He could see their ribs. Through the shadows and the inky blood and the red glowing eyes, they were like starving dogs, too skinny and on the verge of starvation. No wonder they all gathered here where traders could find them. They'd depleted so much of the Earth's population that they were all starving to death now.

"Roman!" Tresa shrieked when the rope dangled uselessly next to him.

Jerked from his trance, he grabbed the rope and pulled himself up onto the roof. He towered over her but not even he could jump straight up onto a steeply pitched tile roof and not plummet to his death.

Only her alien half could do that.

"Now we wait?" she asked as he settled next to her.

He nodded. "Good thing it's in the middle of winter or this could be really miserable."

She laid back, letting the sun-baked tiles warm her back. She bled from a hundred different cuts and scratches but he wasn't sure she even noticed them. "Arizona winters are delightful."

He snorted. Nothing about this was delightful.

For hours, they sat on the roof in silence, waiting for the Garce to get bored and go away. He noticed Tresa watching the sun, counting the hours until the Pys came out, as he was. "If we're still stuck up here when the sun goes down," he started, but she cut him off, shaking her head.

"No. I'll give them a half-hour more and then I'll take care of them myself."

She was a fierce little thing, he'd give her that.

"That's not in the plan. We have your strength carefully mapped out, Tresa. We have to conserve it or we don't make it back."

She rolled her head toward him, the long black waves shimmering behind her. "You really like plans, don't you?"

He nodded slowly, waiting to see if she was mocking him. When she only continued to study him, he said, "I had my whole life figured out. Baseball scholarship, college, city leagues, computer programmer. The aliens kinda messed that up."

Her eyes crinkled when she smiled and this close, he could see the dark brown beneath the black. "No wife and kids?"

"It wasn't a priority. Maybe one day but it seemed like everyone I knew that got married young..."

"They were miserable," she finished when he didn't. He nodded and she continued. "My aunt got married young. Eighteen. He was even younger. Oh, she regretted it. So, so much. I'm eighteen. I can't imagine being married right now."

"Well, we *are* in the middle of an alien invasion. You'd probably feel differently if the end of the world hadn't come and gone. Didn't you have a boyfriend carrying your books all through school?"

She wrinkled her nose at him, and the adorableness of it nearly knocked him off the roof. "I carried my own books, thank you. Not every girl wants to get married right away. Or at all. You have sisters. How do you not realize that?"

He shrugged. "They didn't talk to me about boys because I had a tendency to...look mildly threatening."

"Imagine that," Tresa said dryly. "You apparently haven't changed much since the world ended."

He ignored that. "So no boyfriend?"

She shrugged. "I dated. But I was busy. School. Softball took up a ton of time. I had plans of my own." She grinned at him. Mocking his plans.

"Huh. I figured you were incapable of sticking to plans."

Tresa rolled her eyes. "Plans don't always work, you know."

"Mine do. See? Here we are on the roof of our first building."

"Yeah, and we've got five more and countless miles to run before dark."

"Ah yes," Roman said, and he almost smiled. "But we're out of the most populated area of the city. The Garce tend to stay right in that mile square that our compound is smack dab in the middle of."

"Yep. You sure can pick 'em." Tresa sat up and crawled cautiously to the edge of the roof, using her claws as anchors so she didn't slip and fall off. "I think they're gone. I'll go first."

Roman raised an eyebrow but said nothing, so she leaned over the side, head upside down as she peered through the broken window. He tensed, afraid she'd topple over and land on her head, but she only popped back up. "It's quiet. No sign of Garce. I'll go see."

He made shooing motions at her and she scowled, the dark eyes flashing in annoyance before she slid out of sight. He could hear the crunching of glass and wondered if she'd managed to make it past without slicing more skin or if she even bothered to give caution a try.

And then silence. She made no sound, there were no battle cries and he was starting down the roof when he heard the gurgled shriek of a dying Garce.

And then more silence.

More quickly, he slid the rest of the way down, caught himself at the last second and swung onto the window seal, shattered glass skittering under his feet. "Tresa?"

She appeared below him, splattered with Garce blood. "All clear."

Roman raised an eyebrow. "Really?"

"Well, it is now." She had the audacity to blush, her cheeks pinking around the sparkling tattoos.

It was charming, to put it mildly.

Roman jumped the rest of the way down, landing in a crouch as he surveyed the area. "You were quiet. I don't think it alerted any other Garce. That wasn't part of the plan, by the way."

She was already moving away from him, scanning the shelves and dragging things into her bag. "I improvised. We have to move or the Pys will catch us on the roof. I had no choice."

"Right." Roman picked another aisle, searching for pain reliever, topical antibiotic, fever reducer and anything that would settle the stomach. There was little left on the shelves, though.

He jogged up and down the aisles, grabbing what was left before he found her looking desolately at an empty section where Twinkies and Cupcakes would have been. "We should check the back room. Looters probably wouldn't have gone through boxes when Garce or Pys could show up at any minute. They would have grabbed what they could and run."

She nodded. "'Kay."

"I thought you only eat meat," he said over his shoulder as she followed him through the store. By the way she'd been drooling at that shelf, he'd say that was the epitome of hungry.

"I do, but I still get all the regular human cravings. Twinkies were heaven. My coach wouldn't let me have sugar and sweets so

I didn't get them often..." she trailed off with a dejected sigh. "But now I get new, fun cravings like for Py blood and death. Way more exciting than Twinkies."

He suppressed a shudder. The pain in her voice nearly undid him, and shuddering because she craved Py blood wouldn't help her at all. "It could be worse. Some people crave dirt."

She snorted.

"I'm going to try to get back there," she paused next to the reinforced glass of the pharmacy, where all the prescription medicines were stored. He could see that the shelves had been ransacked but there was still a lot there. Probably pharmacists grabbing what they could before they ran for safety.

He turned to tell her not to make noise, forgetting that when Tresa said *try* it meant she was going to zip from one shadow to the next, even though she was supposed to be saving that energy for emergencies. One second she stood behind him, so close he could feel her warmth, and the next she was in the other room, searching under the counter. "How ya gonna get the meds back out, Hot Shot?" he called after her.

She reached for something, and the door next to his head opened with an audible click that echoed through the empty store. "Like that," she said, grinning.

They grabbed anything either of them recognized or would know what to do with before. Many of the diseases that used life-saving medicine...didn't exist anymore. Because those who needed the medicine hadn't been able to get it.

"My sister..." Tresa started and then hesitated, peeking up at him through the dark waves as she used her claw to slice through the box in front of her. "She had a disease where she had to get iron injections all the time. We ran out of iron and were trying the pills, but we estimated she only had about six months to a year before her iron stores would run out completely. She would have died anyway. But the Garce got her first."

Roman swore. "That's awful. I'm sorry."

"She didn't let it stop her. I don't know how sick she was. None of us did. She just did what had to be done and made it work."

"It sounds like she was amazing." Roman knew he was supposed to be digging through boxes and shelves that hadn't been looted yet, but he watched Tresa, instead. It was rare that she talked about her sister. Or anything, actually, from before her abduction.

She smiled sadly. "She was. So are you gonna help me, or...?"

He rolled his eyes. "I am helping."

They worked in silence after that, but he kept watching her out of the corner of his eye. If she cried, she hid it well.

He was so engrossed in that, and in the random hope that he could find Twinkies in some of those boxes, that he forgot to track the sun until it was almost too late. It was the shadow falling across his box that brought him out of his tunnel of concentration. He jerked up, peering out the window. "Shit. We've gotta go."

Tresa raised her head, shoving the dark waves over her shoulder. They caught the weak light and scattered it around in shimmering rainbows, quite easily the most beautiful thing he'd ever seen. "We're late."

He nodded, shoving himself to his feet. She rose easily in one fluid motion and slung her bag over her shoulder. "Next up, distribution center. We've gotta get inside and hidden before nightfall. Think we can do it?"

Roman mentally calculated in his head. It was two miles away. Before the invasion, he'd been able to run two miles in about twelve minutes, but now, half-starved and while carrying a bag full of meds, he wasn't sure. Still, they had at least an hour until sundown. "Yeah. We can make it. Ready to run?"

She flicked a hand past her face, the nails growing into shimmering claws. "Always."

Chapter Fifteen

Tresa scanned the sky as they left. It was too early for Pys. The sun would still kill them. But they were leaving much later than Roman had planned on. Being stuck on the roof for so long had seriously thrown them off. Originally, the plan had been to hit the distribution center and then the grocery store before nightfall, and then the armory the next day before making their way back and hitting a Walmart and a gas station. Two days, total.

And they were already behind schedule.

Roman apparently meant to make up lost time because he hit the door running, his bag strapped firmly to his back as he raced through the streets on nearly silent feet. Tresa hadn't found anything edible and wondered if he had. If not, he was running on an empty stomach and if she'd learned anything from her many coaches, it was that the body had to have adequate food to fuel it. It couldn't run on the promise of carbs for very long.

He didn't give her a chance to ask, though. He shot out of the parking lot and down the street like they were going for a sprint around the track and not a two-mile run. She followed, but it was easier for her because she wasn't starving and also, alien blood.

Always helpful.

It took her about a mile to realize the Garce weren't following them. There weren't even any Garce around, none hiding in the shadows, none running up the broken street toward them. It was eerily silent and Tresa didn't understand why.

Roman noticed it, too. He paused, breathing hard and turned in a slow circle as Tresa skidded to a stop next to him. The buildings here cracked and crumbled under the onslaught of summer monsoons and desert heat. She didn't even dare lean against them to rest in the shade.

"Where are the Garce?" Roman asked, his voice low. "Can you sense them?"

She was surprised he asked. She was actually surprised he knew she could do that at all. She had no recollection of telling him. But she just shook her head. "Not anywhere near. Only back the way we came, but it's faint."

Roman nodded. "So either they're running from the incoming Pys or something is keeping them at the other end of the city."

Which was Tresa's thought, too. Either their compound...

Or traders.

Roman swore under his breath and then winced. "My mom would have slapped my mouth for swearing in front of a girl."

Tresa rolled her eyes. "I'll live. Should we go back?"

He glanced at her pack and then his dark eyes moved back the way they came. "We don't have any food to take back to them."

"Let's hit the distribution center. See what we can find there and get you somewhere safe. I can go back and check on them —"

"No. We stay together or you'll get halfway there and run out of energy or magic or whatever it is you call it."

"Alien-ness?" she suggested.

He half-smirked at her. "Sure."

"I can handle myself. It's you I'm worried about. You can't fight anything off."

Roman scowled. "And yet here I've survived for three years without your help. It's a miracle."

"It is. We're wasting time. Distribution center before dark. Yes?"

Slowly, he nodded. "Yes."

They ran, but every step Tresa took felt like a betrayal to her father, to her friends, to those who depended on her. What if they needed her? What if the Garce had gotten inside?

But Roman was right. They'd survived without her for all this time. They would be okay. They *had* to be okay. If something happened to them— happened to her dad — she would have no reason to keep fighting.

Roman had picked up the pace and was practically sprinting through the abandoned streets, his breath coming in ragged gasps. "You know," she said as they closed in on their last several hundred meters, "Killing yourself now won't get us back to them any faster."

He glanced over at her but didn't respond, still trying to breathe. She raced ahead, checking the perimeter as they came up on their building. It was in an industrial park, surrounded by other warehouses and storage facilities, but Roman had targeted this one because it looked the most likely to have to have food. Tresa prowled around it looking for the door, looking for Garce or Pys or traders, traders that she was just realizing she had to add to her list of things to be worried about. But it was clear. Wherever the Garce were, it wasn't here.

By the time Roman caught up to her, she was looking for a window, some way to get in through the shadows.

"Front door's on this side," Roman said, which Tresa already knew. She'd passed it on her search but they didn't have a key, obviously, and she couldn't see the shadows inside to jump into. Still, she followed, hoping he'd have a better idea than she did.

He didn't. It was a risk they'd been worried about at the compound, but they had no way of knowing if the place was penetrable or not until they got there.

Roman paced, looked up at the sky and then back to the door, and paced again. "We've got a few options here."

She waited patiently for him to explain said options while her brain scanned through all her knowledge like a Rolodex, trying to figure out something else.

"We can move on to our next target." Roman held up a finger. "We can search through this general area and see if there are any other buildings that we can get into that might have food, although they're all built about the same so I don't know how helpful that will be, or —"

Tresa rammed the door. It was metal, but hollow and caved under her weight. She backed up again and ran, throwing herself at the door with her claws out, embedding them deep into the metal. It screeched and screamed under the onslaught but held.

"One more," Roman said, pulling her back with him. "On three?"

She nodded, rubbing her shoulder. He was twice her size. She should have let him help the first two times.

"One, two, three!" Roman yelled and they both ran at the door, hitting it simultaneously. Roman didn't have claws, so Tresa took care of that, attacking it with her deadly nails.

Still, it held.

Roman panted, rubbing his own shoulder. "Damn. That's a tough door."

Tresa bent to get a closer look, trying to see if her claws had even made it through the metal on the other side. There was just a sliver of light making its way through, but — "Yes," she hissed.

She could see through to the other side, into the darkness.

She zipped.

She heard Roman's yell of surprise and wondered if he would ever get used to her random zipping. Afraid to leave him out there alone, she rushed around the room, looking for anything that would unlock the door. She had no idea how long the Garce would leave them alone, and there was no time to waste. Finally, she found a button underneath the front desk and pushed.

Nothing happened.

Of course, nothing happened. It required electricity, something they hadn't had for over three years. She growled under her breath, sounding shockingly like a Garce, and searched some more. "Tresa," she heard Roman hiss.

"Are you okay?" she called distractedly as she dug through cabinets and drawers. There had to be a key, or a key card or — or something.

"Hurry up," was all he replied.

"Like I'm not doing that already," she muttered back at him, but he couldn't hear her.

Probably for the best.

Frustrated, she stood, blowing her hair out of her face with her hands on her hips. "Why can't you zip like me?" she snapped.

"Give me a few more minutes and that might be an option."

Oh no. She zipped back out, lunging from the shadows just in time to intercept a Garce mid-leap. Roman stood his ground, gun out but he hadn't fired yet. She caught the Garce, lit the fire at her fingertips and plunged her hand into its mouth, claws tearing the skin at the back of its throat. She jerked free before the powerful jaws could clamp down on her arm and struggled away as the Garce fell, her poison burning it from the inside out.

"Are there more?" she gasped, turning in a wild circle.

Roman shook his head.

She smacked him, nearly knocking him over. "Why didn't you say something sooner?"

He raised a dark eyebrow. "I figured you were busy. I had it."

"Right. That was stupid, Roman."

He shrugged. "Did you get the door open?"

She stared at him, infuriated, for several long seconds before she started for the shadows again. "Any more Garce, you tell me right away, got it?"

"Sure."

He didn't sound terrified. He didn't have fear roiling off him in waves. It was like he didn't realize he'd almost been Garce dinner.

Her, he was afraid of. Actual Garce trying to eat him? Not so much.

She wanted to shake him.

Instead, she fell into the shadows, grateful for the cool darkness, and lingered there a second longer than she had to before popping out on the other side. She cleared her throat and called, "The button doesn't work to open the door."

"There should be a backup key. Do they have a key ring or anything?"

"Do they have a keyring. Seriously, Roman? Don't you think I would have looked for that first?" she growled back under her breath, turning to scan all the walls in the room. "Oh."

There, of course, was a keyring hanging on the wall above the desk she'd spent precious minutes ransacking. Tresa snarled as she snatched it off the hook and jogged back to the door, muttering every curse word she'd ever learned as she went. And of course, she went through five different keys before she found one that would fit and by the time she swung the door open, Roman was bent over the Garce, examining it and completely ignoring her. "I've never been this close to a body before. They usually clean them up pretty quickly. Should I cut some up for you to eat?"

Tresa almost gagged. She hated Garce. She hated that they were the only meat left in the world and the only thing she could eat. She hated even worse that she craved the Pys that would kill her. "No."

"Come on. We'll cook it. I found some spices at the last place. Maybe it's edible for humans, too."

She crossed her arms over her chest and watched him suspiciously. "Are you willing to test that?"

"I'm starving, too." His voice was more ashamed than he'd intended and he ducked his head as he dug for his knife. "Did you know they have tattoos like you do? I didn't see it until I was checking its wounds. Even up close, you can't see them."

"Where do you think my tattoos came from?" she asked, trying not to gag. Why on earth was he checking its wounds? Had he lost his mind?

"The Pys," he said distractedly.

"Apparently not. Just hurry. More could be on their way."

"I can't believe we haven't thought of eating these before," he said and Tresa did her best not to hear the slice of his blade against Garce flesh.

"You haven't exactly had an opportunity, given that only Pys and I can kill a Garce." She held a fist against her mouth and prowled the area, making sure there were no more aliens waiting to kill them.

"Good thing we weren't trying for point C tonight. We wouldn't have made it." Roman's voice was muffled as she moved away. "This seems like a pretty safe place to stay."

"Yeah. Maybe." This building was huge, with no windows and lots of darkness. A perfect place for Pys, although she couldn't figure out how they would have gotten in and out. They were smart, but the simplest human technology still seemed to confuse them. Doors and locks still seemed to be a mystery and if they couldn't blow right through it, they usually avoided it.

Still, best to be cautious.

"I'm going inside to look for any threats. Are you good out here?"

"Just about done," Roman said. "I'll be in in a sec."

She left him to it, confident that she couldn't sense any Garce in the area. Of course, she'd thought that before...and Roman had nearly ended up Garce food. She hesitated in the doorway, waiting.

In those few seconds, she heard all of her fears creeping out from the shadowed interior. Pys angelic voices, Garce's growling hiss, her sister's screams. She spun toward it but the vast chamber beyond was silent. She could see no glowing metallic blue eyes, no sparkling wings. No Garce slithering toward her. It was all in her imagination.

Roman finally came inside, whatever he'd been doing outside tucked away in his bag. "I don't know how we'll make a fire without alerting the Pys, though," he said, wiping his hands on a rag. "What have you found?"

"A keyring," she answered drily, hoping he couldn't sense her fear.

He nodded as if that were a perfectly acceptable answer and dug in his bag for a flashlight. "Ready to go exploring?"

She nodded. Her eyes didn't need artificial light. She could see just as well in the darkness as she when the sun was out — maybe even better. It didn't help with her wild imagination, though.

She'd never been a fan of the dark, and now it was her domain.

Suppressing a shudder, she said, "There are barrels there. Maybe we can use them for fire."

Roman nodded. "Ready?"

Ready to venture into the unknown, with their safety depending on her wits and reflexes? "Yeah. Sure. Why not?"

Chapter Sixteen

Roman stayed close to Tresa, swinging the flashlight back and forth, looking for the red, glowing eyes of the Garce or the metallic blue tattoos of a Py. At any second, he expected claws to rip into his back and only hoped Tresa would stop them before the aliens killed him. She'd be able to stop the bleeding, wouldn't she? She wouldn't leave him there to die.

He hoped.

But no Garce attack came and no Pys, either. After they'd searched the whole floor, Tresa finally released a pent-up breath he hadn't realized she'd been holding. "I think it's safe."

"Seems to be. Want to scavenge or eat first?"

She audibly gagged and he swung toward her. "Eat first," she said weakly.

"You don't like Garce?" He checked the big metal barrel they'd found earlier, making sure it hadn't held gasoline or anything else incredibly flammable. That's all he'd need was to send the distribution center up in flames while they were trapped inside.

"I was a vegetarian before, so...no."

"What have you been eating all this time, then?" he went back to the reception area and found stacks of papers, probably important once but not anymore, and threw them in his barrel.

At his dad's company, they'd used these barrels to keep workers warm when electricity had been hard to come by. He was guessing that was the point of this one, too.

"I eat only when I have to. Which isn't as often as you."

He nodded wisely. "No wonder you're craving Twinkies."

She snorted, that sound he'd realized she made when she didn't actually want to laugh but he took her by surprise. It was more a huff of air across the top of her mouth than an actual snort, like the laugh escaped her lips but just barely. It amused him to no end.

"I had no idea you even had a sense of humor." She shied away from his match and he wondered if that move was a Tresa thing or a Garce thing. They'd tried bombing the Garce, of course. Even nukes that had fallen back to earth with disastrous consequences hadn't affected the Garce in any way but to annoy them. So he doubted fire was a problem and had to guess it was Tresa's human half that was afraid, not the alien part of her.

"I would kill for strawberry shortcake. It's my very favorite thing in the whole wide world." She watched the flames grow from a distance and when he pulled out the meat he'd harvested from the Garce, she disappeared into the shadows. He could just see her sparkling hair through the darkness, several aisles over. "I'll see what kinds of things they store here."

"Don't worry," he called after her. "My dad taught me to cook. I am an excellent cook. Garce probably tastes like chicken, right?"

That soft chuff of air was the only response he got.

A half hour later, he pulled the seasoned, cooked Garce meat from the flames and cut into it with his knife, checking to make sure it was cooked all the way through. He definitely didn't need

Salmonella or E. coli on top of whatever weird side effects he might get from eating alien. She returned, interest piqued. "It smells...not so bad."

He nodded. "I told you. I am an excellent cook. Do you think I'll turn into a Garce if I eat one?"

She shrugged, reaching for her half, which was almost as big as her head. "Wouldn't hurt. I could use the help."

He could only stare at her until she grinned up at him. "I'm kidding. You were a big help today."

"Damn right I was." He poked at his first bite. "How does it taste?"

She chewed slowly and her nose didn't wrinkle in disgust. "It's not bad. The seasoning helps. Doesn't taste like chicken, though."

Slowly, ashamed that his hand shook just a bit, he brought the bite up to his lips. In the light of the low burning fire, she looked positively terrified, and he thought again how ironic it was that she could read his emotions because of her Garce blood but he could read hers just as easily because everything was right there in her eyes.

And her fear didn't inspire much confidence.

He pushed the bite past his lips, felt the charcoal against his tongue, and waited for any adverse effects. Nothing happened. He didn't change into a Garce. He didn't develop any cannibalistic cravings, and there was definitely no desire to try to catch a Py and eat it whole. Slowly, he chewed, still waiting.

Nothing.

Except that Garce meat definitely did not taste like chicken.

Tresa watched him, eyes wide and meal forgotten. "Anything?" she whispered. When he didn't respond right away, she leaned toward him and pressed a hand against his heart.

"What are you doing?" Her touch was warm and sent shards of heat ricocheting across his skin, bouncing off his internal organs.

"Making sure your heart is still beating," she said quietly. "Shhh."

"Tresa, if my heart wasn't beating—"

"Shh!"

He waited patiently, wondering when, exactly, her touch had started to affect him the way it was. Maybe it was the dark, or the fact that they were alone, or because of her ethereal beauty. Maybe it had been there all along. The first thing he remembered thinking about her, after she'd ripped the Garce's head off, of course, was how gorgeous she was.

And then she'd opened her mouth.

Now, though, her smart wit and sarcastic comments were what he looked forward to most every day.

"You're still alive." She sat back and nodded with relief, as if she'd been genuinely worried. "We'll have to watch and see about the turning into a Garce thing, though."

He raised an eyebrow and she shrugged. "You never know."

"Am I allowed to keep eating? I'm starving, Tresa." More than she would realize. He couldn't remember the last time he'd eaten, forgoing his portions so the rest of their team would have enough.

She eyed the food in front of him and finally nodded. "I guess so. Let me know if you can suddenly see in the dark, or are able to move cars or crave Py blood. It's poisonous, by the way. So don't try to eat them."

He smirked. "I'll do my best."

They ate in silence while she watched him suspiciously like he might possibly burst into full-on Garce mode at any second. In reality, he didn't feel any different. The meat tasted bland and was more grisly than he would have preferred, but he hadn't had fresh meat in years. The Garce had killed everything — wildlife, humans, pets, livestock. There was no meat to be had. Occasionally, they would run across beef jerky but it was a rare treat.

Garce meat was also lighter than regular meat, but incredibly filling. He wrapped up what he didn't eat and packed it away for later.

"Ready to start foraging for food?" She stretched and stood. Her half was gone and he wondered how hungry she must have been to have eaten what she had so despised.

"Assuming I survive, this changes everything. Do you realize that?" He followed her to the first aisle, where boxes upon boxes were stacked from floor to ceiling on four different rows of shelving.

"You surviving? I think it means everything stays the same." She loosed one claw and sliced open the tape holding the box shut. "This place hasn't been touched. Not sure if that's a good thing or a bad thing."

He wondered that, too. Surely, if food was scarce and employees knew this place held food, they would have come back here and taken what they could have. Either it held no food...

Or they hadn't made it back.

For his team's sake, he had to hope it was that one, even if he felt like a monster doing it. He shook off the thought. "No, I mean that we can eat Garce meat. There will be no more going hungry. No more scavenging far and wide looking for anything edible. You just pop out there, kill one and bring it back and our entire team eats for days."

She blinked up at him, her eyes catching the non-existent light. "Assuming you don't die."

He nodded. "Assuming I don't die."

"Please don't die."

Her plea stirred something in his chest and he wanted, more than anything, to survive just so he could do as she asked. "I'll do my best," he said gruffly.

She nodded and ducked back toward the box. "So you played baseball, huh?"

"Yeah."

"This is an office chair. Next. Were you any good?" She sprang up to the shelf above them and sliced into it while he moved down the aisle.

"Yeah. I was okay." He'd had college scouts watching him. Words like scholarships and potential big leagues had floated around quite frequently.

He'd had plans.

"We took state my sophomore year."

"Nice. This is also office furniture."

He wasn't sure if the nice was because of his state championship or the fact that she'd found another chair. His box held filing cabinets, so he moved on.

"You must have had girls falling all over you." Her voice was muffled and she was another row up, moving with that freakish speed that made his mind blur.

"No. I was busy. Same as you."

He could feel the glowing eyes on him, felt her blink in confusion, and then she went back to her box. "I thought boys had pretty one-track minds. And those minds weren't used for making plans."

He laughed. He couldn't help it. Of everything that could have come out of her mouth, that was the last thing he'd expected. The sound startled him, but it scared her worse. With a screech, she tumbled out of the rafters and plummeted toward the ground.

He dove for her, but he wasn't fast enough and visions of her skull splattered across the concrete floor blinded him. "Tresa!"

He'd forgotten her zipping, though, and she grabbed the shadow before she hit the ground and came out next to him instead of cracking her head open. "You laughed!" she gasped.

"Shit, Tresa!" he yelled, grabbing her arms like she still needed saving. "You scared the crap out of me!"

She grinned. "Sorry." She definitely did not sound sorry. "You laughed, Roman! Did you smile, too?"

He had laughed. Because of *her*. Three years and not one person had been able to make him smile, able to make him forget his pain long enough to feel anything else, and then she waltzed in, the last person on Earth he thought he could trust and...

He'd laughed.

"So I did. Are you hurt?"

She shook her head. "No. I caught myself. I was just so surprised. You knocked me right out of the rafters. That's powerful right there."

He almost smiled again. "You're weird."

Tresa nodded solemnly, eyes sparkling. "All the best ones are."

She skipped away, zipping back up to her rafter to search through more boxes. Some were labeled, some were not, and they spent the next several hours going up and down aisle after aisle. It wasn't until nearly midnight that Roman finally found something.

Tresa was on the top shelf, trying to see outside through the small air ventilation shaft. She said she couldn't feel the Pys, but she wanted to be safe. Roman was still on the bottom row, scanning labels with his flashlight. He'd found batteries before, a huge box of them that would keep their flashlights running for months. But no food, and he was starting to lose hope.

Until he found the aisle.

Because of limited light, they hadn't even realized the aisles were labeled until Tresa had smacked her head on one climbing to the top of the shelving. It was clearly labeled nutriment. It looked promising.

The first box he came across had been perishable and was mostly rotted away. He closed the box and moved on to the next, holding his breath. The label was all numbers so he sliced through the tape with his knife.

Canned goods.

Vegetables. And in the next box, a box he could easily fit inside, fruit. Stews and soups. He let out a whoop that sent Tresa crashing down through the shadows next to him. "Look at this! Look at all this!"

She squealed and opened box after box, dancing excitedly. "They're going to be okay. Roman, you're all going to be okay!" When Tresa threw her arms around him, he grinned and hugged her back, feeling like ten thousand pounds had been lifted from his shoulders. When she'd said he didn't have to fight alone anymore, she'd been serious.

Tresa was a game changer.

ROMAN slept near the fire in a big, plush office chair. It was a tad uncomfortable because office chairs weren't meant for sleeping, but it was better than sleeping on the concrete warehouse floor. He fell asleep watching Tresa, also curled in an office chair, watching the fire.

Damn, she was beautiful.

The fire played tricks in her eyes, reflecting the flames like two little mirrors and he was mesmerized. He wanted to stay awake just so he could watch her in the firelight.

Except that it had been a very, very long day and his eyes, against his will, fell closed.

He woke with a start. The fire had died, and he expected to see Tresa's glowing tattoos, maybe the black eyes shimmering faintly in the dark, but her chair was empty. There was nothing.

Just cold.

"Tresa?" he called, sitting up slowly and trying his best not to topple out of his office chair.

No answer.

"Tresa," he yelled again, sliding to his feet. His legs protested — they weren't used to sprinting several miles and climbing up on roofs and through rafters, and his arms and back were just as sore, but he barely noticed. Rising panic consumed him.

The Pys had to have gotten her. Or the traders. If the Garce had been there, he'd be dead too, but the Pys and traders both would have been incredibly excited at a specimen like Tresa. She was like nothing else in the world.

And he'd lost her.

"Tresa!" he bellowed. His voice echoed and ricocheted off the warehouse walls, coming back to mock him.

Nothing.

Roman grabbed his flashlight, flipped it on and ran for the front. He couldn't believe they'd gotten in without him hearing. The Pys—they usually made quite a loud entrance and traders, well, they would have had to fight their way through that big metal door. But somehow, they'd gotten in silently and taken Tresa.

He shined his light around the front office, his hand shaking, the light shaking, his entire body shaking.

He'd lost her.

He hadn't even realized how much he cared about having her until he'd lost her and he'd never even had a chance to—to get to know her, the real her. He'd finally found something worth opening his eyes for every day, and now she was gone.

The front office looked undisturbed. The door was just as mangled as they'd left it the night before but still locked up tight.

It didn't make any sense.

He wandered up and down the aisles, checked the rafters, and then checked again. It was a huge building, but his voice reached every corner.

She wasn't there.

He finally came back to his barrel, pausing to stare at the low burning embers, his chin on his chest in defeat. He didn't want to go outside in the dark. Who knew what monsters lurked beyond the thick cement walls, all of which could see better at night than he could. But the thought of her out there, scared, possibly hurt — he had no choice.

He smothered the flames and made his way to the front of the building again, to the front door.

It was locked.

Which was the smart thing to do with traders in the area. Except that Tresa must have kept the keys because they were nowhere to be found.

He was locked in the building, and he had no super alien claws to dig his way out.

The door handle jiggled.

Roman jerked back several steps and dug his gun out of its holster, pointing it at the torn, broken metal. As the door swung open, he clicked the safety off.

It was Tresa.

"What the—!" she squeaked, diving back outside when she saw the gun. "Roman!"

He quickly flipped the safety back on and put the gun away. "Where the hell have you been, Tresa?" he roared.

She dragged in a bag behind her, dropped it at his feet and unzipped it, all while glaring at him. "You almost shot me."

"Well, you scared me to death. I should have shot you."

The bag was full of ammo.

"You went—" he said through gritted teeth, "—to the armory. Alone. At night. Without bothering to tell me?"

She swallowed. "Well, I figured you were asleep and we weren't going to have time tomorrow and—"

"Tresa!"

She straightened. "You're really upset I didn't follow your plan, huh?"

He was really upset but it had nothing to do with his stupid plan. He was upset because for several hours there, he thought the light she'd brought into his life was gone. That he'd lost it without having the chance to be grateful for it. That he'd never see those dark, dark eyes and the sparkling tattoos again.

None of which he could tell her.

"I like my plans," he said instead. "Get some rest."

Chapter Seventeen

They loaded up as much as they could carry, enough to get them through the next week, at least. The silver lining to starvation, if there was one, could be that no one ate much at all because their stomachs had all shrunk.

But. Roman had survived the Garce meat, which meant if Tresa could kill them, the humans could eat them.

Hunger could be a thing of the past.

She couldn't even fathom.

"Ready?" she asked, glancing at Roman. He seemed lighter and had hardly snarled or snapped the entire morning. They had a plan to come back with a larger crew and carry back more food before it disappeared. If there were really traders in the area, Tresa wouldn't put it past them to sneak in and take what she and Roman hadn't. Her only consolation was that if the traders were feeding the Garce in the neighborhood by the compound, then they weren't staying in the area.

Hopefully.

"Ready." He checked his gun for the second time, made sure it was loaded, and fell in behind Tresa as she slid through the door. Instantly on high attention, she spun in a circle, using every sense she had to check for Garce.

Dropping her pack while Roman locked the door, she ran the length of the building they'd just come from, making sure no Garce were sneaking up on them from behind. "Safe?" Roman asked as she jogged back to him. He kept his voice low, somehow knowing she had superhuman hearing without her ever having to tell him so.

That's what she liked about Roman. He figured things out.

"I think so." Tresa shouldered her pack again and they left the building behind, but slowly. Saving their energy for when they would have to run. Their packs were heavy now and they had a long run ahead of them with no plans to stop anywhere else.

Since she'd made her little trip to the armory a few hours before.

"Are you scared?" he asked after several minutes of tense walking. She glanced up at him, brushing her hair away from her face.

"No. Concerned. I mean, why are the Garce gone? Why didn't I sense any Pys last night? This is really weird. I don't know what we're going to walk into." And who knew what had happened to their friends and family. But she couldn't force those words past her lips.

Please be okay, Dad.

"They'll be fine," Roman said, as if reading her mind. He did that a lot and it unnerved her to no end. Even *she* couldn't read minds, just emotions. What kind of witchcraft was he playing at?

"I know."

"So, what was it like growing up with Jeff? He's kind of a badass."

Roman was trying to distract her, but she only gave him half her attention. "He was amazing. He was in the Army. I had two sisters, Phoenyx and Cherish. Cherish wasn't his but he raised her as his own anyway. We didn't even know. I'm not sure she knew. He told me while I was trying to recover from the — the abduction. I had to learn to walk again, and I was mad that she hadn't tried to save us, her or my mom. I was mad that she was always so awful. My mom favored her a lot, but he did his best to make up for it."

"No offense, but you guys have weird names."

Tresa laughed lightly. "They're *unique*. Not weird. I'll tell you this, though. He made sure we could shoot a gun and take care of ourselves. He taught us to work hard and dream big. My mom would always say we couldn't do this or become that because it was too dangerous or too risky or we'd get hurt. He just said if we want it bad enough to work for it, we'll get it."

"Sounds like an amazing man."

Tresa nodded. "He is. Wait." She stopped abruptly and raised her head, sniffing the air. Maybe a hint of Garce, but it was hard to tell when Roman still carried cooked meat in his bag.

Cooked meat that could very well attract the Garce.

Slowly, he raised his gun.

"Run. But slowly. I'm not sure..." she frowned, turning in a half-circle. "I can't tell how close they are. If I could get higher..." She dropped her pack and Roman caught it before it hit the ground.

"Zipping?"

She nodded and stepped backward, into the shadows. The coolness enveloped her and pulled as she swam through the darkness, envisioning the shadow she wanted to come out through.

Once, she'd just jumped into a shadow. She'd panicked and it had been her only escape. She'd been lost for hours until she remembered the very shadow she'd fallen into and come back out that way. Horrifying wasn't even close to how scary that had been.

She was more careful after that.

She zipped out of the shadow near the top of the roof and grabbed the ledge before she could fall. Hauling herself up, she first checked on Roman, who still stood below, gun drawn. Safe.

She jogged the square roof, looking for threats, for anything that could be coming for them, eyes straining to see in the distance. They were still too far away to see their building, but the Garce were definitely heavier there. The worry coiling in her chest tightened and she zipped back down.

"We've got at least a mile before there are any Garce at all. This is crazy. I've never been able to walk a whole mile without having a Garce try to eat me," she reported as she took her bag from Roman.

"Are there still Garce out there?" They walked slowly, despite her earlier advice to run. It seemed stupid now, to waste precious energy.

"Yeah." She massaged her temples, fighting the headache that came from squinting for so long into the sun. Her eyes were sensitive now, and the sun wasn't really a friend. Except for the fact that it kept the Pys away. She did like that. "They're still by the compound."

Roman swore but said nothing and they fell into silence for several long minutes.

Still, Tresa couldn't shake the feeling that something was off. She just couldn't tell what.

Until it nearly ran into them.

Kylie, Michelle and Angie flew around the corner, running hard. They all had guns in their hands and raised them instinctively when they caught sight of Roman and Tresa. "Don't shoot," Roman snarled without any real alarm.

"It's just us," Tresa said needlessly as they immediately lowered their weapons. "What's going on?"

"Traders," Kylie said. "There are traders in the city."

Roman instantly went into what Tresa had fondly decided to call full-Roman. The darkness descended across his face and took root in his eyes. "Where?"

"They've been watching the compound," Angie said. "We don't know how much time we've got until they attack, but it's coming. There are a lot of humans there for them to capture and use as bait. They aren't going to just go away."

"And they might tell the Pys where we are. We have to get rid of them." Roman rubbed the bridge of his nose. "Where are they? Tresa —" he grabbed her arm, "— just because we know where they are doesn't mean you run off by yourself and take on all the bad guys alone."

"They've surrounded the building. Two on each side, as far as Jeff can tell. He's been watching them but hasn't shot yet. We're still hoping..." Michelle trailed off. "I guess we're hoping they'll just go away."

"They won't. Have they been feeding the Garce?" Tresa wanted to shake off Roman's arm and go. Attack, like she was created to do. But finding out all the information would be wise, probably, so she forced herself to stay put.

"They did when they first got here." Kylie swallowed hard. "Two people. Barely teenagers, I think. There was nothing we could do."

Tresa's heart clattered to a stop in her chest. Barely teenagers? The traders were feeding the Garce children? "If I had been there..."

"If you had been there, you would have been similarly stuck, Tresa. You can't go up against traders. They have guns, traps —" Roman started, but she cut him off.

"And I'm indestructible and have claws with Py blood. I can take some stupid humans."

"Tresa." Kylie put her hands on Tresa's shoulders. "We all agree that you're a badass hybrid alien, but are we even sure you can't be killed? I mean, have you ever been shot?"

When Tresa just raised an eyebrow, Kylie shook her head. "Right. I digress. You're tough. But there are too many variables. You can't just run in there to kill everything."

"I could have saved them."

"And we could have lost you. And then we'd truly be screwed." Kylie nodded firmly.

Roman ran a hand through his dark hair and stared up at the sky as if traders were going to leap down from the rooftops at any second. "It's true. What if they're like you? Indestructible with teeth and Py blood? We've gotta do more recon work before we go in."

"There's this *we* thing again. Roman, it's not —"

He ignored her. "How'd you get out?"

"By rope while they were asleep. They aren't so good at the shift change." Angie and Michelle shared a glance that spoke more words than any conversation could. "Brittany and Chris Ann kept watch for us, but getting back in could be tricky."

Tresa looked expectantly at Roman. When he didn't speak, she prompted him. "Well? What's our plan?"

He grinned, Michelle and Kylie both gasped, and Tresa was distractedly aware of how devastatingly beautiful that smile was. "Good girl. All things start with a plan. We need to know what buildings they're on. If they're still separated, they'll be easier to take out."

"You smiled," Kylie whispered. Michelle's eyes teared up, and Roman shook his head. "Apparently I'm making a habit of it. Now focus. We can celebrate later.

Kylie knelt in the dirt and Tresa dropped her pack to bend next to her. "He smiled?" she whispered.

"I fell out of the shelving and he laughed. I'm funny," Tresa whispered back.

"Technically, the falling happened after. Kylie, what's this?"

Kylie had drawn squares in the red dirt that had long since blown across everything, settling deep into crevices, reclaiming the desert. If the world ever came back from the edge of collapse, someone was going to have a massive cleanup job. "These are the buildings." She looked in disgust at Roman, because clearly, he should have realized that. "Here's ours." She drew a star in the middle square. "It's the tallest, so they can't see to our roof, but they can probably see when we're on our roof. And from the eighth floor, we can see them. They're in the buildings here, here, here and here." She drew little x's on each building surrounding their compound. "Two in each building. They stay together, and they're on the top floor but not on the roof. If not for Jeff's sharp eye, we would never have seen them."

"Okay. So that building has, what? Six floors? And this one is pretty far away," Roman mused, drawing all over Kylie's sand art.

Tresa stood, straightening her back. The sun was high in the sky now, and they apparently had a lot of work to do before they were safely inside and away from the Pys.

Work that included killing eight people. The thought sat horribly in her stomach. She'd never had to kill another human before, but if it was them or her tribe, well...

It would be them. No matter what.

"We need to go. Roman, we know what has to happen. You can't go in those buildings. They could have let Garce in after them and if you go running inside, you're Garce food. I have to zip up there. They'll never see me coming."

He stood, as well, and shouldered his bag. "I don't like this plan. There are too many variables. What if they have walkie-talkies? What if they have abilities like yours? What if they have a hidden Py with them?"

"Some plans have risk." She wrinkled her nose. "*All* plans have risk. But if we don't move fast, the Pys will be out and these awful people will give us away. We don't have time to assess any more risk."

Roman groaned, his teeth grinding together. "I don't like this plan."

She smiled and bumped him with her shoulder. "You said that already."

"Fine. Ready? Are you guys burned out or can you run again?" Roman's scowl was still dark and slightly terrifying, but Tresa nodded and pretended he was more thrilled about the situation than he was. It was the only way to survive, really.

"Yep," she said enthusiastically, earning her a special glare all her own.

They started running, Tresa keeping pace with the others because the closer they got to the city block, the thicker the Garce were. Like they were either waiting for the traders and their next meal or trying to hunt the traders. Tresa preferred to believe that one. It's not like a human could train a Garce, could they? They couldn't domesticate an alien that could easily and enthusiastically tear them to shreds.

Right?

"Pace yourself," Roman breathed when Tresa launched herself out of the shadows at the nearest Garce. She watched her energy levels, using only the bare minimum to kill it and keep the rest at bay while her friends ran through the abandoned city streets. The only sounds were their ragged breathing and the pounding of their feet against crumbling asphalt.

And the screaming of Garce. Always, the screaming of Garce.

Tresa leaped from shadow to shadow, trying to create a barrier or a wall of Garce bodies blocking the others, distracting them from the humans racing through their midst. If only she could throw her attacks like the Pys did, instead of having to hand deliver every one, she'd save so much energy.

"Progress report!" Roman snapped.

She stared at him briefly before she realized what he meant and fell into step beside him. "I'm okay. I have enough to get us back to the compound and fight the traders."

"Have you ever fought traders before?" Roman raised an eyebrow and she had the distinct impression it was a rhetorical question.

"They're human, Roman. Their guns can't kill me."

They'd been over it already, and Roman apparently decided to save his breath. The compound rose into view, peeking over the shorter buildings around it.

Three more blocks.

The Garce were thick, though, their shadowy bodies closing in from every direction. Roman moved his team closer to the buildings so the aliens could only attack from three sides, but it wasn't much comfort, not when they could leap from the shadows between sidewalk and wall.

Tresa stayed close, so focused on the Garce she forgot to blink and her eyes dried out against the wind and then teared up so she could barely see. Cursing, she swiped her hand across her eyes.

In those brief seconds, gunshots rang out.

At first, she thought it was her dad and wildly couldn't figure out how he was getting a clean shot from so far away. When the bullets embedded in the walls and concrete at their feet, her sluggish mind finally realized that it wasn't Jeff shooting at all.

It was the traders.

"Roman, I've gotta go or they'll kill us. Can you hold the Garce off?" she searched the buildings around them, trying to remember where Kylie had said the traders hid.

Roman blew out a breath, but more gunshots drove them back, closer to the building.

There were Garce everywhere and Tresa had no idea which threat was worse.

"I got this. Go."

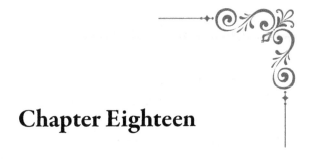

Chapter Eighteen

One second, Tresa roared along next to him with all the force of a hurricane, throwing Garce out of the way like they were nothing and Roman thought they had a good chance at survival.

The next, she was gone, diving into the shadows and zipping away from them. Leaving them to face the Garce alone.

She didn't have a choice, and he knew she was taking what she thought to be the bigger threat. Probably hoping she could take care of the traders and get back before the shadowy aliens realized she was gone. But things never worked out so smoothly, and Roman couldn't wait for her to return.

"We've gotta give her time to get back. The traders knocked out the main doors of that building. If we can get in..." Michelle gasped.

"It will be full of Garce. They'll have followed them in and flooded the floors. We're safer out here," Kylie argued breathlessly. She'd taken Tresa's pack and it weighed nearly as much as she did.

The Garce had caught their scent and came from every shadow, loping through the abandoned city toward them. They had no choice. "In here!" Angie ducked into the doors they'd just decided were too dangerous to go through. It was dark and cool inside, most of the windows boarded up, but the ground was littered with blood-stained shattered glass.

Not a good sign.

The aliens would figure out where they went soon enough, tracking them by their tell-tale scent, feeding off their fear. They kept running through the halls, trying to find another way out, maybe on the other side of the building where the Garce wouldn't be so thick.

Hopefully.

It was like a labyrinth, the hallways twisting and turning and leading nowhere, seemingly endless. Roman could hear the snarling, panting breath of the Garce and knew they were there somewhere. One wrong turn, one unlucky choice, and they could all die.

But in this building above them, Tresa stalked the traders. She'd be able to feel her friends in the floors below her, right? She'd get back to them if they truly needed her.

Roman was surprised how much he believed that.

"We're running in circles. Up there and around that corner is where we came in." Kylie slowed to a walk and Michelle wordlessly took the bag from her, shifting the weight to her own shoulders.

Roman nodded, breathing hard. "We're running blind. Let's take it slow. Listen for Garce."

Kylie and Angie nodded and Roman checked the gun in his hand, making sure the safety was off and it was loaded. They tread more carefully through the building, watching door signs and trying not to notice the rust-colored stains splattering the walls. This building had been hit hard. Much harder than their compound next door. It was weird the way the Garce attacked one building or one area and left others almost completely alone.

Bodies, or what was left of them, still waited in the first conference room they passed. Mostly bones, now, but still hellacious. These people had died at work. There hadn't even been time to leave the meeting they were in. Kylie whimpered and squeezed her eyes shut tight as they edged around the door and continued down the hall. Michelle and Angie shared a grim glance and Roman tried not to see any more than he had to.

Focus on the path ahead.

Funny how the weird little voices in his head that had once belonged to coaches or parents or youth leaders now sounded like a sarcastic Tresa.

He listened, though, leading the way down one hall and then another. He thought maybe they were making progress when the gunshot reverberated from above, echoing through the hallways like a death sentence.

"Tresa!" Kylie gasped and Roman's crazy sister took off running.

More shots, one after another in rapid succession, rattled the windows as Roman dove for Kylie, trying to keep her from making it up the stairs and into who knew what. "She can handle herself!" he yelled, but his own heart thudded in his chest and he kept staring up at the ceiling like he could see through to where she stood.

Kylie made it to the second floor with Roman on her heels. He didn't know when his sister had gotten so fast, but she took the stairs three at a time and darted out of his grasp every time he almost caught her. "She's fine, Kylie!"

But the gunfire kept coming like there was some kind of legendary showdown above, and eventually, he stopped trying to catch Kylie and almost without his knowledge, started sprinting toward Tresa.

What if they wounded her, and then caught her? Something like Tresa in their possession could do a lot of damage. The Pys would pay dearly, he'd bet. They liked shiny, beautiful things.

The third floor blew by as he and Kylie raced together up the stairs. "She's okay. She's okay," Kylie kept whispering, matching her words to her steps.

They almost made it to the fourth floor when the gunshots stopped them again. Gunshots...coming from below.

"No!" Kylie shrieked and froze in indecision, her wild eyes swinging from up the stairwell toward Tresa and back down toward Michelle and Angie. "Roman! What do we do?"

"We have faith that Tresa can handle herself. They need us, Kylie!"

She nodded quickly and whirled, sprinting ahead of him with her gun already out. Kylie hated guns, but she tolerated them because they were more effective than anything else she'd found. She still searched, though, trying to find her perfect weapon. For now, the gun had to do and Roman was grateful their parents had made sure they all knew how to shoot.

And that his sisters both had freakishly accurate aim.

Roman and Kylie hit the first floor, following the sound of gunfire. There was no screaming — always a good sign. He skidded around the corner, trying to remember what way they'd come and what way Michelle and Angie must have been headed and praying he was moving in the right direction. He shouldn't have left them. He shouldn't have gone after Tresa when she was more powerful than all of them put together. He should have believed in her.

Faster, Roman. Faster.

He lengthened his stride, skidding around corner after corner and cursing the layout of the building with each step. "This way!" Kylie yelled and he blindly followed as the gunfire got louder.

That meant they were going in the right direction.

Kylie ground to a stop right before another corner and he barreled into the back of her, nearly knocking her forward and right into the path of a bullet. It shot past her face and embedded in the wall next to her head.

Found them.

He risked a glance around the corner, trying to assess the situation. He obviously couldn't go in shooting — Michelle and Angie were at the other end of those bullets and he could risk hitting them. But the Garce had them backed up against a wall. They'd found the door they'd been looking for, but it was just out of reach.

"Come in low!" Michelle bellowed. She must have seen him or heard Kylie or maybe she was just that intuitive, but Roman rolled out, landing on one knee, and fired into the Garce while Angie and Michelle attacked from the opposite direction. The Garce froze, turning in confusion as it yelped in pain. The goal was never to kill it — that was impossible. Only to hurt it enough to drive it away.

He kept firing, Kylie joining him, both careful not to miss, not to let the alien jerk away because if it did, if their bullets found their way past, they could very easily hit Michelle or Angie, who had nowhere to go, no cover to take. No escape.

It snarled, trying to bite the bullets out of the air, its very essence pulling all the light from around it, making it stronger, healing it before their eyes. This one wasn't running.

A small, dark blur dove from out of nowhere, launching herself through the narrow hallway and onto the Garce's back. Immediately, they all stopped firing and Roman rose to his feet, watching helplessly as Tresa battled the Garce alone.

Wounded Tresa. He could see the bright red blood soaking her entire shoulder, and more across her right temple. She'd been hit. More than once.

He didn't know what to do. He couldn't watch her fight alone, not when she was hurt and weak. But if he kept firing, he risked hitting her.

Kylie whirled on him, dug through his pack and emerged with his daggers. With a battle cry that startled even Roman, she ran in, daggers held high. "Kylie!" he yelled, but she ignored him, diving at the Garce, attacking with the blades one after another. They sank deep into the shadowy flesh as the Garce fought to turn toward her while Tresa held its neck. She struggled to pull enough Py blood to kill it, but she kept fighting, kept distracting it. Kept them alive.

She was spent.

And there was nothing Roman could do about it.

"Run!" he yelled instead. "Everyone run! Tresa, can you still zip?"

No one moved, unwilling to abandon her if she couldn't get herself out of there. Kylie kept fighting, and Tresa barely nodded. "I can. Get out of here!"

"*No*," Kylie hissed. "We're not leaving her alone."

"Kylie, we'll kill her if we stay. We have to go!" Michelle hefted the bag back up to her shoulder. Their compound was one building over. The Garce had been drawn to the sound of gunfire. Roman could hear them invading the building from the opposite side.

"Go!" Tresa screamed, fury and fear carrying clearly in her voice.

The blades dropped to Kylie's sides and she backed away. "I can't."

"We have to. Now, before we lose our chance. Tresa, the shadows outside the building —"

"I got it. Go!"

Roman dragged Kylie out, escaping through the door the Garce had been so fiercely blocking. He backed away, keeping his eyes on Tresa for as long as he could until the wall obliterated her and the image of her clinging to the Garce's back, covered in blood and exhaustion, was imprinted on his mind.

Then he pushed his sisters ahead of him and they ran for the compound. Angie hung back, watching the shadows around them like Tresa would pop out at any second. There wasn't time, though. Tresa could sense them and she wouldn't let go until she knew they were safe. Roman was forced to pull Angie with him, feeling like he betrayed everything good in the world by doing so. He was leaving Tresa behind.

He was leaving her behind so she could escape.

It didn't matter. He felt like a monster. Worse than the aliens they were trying to run from.

"Angie! Roman! This way!" he heard the voice coming from ahead, even though all his attention as still focused squarely behind him. It was Francheska from Tresa's team and Cali Jewel from his, on the third floor with the rope ladder. From the roof, Jeff watched like a silent sentry, gun ready.

Watching for Tresa.

As they raced from the shadow of the building and into the sun, Roman's only focus was getting them to that rope ladder before the Garce figured out that they weren't in the tower behind them. He wasn't expecting gunshots and he dove out of the way, taking Kylie with him while Angie and Michelle dodged the other direction.

Traders.

He risked a glance up, searching wildly for any sign of them, any hint of what direction the attack came from so he could get around it. His eyes strayed to their own roof and saw that Jeff was gone.

They were on their own.

More gunshots, more bullets, and they raced ahead, running in a zigzag, making themselves as small as possible. But the Garce had found them and loped across the cracked and broken street, black drool hanging from their jagged teeth.

They weren't going to make it, and there was still no sign of Tresa. If she zipped out of any of these shadows, it would be right into a pack of aliens. He was torn between the need to go back for her and the need to keep his sisters alive.

Two single gunshots shattered the air, but the bullets didn't scatter at their feet. He looked up, searching the buildings in confusion, but could see nothing.

"Tresa, no!" Francheska screamed. Roman whirled, his eyes straying from the aliens bearing down on them to the small dark object falling from the sky.

Tresa.

That's how she'd gotten around jumping blindly into shadows she couldn't see. She'd gone to the top of the building...

And jumped.

But she didn't have the energy to zip. He saw her, fighting with the shadows, her hand passing through them like her strength and power were completely gone. She was going to die.

Chapter Nineteen

Her power was gone. The Py blood was exhausted. She'd used it to kill the Garce when it wouldn't leave her alone. More of the aliens had filled in behind her after the others had escaped. She'd had to block the exit and then...

Then, she'd had to run. The only way she could, which was up. Higher and higher, knowing she was going to have trouble getting back down. The building had been flooded with shadowy demons and she'd had nowhere else to go. She'd gone up to where she could see the shadows outside and she'd jumped.

Because how hard could it be to zip, right?

Yeah. Not right at all.

She had nothing left. Nothing to grab with. Her hands passed right through the shadows like they weren't even there, and she plummeted toward earth too fast to think of a plan b.

"Come on, Tresa. You're stronger than you know."

Phoenyx's voice startled her and she half-sobbed, seeing the ground so close, knowing there wasn't time. Her dad could see her falling. He was going to watch her die.

After he'd fought so hard to save her.

"Tresa! Find that strength!"

Something shoved a well of power out of her chest, from somewhere she didn't know existed. Maybe it was her sister's anger, maybe it was Tresa's desperation, but she grabbed it, her hand lit, and just as her long hair brushed the ground, she grabbed a shadow and was caught in the cold embrace of darkness. But she had no energy to stay there, not enough to keep her up. She fell out of the shadow she'd been watching when she'd jumped and collapsed on the ground at Roman's feet.

Roman didn't hesitate. If he'd even seen her falling, he gave no indication. Instead, he hauled her to her feet and dragged her along behind him. Garce were coming. After she'd worked so hard to lead them away from the compound, they were fighting their way out of the building she'd just left, some leaping from the same window she had.

They sprinted across the parking lot, her dad's gun roaring in anger every few seconds as he fought the Garce from the roof above.

He hadn't had to watch her die, and for that, she was grateful.

Michelle and Kylie were already scrambling up the ladder Cali Jewel and Francheska held. Angie was bouncing on her toes at the bottom, waving them forward. Kylie paused mid-way up, reaching back a hand, and between the four of them, they managed to push and pull Tresa up, several rungs at a time. She could hear the Garce behind them, could hear Roman roar words but everything in her was so focused on getting away, getting to safety, that she barely registered any of it until Michelle had pulled her through the window and Roman and Angie fell in behind her.

Safe. They were safe.

Roman started bellowing before he'd even pushed himself back to his feet, something about her preserving her energy and she should know better and to never scare him like that again.

She couldn't lift her head, and the pain from her gunshot wounds and the new claw marks across her back found their way through the adrenaline.

"Roman, knock it off," Kylie snarled. "Do you think she would have done that if she hadn't had a choice?"

She was nearly as formidable as her brother.

"Get our medic kits. We've gotta stop the bleeding," Roman barked instead of responding to Kylie.

Footsteps thundered on the stairs and just as Tresa was fighting her way up to her knees, Jeff came through the stairwell. "Tresa!" he roared.

She thought for a minute that she was in for another lecture, but he just scooped her up like she was a little girl and cradled her to his chest.

Safe. She was safe.

"Dad, I hurt," she whimpered without meaning to.

"I know. We'll get it fixed up. You'll be okay."

She nodded because she knew she would and she just needed that moment of weakness, a moment of rest before she had to pull on her brave self again.

Roman knelt next to her. "You're going to be okay, Tres. We'll stop the bleeding, get you something for the pain. Good thing we just raided that pharmacy, huh?" he held up his bag and managed half a grin.

She blinked owlishly at him. A day ago, he hadn't even been able to smile. Now he was attempting it at a time like this?

"I hate to be the bearer of more bad news, but we've still got three sets of traders to take out." Angie paced next to them, watching while the window was boarded up. "Before dark."

"Only two more sets. I took out the ones shooting at you. The others hid after that," Jeff said.

Tresa closed her eyes briefly, counting stars that flitted through the darkness behind her eyelids. "What time is it?"

"Almost three," Francheska answered, whacking the nail she was working on.

"Not a lot of time until dark. Four hours at the most." Roman murmured. Tresa cracked an eyelid and peeked at him. He stared back with dark, worried eyes. "We'll have to come up with a plan without her help."

"What?" she struggled to sit up, brushing her wild hair out of her eyes. "What do you mean, 'without her help'?"

"Tresa, come on. You can't even hold yourself up. You can't go fighting any more bad guys today."

Tracy and Amanda, two from Roman's team, arrived at a full out sprint, skidding to a stop to rummage through the bag Tresa and Roman had brought back from the pharmacy. Carefully, Roman eased her from Jeff's arms to the floor and it was then that she realized how much she was bleeding. Her poor father was covered in it. And it wasn't like they could just throw his clothes in a washing machine with extra bleach to get the blood out.

"I'll take her back. Tracy, you got her shoulder?" Roman asked, pulling out his knife. Without bothering to ask, he cut away her shirt. She started to object, but it was already torn to shreds. Still, she was slightly self-conscious sitting there in only a bra and her many, many sparkling black tattoos.

"Got it."

"Where else are you hurt?" Amanda asked, coming up with gauze and antibiotic ointment.

"She doesn't need that," Jeff said, taking it gently from Amanda's hands. "Save it for someone who might get infected."

"Gunshot wounds might be different," Roman said from behind her, his voice distracted.

Amanda raised an eyebrow, still waiting for an answer to her question. "Just my head," Tresa murmured.

They got to work, Jeff holding her down when she screamed and writhed in pain. The bullet was still in her shoulder — it hadn't gone clear through — and it took all of them to try to get it out without Tresa going ballistic or passing out, whichever came first. Kylie cradled Tresa's head in her lap and smoothed back her hair and even Roman kept mumbling semi-comforting phrases in between snapping at her to hold still.

And while they did that, while their powerful fighters fought with Tresa, the rest of them tried to come up with a plan to take out the rest of the traders. Michelle and Angie finally gave up holding Tresa's feet and went to help the group with their plans, and Tresa had to force herself not to kick whoever was closest. It took too much energy anyway.

Garce, the unstoppable, un-killable aliens she could survive. But a man with a gun? Apparently not.

Well, there had been two men with guns. Men who were not starving and were not war-weary. They'd been too strong and too well fed for this world. This world, where no one could remember a time that there was enough to eat.

Tresa's eyes slid shut and she hid in the darkness behind them, trying to block out the pain and the fear.

But the fear found her.

She slid out of the shadows, watching them while they stared through binoculars out the window. They were laughing.

Laughing at the teenagers who had just run through their barrage of bullets out of sight. Laughing at the fact that they would easily be able to catch them all and use them for Garce bait.

Tresa lost it. She launched herself through the room, not sticking to her carefully made plan, not relying on the shadows that made her so deadly. She screamed and they turned and fired and she was hit before she had the sense to dodge away. The pain tore into her shoulder but she barely noticed.

Those were her friends. Her friends fighting to survive as these monsters laughed.

Tresa heard Roman in her head, snarling unintelligible words about plans and preserving her strength and every other thing he'd ever tried to drill into her, but by then, momentum had taken over and she darted, too fast for their bullets to follow, around the room, jumping from shadow to shadow. She'd thought — she'd been terrified when faced with the prospect of killing a human. She was an alien killer. She was a protector, a guardian. And she'd thought it would be hard, that she'd feel remorse.

She felt no remorse.

Tresa exploded out of a shadow behind one of the men, between him and the window and her claws raked through his throat before he even turned toward her. His gun clattered to the ground and his body fell limp to the floor but Tresa was already moving. The other man wasn't laughing any longer, his face was covered in a sheen of sweat, and he followed Tresa through the room, trying to keep her at bay with his worthless bullets.

"What's your name?" she hissed from behind him. He whirled, his gun coming up too fast. She was sluggish, the shoulder wound threw her off. The bullet grazed her temple but she hardly felt it.

"What's your name?" she screamed at him, diving back into the shadows.

"Ch—Charles. Please. Please don't kill me. We're trying to survive, that's all. We're just trying to survive."

"Survive?" Tresa snarled. "Survival by using your own species as protection? By feeding humans to the aliens? You don't deserve to survive. You deserve to die by the Garce you feed."

"But—but they're— they're so far away. And you aren't evil. You're go—good, right? I saw you protecting the others. You're not a monster. You wouldn't call the Garce up here."

She materialized out of the shadows in front of him. He jerked the gun up again and pulled the trigger, but the chamber was empty. He'd wasted all his bullets shooting at shadows. At nothing.

"I don't have to wait for the Garce to come up here," Tresa whispered, advancing on him, one boot in front of the other. "I am the Garce."

Tresa sat up with a gasp, her heart pounding. She had no idea how long she'd been out. She couldn't remember the last time she'd lost consciousness. But she was definitely not where she'd been. She was covered in a blanket, laying on something soft. Bandages covered her shoulder, her back and wound around her head. But she didn't need them. Beneath them, the wounds were gone.

Tresa could feel it without even having to look.

She was healed.

And more than that, her alien blood had regenerated. The fire was back, the inky blackness craving the shadows and if anything, she was stronger than before.

Give a girl her beauty rest and she could conquer the world, apparently.

She rolled to her feet and reached for her boots, still covered with blood but left considerately by her side.

HER dad was on the roof, and no one else would tell her where Roman had gone. Tresa had two guesses, but she didn't like her fifty-fifty odds. She pushed open the roof door and stalked through the twilight. "Where are they?"

Jeff glanced over his shoulder before returning to the sight on his gun. "You need to rest."

"I'm healed, Dad. I'm stronger than ever. I need to be out there."

Jeff pulled away from the gun to look at her in surprise, which was something. Jefferson was *never* surprised. She half thought he could read her mind and everyone else's most of the time. "What?"

Tresa raised her shoulder, moving it easily in wide circles, and pushed her hair back from her temple. "All gone. The sleep healed me."

"Well. Would you look at that. Get going then. They need your help. They split into two groups, so you're going to have to pick your favorite." His eyes sparkled, just a little. "Roman led Kylie, Cali Jewel, Amanda, Sairaika, Shannon and Kira to the west building. Michelle and Angie took Jessi, Tracy, Francheska, Chris Ann, John and Brittany to the south. I'm calling them the warriors."

Tresa secretly loved that he knew all their names, or that he could remember who went where, but the fact that they'd split up was dangerous. She couldn't be in two places at once and she couldn't run from one building to another very quickly. Plus, that meant limited firepower in each place.

But they hadn't had a choice. The sun was setting and the Pys would be out soon. The traders would give them away if they waited.

"You know..." Jeff said almost conversationally. She looked up at this man she loved so much, her hero, her best friend. He nodded toward the south building. "I can see some shadows through those windows. And there are lots of shadows here on the roof. Just sayin'"

Tresa pulled his gun closer and peered through the sight. "I can see shadows!" she squealed. Leaning up on her toes, she kissed his cheek. "You're the best."

"I am. Get to it but come home less bloody this time, huh?"

She nodded obediently. "I'll stick to the plan."

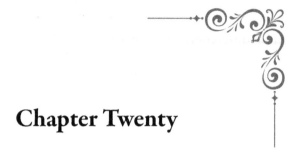

Chapter Twenty

Roman hesitated near the door of the building. They'd gone clear out the west side and around the block, which had involved a lot of running and they were already exhausted, but at least the traders hadn't seen them coming.

He hoped.

"Kylie, your team's got guard duty, yeah?" He glanced down at his little sister, who had her gun holstered and flipped her daggers easily across her fingers like some miniature assassin.

"We've got this. No Garce will get up those stairs without you knowing about it." Kylie nodded confidently. Apparently, her fight with the dark aliens earlier had given her some newfound strength and an alarming lack of fear.

"Okay. Cali Jewel, Shannon, Kira, you guys stay with Kylie." They'd already gone over this, but he felt the need to reiterate. Or he was stalling. Either was plausible. "Amanda, Sairaika, you're with me. That good?"

They all nodded wordlessly, checking weapons. They had a ladder in case they had to escape out the window. They had extra ammo. They had backup weapons.

None of it seemed like enough.

Not without Tresa.

It annoyed him how much he'd come to depend on her. They'd made it just fine without her for *years*. Now a couple weeks in and he suddenly couldn't survive without her? Suddenly couldn't breathe knowing she was back at their compound fighting for her life and he'd had to leave her there?

He'd left her there to protect her. Because he knew damn well if Tresa woke up, she wouldn't let them go without her, and she didn't have the strength to fight.

Not that it would have mattered to her.

She'd whimpered in her sleep. Cried about killing humans, and cried about what the humans had done. Cried about the pain. It had driven him to his knees.

Roman had no qualms about killing the humans upstairs. They were a threat to his team and he wouldn't let them be hurt. He just had no idea how skilled they were, or how deadly. Given that they were human traders, he had to guess they were pretty awful.

"We've got this," Amanda said, her quiet voice steely with determination.

Roman sucked in a breath and nodded. "Let's go."

They slid through the doors in a silent line, Kylie walking backward at the end, not giving anything a chance to sneak up on them.

He glanced back at her when they found the base of the stairs. This building was substantially smaller than theirs, only three floors and one stairwell. She met his gaze and nodded confidently, hiding her fear as easily as she spun the daggers in her hands. He wished she'd go for her gun, but she'd been adamant and he'd given up arguing with her.

Daggers it was.

He took his smaller team and they filed silently up through the darkness on light feet, hands ready. Sairaika nimbly spun every few steps, making sure nothing followed them from the shadows that they weren't expecting.

Jeff had scouted for them and found the snipers on the top floor, where they had the best vantage point without being on the roof and exposed. The traders must have seen when Jeff had taken out the two traders in the north building because they'd been careful to stay out of his range ever since. But with dark fast approaching, they couldn't possibly expect Roman's team to attempt to stop them. Not when the Pys could show up within an hour.

That's why they had to hurry.

They hit the third floor and Roman mentally calculated in his head which room belonged to the window Jeff had seen them in while Amanda scouted ahead, peering cautiously around the corner with her weapon ready. They hadn't been professionally trained for war, but they were soldiers none the less.

"This way," he mouthed, barely daring to breathe. One by one, they slipped down the hall through the darkness. Listening hard for voices, for the sound of life, anything.

Gunshots, Roman hadn't been expecting.

His heart fell and he immediately thought of Kylie and her team fighting the Garce below. It was too soon. He'd hoped they would have had more time before trying to battle the shadow monsters for their lives.

"It's not ours," Sairaika whispered. "It's —"

The west building. Michelle and Angie's team had already run into trouble. His heart crashed painfully against his ribs and the need to keep going, to finish his own mission, warred with the need to go to their aid.

He froze, eyes wide as he fought with himself. How could he leave his sister to fight without him? And Kylie. Kylie must be fighting the same battle he was. They should be by Michelle's side. How could they continue on?

You trust her strength.

Once again, it was Tresa's voice in his head. He nodded and was immediately grateful for the darkness so no one could see him physically agreeing with an imaginary voice. "Let's go," he said quietly.

They'd just started again when a door several feet away from them jerked open and a man and a woman exploded through it, running straight toward Roman and his team. "Did you see who attacked them? Was it Garce?"

Roman didn't hesitate. He had the advantage, his eyes were used to the dark and theirs weren't. He raised his weapon at the same time Amanda and Sairaika pointed their guns, and three single shots fired simultaneously. The traders fell with barely a scream, their bodies collapsing to the floor as momentum propelled them forward.

Amanda gasped, the reality of what she'd just done settling across her face, and Sairaika murmured next to her about how they were protecting the innocent. They were protecting their family.

And all this time, he'd thought his team had no loyalty. That they only had fear holding them together. That Tresa had the amazing team and his...

Well, suffice it to say, he'd been very wrong. His team was freaking amazing.

Roman knelt next to the corpses, checking for a pulse where there wasn't one. He had no idea how they'd been so accurate in the dark, but the two women with him were clearly more deadly than he'd realized.

Good to know.

"I'll check the room. Make sure there isn't anyone else hiding," Amanda said, her voice barely betraying any hint of emotion. Sairaika followed, watching their backs as Roman rose to his feet.

The room was empty. Amanda came back out, frowning. "That was anti-climactic. Where was our big fight scene? I was all prepared for a legendary shootout." She tried to force a lightness into her tone that didn't reach her eyes.

"Not completely empty. They've got supplies here, Roman," Sairaika called.

Roman jogged to her side. They had a myriad of weapons, stockpiles of ammo and plenty of food. They'd been messy — everything was scattered everywhere and all Roman wanted to do was get to his sister's side, make sure Kylie was okay and rescue Michelle. But he had to think of his team. These supplies were desperately needed.

"Hurry. Pack up what you can."

They scrambled through the room, throwing everything they could fit into the traders abandoned bags. Roman's hands started shaking and horrible images of his sisters in trouble kept flashing across his mind, begging for his help and yet he was here, gathering supplies like he was in a video game picking up dropped loot. "It's like Diablo III," he murmured without meaning to.

Amanda and Sairaika barely paused to glance at him in bewilderment, feeling the same trepidation and worry he was.

Minutes later they were bounding back down the stairs. Kylie's team still waited at the bottom in silence, pacing through the small foyer and watching the windows.

"Roman! Michelle is —" Kylie screeched when he came into view.

"I know. I know, let's go. Sairaika, Amanda, can you take the supplies back to the compound? Jeff's watching from above. You should be safe."

They both nodded, slinging the bags higher on their shoulders. "Got it."

"The rest of us will go after Michelle's team. Ready?" He did a quick count in his head as everyone else nodded and readied themselves. Stealth was no longer necessary, and they burst out of the building and sprinted toward the west.

"Where are the Garce?" he asked as they skidded around tumbleweeds, broken asphalt and rusted cars. This had been a huge parking lot once, but now the paint lines were long gone.

"They were coming." Kylie glanced at him grimly before jumping easily over a car door that had been torn from its hinges. She'd run cross country once. Those skills had stayed with her. "But then the gunshots started and the noise drew them to the west."

To Michelle and Angie's team.

"They must have swarmed the building," Kira said. "We didn't dare try to call them back because we didn't know if you guys had found the traders yet."

Roman understood. But he hadn't heard gunshots in several minutes...and yet no one raced out of their building like he and his team just had.

That was a very bad sign.

They hit the concrete that had once been an entryway and slowed, guns raised and ready. From above, he heard a scream and raised his head just as a body plummeted toward them.

"Look out!" Michelle yelled from the window above.

Shannon dove out of the way just as a man landed right where she'd stood. She screamed, several of the others screamed, but the man didn't move. Roman knelt swiftly to check his pulse, but there was none.

Straightening, he peered up at the window his sister had stood at, but she was gone. "Inside. Let's go."

They followed, no one throwing up or even whimpering despite the fact that bodies were now falling from the skies. He didn't know if it was an amazingly brave feat or a sad one. Had life become so grim that this barely elicited a response?

Garce had smelled the blood. They poured out of the cracked and broken doors like a wave of shadow, straight at them.

"Run!" he yelled. Kylie leaped backward and was gone, sprinting away from the chaos washing toward them. The others followed, but not back to the compound. They ran out and around, taking advantage of the Garce's distraction with the dead body, and found another way in.

All while he stood, staring stupidly.

"Roman!"

It wasn't his sisters bellowing his name in fury. As Jeff's gun cracked from above, driving the Garce back, Tresa burst out from behind the Garce, running straight for him.

Too fast, faster than he'd seen her move ever. It blurred his vision as she darted between Garce, sometimes zipping through their very shadows. She hit him like a miniature bulldozer, knocking him back and out of harm's way. "Have you lost your mind?" she snapped as she dragged him to relative safety.

"What are you doing here? How are you moving like that? You were almost dead!" His voice, much to his chagrin, bordered on hysterical.

Before answering, she whirled — claws out — and slashed the Garce closest across the throat. Sparks licked at the sharp ends of her nails, lighting the shadowy monster on fire, devouring its blood with Py flames. He grabbed her hand before she toppled over and swung her back toward him, and they ran, up and away from the Garce and then back around the way the rest of his team had gone. "I'll hold them off," Tresa said, and her eyes sparked dangerously. "Go help Michelle and Angie and get everyone out of here."

"You'll hold them off? There are —" Roman didn't stop to count, but a rough estimate was way more aliens than Tresa could fight alone, especially weak and hurt as she had been. "— Way too many, Tresa."

"Go!" she yelled, and launched herself into the shadows, popping up in the middle of the pack, dangerous claws moving fast as lightning while she dodged teeth and nails. Roman couldn't stay to watch. He raced after his team just as Jessi and John came sprinting down the stairs.

"They got them. Traders are dead. Let's get out of here before dark!" John yelled. The rest of Michelle's team came, as well, but there was no Michelle. And no Angie. If the traders were dead, where was his sister?

He couldn't leave them, and he couldn't leave Tresa, who was outside the building, attacking as fast as she could, taking down as many aliens as possible before she ran out of energy.

She was trying to lead them away, back to the other side of the city and away from the compound. When the Pys came, the Garce couldn't be sniffing around their building trying to get in. It would be a dead giveaway.

The problem was that the Garce were more interested in the humans so close and weren't chasing one single half-breed they weren't even sure they could eat. "We've gotta get out of here," he murmured absently. "Or she's going to run out of energy."

She didn't seem even close to that, though. It was like nothing he'd ever seen before, and after watching her for weeks on end, it was as if he was seeing a whole different Tresa. Stronger, more powerful. More deadly.

"Where's my sister?" he yelled, catching Tracy as she bounded down the stairs.

Tracy kept going. "She and Angie are coming! We had to gather the supplies but they're right behind me."

Belatedly, he realized they had packs similar to the ones he'd found.

Thunder roared above him and seconds later, Angie and Michelle bolted around the corner, running hard straight for him. Roman spun as they passed him and followed them out, checking on Tresa's progress. Their team was half-way across the street, a shorter distance than the one between the building to the south. Tresa was trying to lead the Garce north, away from their compound so that when the Pys came, they wouldn't look twice at their safe haven.

"Faster, go! Get back in the compound!" he yelled, pushing the others along. The sooner they were out of sight, the easier it would be on Tresa.

She'd been fighting for, what? Over an hour now? Usually, she would have crashed hard long ago, but she was only just starting to show signs of fading.

His team picked up the pace as if understanding the urgency in his words, and they ran hard for the compound. Donna, from Tresa's team, stood at the third-floor window with a ladder, ready to pull them up, bouncing anxiously on her toes.

Hurry, hurry, hurry.

One by one, they hit the rope and clambered up, packs weighing them down, holding them back, but they kept fighting. Sairaika and Amanda helped pull them through the opening and to safety.

Roman was the last, just as the sun was fading. He looked over his shoulder, searching for Tresa in the pack. He couldn't yell, couldn't tell her they were safe. It would bring the Garce back and undo all her hard work.

But she must have felt him watching her because her head jerked toward him and she nodded.

And then she was gone.

Chapter Twenty-One

Tresa dove into the shadows and the cool darkness slid over her.

Safe.

At least until the Garce figured out how to follow her in and devour her while she wasn't looking. She needed to get out, find a shadow away from the pack and escape to safety but her mind was fuzzy with exhaustion. The sleep had given her superpowers for a while, longer than ever before, but now she was spent. She tried to remember a shadow she'd seen before she'd jumped in, but she'd been careless. She hadn't seen any and now couldn't envision where to emerge.

She was lost in the darkness.

Maybe that was why Garce only zipped through short distances. They weren't smart enough to remember where to come out.

Focus, Tresa.

She remembered the shadow on the rooftop, next to her dad. But that was over an hour ago and she wasn't sure if the shadow was even still there. What would happen if she tried to zip through a nonexistent shadow?

Panic overwhelmed her and she turned in a circle, or at least, she thought she turned in a circle, but it was so dark she couldn't see anything, and suddenly it was hard to breathe and she didn't even know if her eyes were open or closed.

She screamed. In all her times of zipping, this had been her fear and she'd always been so careful but this time — this time she'd gotten cocky and now she was lost.

"Phoenyx, help me. Help me find the way."

Her sister didn't answer her, not with words. But a calm slid over her heart, and she couldn't *see,* exactly, but her feet knew where to go and the shadow she remembered from the rooftop kept flashing across her mind's eye. *Go there. Keep moving. You can see it.*

She stumbled out of the shadow and into the light without realizing she'd found the way. It was just bigger now because the sun had nearly set and the whole roof was covered in shadow, but it didn't matter. She'd found her way.

Back to the light.

"Thanks, big sister."

"I was wondering when you were coming back," her dad said. He sounded calm enough, leaning against the wall, cleaning his gun, but she could feel the fear and worry dying off him. He'd been as scared as she was.

"I—I got lost."

He looked up, his hands stilling against the barrel. "You got lost?"

She nodded. "Phoenyx helped me."

A soft smile turned up his lips, and he didn't act like it was weird that she was apparently still communicating with her dead sister at all, and maybe he still talked to her, too. "She's always there when you need her, that one."

Tresa nodded, dropping her head against his chest. "I was scared."

He nodded, smoothing her hair with shaking hands. "Me too."

He'd already lost so much. And for those moments, however long they were, he'd thought he'd lost her, too. She didn't want to do that to him. Not ever again.

"I wonder...do you think she blames me?" his voice broke and he cleared his throat before trying again. "I went after you. I tried to save you and I didn't have the chance to look for her..."

Tresa shook her head. "No. She would have been furious if you'd stopped to try to find her."

Besides the fact that she was probably already dead before Tresa had even been attacked. But she didn't say that part. Phoenyx wasn't dead, she lived on within them.

Tresa had to believe that.

The door next to them burst open and Roman crashed through, running straight past to the wall overlooking the city. "She didn't come back. I watched her zip, and I've checked every side of the building but she didn't come out anywhere. Jeff, have you —"

Tresa was touched that he was so panicked. "Roman," she said loudly, trying to talk over him. "I'm right here."

He spun, his dark eyes narrowing. She thought he was going to yell or at least snarl. It was Roman, after all. Instead, he crossed the distance between them in two long strides and swept her up against his chest. "Holy shit, Tresa. You have no idea how scared I was."

She did, though. She could feel his fear. Even without her Garce blood whispering it in her ears, she could feel it in his shaking hands, the pounding of his heart against her chest.

"We need to get down below and lock up here. The Pys will be out soon," Jeff said mildly.

Roman let her go, but his hands stayed close like he was reluctant to lose her touch. "You scared me, Tres."

She blinked up at him. "I got lost," she said quietly. "I couldn't find my way out of the shadows."

He pressed his hand at the small of her back, guiding her inside before he bolted the door behind them. "Don't do that again, maybe."

She half-smiled, too exhausted to do anything else. "I'll try not to."

"Thank you, heavens!" Kylie crowed as she paused at the bottom step. "You found her!"

"She got lost," Roman said before Tresa could answer. "She's okay."

Kylie threw her arms around Tresa, and Tresa could feel her fear as clearly as she had Roman's. They'd been truly afraid of losing her.

That knowledge did all kinds of warm things to her chest.

"Do that again, and I'll hunt you down in those shadows myself," Kylie growled. Tresa couldn't help it, she laughed. Exhausted, hurting, still scared, and yet Kylie had managed to make her laugh.

Maybe this wasn't hell on Earth after all.

"I've got everyone in the common room and ready to go on lockdown. Michelle and Angie are at the south side keeping a lookout with Jessi and Tracy," Kylie reported as they made their way down the two flights of stairs. "But as long as we stay quiet, it should be an easy night."

Tresa shuddered. A statement like that was just asking for trouble.

"Yeah. Let's hope."

"So what happened out there? You were barely clinging to life when we left, and then you went all terminator on those Garce," Kylie said. "It was like a whole new Tresa. On caffeine."

Tresa laughed softly. "Sleep, I guess. I woke up all healed and fully charged. I felt better than — well, better than I can remember, actually."

Roman frowned thoughtfully, the light from the candle dancing in his dark eyes. A stray strand of hair waved across his forehead and something in her longed to push it away, which was a weird little thought. He'd probably break her wrist before she got close, purely out of reflex. "Weird. You can't sleep normally, but when you pass out from blood loss you wake up all bright eyed and squirrelly."

"I don't think that's how the saying goes," she objected but he ignored her.

"So what you're saying is we have to nearly bleed you dry every time we want you to sleep?"

"I think that's not a great idea." Kylie paled in the dim light.

Roman grinned, and once again Tresa was thrown by how beautiful that teasing smile was. It was devastating, heart-rending and soul healing all at once, even if he was talking about trying to kill her on a regular basis. "We'll figure something else out."

Donna took first watch. Tresa had planned to pace through the room like always, but Roman tossed her a sleeping roll. "You need to rest. Maybe you can wake up tomorrow and take out the rest of the Garce population here."

She smirked at him. Jeff nodded in agreement, so she took the sleeping roll and spread it out on the outskirts of the rest of the crowd, in case she had to get up quickly. In case —

She refused to finish that sentence.

Roman did the same, and by the time the sun's rays died completely, the room was silent and she found herself laying on her side, facing Roman. His eyes were closed, the dark lashes swept across the sharp cheekbones, almost hiding the circles of exhaustion under each eye. She studied him for several long minutes, memorizing his features without even realizing she was doing it. Holding her breath, waiting for Donna to tell them the Pys had shown up.

"You can't sleep if your eyes are open," Roman whispered.

She blinked as blood rushed to her cheeks. He hadn't even opened his eyes and she had no idea how he knew she watched him. "I don't sleep."

"Definitely not if you don't close your eyes." A small half-smile played around his lips and her blush deepened.

When she didn't respond, he cracked an eye and raised one eyebrow. "Why can't you sleep?"

"It's a Garce thing. Have you ever seen them sleep?"

He shrugged, propping one hand under his head. "So let your human half take over."

She twitched her lips in annoyance. "Right. Because that's how it works."

"I don't think it's a Garce thing. I think it's a Tresa thing."

She scowled and rolled onto her back. "It's not."

"You're afraid to go to sleep."

"I am not. I'm not five, Roman."

He laughed softly, earning him a glare from Donna and Jeff both. "Shhh!"

Leaning closer to her, so close she could feel the heat of him, he said, "You're afraid. Because if you go to sleep, there's no one to protect us."

"That's—" Exactly true. She didn't dare sleep unless she was forced. Because what if the Pys attacked or the Garce attacked and she didn't wake up in time? Sleep made her sluggish. "Holy crap."

He grinned again, nearly driving the breath from her lungs. "I'm always right, Tresa. You haven't realized that yet?"

She rolled her eyes. "Yeah. Sure you are, Roman."

They were silent for several long seconds. Tresa struggled to breathe, and she wasn't quite sure why. "You're not what I expect-ed," he finally said quietly. She raised her eyes to see him study-ing her much the way she'd been studying him earlier. With one finger, he reached out and traced the sparkling tattoo that ran around the corner of her eye, swirling up and across her forehead.

"Oh yeah?" She could barely force the little words past her lips. His touch on her face was like a brush with fire, sending flames roaring through her blood to her heart.

"I thought you'd be all angry and blood-thirsty and out for revenge. None of this makes you happy and yet —"

"And yet, you're the angry one. And no one even changed you into an alien."

He snorted, burying his head in his pillow to hide the noise. "You've got a smart mouth."

She nodded. "I do. It speaks the truth."

He lifted his head, his eyes shining. "I'm trying, Tres. You stick around long enough, and one day I'll be all sunshine and rainbows just like you."

"We'll see. It takes a special gift to be this optimistic and such a force of good in the world. I don't think you have it."

Instead of the smart retort she'd expected, he nodded. "Yeah. You're definitely a gift."

She let her eyes fall shut because she had no idea how to respond to that. Her heart was all fluttery in her chest and she couldn't swallow. She tried to remind herself that Roman was a jerk, angry, sullen, bossy, and moody. And yet she kept wondering what he'd been like before. Before the world had ended, had he been charming? Flirtatious? Adorable like he was now?

Beside her, his breathing evened and she could hear the heartbeat in his chest. Slow and steady.

Roman slept.

TRESA watched the Pys fly through the sky, attacking Garce at random. Five of them still, and she studied their movements, wishing she had their wings. Or their ability to throw their attacks. They were unstoppable, powerful, faster than the eye could follow, and so beautiful.

And yet, the Garce could kill them. She'd seen it happen when Pys were trapped in the dark with no escape. They were each other's only weakness, and she was made of both.

Well, that wasn't entirely true. When the sun rose and the Pys shrieked and flew away, she remembered their other weakness and the only thing that saved her humans.

The sun.

She heard Roman stir, heard his heartbeat speed up long before he opened his eyes. She was hyper-aware of every movement he made, every breath he took. So when he paused right behind her, so close she could feel his warmth through her thin flannel shirt, she wasn't surprised. "Hey. Ready for training?"

She turned from the slot in the board, away from the sunlight, and her eyes took several seconds to adjust to the dim interior. "What?"

He grinned. "Since you won't sleep to recharge, we've gotta make you more powerful, right?"

"What?" she said again, flatly. This didn't sound like it would be fun for her at all.

"Remember a while ago, we agreed that you would work out in here where it's safe, learn to control your powers and slowly strengthen them? I compared it to training for softball, which you've clearly done many times before?"

"I vaguely recall."

"Well, let's get to it."

"Don't we have more hunting to do? More scavenging? We didn't hit most of our targets on our mission last week. What about the plan, Roman?"

"We're set on supplies for several weeks now, thanks to our little field trip and the traders. They had more than enough for the eight of them. I think *they've* been scavenging from the people they took. Which reminds me. If you have your heart set on venturing back into the danger zone, we do need to see what the traders your dad killed left behind. No one's been to that building yet."

She nodded. "And the first traders I — I attacked. I didn't gather their stuff, either."

"Perfect. Let's get started. I was thinking we could work on your zipping first —"

"Roman, I haven't even had breakfast yet. I might just strangle you if you don't shut up."

Roman laughed, startling several of the others who were just stirring in their beds. They looked at him like he'd been body-swapped in the night, but he didn't seem to notice. "Fine. Eat, whatever. Then we'll get started. Everyone else," he turned, the smile dying on his face. "We've got work to do. Get up already or you can go sleep outside with the Garce."

Nope. Definitely not body-swapped in the night.

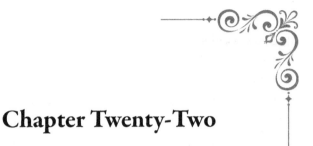

Chapter Twenty-Two

Tresa stumbled ahead of him, still exhausted because unlike the rest of them, she hadn't slept the night before. But the sparkling streaks in her black hair were back, which Roman believed meant her power was back. The Garce blood, as she called it, but he was pretty sure it was the Py blood that made her shimmer even in the darkness.

What an anomaly.

"What are we doing?" Jeff fell into step next to Tresa and she looked up at him fondly.

"Alien practice."

Roman smiled.

"Alien practice?" Jeff sounded understandably concerned.

Tresa nodded. "Like softball practice, but with aliens."

Jeff glanced over his shoulder at Roman, raising an eyebrow. "I like the sound of that."

Roman chuckled softly while Kylie skipped along next to him. "There are no aliens involved today. We're just going to practice zipping. Build up her strength."

"So...this is like weight training between practices. Got it." Tresa nodded, the dark hair cascading down her back, catching the light and creating its own. He'd noticed when she was angry or particularly feisty, she pulled the light in, building the shadows around her like the Garce did. It didn't happen very often but it was terrifying. Now, though, she caught the weak light with the sparkling tattoos and threw it around the hallways in shimmering rainbows.

While everyone else in the compound worked on the garden or building fortifications below, he, Jeff and Kylie set up a course of sorts for Tresa to run through. Or zip through, actually. "Ready?" he asked Tresa, who watched silently, half-enveloped in the shadows.

She turned wide eyes toward him and they were so brown they almost looked purely human and it startled him. His mouth opened but no sound came out.

"Ready." She nodded, letting the shadows fall away from her like a cloak. "What do I do?"

He cleared his throat, trying to work through the confusion. "Zip through here to Kylie over there."

Tresa raised a perfect eyebrow and he nearly strangled himself with the urge to tell her she was adorable.

Right now, while they were focused on training her to be more deadly.

Totally appropriate.

"That's it?" she was still talking while he debated with himself. "That's easy, Roman."

She's a hybrid alien, you idiot. The most dangerous weapon this world has against them. Not some hot high school girl. Focus. "Yeah. You start with the small weights, Tresa."

Kylie waved and bounced on her toes while Jeff watched with interest. Tresa turned, scouting the hallway ahead, and nodded. Humming softly, she slid her hand into the shadow next to her —

And froze.

"I'm scared," she whispered.

Roman had been afraid of that. Actually, he'd hoped she'd forgotten, but apparently not so much. "Because of yesterday when you got lost?"

She nodded.

"Look at these shadows. You can come back to me, Tresa. If you get lost, come back to me."

She peered up at him, a soft smile playing around her lips and he belatedly realized she could feel his emotions. She knew exactly what that sentence had meant to him.

He was acting like a stupid kid. He wasn't a kid. Lives depended on him now and he needed to act like it. But Tresa only nodded, sucked in a breath, and slid her hand through the shadows again.

He'd never watched her do it up close, not unless they were fighting or running for their lives. It was interesting. Like the shadow enveloped her, pulling her into the depths beyond, sliding from the tips of her fingers up her arm, across her chest and spreading down her body and up her neck until she was completely enveloped. It happened in seconds, maybe less, and she was gone from him.

Silently, he counted in his head and hadn't even reached three before she appeared next to Kylie at the other end of the hall. "Hi there," Kylie said with a grin.

Tresa smiled.

"Three seconds for you to go approximately thirty feet. I wonder if that will stay consistent." To Jeff, he said, "Have you ever tracked this before?"

Jeff smirked. "No. We were always trying to stay alive."

Right. Roman had forgotten they'd been entirely nomadic before. This was their first time at a permanent location.

Well, hopefully permanent.

"Ready to go again?" Kylie called from the other end of the hall. Roman jogged backward another twenty feet, checking the shadows around him. Lots for her to come through.

"Ready."

Tresa did it again, sliding into the shadow and disappearing. Roman started counting, got to five, and expected Tresa to come out in front of him. When she didn't, he started to panic.

Because that's what he did now, apparently.

Two seconds later she appeared. "You took longer," he growled.

She raised an eyebrow. "It was further."

"Yeah but last time —"

Jeff cut him off. "He means your timing isn't consistent. Did you do anything differently that time?"

Tresa leaned against the wall, absently playing with a silky strand of hair. Roman watched, mesmerized. "Well, the first time I had more energy so I moved more quickly through the darkness. The second time was further. I was more hesitant because I didn't want to get lost." She shrugged. "There are a few factors going into it. My guess is that it will slow each time I go longer between shadows."

"No," Roman snapped. "We need to get the logistics down. You can't control this if you're guessing, Tresa."

She scowled at him. "Fine. Let's do it again then. Make sure your counting is accurate, Roman."

Kylie snorted at the other end of the hall and clapped a hand over her mouth, trying to suppress a giggle while Tresa jogged back down the hall. "He's just nervous," he heard his sister say.

Nervous. What did he have to be nervous about? He wasn't the one popping through the shadows and risking getting lost.

Tresa shrugged and glared at him. He could see the spark in her eyes even from fifty feet away. "Ready?" she snarled. Had she been closer, she might have ripped his head off.

"Yeah."

She slid in again and he focused very hard on his counting and not panicking and not doing anything else stupid because he wasn't some dumb kid with his first crush. When she bounced out in front of him, eyes still glowering four seconds later, he almost forgot that.

It's a matter of life and death, Roman. This could save her later.

That got him, and he straightened. "Four seconds. What was different?"

"The shadow was familiar. Go another fifty feet and let's try again."

All business. The playfulness from earlier was gone. He'd driven it right out of her soul.

And he hated himself for it.

But now wasn't the time to apologize, and besides, apologies didn't mean anything if he was going to do it again. The important thing to focus on was controlling his mouth and his temper so he didn't kill the sparkle in her eyes and replace it with the fire. "Okay."

He counted the feet as he went and she followed, also counting under her breath. They turned a corner and he worried because now she couldn't see Kylie and what if she got lost?

"Tresa —" he started.

She cut him off. "This is fifty feet. Kylie? Ready?"

"Ready!" Kylie called.

"I'll count." Jeff stood at the corner, being able to see down both hallways, already anticipating that Roman wouldn't be able to see Tresa emerge.

"This is out of sight, Tres."

She nodded. "I do it all the time, Roman. So judging by the last three attempts, I should come out in ten seconds, giving me two extra seconds to adjust for the longer distance."

She didn't look at him and he felt like an ass. "Okay. Just be careful."

She rolled her eyes and slid into the shadows. Roman started counting under his breath as Jeff counted out loud. Nine seconds later, he heard Kylie call, "She's out!"

Tresa was speeding up, which messed up their data.

He jogged around the corner and met her half-way. "Nine seconds. What was different?"

"Nothing. I figured fifty extra feet would equal two extra seconds but it didn't. It must be less than a second per fifty feet of extra time."

And Roman had thought, all those years ago while he was wasting away in math class, that he would never use that stuff.

"But if we can get it to within a half a second, I think that's accurate enough for a science we don't understand using a counting system that isn't exactly computerized." Smiling up at Jeff, she said, "No offense, Dad."

"You kids and your technology," he grumbled in return.

"How much more you got? Wanna go again? Another hundred?"

"Two hundred feet at once?" Tresa gnawed on her lip. "Let's go fifty more. Baby steps, Roman." She almost smiled before she seemed to remember she was still annoyed.

"These aren't baby steps, Tres. They're huge giant steps. If we need to go smaller—"

She shook her head. "I don't have all day, Roman."

That was exactly what she had, though. They were stocked up on food and medical supplies for the time being. Everyone else was working on the garden. They literally had nothing else to do.

Hours later, Tresa leaned over Roman's shoulder in an abandoned office while he jotted numbers down and tried to figure out her rate through the shadows. She'd zipped through so many he would have lost count if Michelle hadn't shown up with a paper and pencil, somehow reading his mind. She'd stayed to watch the rest of the testing, eventually coming up with more questions they needed to explore.

Which was what she and Kylie were bent over now, across the desk from them. "I think it's more important to know the rate her energy deteriorates than it is to know how fast she can move."

"She does slow down, though, when the energy starts depleting," Kylie pointed out, jabbing at a line on her paper and then pointing at Roman's. "We need to know that, too."

"And I'm sure actually fighting with the Garce uses her ability to zip more quickly than bouncing through shadows in an abandoned hallway," Michelle mused.

Tresa stirred and Roman glanced up at her. She'd long ago tied her long dark waves up into a messy bun, but strands escaped, whispering across her skin and he wanted to brush them back except that she probably would have smacked him. "I don't think it does," she murmured, drawing him out of his internal obsession with her hair.

Get it together, moron.

"What?" he asked, brilliantly.

"What I kill the Garce with isn't the same thing I use to zip. Two different types of blood." She held up two fingers like that demonstrated it perfectly. "I mean, I'm not sure, but when I fought the traders and only used the Garce abilities — speed and shadow jumping and claws, I still had the Py fire to fight the Garce when I got back down to you. I just couldn't zip much."

"The speed probably comes from the Pys, as well," Roman mused. "So you're drawing from both when you move that fast. But that's interesting. You have two separate sources of power instead of one to draw from."

She leaned against the desk and smirked at him. "What'd you say you wanted to be when you grew up?"

He glanced down at his very detailed notes. "A computer programmer."

Tresa grinned. "It all makes sense now."

She pulled his paper toward him, stared at the numbers and nodded. "I move at ten feet per second in the shadows, plus an additional half a second per fifty feet, more or less. Tomorrow we'll have to find a way to test the Py blood and see how strong it is. But it's almost dark and I'm worn out. We need to close up for the night."

"Close up? Like we're a shop of some sort?"

"Or a secret lab." She shrugged. "Whichever."

He laughed, pushing himself to his feet, and he wondered if laughing would ever feel natural again. It still felt wrong, like he was betraying everyone he'd lost with his happiness. But with her, he couldn't help it. She had too much light and it was contagious.

"You're adorable." He spoke the words without meaning to.

She nodded, bumping him lightly with her shoulder. "I know."

Chapter Twenty-Three

Roman had taken the opposite side of the building, and Tresa sat at her slot in the window and stared into the darkness. Waiting for the Pys she knew were coming. The Garce blood in her craved them and it grew the closer they got.

But this time she had a distraction. She was exhausted, yes, but she couldn't keep from smiling. It had been a good day.

Sure, Roman liked to panic and yell at everyone and use his anger as a shield, but eventually she saw through it. He worried about her. And something small and shy inside her hoped he worried because he liked her, but it was probably more that he'd adopted her into his tribe. He worried about them all.

Still, he had called her adorable.

She felt the Pys — too close— and it momentarily took her mind from Roman. She watched through the slot as they tore across the sky, hunting the Garce with a ferocity that she could never match. One well-placed hit of their blood ball took it down, and that was from twenty feet away. They never risked their life. They never got bit.

And their wings...

They were glorious. Huge, black with blue sparkling streaks running through them, streaks that matched the twining tattoos on their skin. The Pys were something dreams were made of, so beautiful everything around them paled in comparison. Small, dainty, fairy-like. But Tresa also knew they were more like vampires, the way they sucked their victims dry. The men, at least. No one knew what they did with the women and girls. The Pys took them and never had anyone returned. Millions, just gone.

There were only two Pys this time. Tresa couldn't see any trace of the other three, and she watched for hours while they feasted on the Garce below. Waiting for them to leave so she could breathe again.

Something distracted them, though, and Tresa squinted, forcing the Garce DNA to take over so she could see better. Something in one of the buildings to the north of them. They both darted, lightning fast, out of sight.

Odd.

Something coiled in her chest, clenching her heart. She glanced uncomfortably around the room where everyone slept or if not, at least lay silently. They were safe. The Pys wouldn't find them.

She turned back to the slot but the Pys didn't reappear. For almost an hour she watched, growing more concerned by the second.

The explosion from above was barely a surprise.

She heard them blast through the door above, leading to the roof. Pys didn't seem to know how to work handles. If something stood in their way, they burned through it. Tresa spun, her heart pounding. She had to stop them and protect these people.

And then from below, another explosion rocked the building as the blood ball hit one of the boards covering the wide windows.

They were coming from both directions.

"Into the offices. Hide, now!" Tresa bellowed because the Pys knew where they were and there was no point in being stealthy.

Kylie was on her feet first, handing Jeff his gun before he even made it to his feet, and then there was chaos as people ran in many directions at once, looking for a safety, a shelter, that didn't exist. There was no escaping the Pys.

There was nothing that could keep them out.

"Tresa!" Roman burst into the dim light, wading through the confusion. "How long do we have?"

"Seconds. We've got to get them out of the common room and into one of the back offices. Separate them so the Pys can't take them all —"

Because the Pys would take whatever they could carry. Which meant some would die, but if they weren't all in the same place, maybe some would survive, too.

Roman moved, barking orders while he loaded his gun. But these people, their tribe, they'd all been attacked by Pys before. They knew how to respond. They knew the likelihood of survival. Fear drove them, fear made some crazy and others strong. Kylie, Michelle and Angie directed traffic, keeping themselves directly in harm's way to make sure others were safe.

Tresa stood frozen in indecision. She couldn't get to both Pys at once. They'd come from different directions, almost like they were expecting her. Like they knew there weren't just defenseless humans here.

Had she been so careless that she'd left clues behind of what she was?

"Traders. We missed one," Roman barked. "Go, Tresa. Be safe."

"We'll hold the other one off," Jeff promised, his gun loaded and ready. Roman stood next to him.

Fearless. Beautiful.

Tresa nodded and ran. She'd spent all her energy earlier that day, training. She had very, very little left and she had to save it all or she wouldn't be able to kill them. She sprinted up the stairs, letting the craving lead her. With every step, it got stronger until it consumed her. She heard the Py singing before she actually saw it, calling the humans in the building. Its voice, siren-like, didn't lure Tresa like it would the others.

The only thing driving her was the Py's blood.

"You're so strong, little ones," it purred, which was ironic since Pys were small and most humans towered over them. Except the wings, which were big enough to fill the stairwell. "You've survived so long. So much longer than many others. Come to me. I'll make you pretty."

It seemed startled when Tresa came pounding up the stairs, spinning around the landing toward it. "I'm already pretty," she snarled.

"What—what are you?" the Pys stuttered. It was the first time Tresa had ever seen one's absolute confidence shaken. "You're not human."

"I was. If you leave now, I won't kill you."

The Py tilted its head, long sparkling blue hair tumbling in thick waves across its shoulder. "Kill me? Nothing kills me, little one. Come to me. We'll find your friends, we'll take you away. We'll make you beautiful."

But there was fear in her voice. It recognized the darkness in Tresa. It was Garce blood, but not how she was used to it.

"Take me where? Where did you take everyone else?" Tresa didn't have time to make conversation, but she could already see the sparks in the Py's hand. They moved so fast, Tresa wouldn't see that blood ball coming until it was embedded in her chest. If she blinked, she could be dead.

Fear made her arms stiff as her brain raced, trying to find a way to stop the Py and get back down to Roman.

"We'll take you home." The Py motioned toward her, some of the fear fading. They couldn't sense emotions, not like Garce could. Tresa knew this, and she struggled to make her head connect the dots — to use that to her advantage. "You're so pretty. You'll be so pretty as one of us."

Tresa took a hesitant step forward, watching the Py's hands. "Are you going to hurt me?"

The Py smiled, revealing rows of razor sharp teeth and delicate white fangs. "No, pretty one. I will not."

She lied, but Tresa already knew that. She took another step forward and the Py held out her hand. "How many of you are there?"

"Just me."

The Py narrowed her eyes. "Don't lie to me," she hissed. "I know there are more of you. We were told there are many here."

Roman had been right.

Traders.

They must have missed some.

"There—there are many. Like me. Lots. Like me."

The Py watched her. "What made you, pretty one?"

"A Py, like you." Tresa inched closer, trying to judge how much energy she had. "A Py in a Garce ship."

"Nathalia." The Py hissed, the flames dying in her hand. "Our lost sister. What is she doing now?"

Tresa launched herself just as gunshots exploded below and the infuriated scream of the Py below shook the building. The one in front of her blinked, too slowly, unprepared for Tresa's speed, and raised her hand. The fiery ball shot through the air but Tresa twisted out of the way as it flew past her face, singeing her hair as everything in her zeroed in on the blood of the Py in front of her.

The Py shrieked, clearly unused to missing. Unused to anything being able to dodge her, to be able to move as fast as she could. Her wings fought to pull her back up the stairs and out of Tresa's reach but the stairwell was too small and her wings were too big. They slid uselessly along the walls and her feet tripped in confusion.

Tresa landed hard, crashing into the Py as the screams from below filled her ears. They both tumbled backward, the wings twisting, cracking, tearing under Tresa's claws. The Py fought back with claws of her own — long, sharp, dagger-like nails that tore at Tresa's arms and chest, trying to force her back.

Fire erupted across Tresa's skin as the blood ball hit her chest, but she dug it out before it could seep inside and light her very soul in flames. She threw it back at the Py, ducking away from the claws and the sparks and the pain.

The blood ball hit the Py in the face. She screamed and thrashed and in those few precious seconds, Tresa slid past the wings, past the claws —

And stabbed her in the chest.

The Py gasped in genuine surprise as she flung the blood ball weakly back at Tresa. Her beautiful face was charred, her body covered in blood. As she stared down at the gaping hole in her chest, the tattoos winding across her skin faded and she whispered, "Nathalia. What have you done?"

The need to devour her blood nearly drove Tresa to her knees, even knowing as she did that the blood would poison her. It might not kill her, not like it did the Garce, or at least as quickly, but it wouldn't be good. Every minute, every second her body waged war against itself, Garce blood and Py blood within her fighting to eradicate the other while her human half struggled to survive.

And yet...

The Py's blood was everywhere. Tresa could easily —

More gunshots and more screams. Tresa was jerked from her trance and she spun, racing away from the dead Py and back down the stairs. "Tresa!" Roman bellowed.

She ran faster, leaping down the staircase, from landing to landing. She hit the sixth floor and shoved through the door, nearly ripping it from its hinges. She bolted down the hall, the smell of scorched paint and burning carpet hanging thick in the air.

The Py laughed.

"Come out, pretty ones. I can take care of you. I can take care of you better than him. I can make you beautiful. You can live forever."

Her voice was soothing, comforting, warm, and Tresa knew how much of a fight it had to be for those in her tribe to stay behind their doors.

"Tresa! Anytime!" Roman yelled.

"Your Tresa is gone. She left you. But I will take care of you," the Py sang.

Tresa rounded the corner, trying to keep her feet silent on the thick carpet, gauging her energy levels, praying she hadn't lost so much blood she'd be unable to fight.

The Py hovered in the air above her, just around the corner and out of reach of Jeff's big gun and Roman's deadly accurate aim. She was too high for Tresa to reach.

If only I had wings. Or blood balls.

She didn't have those things. She couldn't fly, she couldn't throw attacks.

But she was deadly.

The Py shot around the corner, blood ball in her hand. Jeff and Roman both fired, but they were forced to dive out of the way. Again and again, she drove them back, clearing a path straight for the offices.

She'd apparently gotten tired of waiting.

Tresa threw herself against the wall as a stray bullet shot past her face, dangerously close to burying itself in her forehead. Jeff and Roman couldn't see her yet, they were so focused on taking out the Py in the air between them.

The Py, who still had her back to Tresa.

Tresa skidded to a halt, staying close to the wall, taking in the scene before her, looking for shadows. She didn't have wings, and she couldn't throw blood balls, but she could slide through shadows within seconds, and there was no way the Py would have time to fight back.

Not when there were shadows hanging right above her head.

She moved quickly, though, and Tresa watched her for seconds more, judging her directions. It would do no one any good if Tresa came out of a shadow three feet too far to the left because the Py had moved while she was zipping through the darkness.

There was a pattern. Of course there was a pattern — Pys loved patterns. They were probably the most OCD aliens in the galaxy. Left, dodge Jeff's bullet, right, throw a blood ball at Roman, forward, throw one at Jeff, back, dodge Roman's bullet.

"Got it." Tresa dove into the shadow in front of her, counting seconds and matching them to the Py's pattern. When she emerged from the ceiling, she dove, hitting the Py and knocking her out of the air.

She felt the bullet hit her in the shoulder and some crazy part of her thought how good it was that she didn't have wings, but the rest of her, the sane, functioning part of her, attacked the Py.

This Py fought back, but sluggishly. She'd been hit by bullets, too, but mostly her brain couldn't fathom what Tresa was, and couldn't figure out how to fight back. Not fast enough. They rolled across the floor, Tresa wrapped in silken wings that threatened to suffocate her. She slashed out with her claws, tearing through the wings like silk. The blood balls hit the floor on either side of Tresa's head and she jerked away, curling in on herself before she lashed out again.

So tired.

So tired.

She had nothing left, all her energy spent. No more Garce power to fuel her fight, no more Py power to attack with.

The Py screeched and threw another fiery attack that burned across Tresa's temple before hitting the wall behind them. But it left the Py vulnerable, so surprised she had missed that she froze in confusion. Tresa pounced, claws tearing across the Py's throat, but still, the alien fought, long nails raking across Tresa's already wounded chest, across her arms and stomach. Their blood — the

Py's shimmering blue and Tresa's inky black, pooled on the floor beneath them.

Kylie burst out of the door just next to Tresa, daggers blazing, nailing both the wings to the floor. Roman threw himself over the Py's arms, pinning her claws beneath him while Jeff pulled Tresa to safety.

The Py's shrieks gurgled in her torn throat, growing softer and softer until it was barely a whimper.

Tresa sank into her dad's arms, finally safe. She was bleeding from she didn't even know how many injuries, weakened beyond repair. "Daddy? I'm not sure —" she whispered. "—not sure I'll come back from this one."

Jeff choked on a sob, cradling her against him.

Roman's voice fought with the darkness at the edges of her vision. "Yes. Yes, you will, Tresa. Dammit, do you hear me? You're going to be fine. Because I can't do this without you."

Chapter Twenty-Four

Tresa fought to stay with them, but every time Roman stopped swearing at her, the dark eyes fluttered closed.

So he kept swearing.

She'd lost so much blood. Kylie and Michelle had gone to check the Py above and said the hallway was soaked. Mostly Py blood, but too much of Tresa's.

And the common room. Where he and Jeff had made their stand. They were both burned, injured, but still on their feet. It had been Tresa who flew in from the shadows and knocked the Py out of the air. Tresa who had fought tooth and nail to kill it while they'd been helpless to do anything but watch because one wrong bullet would have weakened her beyond what even Tresa could have fought back from.

"Tresa, stay with me," Roman snarled again and sluggishly, the dark eyes opened.

Kylie, Michelle, Angie, Jeff, they all worked tirelessly, trying to stop the bleeding. Trying to keep her alive.

Others, their warriors, they came and went constantly, bringing supplies, food, water, support.

Roman held her head in his lap and smoothed the silky black hair away from her face, always careful of the burns. Everyone else watched silently, some crying, everyone realizing what she'd done.

She'd saved them.

There was no fighting back against the Pys. Guns would only annoy them. While it was possible to run from the Garce, to hide from the Garce, it was not possible to run or hide from Pys. It was the first encounter Roman had ever had with them that he hadn't lost half his team.

"I hurt," she whimpered.

Roman nodded, letting his fingers trace her cheekbone, across her ear and down her jawbone. "I know. I know, Tresa, but you're stronger than this."

"If she falls asleep..." Angie started. She hesitated, glancing up at Tresa. "She could wake up supercharged and stronger than before..."

"Or she could not wake up at all. Keep her alive, Roman," Jeff said quietly.

Roman swallowed hard. He'd been scared many times in his life, but watching Tresa fight with the Py, taking so many hits, trapped within those wings...

It would haunt him for life.

Her eyes slid closed. "Tresa! Open your damn eyes!"

She fought. He could feel more than see the fight within herself to come back to him. But she did because she was Tresa and she always came back to him. "That's my girl."

"Trader," she whispered, her lips cracking and bleeding. "Trader told them where we were."

"We missed one, I guess. We'll find him. We'll find him and I'll kill him but only if you stay with me, Tresa," Roman promised. He would have promised her the damn moon if it would keep her eyes open.

She leaned into his hand, whimpering against the pain as Jeff dug the bullet out of her shoulder.

Roman's bullet.

He hadn't realized she was there. Hadn't seen her zip out of the shadow until he'd already squeezed the trigger. "I'm sorry," he whispered. "I'm so sorry."

"It won't be what kills her," Jeff said, his head bent over the wound. "Bullets can't kill her. Only aliens can do that."

But it definitely didn't help.

"Just be glad it was your bullet and not mine," Jeff murmured, trying to give Roman comfort when his own heart had to be breaking.

For hours they worked on her, and for hours Tresa fought to keep her eyes open, even if oblivion would have given her an escape from the pain. The sun rose and no one moved, and Roman couldn't muster the will to care about the garden or the shattered points of entry or anything beyond the broken little half-breed alien in his lap.

It was Michelle who finally directed them to the garden. Tresa's wounds were cleaned and bound. It seemed that more skin was bandaged than not. Her breathing was still ragged with pain but the dark eyes watched him quietly. He smiled down at her. "Hey."

"Hey." She didn't smile, but he felt the warmth of it anyway.

"You're pretty tough."

"I am."

"Roman?" Jessi asked, drawing his attention from Tresa's dark eyes. "What do we do with the bodies?"

He frowned. The Py was tiny. Lifting her wouldn't be hard, but the giant wings would be a problem. And then what did they do with her that wouldn't alert other Pys to her death?

"Bottle the blood," Tresa gasped around the pain. "We can use it to fight the Garce."

Jessi's eyes widened and Roman could only gape down at Tresa for several long seconds. "That's genius," he finally managed.

She closed her eyes in agreement. "Then throw the bodies to the Garce it will kill them but not until they've destroyed any evidence."

"One would think she's done this before," Jessi murmured as she turned away. "One would be wrong."

Roman leaned back against the wall, careful not to jostle Tresa, and closed his eyes. Exhaustion, now that fear didn't drive him relentlessly, nearly crippled him. "You should sleep," she whispered.

"Yeah. I'll go ahead and do that after four hours of not even letting you close your eyes."

"She'll get chilled on the floor," Kira said, kneeling next to them with blankets. Carefully, she spread first one across Tresa's body, and then the second, before she moved away to something else.

"Here, Roman. This might help," John said several minutes later, dropping a bedroll next to him.

"You both need water. See if you can get her to drink," Brittany said quietly, setting a bottle next to him. "She'll be okay. She's strong."

Someone else brought him food. They kept coming throughout the day, checking on Tresa, making sure she was as comfortable as possible. Before the end of the world, she would have been in a hospital, but now all they could do was watch and pray.

"You know, before I met you I thought my team...well, I thought they were here because I could protect them. If someone else could protect them better, they would leave." He talked just to give her something to focus on, but it needed to be said. "I sorely misjudged them. I projected my own disinterest onto them. They're fierce, Tresa. Like your tribe. They're fierce and strong and loyal." He chuckled, but it was forced. "Probably because of my sisters."

Tresa tried to smile, but she didn't succeed.

It was late evening when she finally gave up her fight to stay awake and tumbled into sleep. Roman had dozed off before she had and woke to Kylie and Amanda's quiet, panicked murmurings. "Her pulse is steady. Should we wake her up?"

Kylie shook her head. "It might be better for her to sleep. She heals faster."

Roman swore, running a hand over his face. "I didn't mean to fall asleep. How long has she been out?"

Kylie shrugged. "I don't know. You were both asleep when I came back up. It's okay. She's breathing and her pulse is — well, it isn't strong but it's steady."

"But what if she doesn't wake up?" Pure fear ran over and under Amanda's words. "The longer she's asleep, the more dangerous it could be."

Kylie watched her silently for several long seconds. "She'll wake up. She has to. We still need her."

Roman gritted his teeth, furious at himself for falling asleep. If he lost her because of his own carelessness, he would never forgive himself.

"Roman, she needed to rest," Kylie said, reading him too easily.

He rolled his head toward her. "I can't lose her, Kylie."

She smiled, too understanding. "You won't. You should sleep while she sleeps."

"No one else is sleeping."

Kylie sighed and slid down to sit next to him. "You're pretty attached to this one. I didn't know you had it in you."

"She nearly died to save us. Again."

"Yeah. That's not why you're freaking out." Kylie slid him a sly smile.

"I shot her, Kylie. And that wasn't even the worst of her injuries."

"That was rude."

He scowled at her.

"I was kneeling right next to you, Ro. Trying to stop the bleeding on her chest and throat. I heard everything you said."

"Why were you listening to me and not trying to save her?" he snapped without vehemence. He was too tired.

"I'm a woman. I can multitask. You like her, huh?"

"Of course I like her. Everyone likes her. I don't think she's got an enemy on this entire planet." He smoothed Tresa's hair away from her face, keeping it off the bandages. She half-sighed and leaned her forehead into his hand.

"Well, the Garce probably aren't fond of her. And not the Pys, after this. But that's not what I meant and you know it." Kylie adjusted the blanket, trying to keep the chill away.

Roman stared down at Tresa's face. Even so injured they'd almost lost her — burned, clawed, broken — she was still mindnumbingly gorgeous. It wasn't the alien part of her, but the human half he could see through it. The brown eyes under the black. The freckles under the Py's flawlessness. The sweet smile under the Py's coldness. "Yeah. I like her. I tried not to. I failed." He turned tortured eyes on Kylie. "Getting attached is dangerous, Kylie. You're not supposed to have feelings in an apocalypse. That's how you lose the will to fight anymore."

Kylie snorted. "I don't know what crappy apocalypse movies you've been watching, but in every one I've seen, that's what *gives* them the will to keep fighting."

"Real life, Kylie. Not movies. I lost mom and dad. And I— I couldn't —"

She cut him off. "But you had us, so you did. We forced you to keep fighting. Tresa's just one more reason."

"Yeah, but I almost lost her today, Kylie. And I don't know if I'm strong enough to lose anyone else."

Kylie nodded toward Jeff, who had been the only one who actually dared touch the dead Pys and so been busy with that all day. "He lost two daughters and a wife. He almost lost Tresa. He's still the strongest guy I know."

Roman watched Jeff work. He stayed close to Tresa, but he trusted that she'd stay with them. He had faith in her strength, faith Roman didn't. He'd been scared, yes, but he'd done what had to be done and...

He'd trusted Roman to take care of his daughter.

"Why?" Roman said aloud without meaning to.

"Why is he strong?" Kylie raised an eyebrow. "Because of all the reasons I just said."

"No. Why did he trust me with her?"

Jeff barely glanced up at him before he went back to work. "Because you've been there for her from the very beginning. I'm not stupid. I have eyes."

"It's not the end of the world to let someone else in. She's my best friend, and I'm still fine."

Roman rolled his eyes. "Does she know she's your best friend?"

"Yes," Kylie growled.

He snickered.

"See? A best friend is way more important than a crush, so..."

Roman ran a hand through his hair. "This isn't just a crush, Kylie."

Kylie's eyes widened. "I see. Well, then we need to be having a whole different talk and we probably need to involve Michelle."

Roman laughed half-heartedly. "No. What is it with you two and your talks? We don't need any more talks."

"Says the boy who was just saved by one." Kylie smiled triumphantly and bounced to her feet, checked Tresa's blankets, and went back to helping.

It was nearing dark when Michelle approached and at first, he thought he was in for another 'talk'. "We can't stay here through the night, Roman. We've got the boards back up downstairs. I think we should move down a floor."

He blinked up at her. That meant moving Tresa and he wasn't sure she would survive that. "Why?"

"They're scared. And rightfully so. This room might as well be haunted now. Plus, I'm not really sure how sanitary the Py blood-covered walls and floor are for sleeping. And everything's burned."

He sucked in a breath and straightened, seeing the room clearly for maybe the first time. She was right. It was a battlefield and forcing them to stay there another night was asking too much.

"Okay. We'll go down a floor. We've just got to figure out how to move her without causing her too much pain."

Michelle nodded. "I'm on it."

Tresa had been asleep for hours. Roman checked her pulse every half-hour, making sure it was still steady and he knew it was slowly getting stronger and stronger, but he couldn't let go of the fear that she might not wake up. Even as he did everything in his power to keep her asleep. Like sitting in the same position for hours and hours on end. He'd long since lost all feeling in his legs.

Michelle came back an eternity later. Or hours, Roman wasn't sure. He had no way to tell the passage of time. He could hear her tugging something toward them, something big and watched the darkness until she appeared pulling not a board like he'd assumed, but the top of a desk. He had no idea how she'd even ripped it off. The strength of his sister apparently knew no bounds. She dropped it unceremoniously on the floor and settled next to him, watching Tresa for several long minutes before she finally spoke. "What do we do if they attack again tonight?" She spoke quietly so only he could hear her, trying to cause as little chaos and panic as possible. "They'll come after her. They probably won't even care about us now, not after they realize she can kill them. We can't protect her and she sure can't protect herself."

Roman watched Tresa's still not steady breathing. "We hide her. We hide all of us and if that fails, we fight for as long as we can. If they get their claws on her, Michelle..."

She pressed a hand to her forehead. "It would be catastroph-ic."

Catastrophic was an understatement.

"They won't though. They probably didn't even notice the other two didn't come back today," Roman said with a conviction he didn't feel. "They'll eat whatever Garce they can get and they'll leave."

"The trader's still out there, Roman. If any Pys come tonight..." Michelle couldn't finish the sentence.

Roman didn't blame her.

They wouldn't survive it.

"We'll hide. It's all we can do. And protect Tresa at all costs." He was amazed at how important those few words were. Not long ago...weeks, maybe? He couldn't even remember. It felt like a lifetime. But he'd hated her. He'd feared her. Now, he couldn't stop thinking about her. He made stupid mistakes and couldn't concentrate because she was always in his head. Hell, when some-one was screaming at him in his own mind, it was usually her voice he heard.

"Can you help me move her?" Roman asked. "Without caus-ing her any more pain than necessary?"

Michelle nodded. "That's what my desktop is for. Like a stretcher...with no wheels."

Roman nodded. "Nice."

"Maybe we should pad it a little. One sec, I'll be right back." She disappeared again and he stayed, watching Tresa sleep, occa-sionally brushing her hair back from her face and marveling at how beautiful she was.

It's not just a crush.

He didn't know what it was. It was too soon to give it a name. All he knew was that she brought light back into a dark world and the thought of losing her scared him more than he wanted to admit.

"Keep fighting, Tres. Please keep fighting."

"Ready?" Michelle asked breathlessly. He hadn't even heard her come back, and she'd already arranged the blankets and pillows on the desktop.

"Yep. What floor are we moving to?"

"Just the one below us. Almost everyone is situated now. Getting ready for lockdown." Michelle aligned the desktop next to them and awkwardly, he shifted Tresa's weight from his legs to the board. Blood rushed through his long-numb extremities, spiraling into pins and needles that he tried to shake off. Tried, and failed. Pins and needles didn't care that he had stuff to do—

There was a whistle and crash that already haunted his every waking move. And from above...

Their freshly boarded up door to the roof exploded open.

He heard them screaming, his team, defenseless below. He heard the terror and the erupting chaos as the Py found them too quickly. He heard it all and knew they needed him...but how could he leave Tresa? She was alone and unable to defend herself.

He was torn. Them, or Tresa?

Michelle stared helplessly at Tresa, still unconscious at her feet despite being moved. "What do we do?" she whispered.

"We've got to hide her. Not here. The Py—it will smell her. It will smell the humans on this floor. We've got to get her out of here."

Michelle nodded and Roman swooped down and scooped her to his chest, barreling down the hall to the stairwell. She weighed nothing. For her size, she should have weighed over a hundred pounds, but it was like lifting a doll. Her bones, her body, were made of the very shadows she hid in.

He had to get her out of there. He couldn't let the Pys hurt her.

He couldn't lose her. His heart wouldn't survive.

Chapter Twenty-Five

Roman could hear them below, screaming for him, and he could hear the sweet, lyrical voice of the Py coming down the stairs above him. He bolted past the fifth floor, past his people, those who needed him, and hit the fourth. There, he hid Tresa in an abandoned office with a sturdy desk. Laying her gently on the floor, he allowed himself one last look, trying in those precious seconds to memorize her face before he forced himself away, running back for the stairs, loading his gun as he sprinted up.

The Py hit the landing just behind him.

She shrieked — they didn't like men — and flung a blood ball just as he slammed the door shut behind him. It whistled through the air and hit the door in a fiery explosion, but Roman was already sprinting down the hall toward his team.

His sisters.

Kylie, Michelle and Jeff held it off while Angie herded the rest of them away from the Py, trying to get them to focus on her voice and not the sing-song plea that came from the alien. Roman ducked through a side hall, hoping this floor was the same as the floor above and it would take him around to his family.

Thankfully, he was right—which never happened. He rounded the corner as the Py attempted to dart in, reaching for Kylie, whimpering when their bullets pushed it back. He jerked the gun up and pulled the trigger. The bullet lodged in the center of its forehead, knocking the Py end over end backward and into the wall. She slumped to the floor but wasn't dead. Not even close.

From down the hall, the other one screamed, and as she came into view she was clawing at her own forehead, blood dripping past her eyes. He'd seen it before — that the Pys were connected somehow, and it came in handy now but wouldn't stop them. Eventually, he and his sisters and Jeff would run out of ammo and the Pys, no matter how bullet-ridden, would take what they wanted and kill what they didn't.

There was no stopping them.

"Run," he told his sisters. "I'll give you a head start."

"To where?" Michelle snarled. "There's nowhere to run and besides, we're not leaving you."

"There's nowhere they won't find us, Roman. We'll hold them off and do as much damage as we can. Hopefully, the others will have time to escape," Kylie said breathlessly as she reloaded her gun.

Jeff remained silent, his weapon trained on the Pys. Waiting for them to make a move.

Growling, her blue metallic eyes suddenly red, the Py crawled back to her feet, using her wings to rise into the air. She bared her teeth at him, hissing.

The second one darted from behind her, shooting too quickly through the hallway. Jeff fired, the big gun shaking the walls as plaster rained down on their heads. It hit her in the chest and she fell backward, the first one screaming again, trying to clutch at her own chest and her forehead at the same time.

"Leave us alone and we won't hurt you anymore," Kylie called, a half-beg that broke Roman's heart. "Please."

"We'll take you away," the second one hissed, blood bubbling around her lips. "And we'll watch as our children tear your bodies apart from the inside, and break every bone until your weak, stupid hearts shatter under their strength. We'll watch, and we'll smile."

Kylie's eyes widened and Michelle sucked in a breath. Roman couldn't utter a word.

"That's after we tear your men apart in front of you, devour their blood and leave their rotting carcass as bait for the Garce," the first one whispered, but her voice carried through the room, seeming to echo from every corner.

"You can't kill us," they said together, rising higher. The fire licked at their fingertips and the bright blue tattoos that wound across their skin seemed to vibrate with angry energy.

Something small, dark and ferocious exploded from the shadows, landing on the first Py. They toppled to the ground as she screamed. Tresa shredded her wings, her claws moving so quickly Roman couldn't even follow the movements.

The second Py crumpled out of the air as her own wings tattered and bled, confusion making her slow.

The first tried to fight back, but Tresa was too ferocious, too fast, too powerful. She tore out its throat, ripped out its heart, and before its lifeless body even hit the floor Tresa had launched herself at the second Py, who was writhing in agony already.

It didn't stand a chance.

Breathing hard, Tresa pushed herself away from them. Her hair sparkled in the darkness like a beacon, and her own tattoos glowed and sparked. "They can't kill you," she gasped. "But I can."

"Tresa!" Kylie's gun clattered to the floor and she dove at Tresa, locking her in a death grip Tresa may never have escaped from. "You're okay!"

"I just needed a nap," Tresa said as Michelle and Jeff joined Kylie. She met Roman's eyes, her sparking black ones still furious. "That's all. I've got to get away from the blood."

She slid into a shadow before anyone could object.

"The blood," Jeff said hoarsely. "She craves it but it would kill her."

"Right. We'll move to the seventh floor after we get this cleaned up." Roman stepped gingerly over the Pys and started down the hall. He had no idea where Tresa was but he needed to find her. To make sure she was okay.

He heard Kylie behind him, coordinating efforts to get the Py bodies out of the building to the Garce. He heard Michelle telling Jeff that Tresa was amazing and strong and asking if they should go after her.

He heard Jeff's voice just before he rounded the corner into the stairwell. "No. Roman's got her."

Roman searched the fourth floor where he'd left her first, but she wasn't there. He logically skipped the sixth and fifth floor but jogging up and down the rest of the floors yelling her name didn't magically produce her out of the air. It wasn't until he noticed the shattered board leading to the roof —what they'd attempted to use to hide the doorway since the first set of Pys had blown up the door and thought he should try to nail it back together— that he found her.

She stood on the roof, in the dark, glaring out over the city. He approached cautiously because she still hummed with the rejuvenated alien blood. "Tresa."

She turned and the anger faded, although she barely let her eyes land on him before she was back to searching the skies. "There's one more."

"What?" he, too, frantically turned toward the sky. She'd be able to handle another one in the building, maybe, but not out here. Not where they could stay out of her reach and throw blood balls from a distance. "Where?"

She shrugged. "I don't know. But there were five, and we've killed four."

"We've. Right."

She glanced at him, a small smile forcing the darkness from her face. "We've." She said again. "It was a group effort."

Roman scanned the dark night around them, but there was no sight of sparkling blue wings or fiery blood balls. "Maybe you scared it away?"

She gnawed on her lip, dark eyes unreadable. "I don't think so."

He stayed with her, and even though the night sky meant vulnerability and death, he enjoyed it. He couldn't remember the last time he'd stood fearless under the stars. It felt like...like freedom.

Because of Tresa.

"Thank you," she finally said, so quietly he almost didn't hear her.

He glanced at her in surprise. "For what? Not shooting you this time?"

Tresa smirked, a soft laugh escaping her lips. "No. I mean yes. That was nice of you. But that's not what I meant."

He raised an eyebrow, waiting. She slid closer, half zipping through the shadows and half staying in the light of the moon until she stood next to him. Hesitantly, she leaned her head against his shoulder. "For — for staying with me all day. For giving me the strength to keep fighting. For trying to save me when I couldn't save myself."

Roman swallowed hard. "You—you were awake?" Holy crap, had she heard everything he'd said to Kylie? To Michelle?

"In and out. I just know every time I did manage to fight my way to consciousness, you were there, telling me to keep fighting. So thank you."

He reached down, found her hand at his side and slid his fingers through hers. "Anytime. It was nice of you to wake up and save us, too. I should say thanks for that."

She snickered, and it was adorable and he could barely hear it over the racing of his heart. Before the world had ended, he'd had girlfriends. He'd kissed his fair share and back then, holding hands was just something he did — it never really meant anything.

But now, holding her hand, it felt like something shifted in the universe and suddenly, despite the constant alien attacks, the fear, the starvation, the death, suddenly, there was hope.

She was hope.

"We've got to find that fifth one," she said, completely oblivious to his racing heart or the way he suddenly couldn't swallow.

Trying to keep up with the conversation, he nodded. Her dark hair seemed to caress his skin as he moved. "Yeah. And you've got training again tomorrow. You missed today."

She half-laughed, "I'm so lazy."

"Totally. Sleeping the day away. Teenagers these days."

"Roman?" she whispered.

He glanced down at her. "Yeah?"

"I feel your emotions."

He sighed. "I forgot about that."

She didn't respond, and her silence spoke volumes. She didn't feel the way he did.

"Can you just turn that sixth sense off, maybe? That'd work out so well for me."

She giggled, sounding for once like the actual teenager she was. "I can feel them but I don't understand them. You're very conflicted. And you have no idea how often I try to shut that little gift off. Maybe one of our practices can be trying to figure out how to do that."

"Yeah. I'll schedule that in, just as soon as I figure out how."

She didn't release his hand, didn't move from his side, and yet she knew how he felt and didn't return it? And she said he was conflicted. His heart felt like it was mildly shattered. Like being rejected by her hurt, but wasn't as bad or terrifying as losing her completely.

"How am I conflicted?" he finally asked.

She finally raised her head and met his eyes. "Well, there's fear there."

"We were just attacked twice in twenty-four hours. I almost lost you."

She tipped her head, her eyes widening like it hadn't even occurred to her that his fear might stem from losing her. "That's what you're afraid of? You're not afraid of me?"

He snorted. "Tresa, I stopped being afraid of you the second I had to drag you off the back of a Garce."

She rolled her eyes. "That's not true."

He shrugged. "Says you. Are you conflicted?"

She ducked her head. "Yes."

Another sharp pain through his heart. "Why?"

"Because it seems really weird to have a romantic relationship in the middle of an alien apocalypse."

He shook his head, hiding his shaking hand in his back pocket. Staring up at the sky he said, "I don't know. It seems like maybe that's what gives people the will to keep going in an alien apocalypse."

She smiled.

"We had a rocky start. We kind of hated each other. I get it. If you need more time to get over that than I do, I'm okay with that." He reached out, tipping her chin up so she would meet his eyes. "I'll wait, Tres. I've got nothing but time."

She swayed toward him and it felt like they were the only two people on Earth.

"How do you feel, Tresa? How do you feel about me?" the words escaped his lips without his consent, but he didn't regret them.

She sucked in a breath and he felt like his heart was balanced on whatever came out of her mouth. "I kind of like you. You're pretty hot, Roman."

He laughed. He couldn't help it. It was completely unexpected. He slid his arms around her waist, pulling her against his chest. She laid her head against his collarbone, fitting perfectly under his chin like she was made to be there.

Like she was made for him.

"You're kinda gorgeous, too, Tres."

"So...if I'm kinda gorgeous does that mean you're going to kiss me?" Her voice shook, just a little. And then she frowned, backing away from him. "You're scared."

He grabbed her hand, pulling her back. "Hell yes, I'm scared. This," he motioned between them, "is stronger than anything I've ever felt, Tresa. It scares the shit out of me."

"You're not scared of me?" she whispered.

"Not even close." He lowered his head, capturing her mouth with his own. Her lips were satiny smooth and he pulled her closer so he could feel her racing heartbeat against his own. He slid his tongue against hers, his hands clenching her hips, holding her to him.

They were supposed to be watching for the last Py, but he forgot everything, could think of nothing but Tresa. Her touch sent fire burning through him, her curves haunted him, and her hair.

Her hair.

He couldn't keep his hands from it. Twisting the strands around his fingers, clenching his fists in it. It tumbled down her back in reckless waves, silk against his skin.

For an eternity, for hours, for mere minutes — he didn't know — they stayed that way, exploring each other in the sliver of moonlight across the roof.

Chapter Twenty-Six

They spent the next day and the next training. While everyone else worked, building barricades on the lower floors with whatever office furniture they could move, coaxing their garden to life and rebuilding their lives on the seventh floor, Roman ran Tresa through exercise after exercise and test after test.

To say she was distracted was an understatement. Several times, she nearly lost herself in the darkness because she watched Roman instead of the shadows when she zipped. She knew she should be focusing on the aliens, the threat of death and the remaining Py, but all she could think about was him. His touch, his kiss.

They kept up a front, Roman snarling and snapping at everyone around him, but Tresa could feel it — no one bought it. They all suspected something had changed between their two leaders, but no one dared come out and ask.

At least, no one but Kylie.

They were studying his notes after another day of exhausting tests when she walked in. Tresa wasn't even touching him. Roman was scowling, in the middle of a sentence. "You were a lot stronger yesterday, even after fighting the Pys, than you are today. If we could figure out a way to get you to sleep on a regular basis without having to nearly die first—"

"So you two are together now?" Kylie asked brightly, perching on the edge of the desk.

Tresa jerked upright and Roman leaned back in his chair. "What?"

"We all know it. We're not blind, you know." Kylie grinned.

"What do you mean?" Tresa objected. "We've been so careful."

"Yeah. The way Roman looks at you? Can't really miss that, Tres."

Tresa glanced down at him, her cheeks warming. "How he looks at me?" she asked softly.

Roman smiled, brushing the hair from her temple.

"And you're not exactly subtle. You literally zipped through the wrong shadow today and nearly fell to your death outside the building. Remember? Because you were watching Roman when you went in?"

"That — that was an accident. I didn't know anyone saw that."

Kylie laughed. "Oh honey. We all saw that."

Roman pushed to his feet. "Fine. We're together, but — Wait." He glanced at Tresa. "Are we together?"

Tresa's heart bounced against her sternum and she swallowed hard. "I—I hope so."

He nodded, turning back to Kylie. "We're together but it doesn't change anything. We're still fighting for survival, there is still a Py out there that we're waiting for and traders somewhere nearby who keep giving away our location. We have to focus on that."

Tresa nodded solemnly.

Kylie's smile just grew. "Whatever. This changes *everything*."

She bounced out of the room to do who knew what, and Tresa watched her go, gnawing on her lip. "Should we be worried?"

Roman shook his head, still watching his sister. "No. Even if they know, what are they going to do? They all love you and are afraid of me. That hasn't changed."

She frowned. "There are some strange ones that don't seem to fit in either of those categories."

"Kevin? And Roanna?"

She nodded. "Yes. They're both in your group, by the way. My tribe is full of saints."

He smirked, pulling her back to him and her blood roared through her veins at his touch. "They are. That's the difference between love and fear, I guess."

She rose up on her toes, kissing him the way she'd imagined ten thousand times already that day. He was strength and sarcastic wit and anger all wrapped up in a fierce loyalty, and she loved every facet of it.

And the muscles.

His muscles were tight under her fingertips, his arms and chest well developed under the faded black t-shirt.

Kylie's laugh echoed through the hallway. "Yep. It changes everything."

"Just don't exhaust her completely," Michelle said. Roman paced around the small office, sometimes peering through the slot in the board. Tresa watched him, watched the muscles ripple under his shirt as he dragged a hand through his dark hair. "In case the Py shows up. She's gotta have something to fight with."

"The Garce population is dwindling. Fast. There's not much to lure the Pys here anymore. And it's been over a week since the Pys attacked. Maybe that one isn't coming back." Roman hesitated before he turned his dark eyes on Tresa. "Can you feel anything? Do you still have enough strength to fight if one does come?"

She smiled. He'd asked her that about fifteen times since he'd let them quit training for the day. "It's been almost two weeks. No. And yes."

But she did feel something. The familiar craving, but it wasn't as strong. It was a ghost of what she usually felt when the Pys came to their city. It wasn't something she could explain, so she didn't.

He nodded, all business, but his eyes softened when he looked at her and butterflies danced in her stomach. "Good. We can't push you too far."

"If you don't, she won't get stronger," Jeff said. "That's how you grow. Leave the comfort zones behind."

"It's true," Tresa agreed with a smile.

"Just judging by our data, you're growing by leaps and bounds. I'm a proud coach," Roman said. He was distracted, checking the slot in the board, and Tresa wondered if somehow, he could feel what she felt. The odd unsettling of maybe a Py nearby, but not exactly.

She pushed to her feet, tired and ready to be done with all things alien for the night. "I'm heading back upstairs."

Roman had made the fourth floor into a training hall of sorts, had marked it all up for different exercises he ran her through, and even had protein bars and water stashed away in the office for when she got tired. He had a whiteboard with her speed, both in and out of the shadows. Another with math calculations trying to figure out how fast her energy deteriorated. Basically, he'd turned the whole floor into a resource center for human/Garce hybrids.

Kylie slid her hand along the metal stair rail. "We're going to have to go hunting soon. We're running out of fresh meat. And the canned vegetables are running low. Do you guys think you're up for another warehouse run?"

That warehouse could feed them for months.

"Yeah but it can't be a two-day trip. Not until that fifth Py is found and I kill it." Tresa stomped up the stairs a little harder than necessary. "We'll have to figure out how to make it back before the sun goes down. Maybe tomorrow?"

When Roman didn't respond, she glanced over her shoulder at him. "I can go alone if you need me to."

She had no idea why the thought of being out of his presence for a few hours made her heart hurt. It was a stupid notion in an apocalypse.

And yet, there it was.

"What?" he blinked owlishly at her, his dark hair tumbling across his forehead.

"We need to go back to the warehouse. Do you want me to go alone?"

He scowled, eyebrows clashing. "That's a stupid question."

With the Garce population outside so depleted, it wouldn't be nearly as dangerous as before. She could manage it by herself but she couldn't carry as much as two people could. Before she could answer, Kylie said, "We need a car. That would make life so much easier."

"A car. The only thing besides Tresa that can outrun a Garce."

Tresa hit the seventh floor and turned to the common room. "That's not true. Lots of people can outrun a Garce."

"Lots?" he asked with a teasing grin, his hand resting at the small of her back.

She smiled up at him, "Lots of very fast people."

He chuckled but even then, she could feel that he was still distracted. "What's up, Roman?"

He kissed her temple. "Nothing. Just trying to figure out how to get you to sleep without almost killing you."

He'd been obsessing over it for days. She didn't understand why. The power she had without sleep was fine for what they'd had to fight.

Sort of.

"I'm strong enough without it, Roman." It sounded stiff even to her own ears.

He leaned against the wall, watching her quietly while she snapped out her sleeping mat. Before she could brush past him, he reached out and caught her arm. "It's not that, Tres. I don't care how strong you are."

She raised an eyebrow. "Says the boy who's spent the last two weeks training every day to make me stronger."

He shrugged, tugging her toward him. She leaned into him, her hands on his chest so she could feel his heart raging under her touch. "That's to keep you alive since you're so determined to jump right into the middle of a Garce pack."

"And the sleep thing isn't?"

He sighed. "It's to keep you alive, too."

"By making me super Tresa?"

"No. Py blood kills Garce. Garce are also the only thing that can kill Pys, although we have no idea why that is. You have both their DNA running through you, Tres. I'm afraid it's slowly killing you and when you sleep and wake up all recharged, it's because your human half had the chance to heal. If you don't sleep, the Py blood will slowly kill you."

It was probably the sweetest thing anyone had ever said to her. "Roman, I've been this way for three years. If it was going to kill me, it would have."

"Maybe it has been."

She leaned her head on his shoulder. "While I do enjoy sleep, especially when it's not blood-loss induced, I would be dead by now. It's been over three years."

He kissed her temple before letting her go. "Knowledge is power. So is sleep, apparently."

She smiled, shaking her head.

Tresa checked the slot again for Pys outside, but there was no sign. The next day, she would go hunting again, bring back fresh meat and then hopefully sneak away from Roman and go back to the warehouse. It was safer if she went alone. He could protect the compound while she zipped through shadows and brought home food.

He wouldn't like it. But it was better that way. She was faster and he was needed at home.

Home.

She never thought she'd have one again.

He sighed as he laid down next to her, stretching his long body across his mat. She rolled on her side to watch him. "How many girlfriends have you had?"

He raised an eyebrow and propped his head up on one hand, regarding her. "So...we go from trying to keep you alive to my romantic history?"

She nodded. "It's a legitimate question."

He flopped onto his back and stared at the ceiling. For several long seconds, she could practically see the gears turning in his head. "That many?" she asked, exasperated when he took too long to answer.

He chuckled. "No. Four. Five if you count Janessa Rogers in kindergarten."

Tresa smiled. "Did any of them break your heart?"

Roman glanced at her out of the corner of his eye. "I feel this is a dangerous question."

"It is. I'll probably use it against you later when we get in a fight."

"We're going to get in a fight?" he asked in mock horror.

Tresa pursed her lips, waiting until he noted her fake annoyance before she continued, "We fight every day, Roman. Usually about me scaring you."

He nodded. "Yes. You do that a lot. Okay, let's see. Janessa broke my heart because she married my arch nemesis at recess while I was home with the flu."

"Rude."

"Yep. Other than that, no. No one broke my heart."

"In other words, you broke their hearts?"

Roman laughed. "I knew this was a dangerous question."

She gave him her most innocent look.

"Fine. So Mary had a temper and I didn't have time for her crap. We didn't part as enemies, and her heart wasn't broken. Nadia wanted to get married while we were still in high school and I freaked out. I had a life to still live, you know."

"Of course."

"Sasha and I were just too busy and never saw each other. And Izzy...we were together when the first Garce wave hit. I never saw her again."

Tresa swallowed. "You never saw her again?"

He shook his head.

"That's so sad."

"I was trying to keep my sisters alive. A high school girlfriend wasn't high on my list of priorities."

"My sister's boyfriend, Cole, would say differently."

"Oh yeah? Maybe they're soul mates. Izzy and I were definitely not."

She smiled. "You believe in soul mates?"

He rolled onto his side again so he could face her, the playfulness dying from his face. "Yes, Tresa."

She swallowed hard. "Do you believe in love at first sight?"

Roman frowned. "That's harder. I don't think I do. Maybe you see someone and think, 'wow, she's hot. And also moves like an alien but holy crap I can't stop staring at her because I've never seen anything so beautiful in all my life.' Was it love? Who am I to say?"

Tresa laughed softly even as her heart raced in her chest and she couldn't breathe properly.

"Your turn. How many boyfriends?" He raised a dark eyebrow, his hair falling recklessly across his forehead. She brushed it back, her fingers splaying against the soft curls, and he caught her hand, kissing her fingers. "So?"

"Two boyfriends. My mom didn't like us to date. Phoenyx did it anyway but I was a much more obedient child. I actually think it was more fun that way. I had a lot more experiences and adventures than if I'd been stuck with one guy."

"Having a boyfriend is being stuck?" Roman struck his hand to his chest like she'd shot him with a fiery arrow. "Good to know."

"It was then. I was young. I had stuff to do."

He grinned. "I see. So what happened? Is heartbreak in my future?"

She pushed on his shoulder, giggling softly when he toppled over onto his back. "One split amicably, the other threw a fit but backed off real quick. Phoenyx was formidable."

"Big sister to the rescue?"

"Always," Tresa said softly. "Always."

Chapter Twenty-Seven

Tresa got up as soon as the sun rose over the buildings in the east. She sat on her bedroll, watching Roman sleep in the dim light. He was beautiful. Especially in sleep, when he didn't carry the weight of the world on his shoulders. His thick lashes laid against his pale cheeks, hair falling recklessly against his forehead. She almost couldn't look away, but she had much to do that day and wanted to be back by dark.

Just in case.

She smoothed Roman's hair off his forehead and pressed a light kiss against his skin before she rose to her feet and slid from the room. She had just grabbed her pack and was sneaking through the hallways, rounding a corner silently and nearly ran into her dad. He leaned against the wall with his gun. "Going out early today, aren't we?"

She jumped, squealed, and clapped a hand over her mouth. "Dad!" she gasped through her fingers.

"It was my turn to keep watch." He sounded amused in the darkness.

"I'm going to kill some Garce. For fresh meat. Then I'm heading to the warehouse for more supplies. I should be back by nightfall."

"You could carry more with more people."

"I know. But I'm faster on my own. I'll try to lead the Garce with me so it's safe for you guys to go get the meat."

"Sounds dangerous," he said, unassuming. Always.

"For me or for you?" she asked teasingly.

"For you. We'll be all right. Be careful, okay?"

"Of course. Love you, Daddy." Tresa kissed him on the cheek and he patted her head before she could escape, secretly loving how it still made her feel like a little girl.

Seconds later, she was on the roof and jumping down, zipping through the shadows before she could over think it. Before she could be afraid that she wouldn't come back.

She hit the ground with a soft crack and searched the parking lot around her. It was full of cars, lots of places for Garce to hide, but nothing came out and pounced on her. She almost missed the days when Garce roamed freely and she could lead them around as a pack. When they waited eagerly for anything that moved and a whole bunch of them attacked at once.

Wait. That wasn't right.

She didn't miss that at all.

Back to her senses, she snuck through the twilight, looking for monsters. Given how many there had been just a few short weeks ago, they were hard to find now.

Unless the traders had come again and the Garce were at the far west side of the city waiting for their next meal.

She looked for a few minutes and when there was still no sign of Garce, she rounded back to their compound. Her dad was on the roof, watching her progress. Because of course he was. She raised her hands in a silent question and he shook his head.

He could see no Garce.

Plan B then. She'd go to the warehouse first and find Garce when she got back. It made more sense anyway.

Hopefully.

Shrugging her bag higher up on her shoulders, she started to run.

She was fast and she had freakish endurance. What had taken her and Roman most of the day now took her less than an hour. She saw Garce in the distance, but they didn't notice her. At least she knew they were still in the city. She found the warehouse and sprinted around it quickly, making sure there were no exploded doors or windows that would prove a Py had been there. Everything was intact so she zipped into the shadows on the other side and paused, letting her Garce vision take over in the sudden darkness.

Thanks to their earlier exploration, she didn't have to spend hours searching boxes and aisles upon aisles. She hit the one they'd found earlier and loaded her bag with as much as it could hold.

A car would have been awesome. No more dangerous trips out on her own or sneaking away from Roman.

She jogged back, weighed down by the heavy pack. It wouldn't keep them fed for months, but it would do for now. Maybe one day they should work on finding a gas station, getting one of these cars started. She had no idea if a car that had rusted out, doors hanging off its hinges and seats torn would start after three years, but it was something to look into. A car could outrun a Garce...as long as it never had to stop or slow down or swerve through the hundreds of other cars littering the roadways.

Roman was waiting on the roof and she could feel his anger before she even grabbed the ladder Kylie strung from the third-floor window. She clambered up and handed her pack off to some of the others who took it to their food storage.

He stormed down the dark stairs with all the force of a hurricane and everyone else scattered.

"What the hell was that, Tresa?" he bellowed.

She crossed her arms over her chest. "I went to get food."

"Without telling me? You snuck out like a spoiled teenager." She could feel that he was trying not to yell. He was failing, but at least he was trying.

"Except a spoiled teenager sneaks out to party and I went to get food for our people, so not like a spoiled teenager at all."

"You could have cleared it with me first! You didn't ask. Not a single freaking word."

"Last time I checked, you aren't my boss, Roman." She raised herself to her full height, annoyed that it was still over six inches shorter than he was.

"Dammit, Tresa! We're supposed to be a team. Teams don't sneak off without telling each other. What if something had happened? We wouldn't have known. We wouldn't have had any way to find you." His broad chest rose and fell with each harsh breaths but underneath all the anger, she could feel his relief. And his hurt.

She'd hurt him.

Her own anger melted. "Okay. You're not trying to control me. I get that. I'm sorry I thought you were. We *are* a team, Roman. I left because I knew we needed food and I knew you wouldn't let me go alone—"

"Damn right I wouldn't," he growled.

"—But I knew we needed you here. You would have been torn between protecting me and protecting them. I was just trying to keep you from having to make that decision. I don't need protection, Roman."

"It's not protecting you, Tresa. It's working together. I thought that was your idea." He threw up his hands and turned on his heel, storming back the way he'd come.

She darted after him, slipping past him in the stairwell and blocking his exit. "You don't get to walk away from me in the middle of a fight, Roman. Don't make me bring up the ex-girlfriends."

His eyes widened and at first, he was angrier than before. It took a few seconds before what she'd said sunk in and he fought to hide a smirk. "I don't want to yell anymore. I need some time to cool down."

She nodded. "Fair enough. But we need fresh meat. I was going to go hunting..."

Roman sighed, running a hand through his hair and staring anywhere but her. "How much energy do you have left?"

"Enough."

"We'll get a team to follow you and pick up the meat so you can move faster. Can you keep the Garce away from them?"

She nodded. "I'll lead the Garce to the north. They can come when it's safe."

"Fine. I'll go ask for volunteers." He shouldered past her and left her standing in the stairwell alone.

She sighed, sinking down onto the top stair and leaning her head against the wall. She heard Kylie's boots thunking down the stairs, and she paused beside Tresa. "He was scared out of his mind, Tres. Don't judge his anger too harshly."

"I know."

"He's been in charge for a long time. Usually when someone goes off on their own, they don't come back."

Tresa opened her eyes and peered over at Kylie. "It's happened more than once?"

Kylie nodded sadly.

"I've been in charge for a long time, too, Kylie. I'm not used to having to run my plans past other people. I see what needs to get done and I do it."

"You deliberately snuck out, Tres. You can't tell me you weren't planning this when he fell asleep last night. It wasn't a spur of the moment thing."

Tresa hung her head. "No. It wasn't. I was trying to keep everyone else safe."

Kylie patted her on the shoulder. "I know. But you're the only light in his life. He's so scared to lose you. I think even he is surprised at how much he—he likes you."

"He has you. And Michelle. And yeah, you have some Strange Ones on your team, but you also have some Amazing Ones."

"Yeah. But none of us could even make him smile. You make him laugh. You make his face light up. There's no point to survival if you're trapped in the darkness of your own soul. He's finally living again." Kylie leaned against Tresa's shoulder and they sat in silence for several long minutes. She could hear Roman above, organizing her hunting mission. She could still feel his anger and his hurt, even through the walls and the ceilings and everything in between.

She could feel Kylie's, too. Kylie, who tried so hard to be the mediator. The peacemaker. Kylie, who jumped to her defense, whether it was Roman or a Garce she was defending Tresa from. She'd hurt her, too.

"I'm sorry, Kylie."

Kylie nodded. "I know. Your tattoos are pretty telling."

Tresa sat up. "What?"

Kylie's eyebrows raised. "You don't know?"

"I don't spend a lot of time in front of the mirror. I have no idea what my tattoos do."

Kylie laughed, bright and infectious. "Oh yeah. We can see you in the dark better than you can see us. When you're mad, they spark. When you're happy, they're bright. You might be able to feel our emotions but we can see yours right there on your face."

"What are they when I'm sad?" Tresa asked. "What do they look like now?"

Kylie sat back, studying Tresa. "They're almost blue. Ready to go up?"

"Yeah. Thanks, Kylie."

"That's what I'm here for." Kylie pulled Tresa to her feet. "I'm going hunting with you. If you need help, just scream." She spun her daggers in both hands like a legendary gunslinger and winked.

Tresa smiled. "Yes ma'am."

She followed Kylie up the stairs, pausing only when Roman appeared in the doorway, silhouetted against the weak light behind him. He looked like an ancient god, chiseled, strong and flawless. "Your team is ready."

"Okay. Thank you." She hesitated, watching him but he seemed to be reigning in his emotions and it was hard to read.

Tresa wondered when he'd picked up that little trick. "Roman, I—"

"I'm going with you. Don't argue with me."

"I know. I—listen, I just wanted to apologize."

He was surprised. Apparently, an apology from her hadn't been what he'd been expecting, but he remained silent.

"I'm sorry I deliberately snuck out and I didn't consult you. We are a team and I'll do better from now on. Okay? And I won't bring up any ex-girlfriends."

Roman chuckled, one short bark of laughter before he straightened again. "That's very nice of you, not using ex-girlfriends against me. And I'm sorry, too. I didn't mean to freak out at you like that. I just—you make me crazy, Tresa. When I couldn't find you, I thought—I thought a lot of things. None of them good."

She snorted. "Apology accepted?"

"Please forgive me. I am sorry, even if I suck at apologizing." His voice was more vulnerable than he'd intended and she quickly shook her head.

"It's not you who should be apologizing. I'd still be yelling if you pulled a stunt like that."

Roman cocked an eyebrow. "Good to know."

It was still stilted between them, but the anger was fading, and for that she was grateful. Maybe after their hunting mission, things would be back to normal.

She hoped. Having him mad at her hurt more than she'd been prepared for.

It wasn't just a crush for her. She didn't just like him. Maybe she never had. Maybe she'd hated him so much because she was afraid of what she really felt.

Maybe she'd never hated him at all.

"Ready? Or do you need to rest first?" Roman asked, breaking into her thoughts. He watched her, his head tipped to the side, and she wondered what her tattoos looked like now.

"No, I'm ready. I'd like to get done before dark. And I wanted to talk to you about my car plan when we get back."

"Car plan?"

She waved her hand through the air. "Yeah. I'll tell you later."

He smiled, but it still didn't reach his eyes. "Okay. Let's move."

TRESA caught the first Garce to the east of the building, not far at all. It must have been stalking her on her earlier mission. Before the other Garce came at the smell of the blood, she caught Roman's attention. He nodded and the recovery team landed on the ground. John, Roman, Francheska and Brittany sprinted across the cracked asphalt and she ran in the opposite direction, leading the Garce away.

She left two more bodies in her wake and then focused on just keeping the aliens attention and drawing them away from Roman.

She brought them around the northern building, through an alleyway of what had once been a strip mall and the high rise the traders had been in. The Garce roiled after her like an inky black wave, salivating dark blood.

Something shimmered, sparkling blue, at the corner of her vision.

Tresa froze, jerking up against the wall as she peered around her, waiting for gunshots, for an attack, for a trap.

Nothing moved but the Garce that came steadily closer. No lyrical voice called out to her. No blood ball shot out of the darkness.

"Is someone there?" she called. The Garce responded to her voice and came faster.

This time, she saw the metallic blue glow sparkling from inside, but it shook so terribly. It was a Py—

But...not. She didn't crave it. More like a dull ache at the back of her throat that she barely noticed.

Whatever it was, it was hurt and scared. She could feel that.

Tresa broke away from the wall and sprinted for the tower. It had been offices once, full of glass windows. Unlike her building, most of these windows had been blown or torn out. Scorch marks were burned into the broken tile inside and marked the walls. Claw marks were embedded in the floor and rose almost to the ceiling. When they were on their back feet, the Garce were almost ten feet tall.

Tresa slid through the broken glass and ran into the darkness, letting her eyes adjust before she ventured further. "Where are you?" she asked again.

There was no answer, but the blue tattoos sparkled more frantically, leading her inside.

The heels of her boots crunched on the glass beneath her feet and she froze. Whatever it was didn't make a sound, but it didn't attack, either. She heard Roman's voice screaming in her head, telling her it wasn't safe, telling her to get back, but she didn't feel a threat from it. Whatever it was, it needed help. And who was she to turn her back on it?

"It's okay. I'm here to help you. I can take you to safety." She inched closer until she could see it clearly.

Definitely a Py, but...but not. Yes, there were the blue winding tattoos. The ethereal beauty. The huge blue eyes. But the hair and skin weren't blue. Pale skin, black hair that fell to her shoulders.

And no wings.

"What are you?" Tresa breathed.

The Py shook harder, trying to press herself into the wall behind her. Still no sound escaped her lips.

"It's not safe here. The Garce will tear you apart. We have to go."

The Py shook her head frantically and pointed up.

At the sun.

She couldn't go in the sun.

Of course.

"Okay. Okay, let's just get up higher, to safety. We'll go at dark. I have friends. We can help you. But now we've just got to get away from the Garce." Tresa spoke in slow, careful sentences, trying not to scare her any more than possible.

The Py nodded, backing away. Further into the shadows. Tresa zipped into one, sliding out next to her. The Py's eyes shot open in surprise but she didn't make a sound. Tresa grabbed her arm, surprisingly cold to the touch, and pulled her away. Up the stairs, barricading the doors behind them.

The Garce hit a second later. She hadn't realized they were so close, but they attacked with a frenzy.

Because of the Py blood. They craved it.

The Py gripped her hand and pulled her away from the door just as Tresa was preparing to fight. She stumbled backward, twisting so she could run with the silent Py. They hit the elevator shaft and instead of going around, the Py sprang inside.

At first, Tresa thought she could fly after all, but instead, she caught the heavy metal cable attached to the elevator car below them and scrambled up, hand over hand. Tresa followed her as the Garce burst through the door.

Higher up, out of the Garce reach, Tresa finally understood. "I've seen you before."

The Py nodded next to her, clinging to the cable. She had the same freakish strength as Tresa, and hanging there would be no problem except she was shaking like a small dog in a hurricane.

"This is how you've survived all this time?" Tresa asked.

The Py, a single tear escaping to shimmer against her pale skin, nodded.

Chapter Twenty-Eight

Roman paced on the rooftop, his heart in his throat. He'd still been angry at Tresa when they'd left. He knew she could feel it, despite how hard he'd tried to hide it.

And now she was gone.

The Garce pack that had been following her was out of sight. He could hear them, snarling and screeching, frenzied but not in pain. She was trapped out there somewhere and he had no idea how to save her.

Jeff stood silently next to him, and Roman could only imagine how horrific it must be for him, knowing Tresa was out there in trouble and not being able to do anything about it. The big gun rested next to him, but there wasn't anything to shoot at.

"She'll be okay," Kylie said, more confidently than Roman could understand. Tresa was definitely not okay. They'd brought the meat in from the three bodies hours ago. He'd expected Tresa would take a half hour longer, an hour at most, before she circled around to their building. To make sure they were all inside and safe.

Four hours later, and nothing.

"She's alive. She's fine," Kylie said again. She'd been standing as a silent sentry on the rooftop with them. While everyone else prepared the meat so they could store it, he, Jeff and Kylie waited.

There was no sign of Tresa.

He wished he would have kissed her. Instead of trying so hard to hide his anger, he should have kissed her before he let her go. He should have told her how he really felt.

He was in love with her.

Not just in love with her. He was so crazy, stupidly, completely in love with her that she was all he could think about. All he could see, all he could hope for.

But he hadn't told her, and now he might never get the chance.

"She'll be back," Kylie said, and he wondered if she'd somehow picked up on Tresa's ability to read emotions.

Neither man responded. Roman stared out in the quickly fading light, watching for the inky black tattoos that would light her way back to him.

I love you, Tresa. Please come back.

The sunset. The Garce's frenzy died slowly as the moon rose in the sky, and through the binoculars, he could see them reappearing in the city from wherever they'd been. Wandering the broken streets.

Still, no Tresa.

"She's—she's okay," Kylie said, but her voice broke. "She's okay, right? Roman?"

"Yes," Roman said with more conviction than he felt. "Yes, she's fine. It's Tresa. If she's not back yet, it's because she's keeping us safe. There must still be a threat or she'd be here."

Kylie nodded firmly. "Right. Yeah. Of course."

"There!" Jeff jerked the gun up, peering through the scope.

Roman didn't need the binoculars. He could see the sparkling black tattoos emerge from the shadows, running with blinding speed toward their compound. Kylie sprinted away, yelling for the ladder to be dropped down, but Roman stood frozen.

Right behind Tresa was a sparkling blue blur.

She was bringing a Py back to their safe haven.

ROMAN left the roof, sprinting down the stairs to the third floor. Jeff was right behind him, but neither spoke. When he finally rounded into the hallway where the rest of their tribe was assembled, it had fallen deathly quiet, despite being full of people.

In their midst stood a sparkling, wingless Py. She had black hair and pale skin, but there was no denying the tattoos or the eyes. Tresa climbed in through the window behind her, breathing hard.

"Tresa, what is this?" he demanded, blocking their way. The Py was tiny, smaller than Tresa, staring up at him in horror. She stumbled backward to hide behind his girlfriend.

"I think she's a hybrid, like me. She's been trapped in that building for weeks, Roman."

"So you thought it was a good idea to bring her here? We don't know anything about her, Tresa!"

She scowled at him, her tattoos sparkling dangerously. "Did you want me to leave her there alone?"

Everyone around them took several steps back, inching away from the Py among them and Roman's anger all at once. He barely noticed. "*Yes,* if it keeps our people safe. At least until you know more about her!"

"What is there to know? She can't speak. I saw her weeks ago—"

"She could be a trader, Tresa!"

"She was here long before the traders showed up—"

"The traders have been coming here for months. Maybe years. You could have just compromised our entire compound. Once again, you acted on your own without thought to anyone else and now we're all in danger. She has to leave."

"What?" Tresa gasped. "No! Roman, she has nowhere to go!"

"She can go back where she came from," he hissed.

Tresa sucked in a breath, running a shaking hand through her hair. He noticed but didn't care. He'd never been so angry in his entire life. Never felt more betrayed. She'd risked all of their lives *for a Py*? "Look, you thought I was dangerous, Roman. And now, we're—we're—you like me now. Can't you give her that same courtesy?" she bit her lip, her dark eyes wide and hopeful. Vulnerable.

"You saved us and came with a bunch of people willing to vouch for your not being evil, Tresa. She doesn't. She comes from the same building we killed traders in a few weeks ago. Did you miss that?"

"Give her the same chance you all gave me. That's all I'm asking."

"No, Tresa. Get her out of here. That's final."

Tresa rose to her full height, eyes flashing. "That's final? Did you forget we're a team, Roman? You don't get to make all the decisions."

Roman clenched his teeth. "No, Tresa. We're not a team. You've made that clear. This is my compound, not yours, and it's my job to keep these people safe, since you don't care. Get. Her. Out. Of. Here."

Tresa blinked at him, the tattoos paling to a light blue, and she looked more like the thing behind her than herself. "Those are my people, too."

"Then take them with you, if they're willing to risk their lives for your blatant disregard for their safety or anyone else's opinions." He wanted to walk away. He wanted to beg her to stay, to realize what she was asking of him, of their tribe. But he couldn't. For the first time since he'd met her, she truly was a threat to them all, and he couldn't walk away from that. He had to stop her.

"Wait, wait, wait." Kylie pushed her way through the crowd to stand next to them. "Look, did she—how has she been protecting herself from the Garce? What has she said?"

"She doesn't speak," Tresa said quietly. "She's been hiding in an elevator shaft where the Garce can't reach her. As far as I can tell, she doesn't have the Py's blood balls."

"If she doesn't speak, then she can't be a trader, right?" Kylie asked hopefully, glancing at Roman.

"She's not. She's terrified and she needs our help. Can you please give her a chance like you gave me, Roman?"

"It was a mistake," he growled. "I never should have let you in."

Kylie gasped. Tresa paled, stumbling back, and though her mouth moved, no sound came out.

"She already knows we're here. We can't leave at night. You can keep her on a floor away from us." To those assembled around them, he said, "We leave at dawn."

"This is your compound, Roman. It should be me that leaves." Her voice was so quiet he barely heard her, and still, the words shattered his heart.

"She knows where we are. She'll lead the Pys right to us. We have to leave. At dawn." As he walked away, he said over his shoulder, "Make your choice by then, Tresa."

He made it to the common room before the weight of what had just happened hit him. He'd walked away from Tresa. She'd betrayed them all — what choice did he have? Silently, he went to the lookout to keep watch and everyone left him alone. Most started packing.

But not all.

He expected his sisters to come with their lectures, waited for them to tell him he was wrong. He needed them to tell him to change his mind, but they didn't come.

They gathered their things.

He didn't hear her approach and assumed she zipped out of the shadows next to him. Her eyes were wide but her tattoos were black again. "Where's your friend?" he growled.

"Downstairs sleeping."

"I'm not changing my mind, Tresa. This—"

"I know." Her voice was quiet. "I'm here to talk about us."

Us. The word sliced through him like a knife and he had to force himself to speak while trying to hide from her how much it hurt him. "What about it?"

"We're done then?" she asked, barely above a whisper.

He couldn't look at her. If he did, he'd beg her to choose him over the Py. He'd beg her to undo everything she'd done, but they both knew that wasn't possible. "Are you keeping the Py?"

"She has nowhere else to go, Roman."

He hurt. More than he could remember hurting. But what choice did he have? He had to protect his people. They depended on him, and now he had to protect them from her. He had to protect them from their very own guardian. "Then yes. We're done. When I leave in the morning, you'll never see me again."

"Okay."

And she was gone. No argument, although he'd just caught the pale blue of her tattoos before she disappeared into the shadows. He'd hurt her.

Fine. He hurt, too.

He stared out at the night sky for hours, fighting to hold onto his anger because if he let it go, the pain took over and his mind was consumed with memories as he tried to pinpoint the exact moment he'd fallen in love with her.

He couldn't.

It was a myriad of light, of hope. He'd been afraid of her, but it seemed like it was never enough to block out the bright sound of her laugh, the beauty of her smile. The absolute adorableness. The freckles across her nose that seemed to represent everything she was. Alien blood had tried to conquer her, erase what she'd been, but the freckles refused to fade.

Like her human spirit.

It was nearing dawn when he swung away from the window. "Keep watch for me?" he asked Michelle as he passed her in the hall. Her bags were stacked neatly, the food storage divided among their most trusted members. The garden, that had just started to really thrive, was waiting by the stairwell.

Michelle nodded and he jogged down the stairs. She'd stayed on the third floor, and not alone. There were others from her team down there. Not all of them, though. He'd seen some, most, all packed up and ready to go above.

The Py slept in the corner, curled up in a ball. Tresa watched her silently while everyone else slept, or pretended to. He didn't know how they could with a Py so close.

Tresa looked up when he paused in the doorway. Hope flared briefly across her face before it faded to nothing, and she pushed away from the wall and zipped through the shadow, coming out next to him. It was easier than picking her way through the sleeping bodies, apparently.

He swallowed. Everything in him wanted to touch her. To smooth the pain from her face and brush the hair off her skin, off her neck. To trace her mouth with his lips. Instead, he motioned her with his head back down the hall. She sent a worried look behind her, at the Py, and he realized she wasn't comfortable letting her out of her sight.

And yet she was giving up everything to stay with her.

She followed him, but he made sure they stayed where Tresa could keep an eye on the Py. And then he begged. "Tresa, please don't do this."

"I'm not doing anything. You're the one leaving. You're the one who ended this." She motioned between them.

"You're the one choosing her over all the rest of us. Why, Tres? I don't understand. What if she goes ballistic and kills us all? What if she tells the other Pys where we are? Why are you risking everything for her?"

Tresa's eyes were infinitely sad when she finally looked up at him. "When I was changed, the only thing I had in the world was my father. Do you know how many people tried to kill me? Someone tried to slit my throat. Someone shot me in the head.

Right after I saved their camp from a Garce pack. When I didn't have my tribe to 'vouch' for me. They attacked my father. Because I was too alien. No one gave me a chance, Roman. Not for over a year. She—" she pointed back toward the Py. "—is a hybrid. She was human. I can see it, I can see her human 'flaws'. And I'm giving her the chance no one gave me."

Roman sighed, running a hand through his hair. "I didn't know, Tresa. After all this time, you never told me."

She shrugged and looked away. "It hurts to talk about."

And he'd dragged it out of her.

"I can't—I can't condone this. But I'm not leaving you to face whatever this is alone. If you really think she's not going to hurt us, we'll stay. We'll keep working together. I trust you that much. If my people are willing, we'll stay. But you have to keep her away from us, Tresa. And you have to protect them from her. That means —"

"That means I stay away, too. I understand." Tresa squared her shoulders and raised her chin. "Thank you."

It wasn't what he wanted, but it was a truce. He nodded and backed away, although everything in him screamed to go back.

Instead, he turned and escaped into the darkness.

Chapter Twenty-Nine

Her name was Raya. She could write, just not speak. And she was afraid of everything. Loud sounds sent her cowering into the corner. Someone dropped a pan and she nearly had a meltdown. This girl who had survived on her own for who knew how long freaked out when Chris Ann coughed.

Yeah. She was super threatening.

"So they're not leaving?" Francheska asked, helping Tresa scrub dishes after breakfast.

Tresa shook her head. "Apparently not. They chose to stay. They—they think I can contain her."

A feisty kitten could contain her, but whatever.

Tracy slid an arm around Tresa's shoulders and squeezed. She'd been one of the first to leave her camp and stay with Tresa and Jeff. She'd been loyal from the beginning and she stuck with her now. "How are you holding up?"

My heart is in a thousand shattered pieces and I feel like I lost my whole world. My best friend. He was everything to me. And now he's gone. "I'm okay," she said instead. "It's not the first time I've been kicked out. It probably won't be the last." She forced a smile but knew her tattoos betrayed her.

"Have you gotten her story yet?" Brittany asked. "I saw her writing."

"She got tired. I let her go back to sleep. I have no idea what she's been through but it hasn't been easy." Tresa sighed. She'd actually asked her to write it down and Raya had started crying.

Awesome.

Jessi came down the stairs with more supplies. Rather than have their team travel up and down the stairs and possibly endanger his team, Roman had divvied up the supplies and sent their share down to them.

He wanted to keep her as far away as possible.

John had stayed with Roman. His parents had been killed by Pys and he couldn't even look at Raya without losing it a little bit. Tresa didn't blame him for leaving. He'd been apologetic and promised to be her spy if she needed it.

A few others had left, too. Angie and Jeff, of course, had come with her and now worked to make this little area home. It was close to the barricades and if the Garce got in, they weren't safe by any means. But that was what Tresa was for. She was for protecting. It was stupid of her to think she could have love. That she would ever be seen as more than a weapon.

That's all she was.

Raya appeared next to her. Tresa hadn't even realized she was awake. She had the light movements of a Py and seemed to waft around the air currents from the storm outside. She handed Tresa a paper and disappeared back to her corner.

She was scared, but never more than when she had to interact with Tresa. The one protecting her scared her the most.

How was that for irony?

Tresa lifted the paper. There were just a few sentences in square, blockish penmanship.

You asked me for my story. My parents were killed by aliens. My boyfriend was stolen by an alien. I was taken by the Empyreans but escaped half-changed. I've been alone for over a year. No one wants a Py around. I can't throw blood balls and I can't defend myself. All I can do is run and climb. If I eat Garce, I'm immortal.

That last line, though. Like an afterthought. *If I eat Garce, I'm immortal.*

Holy crap.

Tresa raised her head. Raya watched her, fear radiating from her in waves. She'd lost loved ones just like everyone else. At least when Phoenyx had been killed, she'd been outside. Tresa hadn't had to watch her die.

She smiled encouragingly. "Thank you," she said, keeping her distance. That seemed to be the theme of the day.

THEY fell into a pattern. It wasn't comfortable, really, but it was a routine that got Tresa through each day. Kylie came to visit, fearless as ever. She was torn between them—Roman was her brother, her hero, her favorite person on the planet, but Tresa was her best friend. And, Kylie being Kylie, she believed the Py was adorable and not a threat at all. How could anything that slept curled in a ball in the corner be a danger to their compound?

They ate, they cleaned, they gardened, except for Tresa, who couldn't leave Raya, and Raya couldn't go in the sun. So Tresa stayed in the dark.

Day after day after day.

Raya didn't come out of her shell. Even surrounded by safety, warmth, and kindness, she kept to herself, ate her Garce meat, and watched them all suspiciously. She didn't offer any other info, no other notes, and she cringed when Tresa even looked at her.

I'm the one who saved you, don't forget. You had no problem with me then, did you?

Of course, that had been before Tresa had killed two Garce right in front of her. But if she'd been hiding in that building all this time, she already knew what Tresa could do. She'd seen her before.

"What are we going to do when you have to go hunting or for more supplies?" Kylie asked, keeping her voice low. "She obviously can't go with you. She'd never survive. But Roman won't let you leave her here."

Tresa nodded. "I know. I'll figure something out. She's survived for over a year on her own. She's tougher than we give her credit for, I think."

"She's scared out of her mind." Kylie sighed. "Poor thing."

"How long do we have until I need to go again?" Tresa checked through the slot she'd cut in a board, far away from Raya, who couldn't be near the light. The Garce mulled around like stray dogs looking for scraps. Always in a pack, but the pack was dwindling.

"We're about a week out, I think. How are you down here?"

Tresa did the math in her head. "Raya and I only eat Garce, so we're low on that, but everything else should last a week, at least. Roman was generous."

"Good. Otherwise, I'd have to kick his ass. That wasn't generous. You're the one who got that food and then got yelled at for it." Kylie crossed her arms over her chest and glared, the spitting image of her brother.

Tresa smiled despite the fact that it made her heart ache. She missed him so much it felt like it was constantly eating away at her heart. Knowing he was only a few floors up, so close she could hear his voice sometimes when he was particularly angry.

It drove her insane.

He hadn't come down. Not once, not to talk to her, not to train her, nothing. He stayed away from her and life went on as usual.

Clearly, she'd never meant that much to him, if he could forget her so easily.

He holds onto his anger like a shield.

It was Phoenyx's voice in her head. Tresa didn't know if her dead sister had finally found a way to communicate or if she was just that crazy, but it was a comfort to hear her.

"I'm bored. Wanna play a board game?" Kylie asked brightly. "It's raining outside. I think it's gotta be close to Christmas now." She wrinkled her nose. "It's hard to tell, though."

Tresa wondered if anyone ever celebrated holidays anymore. Her favorite had been Halloween, but she was pretty sure she'd missed the last one. And the two before that. "There are board games here?"

Kylie nodded. "I found them yesterday while I was exploring in one of the offices. Maybe they played them on lunch breaks. Or during meetings! That's the kind of job I want. You know, if the world hadn't ended."

"Right. We can totally play. What'd you find?"

Tresa, Phoenyx and their dad had had mandatory family game night every Sunday before the invasion. She'd looked forward to it every week. So she wasn't surprised when he settled next to them, looking more excited than she could remember him being.

To play Life.

It took her back to a different time, a time when there was still hope for the future, where they weren't trapped in a building, locked away by aliens and fear. Where she could have twins and an SUV and a great job and her dad sued her on a regular basis.

Tresa had always wanted the lawyer job and four kids. Now, she was fairly positive kids would never be in her future, and though she liked to argue, there was no need for lawyers in this new, hopeless world.

Still, it was an escape, and when Jeff was the first one to retirement, he laughed and said how scarily accurate the game was.

Just like before.

However, it was Kylie who won, sneaking in under the radar with her job as a vet. She giggled as she put the game away and told them they had to call her ninja Kylie from now on. Tresa agreed. Her accuracy with those daggers was deadly.

They spent the rest of the day working. Dragging desks to the barricades, repairing holes in the boards, cleaning clothes and preparing meals. Tresa longed to see the sun, but more than that, she longed to see Roman. She wasn't sure how much longer she could keep up the happy facade she'd kept plastered on her face.

It was exhausting.

"Did you notice the Garce?" Michelle asked. She didn't hang out as much as Kylie, but she also showed zero fear of Raya and came and went as she needed to. "They're anxious. Something's up."

"Maybe it's the rain?" Amanda asked, peering through the slot. "It's pretty bad out there."

"Yeah, we've had flooding on some of the upper floors where the windows are broken. How are you guys down here?" Michelle brushed the dirt off Kylie's cheek. "Ninjas aren't supposed to be dirty."

Kylie's lips twitched to the side and she frowned.

"Nothing yet on this floor, but I haven't been down below for a while. I think it's impossible to get through the barricades unless I could see the shadows down there." Unless she tore through them all with her claws and freakish strength. Which would be counterproductive.

"Well, hopefully, it's the rain. We'll keep an eye on them. Do you need anything down here?" Michelle asked.

Tresa shook her head, distracted by Raya, who had ventured out of her corner to peek out of the slot next to Jessi. Her sparkling blue tattoos shimmered a little brighter at the sight below her, which was odd until Tresa remembered those Garce kept her immortal.

She'd wondered, after reading Raya's note, if Garce kept *her* immortal, too. She was partly Py. Maybe it just slowed her growth? It was something she would have discussed with Roman since he loved data so much. But now it wouldn't happen.

She sank to the floor and drew her legs to her chest, dropping her forehead onto her knees. For just a few moments, she needed to let the facade fall. Her heart was breaking and she would hide it again in a minute, but for those few seconds, she let it go.

"Hey. You okay?" Kylie asked, sliding down next to her. Tresa felt Kylie's arm slide around her shoulder and Tresa leaned into her.

"Yeah. Just tired."

"Want me to kick his ass just because?" Kylie asked softly. "I can do it. I'm a ninja."

Tresa giggled despite herself. Kylie had proclaimed them best friends weeks ago, and Tresa had gone along with it because Kylie was best friends with everyone and she'd never had a best friend herself. But Kylie had been her defender—against the Garce, against Roman, against herself. Now, when Tresa had lost Roman and divided their team, at her lowest point, Kylie was there.

Tresa would have been lost without her.

"No. I don't blame him. He's being more than fair."

"And you're being kind. Kindness wins. Hashtag team kind, Tresa."

Tresa smiled, raising her head. "He's being protective. I think that's what he was born to do. And I can't blame him for that."

"It was a mistake. I never should have let you in."

His words haunted her. They tore at her chest and stole her breath. After everything she'd done, everything she'd tried so hard to do for them, to protect them, to feed them, to save them, she was a mistake.

She couldn't blame him for being protective, but she could blame him for his words. That little teeny bit of anger was all that kept her from going up to his floor and telling him she'd send Raya away. Anything, to stop that pain.

But she didn't. Because of the anger, and because she'd been there, and she couldn't put Raya through what she'd gone through. At least Tresa had her father. Raya had no one, and no one deserved to live in this horrible world alone.

Chapter Thirty

Kylie trudged up the stairs like the weight of the world rested on her shoulders. Roman hadn't seen her all day, although Michelle had reported back that Kylie now called herself a ninja and expected everyone else to, as well. That had sounded encouraging. Like maybe she was happy. Maybe she was enjoying herself.

She straightened when she saw Roman watching her, and pulled a smile back on her face, and suddenly he understood. Kylie was acting. She was trying to be the positive force they all needed right then, at the cost of her own spirit. "Hey Ro. What's up?"

He pulled her into a hug. She stiffened in surprise at first and then melted against him. She didn't cry and he was impressed by her strength because he could see the tears shimmering in her eyes. She didn't let them fall by sheer force of will. He held her until she pulled away, trying to absorb the pain he was responsible for. He would have given anything to take it from her.

To take it from Tresa.

"I heard you yelling earlier. Everything okay?" she asked, playing absently with her hair.

Roman nodded. "Just the usual."

"Meaning Tresa's gone and you're back to your angry, sullen, miserable self?" She peeked up at him, gauging his reaction.

He frowned. "I'm not any of those things."

Kylie raised an eyebrow and he sighed. "We just had flooding issues. I was yelling to be heard over the rain."

"Right."

He draped an arm over her shoulder as they went to the common room. "Have you eaten?"

"Yes."

"Do they have enough?" The thought of Tresa going hungry nearly drove him to his knees.

"For now." Kylie thunked down on her bedroll. "Are you going to sleep tonight?"

He hadn't, not since the Py had shown up. But that had been days ago. Surely, if something bad was going to happen, it would have. Maybe...maybe they could call an end to this division. Maybe Tresa would come back.

Except she wouldn't. Not after the things he'd said. Not after what he'd forced her to do. "Yeah. I'll take first watch and catch some sleep when Shannon takes over. Deal?"

She nodded. "Which side?"

He didn't want to be around people. He always chose the south side because he was usually alone. Tonight was no different. "I'm going to head over that way. Give Cali Jewel a break."

Without a word, Kylie gathered her sleeping roll and trudged off into the darkness, disappearing around the corner. He followed her, catching up just as she found Cali Jewel. "Ready for a break?" he heard his sister ask.

"Definitely. There's nothing out there. The Garce all left earlier today."

Roman frowned. "They left?"

"Yeah, they ran all excited out of my view. I'm not sure where they went, though."

"To the northwest." Kylie rolled out her sleeping roll. "We think it's because of the storm. They're anxious about the rain."

They'd been there since before the monsoon season and never had the Garce acted strangely before. It was almost like—

"Traders must be coming. Or this was the time they usually came. The Garce are waiting for them."

"Well that sucks worse than my theory that they were just playing in the puddles," Kylie muttered from the floor where she'd curled up on her mat.

"It could be that, too," Cali Jewel said encouragingly. "I'll give Michelle a heads up."

"Thanks." Roman went to the lookout and peered through. It was true, there was no sign of Garce anywhere. "Weird."

"Just because they're gathering doesn't mean the traders are coming. It could just mean that's when they're expected," Kylie mumbled. "But we killed them all." She rolled over onto her back, her eyes barely visible in the darkness.

"Yeah. They're creatures of habit." He watched out the slot for several more minutes, listening to Kylie breath and wondering if she was asleep. When she growled and threw herself onto her side, he finally gave up. "How is she?"

Kylie was quiet for so long he thought maybe she really was asleep. "Do you really care?"

"You know I do, Kylie."

Kylie sighed and pushed herself into a sitting position, watching him suspiciously. "Then why are you doing this?"

"I have to keep them safe," he answered automatically. "I can't put them in danger."

"You did it for Tresa."

"Tresa saved our lives. It was the least I could do."

"Right. But you were scared of her."

He sucked in a long, anger-cooling breath. "Tresa has a light about her. Even though she looks like an alien, there was a goodness that was undeniable. This Py—"

"Raya."

"—This Py has no such light."

Kylie gnawed on her thumbnail and Roman went back to watching the window. "It's true," she said finally. "There's a darkness in her."

His heart sank. He'd been hoping Kylie would have raving reviews and he could, with a clear conscience, invite the Py into their fold. But not when even Kylie didn't trust her. Kylie accepted everyone immediately.

"You didn't answer my question," he said quietly when she didn't elaborate. "How is Tresa?"

Kylie rolled her head toward him and her eyes glinted in the darkness. "She's hurting. She pretends she's not. She tries to hide it with smiles and laughter because she's not addicted to anger like you are. There's no yelling downstairs, you know."

"You didn't have flood issues," he murmured distractedly. *She's hurting.* She was hurting because of him. Because he'd forced her out, made her choose, and torn her heart to shreds with his horrible, horrible words. "Is she getting enough rest? Is she still training?"

"She gets no rest, and no, she's not training. She watches Raya all the time. She doesn't let her out of her sight. All Raya does is sleep. When she's not sleeping, she's pretending to be asleep. Tresa's protecting us and her."

Roman nodded. Of course she was. "Do you think she'll come back? So she doesn't have to do it alone?"

Kylie smiled sadly. "Would she come back? Yes. She's emotionally exhausted. Would she forgive you?" She hesitated. "Probably not. Those were some pretty awful things you said to her, Roman."

He leaned his forehead against the wall, squeezing his eyes shut tight. He'd lost her.

He'd really lost her.

"I know."

"Did you mean them?"

"No. Of course not. Letting her in was the best thing I've ever done."

Kylie slid down under her covers. "I miss heat."

He blinked at her sudden change of subject. "Give it a few months and you won't be saying that."

"We'll have to move north. Maybe Canada?" she mumbled.

"Yeah. Maybe."

"You should tell her, Roman. Sign a peace treaty. Work together." Kylie's voice faded until she was talking in her sleep. He reached over and pulled her blanket up around her neck.

"Yeah. I'll talk to her."

TRESA was leaning against a wall, her knees pulled up to her chest, watching the Py when Roman came around the corner.

Raya.

Tresa climbed to her feet, shoving the silky black hair away from her face. He knew he'd missed her, but he didn't realize how much until his hand almost reached out without meaning to to stroke the hair off her neck. It was a very real fight to pull his hand back.

"Roman. What are you doing here?"

Raya looked up from her corner, huge blue eyes narrowing. She braced both hands on the walls next to her as if preparing for flight.

"I've come offering a truce." He waved the little white flag he'd made, hoping she would remember that he could be adorable and not always hard-hearted. "If you'll talk to me."

"Of course I'll talk to you." Her eyes were guarded, tattoos black and shimmering. Unreadable. "What's up?"

"Come back upstairs. Let me help you watch her."

Her jaw dropped and she shook her head as if trying to knock his words into place. "What?"

"I don't like you down here alone."

She glanced around him at the room full of people. "I'm not alone."

He stepped closer, unable to stay even that short distance away from her. "But you are."

She swallowed. "I don't know if that's a good idea."

He frowned. "Is she dangerous?"

"No. All she does is sleep." Tresa ran a hand through her hair. "Everyone knows about our—falling out. Won't it be awkward?"

"They were fine when we hated each other—"

She winced, cutting him off. "I never hated you. It was always one-sided, Roman."

"Sorry," he said quickly. "Poor choice of words. I could never hate you, Tresa. You know that, right?"

Her dark eyes flitted from his face to her feet. "Why would I know that, Roman?"

"Because I—we—after—"

She sighed. "We have to leave our personal lives out of this. Will your people be okay with her?"

He'd asked. They'd discussed it. John had pointed out that it had been a week now and nothing had happened and Pys weren't known for their patience. "Yeah. They're fine. They promised to be on their best behavior. *I* promise to be on my best behavior."

She almost smiled. "I'll talk to my team, then."

He nodded, his heart in his throat. Now he had no choice but to walk away from her, and how was he supposed to do that when everything in him wanted to pull her against his chest and hold her until she forgot the awful things he'd said?

"Thanks, Roman," she said quietly.

He tried to swallow and failed. "Yeah. No problem. Let me know."

Roman made it to the stairwell, where he sunk onto the top step and dropped his head into his hands. His legs were weak and his heart still pounded like he'd been attacked by an alien. Maybe he had...a beautiful little hybrid full of hope.

Angie came around the corner and he realized he'd been sitting like that for much longer than he'd meant to, unable to move any further from Tresa than he had to. She paused in the doorway before her boots slowly came into view. "We would be grateful to come back upstairs. Heat rises and it's warmer there."

"More bodies, too. To produce more heat," he mumbled. "I'll send people down to help you move."

"No need. We don't have much." She turned and was gone and still he sat on the steps.

"So...are you just going to sit here all day or do you think you can use those stupid muscles for good?" Kylie asked, popping into the stairwell carrying a box full of food. Canned beans, mostly, and fruit in syrup. They hadn't eaten so well in all the time Roman had been leading them. Now they ate almost balanced meals every day.

Because of Tresa.

"Yeah. Sorry." He pushed himself to his feet, stretching because he'd been sitting there so long. "My muscles aren't stupid. They do just what they're supposed to."

She laughed over her shoulder at him, positively delighted that they were moving back together. Roman jumped back down the steps and jogged through the darkness, nearly running over several others carrying supplies back upstairs. They moved out of his way, mumbling apologies and he realized the rift between the two groups wasn't going to heal easily. It would take time. And it had to start with him and Tresa.

She was balancing two boxes full of cans when he came in. "Here. Let me help." He took one of the boxes and she peered around the other at him.

He nearly fell into her dark, dark eyes.

"Thanks," she said politely, with more cold than warmth but she wasn't icy. "Raya, ready?"

Roman glanced over his shoulder. Raya still stood in her corner of the common room, shaking her head.

"It's warmer up there," Tresa said gently. "And safer. Away from the Garce."

Raya stared at Roman, her entire body shaking, and he wondered how he could possibly have been afraid of something that small and terrified. "It's okay. We won't hurt you," he said.

Tresa nodded.

Raya shook her head.

Sighing, Tresa set her box down. "I'll wait with her."

Roman stacked his box on top of hers and picked them both up. "I'll be back."

He carried the boxes up, deposited them in food storage and found more of his team to go back down to help move. It only took a few more trips before everything but Tresa and Raya were upstairs.

And then it took four more hours.

Roman was watching the storm. In a city that averaged about four inches of rain per year, this never-ending storm was unexplainable. The Garce didn't seem bothered by the downpour but they did stay near the northwest side of the city.

Waiting.

There was a ripple of murmurs behind him and he turned to see the Py shimmering in the doorway to the common room. Tresa stood behind her, more beautiful than he remembered her being even those few hours ago. Her long dark hair, almost to her waist, caught the weak light, throwing rainbows behind her and the tattoos that curled around her eyes seemed more lit than normal.

"Here," Kylie said brightly. "I made you a corner."

He glanced at his sister, who had all of Raya's blankets arranged around her feet in what could only be described as a nest in the corner of the room. No one else had their bedrolls nearby, but he didn't know if that was for Raya's benefit or theirs.

Raya edged around the room, watching them all with wide, suspicious eyes before she sank into her corner. Tresa sighed and leaned against the door jamb. He could feel the exhaustion radiating from her and he didn't even have her alien gifts.

He crossed the room and stopped closer to her than was appropriate. So close he could feel her breath on the skin of his neck and it nearly drove him to his knees. "What do you need? Can you sleep?"

"No."

"Then what, Tresa? How do you recharge?"

She ran a hand over her face. "I want to go outside. I want to see the light."

He hesitated. "It's pouring out there. The streets are underwater—the whole south side is flooding because the windows are broken—"

She nodded. "I know."

"Okay."

She blinked up at him, her hand paused over the bridge of her nose like she'd been about to try to rub a headache away. "What?"

"I'll watch her. Go see the light. Dance in the rain. Just don't fall off the roof."

She smirked. It wasn't a smile, but he would take what he could get. "Yes sir."

She slid into the shadows and was gone and he would have given anything to watch her emerge onto the roof, to watch her lift her face to the sky and maybe, finally, some of the weight would slip from her shoulders. Instead, he watched Raya and waited for Tresa to come back.

Raya sat in the corner, her head against the wall and her eyes closed. That was what Kylie had meant—either she was asleep or she pretended to be. She sat up when he brought her food, taking it from him without touching him, and then curled in on herself as soon as she was done. The sun set and still, Tresa didn't return.

"I'll go check on her," Jeff said. He'd been watching the Garce out the window, but when it got too dark to see, he left and disappeared into the gloomy hallways, gun on his shoulder. Several minutes later, they returned, both soaking wet.

"Are you okay?" Roman asked, catching Tresa before she could slide past him. "You were gone for hours."

She met his eyes, the weight and the darkness that were there before gone. She shivered a bit against the chill, her hair plastered to her head and her clothes clinging to her skin, but she looked more like the Tresa from before than he could have hoped for. "Yeah. I lost track of time. How is she?" She slid her arm free of his grasp.

He nodded, his hand still burning from where he'd touched her. "She ate. She slept. Does she do much else?"

Tresa shook her head. "Not really."

Chapter Thirty-One

Tresa had gone hunting and left Roman in charge of Raya. She'd been with them for weeks now, weeks of cowering in the corner, watching them all suspiciously. They'd moved on with their lives, trying to create some semblance of purpose in their compound.

At least, some of them had. Tresa and Roman did their best to put up a polite, yet cool, front. She stayed away from him when she could, and tried her best not to look at him when she couldn't.

Because he was gorgeous. Mind-numbingly gorgeous and she said stupid things like how much she missed him when she was forced to look at him.

And every day, her heart broke a little more.

But every time he opened his mouth, she heard him again. *Letting you in was a mistake.*

So she kept her distance and they ran the compound as well as they could.

It was a relief to get out of there and away from him, though. A relief to escape through the shadows and run free through the cool air.

A relief to kill the aliens.

She left two of them in her wake and was hoping for one more. They ran from her now, after all this time. They finally had figured out what she was—and it wasn't a friend. They were stupid, but apparently, they did have some form of recognition and remembrance ability. Another thing for Roman to track, since he seemed to obsess over everything he could plot on a graph or write on the whiteboard.

She understood, though. It gave him a sense of control in a world where there was only chaos. Trying to understand the aliens and her, it made him feel like he wasn't just a victim of his circumstances.

"Tresa!"

She froze, whirling in a circle, hoping she'd imagined Roman's voice. It wouldn't be the first time.

Not even close.

But no, he was sprinting toward her, outrunning the Garce on his heels. Not even trying to shoot at them.

Just trying to get to her.

"Roman!" she shrieked and abandoned her chase, diving into the shadows and zipping out behind him. The Garce chasing him skidded to a halt with a panicked bark and tried to turn, but it was too slow. Within seconds, she'd pounced and its lifeless body fell at her feet. She whirled away before its last breath left it. "What are you doing? Have you lost your freaking mind?" she yelled.

Roman shook his head, breathing hard. "It's Raya. She's gone."

"What?" she gasped. They were in the middle of Garce territory. It was no place to have a conversation, and yet she suddenly couldn't will her feet to move.

"There was a fire. In the common room. She was on the other side of it and by the time I got it put out, she was gone. I don't know how or why. Sometime in all the chaos, she escaped. We've searched the building and the surrounding area. She's just not there. I'm sorry, Tresa. I know how this looks—"

She blinked at him. "Know how this looks? How does it look?"

He shoved a hand through his dark hair. "Like I did it on purpose to get rid of her."

She gaped at him. There were Garce stalking in. She could feel them behind her and knew they were not far off behind Roman, as well. But she couldn't even. "You honestly think I'm that low, Roman? That you'd set fire to your own compound to drive out a Py I'm trying to save?"

He stared at the ground. "I don't know what happened."

She didn't know—by the way he said it, he could have meant just now with his words, or the fire, or his original anger when she'd brought Raya back. "There's no time for this right now. We need to go. Can you make it back?"

"It's a half-mile, Tresa. I'm not completely useless."

She almost smiled at his offense, but that would be wildly inappropriate. "Let's go, then. I'll see if I can track Raya."

Roman ran. Tresa launched into the shadows, coming out next to the Garce behind her. It hadn't realized what she was, not until it was too late. As it fell lifeless at her feet, she ran for the next one, clearing a path for Roman to barrel through and thanking the heavens that he was freakishly fast.

For a human.

By the time they made it back to the compound, Kira and Brittany were waiting with the ladder. Roman clambered up and

Tresa jumped through the shadows, beating him to the top. "It happened in the common room?" she asked.

Kira nodded. "Just after you left. It took us twenty minutes to put it out. The room's a loss."

"Was anyone hurt?" Tresa asked, bolting up the stairs. Kira easily kept up with her, rattling off answers to every one of Tresa's questions.

"Minor burns. Mostly loss of goods. Blankets, clothing. Bedding."

"But no sign of Raya?"

"No. We've scoured the building from top to bottom. Even floors one and two beneath the barricades. She's gone."

Raya was part Py. She moved as fast as Tresa. If she wanted to get where they couldn't see her, she could do it easily, especially under cover of a fire.

"Any idea of how the fire started?"

Roman had caught up to them just as they reached the seventh floor. Tresa could smell the smoke and it was buzzing with people getting undamaged items out. Moving again. "No. There are no matches, no fire starters, nothing in the area. It just started," he responded.

Nothing to start a fire except Raya. Who had fire roiling through her blood.

"Where are they moving to?" she asked, edging out of the way.

"Fifth floor. The smoke rose, so the eighth floor is almost as bad as this one."

"We need to get out of the building," she murmured.

Roman sucked in a breath, rubbing the bridge of his nose. His muscles bunched under his shirt and she longed to run her fingers across them.

Which was totally inappropriate given the current situation.

"You think she'll turn on us?"

"If that wasn't her intention all along." Tresa hated admitting she'd been so wrong, but it would be risking their lives if she didn't. "I'm so sorry."

"We don't know that. She was terrified, Tres. I've never seen anyone so incapable of being an evil genius before. You can feel her emotions, right? You would have known if she was faking that fear."

She shook her head. She'd failed them. She'd failed them all.

"Hey." Roman grabbed her wrist, his thumb tracing soft skin in a move she wasn't even sure he knew he was making. "You see the good in people. Even aliens. That's not something to apologize for."

She forced a smile. "Thanks. But we need to move. If there are traders out there, or other Pys coming...we aren't safe here. Not anymore."

"Okay." Roman spun away and in the next few hours, he somehow got everything in their compound loaded up—food storage, bedding, clothing, even their garden—and they started out.

Tresa ran ahead and around, clearing a path while Roman pushed their team relentlessly through the twilight. She didn't know where they were going, but he apparently had a plan. Maybe he'd had one all along.

That boy always had a plan.

They ran hard, following him blindly, depending on him to keep them safe.

When Tresa could see no more Garce, she went looking for Raya.

She'd been able to sense Raya for weeks. Months. She didn't even know how long now. She'd been so busy trying to fight it, to ignore the cravings, that she'd flipped a switch on that sense.

Now, she woke it up. Keeping an eye on Roman and where he was going, she sprinted back the way they'd come. Past their building, past the one next to it. Raya had gone to the northeast.

Where the Garce were gathered.

"Tresa!" Roman bellowed. She froze, whirling on her heel.

"What are you doing? You're supposed to be leading the others!" she jogged back to him. He'd raced after her, and his chest rose and fell in angry gasps for air.

"What the hell are you doing? You don't just run off, Tresa! You have no idea how dangerous it is right now."

"I was trying to find Raya! I made sure you guys were safe and now I'm going to find her and stop her."

"You have no idea what to expect, Tresa! You don't even know if she's bad. Maybe she's just too scared of people to stay with us any longer. Maybe she likes her solitude."

"Or maybe I was wrong all along. I got everyone into this mess. You get them out and I'll try to clean it up."

"No. You come back with me to our team, and we'll find somewhere new and safe. Do you understand me?"

"Roman, they *are* safe. I made sure they were safe. Why are you so angry at me when all I'm trying to do is keep them alive?"

"Because I'm in love with you!" Roman yelled.

Tresa's heart stuttered in her chest as warmth slid over her ice-cold soul.

"Because the thought of you hurt or scared or alone makes it impossible to think straight, and because if this world loses you, there's nothing left to fight for."

She stared at him, fighting to come up with some response. Any response. But no words would come, at least no intelligent ones. "You're—you're in love with me? I'm part alien. You hate aliens."

Roman ran a hand roughly through his hair, looking over his shoulder. She wanted to tell him that Jeff and Kylie, they would keep their team safe, but she couldn't force her mouth to speak.

Because I'm in love with you.

"I hate aliens. You're not alien. You're Tresa and the best thing that's ever happened to me. I don't know how you don't realize that. You're the one who senses all the emotions."

"Roman, I—" She couldn't figure out how to phrase it. So he would realize she wasn't just repeating the words. That she'd loved him from that very first Garce attack when he'd dragged her off its back.

Something swooped through the darkness. Something fast and small with huge, powerful wings. "Run."

"What?"

"Run!"

There were more. Three of them, shooting through the twilight. The thick cloud cover had let them out of the shadows early. The blood balls came hard and fast and Roman dove out of the way, scrambled to his feet and ran for the nearest building.

"Tresa, come on!"

There was no hiding from the Pys.

Tresa couldn't fight them. Not from the ground, not when they had the entire sky to escape to. She couldn't throw her attacks, she couldn't pull them out of the air.

She was helpless.

She dodged their blood balls, but they weren't trying to hit her. They were trying to take out Roman and only keeping her away from him. She didn't understand it, but she had to stop it.

She just had no idea how.

She had no gun. She had no way to reach them. It wasn't like she could jump into a shadow and fall out of the sky.

Wait.

Roman had led them over by a building. They swarmed it now, trying to get to him and still stay out of her reach. It was like they knew exactly what she could do.

But they didn't realize the extent of it. She ran toward the shadow of a car, zipped into it and raced through the darkness, focused only on the last thing she'd seen when she jumped in.

The shadow at the top of the building.

She came out mid-air and fell, wanted to scream but couldn't. Maybe she hadn't thought her brilliant plan through because there was nothing below her for three hundred feet.

Except a Py who wouldn't hold still.

She hadn't seen Tresa coming and swooped right below her. Tresa had hoped she would stay in place but she'd never zipped so far before. It had been a huge, stupid risk.

But it had paid off.

She landed hard, tore viciously at the huge, silky black wings, and then at the Py's throat. They fell, fluttering sideways like a helicopter with a broken rotor.

A second Py jerked toward them in shock while the third fell with them. Tresa didn't understand — their weird connection thing, it didn't make sense — but she used it to her advantage, tearing at the one she fell with to bring down the third.

The second, bigger than the other two, shot through the air, abandoning Roman. Tresa waited, the ground coming up to meet them, too fast, too fast, and she wasn't sure the second Py would get there in time but she did, she did, trying to catch her sister before she hit the ground. Tresa launched herself from the broken alien beneath her, flying through the air like she had wings herself, and hit the not-dead Py, clinging to her neck, claws in her wings.

The Py had her hands full, trying to save her dead friend, and the blood ball she threw at Tresa went wide, slamming into the building behind them. They toppled toward the ground as the Py screamed, over and over as Tresa attacked. She couldn't let her survive. If they survived, they would kill Roman.

She couldn't let that happen.

Tresa was soaked in blood—hers, the Pys, but thankfully not Roman's. The Py blood burned her, scalded her skin and ate away at her flesh everywhere it touched. She wasn't going to survive this, but that was okay. She'd killed them. They were dead, and Roman was safe.

She fell because she had no more strength to fight and there were no shadows to zip into. Nowhere to jump, nowhere safe to land. She braced for death, wishing she could see Roman one more time.

Instead, she was jerked out of the air, her neck snapping forward as the Py below her fell away. Screaming, she twisted, trying to see what held her.

The third Py. She hadn't been dead after all.

"They want you alive. Stay alive until we can fix you," she snarled.

Tresa could only blink in pain and fight to stay conscious as they shot through the dark air.

Below her, Roman emerged from the building. He ran, trying to catch her, yelling her name. She heard gunshots and knew her father fought for her too, but she was out of reach.

They couldn't save her.

Chapter Thirty-Two

" *She's not going to make it."*

"Her heart keeps stopping."

"We'll stop up here and do what we can. Thelenia will be so angry if she's dead."

Tresa heard flashes of conversation between bouts of consciousness as the Py blood burned its way through her and she fought to stay alive. She didn't know when the other two Pys had shown up, and she had no idea where they were.

Even worse, when she was awake, fighting the agonizing pain and the overwhelming sense of despair, she was attacked constantly by flashbacks.

It was all too real. All too familiar. She'd lived this before, and the hands of the Pys were no kinder than the mouths of the Garce.

She was ashamed, but she welcomed the dark that unconsciousness brought.

She woke in what had once been one of those huge furniture stores. She was on a bed still covered in plastic, and the rotting corpse of someone long-since dead fell across the one next to her.

Actually, the room was littered with dead people.

Tresa whimpered, rolling onto her side and finally pushing herself to a sitting position. The Pys were across the room, hiding from the dim light at the front of the store.

No, not hiding. They were eating.

They'd found a Garce in the darkness, apparently.

The pain was gone. The torn skin had healed, the bruises had faded.

But her tattoos were blue now, not black.

And her overwhelming craving for Py blood was almost gone.

They'd nearly erased the Garce DNA. She could feel the imbalance and wondered if she'd still be able to fight them. If she'd still be able to escape into shadows. The room was so dark it was all shadow, and there was nowhere for her to come out of. She squinted, trying to see out the front doors, but they were covered in hastily erected boards, trying to block out the light. She couldn't see the other side. If she could just get closer...

She rolled onto her feet, the Py DNA roiling through her system, and tried to settle herself before she crept forward.

"Zerias, you promised! Let me in!"

Tresa froze. She'd never heard that voice, and while it did have the lyrical quality of the Py, it was human.

She knew only one Py/human hybrid, and she supposedly couldn't speak. She said she couldn't throw blood balls, either, but Tresa was pretty sure she had.

"Go away Rayanna. We will come for you when you're ready. You're not yet."

Ray. Anna.

Raya.

They hadn't known her full name. Why on earth would she not tell them her real name? It wasn't like they could look her up on Google.

"You promised! You said if I got you the one that was killing the Pys, you would finish turning me. So I could be powerful and beautiful like you. You promised! The sun hurts, Zerias. Let me in!"

One of the Pys in the back snickered to the others and rose into the air. Tresa crouched on the floor, waiting for an opportunity to bolt. They didn't seem to walk, using their wings instead of feet unless absolutely necessary. "I don't know why you want to be one of us. At least you can still go into the sun without dying," Zerias said. The other two laughed.

"So I can kill her when I find her. And right now I don't stand a chance. Let me in!"

Zerias threw a blood ball from the depths of the warehouse, shattering the boards and letting in a flood of light. Rayanna screamed and Tresa just caught a glimpse of her diving out of the way. Zerias and the other two laughed. "I thought you wanted to come in, Rayanna?"

Rayanna climbed back to her feet and hesitantly stood in the doorway. "Don't do that again."

Tresa could feel her fear radiating from her in waves, but she came into the shadowy interior willingly.

"Did you save her?" she asked.

Crap.

Before Tresa could throw herself back on the bed, all three Pys looked over to where she should have been. They shrieked in unison and shot into the air. Tresa could probably have fought one, maybe two of them if she could get them in separate parts of the store, but all three at once?

Probably not.

All she could do was run and hope she could catch sight of the shadows beyond before they could catch her. She leaped over furniture, tumbled over fake potted plants and crashed into coffee tables, weaving in and out between an obscene amount of couches, all covered in dust and dried blood.

It was stepping on the human bones that did her in. She tried not to, and that made her slower.

Too slow.

Zerias caught her by the hair and jerked her back, throwing her onto a couch. Tresa hit it and toppled over the back, landing hard on her back and neck. Gasping, she rolled and crawled around the side. As Zerias flew behind the couch to look for her, Tresa sprang to her feet and sprinted for the door.

She was caught again by a different Py, who grabbed her by the neck and flew to the ceiling while Tresa fought to breathe. "Stop running away," the Py cooed. "We just saved your life. You should be grateful."

Tresa clawed at her hands, kicked and wriggled, but made no headway. The edges of her vision went black.

She let her body go limp.

"Don't kill her!" Zerias screeched like a harpy. "We need her alive so we can see what Nathalia has done!"

The Py loosened her grip and Tresa lunged, her claws sparking against her palm. She slashed the Py's throat and they plummeted to the ground while it fought and gurgled and tried desperately to draw in one last breath.

Tresa hit a couch and bounced off onto a coffee table. The glass shattered under her weight and she gasped against the pain, still struggling to see clearly.

Zerias grabbed her by the hair and shot back up toward the ceiling. "I'm going to hurt you for that," she hissed. "You have to be alive. You don't have to be in one piece."

The blood balls shot out of nowhere, fast like lightning, faster than any of theirs had been. It hit Zerias and Tresa fell the several feet, landing half on a bed before toppling to the floor, landing hard on her back with no air in her lungs.

More blood balls lit up the room, one after another, knocking the Pys out of the sky like bowling pins. Rayanna screamed and ran, but Tresa could only lie on the floor, gasping for breath. Waiting for this new super Py to come for her.

She did. The huge black wings blocked Tresa's vision as the Py landed next to her and Tresa cringed away.

"It's okay. I won't hurt you."

Tresa's entire body stuttered, her heart stilled in her chest and her mind froze. Everything froze. The world stopped moving. She knew that voice.

She knew that voice because she heard it in her head every single time she was scared or angry or lost or hurt.

She knew that voice because she'd heard its final words over and over and over again in her head for three years. *Tresa, get to the roof.*

Tresa sat up so she could see her face. Only, Phoenyx didn't stare back at her.

A Py did.

Tresa screamed and crab-walked backward, while the Py who had her sister's voice straightened in shock, her blue-brown eyes huge in her face, the tattoos sparking and the huge, huge wings fluttering anxiously.

"Tresa?" she whispered.

Tresa ran into a couch and stopped. At some point, she'd started sobbing, but she didn't know when.

"Tresa, it's me. It's Nyx—Phoenyx." She moved closer one incredibly slow step at a time, folding her wings back like she could possibly hide them. "It's okay. I won't hurt you. I'm a good little alien."

"You're not little," Tresa said stupidly. When she'd known Phoenyx, her sister had been just taller than her. Maybe 5'6". Now, this creature towered above her, well over six feet.

The Py smiled. "Yeah. When I take their powers, I grow. It's a fun little gift."

The smile was what did it. Tresa remembered that smile. Phoenyx always smiled, always had a kind, encouraging word for her. She'd had every boy in school after her because of that smile and Tresa had wanted to look just like her.

Slowly, she crept to her feet and came closer. Phoenyx went very still, the wings behind her minutely fluttering back and forth, like they were anxious. Tresa reached out, touched her hair, black like her own but with shimmering blue streaks running through it. She touched her cheek, her nose. "Phoenyx?"

Phoenyx sobbed and threw her arms around Tresa. "It's me, Tres. It's really me. I've missed you so much. I thought you were dead!"

Tresa hesitated, but the warmth of her sister's arms, the strength in them, the familiarity, it was all she needed. Tears soaked her cheeks as she hugged Phoenyx back, holding on for dear life.

"But—but I heard you. In my head. I heard you talk to me. I thought you were dead, too. I saw you go out the door and—and when the Garce took me you weren't there—"

Phoenyx kissed the top of her head. "I ran. I climbed the neighbor's tree down the street. It was the only one big enough. By the time I got back, all I found was blood. I looked and looked, but I thought—I thought you were dead."

"Mom didn't tell you I was taken?"

Phoenyx's wings fluttered harder, vibrating with anger. "No. No, she did not."

"Is she—are they alive?"

Phoenyx leaned back, her hands on Tresa's shoulders. "No. I'm sorry. They gave themselves to the Pys and didn't survive. As for hearing my voice in your head, I guess you just knew me so well you knew what I'd say without me saying it." She smiled, and it radiated, brightening the dark room. "Did—did Dad...I mean, of course he did. Or he'd be here and I wouldn't have had to kill those Pys. I was just hoping, I mean—"

Her shimmering tattoos faded, just a bit.

"Dad's alive! He saved me! I'll take you to him. We can go now!"

Nyx's whole face lit up, more beautiful than any Py Tresa had ever seen. Like hope had returned to the world. "He's alive? He's alive," she whispered.

"Yes! He'll be so happy, Phoenyx! Let's go. I think I can run."

Phoenyx turned toward the door, skidding to a halt before she took a step. "I can't. Sunlight is not my friend."

"But...but you—you were in the sun earlier. How were you in the sun?" Tresa asked. Her sister must have the same weaknesses as the Pys.

"I was hunting an old...friend. I saw her come in and I didn't want to lose my chance. I just ran for it."

"Ran for it? Through the sun?"

"I have a suit, but there wasn't time. I was afraid I'd lose her. So I risked it." Phoenyx gave her a teasing smile. "I'm faster than the sun."

"That's a risky little move."

Phoenyx grinned. "That's what I do."

"But—but your friend—was she—is she..." Tresa motioned around them at the dead bodies.

"No. She's not quite a Py."

"Rayanna?" Tresa guessed.

Phoenyx nodded.

Tresa had seen her run when Phoenyx had started killing everything. "And you lost her. I'm so sorry."

"Are you kidding? I *got my sister back!* Rayanna can wait. I've been hunting her for a year. A few more days won't hurt. How do you know her?"

"She sold my whole team out. We tried to help her and she turned the Pys on us. Apparently, so they'll turn her into a Py. So she can kill...oh my gosh."

"Me?" Phoenyx asked softly.

"Yeah. Why does she hate you so much? That's pretty extreme, Phoenyx."

Phoenyx winced, something Tresa had noticed she did every time Tresa said her name. "First, I go by Nyx now. Phoenyx...Phoenyx is dead. The wings and stuff. The name hurts," she whispered. "Second, uh...remember my boyfriend, Cole?"

"Yeah. Cole, of course I remember."

Nyx. Tresa tried the name in her head. It fit. This super powerful, terrifying, beautiful creature in front of her was her sister, but so much had been lost.

So much had been gained.

"Well...while I was taken, he found Rayanna. They were together until he found me again and then they broke up. Because of me. She hates me. Just a little. She sold our compound out, too. Many were lost."

Tresa sat back. "She said an alien took her boyfriend. I thought he was abducted. Like everybody else. So Cole—is he alive? Enika? Keven?"

Nyx smiled broadly. "Oh yeah. Hang on!"

She got up and flew to the door, hesitating just beyond the reaches of the light.

She *flew* to the door.

Tresa's sister could fly.

"They're not as fast as me," Nyx said over her shoulder. "I'm stuck here for at least another hour. Want to tell me your story while we wait for them? Then you can take me to Dad?" There was so much hope in her voice. "I thought I was alone. I thought I'd lost everyone," she whispered. The tattoos around her eyes, shimmering blue, faded to a pastel.

Like Tresa's.

Phoenyx straightened.

Nyx.

Nyx straightened, plastering on a bright smile that lit the dark room. "So tell me you're story. What exactly are you?"

Tresa laughed. No one had ever come right out and asked before. "So the Garce took me that night. Dad stopped it from killing me so it just kept running away. It took me to a ship."

"A Py ship?" Nyx settled on one of the beds, crossing her long legs underneath her, the huge wings waving back and forth and Tresa realized the wings moved like a personification of Nyx's mood. She didn't even have to use her Garce emotion sniffing abilities to know exactly what her sister felt.

"No. I don't think so. It was a Garce ship. Big and black. But there was a Py in it. She controlled the Garce."

"Ah, I've heard of her. She betrayed the other Pys, enslaved the Garce, bred them to be killers, and runs from planet to planet, destroying everything."

"Well, I don't know what she was doing in Idaho of all places."

"She travels from ship to ship. Keeping the Garce under control. Continue." Nyx grinned.

"You're a wealth of information."

"I know stuff." Nyx's grin widened.

"She tried to turn me, but I was in too bad of shape. The Garce blood almost killed me so she added her own Py DNA, as well. Dad saved me. He followed the Garce in, shot them with his big gun when they tried to eat him and dragged me out. The Py didn't even know I was still alive. It took me a year to learn to walk again. We've been traveling ever since with our little tribe of humans. So Dad doesn't get lonely." Tresa winked.

"Look at you, all grown up and saving people!" Nyx clapped excitedly.

There was a noise outside, something that took Tresa far too long to place. She hadn't heard it in so long.

An engine. It was the roar of an engine.

"There they are. It's about time." Nyx pushed herself to her feet and wrapped Tresa in a hug. "I'm so proud of you. And I'm so glad I found you."

"Me too," Tresa said, burying her head against her sister's shoulder. "Dang, you got tall."

Nyx laughed, releasing her to catch her hand and drag her to the doorway. "Enika! Cole! Hurry up! You'll never believe who I found!" She bounced on her toes, her wings dancing behind her. She nearly knocked Tresa over a few times.

"Sorry," she said with a sideways smile. "You'll get used to them."

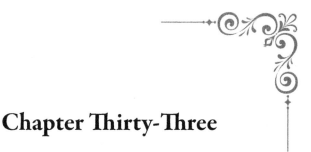

Chapter Thirty-Three

The truck door slammed once, twice, and then Tresa could hear the sound of running feet. Seconds later, Cole appeared in the doorway, tall, gorgeous Cole with his light brown hair and beautiful eyes. He was barely taller than Nyx now, but still human.

He skidded to a stop, the light eyes widening in shock.

Enika appeared next to him, curls tumbling to her shoulders. Carrying an...ax?

"Tresa?" Cole breathed, and in two strides he'd left the sunlight and caught her up in a hug, twirling her around and around. "Little Tresa! Look at you!"

"I knew it! I knew she was still alive! We could never find the bodies and didn't I tell you—didn't I tell you she was still out there somewhere?" Enika squealed.

"Enika is the queen of not believing people are dead," Nyx whispered, but loud enough that Enika could still hear her.

"So, you've grown. And got tattoos and stuff," Enika said, dragging the ax behind her.

"The Py leading the Garce got to her," Nyx explained.

Enika sucked in a breath. "You poor baby!"

"It's almost dark. We need to find somewhere safer than this to hide from the Pys." Cole set Tresa back on her feet.

"Where are we?" she asked. She remembered almost nothing of their flight there. Except pain. So much pain. "And does Pho—Nyx really need to hide from anyone?"

"Mesa. And yes. The Pys send lots after her at once. They've heard of her." Enika beamed proudly.

Apparently, Tresa's big sister was a famous badass.

"Where is Dad, Tres?" Nyx draped an arm over her shoulder, wrapping a wing around them both.

"Scottsdale."

"Your dad is alive, too?" Enika squealed again, her ax clattering to the floor. "Nyx! They're alive!"

Nyx smirked. "Yes, I realized."

"Scottsdale is about an hour from here, depending on how bad the freeway is." Cole shook his head. "I would sell my soul to be able to say that about an actual traffic jam where there were people in those cars. Honking. Swearing. I miss that."

"It's not bad. We came through there on foot a few weeks ago. Months ago. I'm not sure." Tresa gnawed on her thumbnail. She felt like she'd known Roman forever. Had it only been a few months?

"I'll back the truck up to the door. That should limit your time in the sun." Cole started out but paused and smiled back at Tresa. "Wait until you see her fly."

"Well, I mean she's flown around here," Tresa said, confused.

"Nah," Cole called as he jogged away. "That's not *flying*."

"So...Cole is full human?" Tresa asked as he started the truck and the unfamiliar sound reverberated through the building.

"Yep." Nyx watched the truck back up, her eyes moving between it and the sun.

"But Enika's not."

Enika raised an eyebrow. "How'd you know that?"

Nyx watched her, too.

Tresa shrugged, nervous under their stares. "I—so I'm part Garce now. I crave Py blood."

"Oh dear," Nyx murmured. Enika backed away.

"I can sense it," Tresa rushed on. "I can track it."

Her sister stayed firmly at her side, despite this alarming news. "Are you wanting to eat us?"

Tresa shook her head. "No. For hybrids it's different. I can sense the difference. Like the human blood muffles the Py blood or something. But I can still tell when one is close."

Enika breathed a sigh of relief and Nyx smiled. "That's good. That would be super awkward seeing as how I'm not letting you out of my sight for the rest of forever."

"Ready!" Cole flipped the tailgate of the truck down. It had a cushy interior and a shell over the back with something heavy over the windows so it was pitch black inside.

To protect Nyx from the sun.

She dove from the interior of the warehouse into the truck, but Tresa still heard the distinct sizzle as the sun hit her skin and her sister's whimper of pain.

"Nyx," she murmured.

Enika hugged her shoulder. "She's tough. And she heals fast. Do you have that ability? Can you go in the sun?"

"Let's go!" Cole called.

Tresa followed Enika as they ran from the building and climbed into the front seat.

"I guess that answers one of my questions," Enika laughed.

"What question was that?" Nyx asked from the back. They had the back window open so she wasn't completely cut off. "I can't get my stupid wing—there."

"I asked if she could heal like you and go in the sun."

"The sun is uncomfortable but not painful. Just super intense, I guess? I heal fast but if I lose enough blood so I lose consciousness, I heal super fast and wake up really strong. It's fun."

"Wait," Nyx rustled around in the back, staying in the shadows. "Why can't you just go to sleep? Instead of nearly dying? That's when I heal the fastest."

"I don't sleep," Tresa said. "Unless I almost die."

"That's not great," Nyx muttered. "We need to work on that."

Cole pulled the truck out onto the road, weaving it in and out of stalled, broken down and rusting cars. It was worse once they got on the freeway, and Tresa probably could have run faster but she would have gotten tired long before they hit Scottsdale.

"So Tresa, you're all grown up and gorgeous. Am I gonna have to have a talk with some boys?" Cole teased, risking a glance over at her as they picked up speed. The freeway wasn't nearly as cluttered as the city streets.

She blushed and tried to hide behind her hair but too late. Enika saw her and bounced in her seat. "There is!"

"Well yeah. Are you surprised?" Nyx asked. "Look at her. She's freaking hot."

Tresa laughed, pressing her hands to her cheeks. "I—I mean, there was. We fight a lot. He's super cranky and carries the weight of the world on his shoulders. When I brought Raya—Rayanna back to our compound—"

"Rayanna! You know her?" Enika asked.

"Shhh! Long story. I'll tell you later," Nyx said, her wings fluttering against the sides of the shell. "This guy, Tres?"

"He wasn't happy. He said I put everyone in danger, which I did. We stopped whatever it was we were doing before. We broke up, I guess? But—but right before I was taken, he said—he said he loved me."

Nyx shrieked. "Did you say it back? Do you love him too?"

It was like before the apocalypse all over again. Talking to Nyx and Enika about boys while Cole sat uncomfortably, probably wishing he hadn't brought it up. Tresa's throat swelled and she tried to swallow the tears, but it took her several tries. "Yeah. I do. But I didn't get a chance to tell him. The Pys attacked. Because of Rayanna."

For the next hour, she answered their never-ending questions as best she could, everything from Roman to her Dad to Rayanna to the Py activity and the traders in the area.

"That's how we find Rayanna. She works with the traders. She can contact the Pys and she's not afraid of the Garce. We find the traders, we usually find her not far off. They were traveling back this way. That's why I was in the area," Nyx explained.

Horror nearly drowned Rayanna. "Traders are back? I thought we killed them all. Cole, you have to drive faster. My team, Roman. My dad, they could be in trouble—"

"I took care of the traders," Cole said grimly. "They won't be hurting anyone else. You should move your team up to Utah. Keven's got a huge compound there. Safe from the Garce and one of The Nine is usually there protecting it from Pys, but since we destroyed their ship—"

"What?" Tresa gasped. "You destroyed their ship? How is that even possible? Exit here. We were in that tall building, but we had to leave after Rayanna sold us out."

Cole did as he was told while Enika answered her question. "With a bomb from the inside. It forces the Pys out into the sun, and they die. It's pretty simple."

Right. Simple.

"We've done it to all the ships in Utah and part of Nevada as we come across them while we're hunting Rayanna. That's what all The Nine are doing now. Eradicating the Pys from the US. Then we'll probably head up to Canada or down to South America," Nyx mused. "Depending on what season it is."

Tresa felt like her mind was going to explode. So. Much. Information. "The Nine?"

"The Nine. Ten of us escaped the Pys after we were changed. I call them The Nine because they stay together but I—"

"She came looking for us," Cole said quietly.

And he'd been with Rayanna. Oooh, awkward.

"This building was our compound. They were running east when I left them. I don't know—I don't know if Roman is even still alive," Tresa whispered. "I don't know how long I've been gone."

"After dark, I'll fly through the city and see what I can find," Nyx shifted her weight, her wings smacking the sides again. Tresa had always thought it would be so cool to have the Pys wings, that of everything she'd been given, the wings would have been better.

Now she was rethinking that a bit.

"You can't fly through the city. Dad's got a big ass gun and he'll shoot you right out of the sky. You know how he gets when he's angry."

Nyx snickered. "We'll think of something."

Cole pulled into a parking garage where it was covered in shadows and protected from the sun. Nyx slid out of the back, stretching her wings. They towered over her, brushing the ceiling above. Tresa could only stare for several long seconds.

Her sister had *wings*.

"It's weird that you and Nyx both survived the change and your mom and sister didn't," Enika mused. "I mean, only one percent of the population actually survived the procedure in the first place, and two sisters surviving it would tell me there's a genetic makeup of some sort." Enika's lips twitched while she mulled over possibilities.

"Cherish wasn't our real sister," Tresa answered, distracted as she searched the city below them. She hadn't realized Nyx didn't know that until her sister gasped behind her.

"What?"

"She wasn't Dad's. So, I guess she would have been a half-sister."

"Explains so much," Cole murmured, standing next to Tresa in the quickly fading light, searching the city below them.

"I'm going to look for them. Can you—can you stay here? I'll come back when I find them or at dark. Whichever comes first." Tresa wouldn't admit she might not find them at all.

The last she'd seen, Roman was running recklessly after her, unmindful of the Garce stalking him. How had he survived that?

"Wait. I'll come with you. I can handle the sun." Enika grabbed her ax out of the truck.

"That's nice of you, but I can move faster on my own," Tresa said, wincing when she realized it didn't sound very polite.

Enika just grinned. "I doubt that. Ready?"

Unsure how else to dissuade her, Tresa nodded.

Enika started to run.

She was fast. Py-fast, freakishly fast, darting through the shadows and into the light. Tresa had known Enika had Py DNA but she hadn't seen any indication of it.

Until then.

Tresa ran after her, and they sprinted down the corridor and out into the street. Enika leaped easily over the cars in her path and Tresa followed, vaulting off the hood. One day, she would ask if Enika was one of The Nine, and why she didn't have the wings and blood balls that Nyx had. But now wasn't the time. She had to find her dad.

She had to find Roman.

"Think," Enika said, hesitating at a four-way stop. "When you were taken, can you remember anything? Anything that might tell you where they are?"

Tresa ran a hand through her hair, gnawing on her lip. "I remember Roman chasing me,"

"Good," Enika smiled. "What else?"

"My dad! I remember him shooting at the Pys!" Tresa spun in a circle, eyes closed, trying to remember what building he'd been on. "This way!"

She sprinted to the right and Enika followed, both keeping their eyes peeled for any sign of life. *"Come on, Dad. Where are you?"*

It was Roman who answered. "Tresa!"

She skidded to a halt, praying she wasn't imagining his voice because she wanted to hear it so badly, and Enika nearly ran her over. "Roman!"

"This way," Enika said, tugging her arm to toward the next street. They ran again, watching for Garce, watching for any sign of life. The warehouse they'd gotten supplies from was just ahead, and it was there that Roman slid down the ladder from the roof.

"Roman!" Tresa shrieked. She bolted ahead, leaving Enika behind, and met him before he hit the edge of the parking lot. She threw herself into his arms, sobbing, clinging to him like he was a lifeline.

He *was* a lifeline.

He kissed her forehead, her temples, her eyes, her cheeks. "I thought you were dead," he said between kisses. "I thought I'd lost you forever."

"I escaped. I found—my sister! She found me. She saved me! I was so worried, Roman. Is my dad—"

"Tresa!" Jeff jumped down the last several rungs of the ladder and ran for her. He caught her in a hug that healed all the pieces of her broken soul, all the wounds, all the tears in her heart. "We looked for days. There was no sign—I didn't know where to keep looking. I thought I'd failed you."

"Never, Dad. Never. Phoenyx is alive! She found me!"

His face was torn between pure joy and utter disbelief. "Phoenyx...?"

"She's alive. She goes by Nyx now, and she's here. I have to go back and get—"

"Py!" Roman shouted. "Get down. Everybody back in the building!" He grabbed Tresa, hauling her with him. She struggled to see over her shoulder.

It was Nyx. When Cole had said Tresa needed to see her fly, he hadn't been kidding. It was beautiful, like she'd been born in the air. Powerful, so much more powerful than the other Pys. She rocketed around the buildings, her wings shimmering in the darkness and her hair brilliant against the night sky.

"Wait! That's—that's my sister! It's okay!" Tresa dug in her heels, pulling Roman to a stop next to her. "She's a good Py. A *real* good Py. Not some random Py I picked up and brought home." She grinned lopsidedly at Roman.

He could only gape at Nyx as she hit the ground in front of them, so hard it cracked the broken asphalt even more. She straightened, looking for all the world like a terrifying, beautiful, deadly creature that Tresa knew her to be.

Until her eyes landed on Jeff. "Daddy?"

Chapter Thirty-Four

Tresa had thought Roman would be angry at her for bringing another hybrid back to their new home. He could see it in her face when she'd met his eyes after Nyx had shown up. But he had Tresa back. He'd thought he'd lost her, that he'd never see her again, and it took everything in him to keep going.

Now, she was in his arms, watching Nyx and Cole explain everything they'd been through to the rest of the tribe, and all he could think was that she could have brought a whole herd of hybrid Pys back—and Garce, too, if she wanted, and he would have only been grateful that she was with them.

But to see her face. It was like someone had taken away all the pain she carried on her shoulders, all the weight. She smiled so much more than before — and she'd smiled a lot before. She giggled, and she teased Cole and admired Enika's ax.

It was the same with their father. The darkness, the hopelessness, the solemnity in his eyes was gone. Hope replaced them. Hope for the future.

It was a good hope since Nyx seemed to be pretty damn undefeatable. Roman was 6'2" and she was barely shorter than him, maybe by a quarter of an inch, if that. Her wings took some getting used to, though. They were massive and knocked people over and towered way over her head. She looked...formidable.

Maybe she was, but Tresa had the indomitable spirit. She protected them without Nyx's wings, without her blood balls, with nothing but claws and a fierce loyalty. She was small and fast and braver than anyone he had ever met.

And he had her back.

She was different, though. Less black now, more blue. He hadn't asked her about it, hadn't asked what she'd endured. She would tell him when she was ready and until then, he was content to have her curled against his chest, so he could feel her heartbeat and knew she was alive.

Those few days without her had been hell. So dark he didn't think he'd find his way through. Kylie had tried to be brave for him, Michelle had been strong, but Roman...he wasn't brave or strong. He'd been lost.

He'd given up.

It was why he hadn't let anyone in after his parents died. Why he hadn't let anyone get close. But Tresa had slipped past his demons and his walls somehow and even though he knew the pain of losing her, it was worth it. Those few weeks of loving her made any pain worth it.

But he had her back.

The pain was a memory.

"So there's a Py ship not far from here. We're going to take it down, drive the Pys out and hopefully rid this area of them for good. If anyone is willing to help, we'll take it, but no one is required," Cole said. "We're not drafting an army."

"I'll help," Tresa spoke up at once, as Roman had known she would.

"Me too." He smiled down at her and her dark eyes sparkled.

"Look at you," she said quietly. "You went from just trying to keep these people alive to jumping on the danger bandwagon. My, how things have changed."

"Well I can't very well sit at home and wait for my little alien hunting badass to come back, can I?"

Tresa beamed at him.

Many, many others decided to join, too. Roman was moved. He knew they loved Tresa. He knew they feared him. But this went above all that. Risking their lives to drive the aliens out. They were *strong*. Much stronger than he'd ever given them credit for.

The Strange Ones did not volunteer.

Huge surprise.

"We'll leave at first light, but we've got to find another truck or SUV. It's too far for all of you to walk in a day," Cole said.

John snorted. "If it were that easy to find gas and a working vehicle, we would have done it years ago."

Cole nodded. "Yeah. True. But I've got gas and a running truck. We can jump a car. We've just got to find a good candidate. And have some willing guards to hold off the Garce. They're thick in this area."

"Traders," Tresa growled. "I can be a willing guard."

Enika hefted her ax. "Me too."

Kylie watched her with interest before pulling her daggers out. "Me too."

"What?" Roman asked, sitting up and nearly dislodging Tresa. "No. You don't have magic alien powers."

Kylie raised her chin. "No. But I have daggers. Enika has an ax."

"And magic alien powers," Roman argued.

"But she was just a human with an ax for a very long time," Nyx said softly. "And very, very dangerous."

Enika grinned wickedly. "Ready?"

Roman stood, pulling Tresa with him. "I'll help you look for a car. My dad and I worked on cars growing up. I'm not sure how much help I'll be, but..."

"Thanks." Cole nodded to him.

Jeff, of course, came with his monstrous gun.

Surprisingly—or suspiciously— enough, Kevin and Roanna came, too. They'd never volunteered for any of these missions before and usually stayed to themselves in the compound. But Cole needed eyes to help protect and search for cars, so Roman didn't complain.

He followed Tresa's flying sister and her band of merry travelers outside. Cole was just taller than he was, but a few years older and Enika was small and fast. Kylie took to her right away, comparing dagger blades to ax blades and discussing — at length — the pros and cons of each.

"Look for one with doors shut, minimum damage and the less rust the better," Cole directed. "Also, check the tires. The summer heat will probably have ruined most of them." They split up, wandering through the parking lot looking for SUVs big enough to carry all those who volunteered to go on what Roman really hoped wouldn't be a suicide mission.

But if they could do it. If they could pull it off...it would change everything.

"How many ships have you guys taken out?" Kylie asked Enika, who was just a few cars over from Cole, wandering up and down the aisles, inspecting the tires of the cars she passed.

"Five or six. Nyx left us for a while and went hunting with The Nine while we helped our friend stabilize his compound. Then she came back for a while and we had word that Rayanna had been seen down this way, so we went after her. We took out the ships as we found them."

"Wow. And you've never failed?"

Enika laughed lightly. "Trust me, failure means death. We wouldn't be here if we had. It's been close a few times. When we attacked the ship near our home, we grossly overestimated how many Pys were in each ship and brought a whole bunch of Garce with us. Nyx almost died. It was a mess. We're smoother now."

"I see. So we won't be doing the Garce thing this time?"

Enika shook her head. "There are only a few Pys in each ship. And where Tresa's been killing them left and right, this ship probably won't be fully stocked. Do you have any idea how many Tresa has fought?"

Roman did some quick calculations in his head. There had been so many attacks by Garce and Pys lately..."There were the two that came into the building that first time," Kylie started, apparently doing the same thing he was.

"And then the two the next night," Roman added.

"And the three that attacked in the street. But she only killed one."

"I always knew she'd grow up to be tougher than everyone else," Enika grinned before she went back to counting. "Nyx killed three in the furniture store," Enika murmured. "That doesn't leave many in the ship." Brightening, she smiled. "This should be a piece of —"

"Don't finish that sentence," Nyx said, landing next to them. "Do *not* finish that sentence."

She flew as silently as Tresa walked. Roman hadn't even heard her coming.

"It's kinda disconcerting that you fly," he said. "And so silently. We need to hang a bell on your neck. And Tresa's, too."

Tresa was off killing things. He could hear the Garce scream.

"She's pretty fearless." Nyx beamed. When she was happy, her tattoos went lighter and sparked more, her wings fluttered in little beats. It was impossible to hide her moods with those giant wings. "She always has been, but wow. I mean, I can't even with her."

"You have no idea," Kylie said proudly. "She zipped through the shadows of a building and dove out twenty stories up just to take out a Py in the air. It was mind-blowing. And terrifying."

"What do you mean, zipped through the shadows?" Enika asked. Nyx tipped her head, listening with interest and her silky black and blue curls tumbled across her shoulder. So much like Tresa.

"Like the Garce do," Kylie explained. "But she actually has a brain and uses it to her advantage. She grabs onto one shadow and comes out in another. It's cool. Kinda scary, especially when she comes out right next to you. But cool."

Nyx grinned. "She hasn't changed much, then. She climbed a tree to save a cat once. Way too high, I was trying to call the fire department, cat scrambled back down and saved itself and she just..." Nyx shook her head with a rueful smile. "She just jumped."

"So she's been scaring you longer than she's been scaring me. That's...not comforting," Roman said.

Nyx laughed and rose back into the air, big wings pumping effortlessly. "I think I'll go watch her in action. She sure doesn't need my help."

"Hey Cole," Jeff called and Roman turned toward him. "I think I got something. Wanna check it out?"

Cole jogged over and Roman, Enika and Kylie followed him. "Looks promising," Cole said. "Let's see if it will start up with some fresh fuel in the tank."

Roman searched for keys while Cole and Jeff worked on the gas tank. "No keys in the ignition," he muttered. "That would have been ni—"

"Stand against the car with your hands behind your head. Don't make this difficult."

Roman froze.

"Are you kidding me, Kevin? You're seriously doing this? Knowing what you know?" Kylie yelled.

"Now, Kylie. Get down and no one gets hurt."

"Until when, Roanna? Until you feed us to the Garce or turn us over to the Pys? That'll hurt, don't you think?" Kylie responded.

Roman felt the barrel of the gun in his side. "Get out, Roman."

He slid out of the big SUV, glaring down at Kevin. "We saved your life, Kevin. Many times. And you're running to the traders?"

Kevin shrugged. "They *have* a life. They don't run from the Pys, they make the Garce do whatever they want. They're not always afraid of death. They're at the top of the food chain."

"Where are they?"

"At the northwest side of the city. Did you really not realize that? When the Garce have been gathered there for days?"

"And the Pys?" Roman growled through his teeth. He joined the others at the side of the SUV. Jeff looked angry. Cole and Enika didn't appear to be overly concerned with anything, and Kylie looked like she might rip their heads off with her bare hands.

"They came. Your stupid little girlfriend scared them all off."

"She didn't scare them off, she *killed* them," Kylie snarled. "And you know what she'll do to you."

"By the time they get back, we'll be gone. Let's move."

Not far in the distance, there were four men, standing with guns trained on Roman and his team. "You've met Tresa, Kevin. You know she can track us."

"She can track Garce and she can track Pys. She can't track humans."

Enika snickered.

"Something funny, stranger?" Kevin nudged her with the barrel of a gun.

"Nyx can fly, dumbass," Cole said. "She can see us from the air no matter where you go. And if you'd listened to any of her stories you'd realize she will find us no matter where we go."

"Besides the fact that Nyx is right behind you."

Roman smiled. He knew she'd come, knew she'd find them. Kevin whirled, but it was too late. Nyx floated easily in the air and Tresa stood right behind him, in and out of the shadows so even when he pulled off a shot, he was too slow. She grabbed the gun and tossed it to Jeff, who quickly pointed it at Roanna.

The men in the distance started firing. Roman shoved Kylie back, away from the bullets and scrambled after her under a car.

Tresa zipped into a shadow and was gone just as Nyx landed so hard behind them that the asphalt cracked, her wings huge and a blood ball spinning in her hand. "I have a friend named Keven. You're not at all like him."

Kevin lunged at her, but she was too fast. He was dead on the ground before he made it two steps. Roanna screamed and started to run, but Tresa had already made it to the other traders. They tried to fight her off, bullets flying everywhere, but like her sister, she moved too fast. And in seconds, Nyx was flying after her.

Roanna ran right toward them. Even after she realized that Tresa and Nyx were both there, she kept running several steps. She finally skidded to a halt, but too late. A stray bullet hit her in the head and she fell.

Almost as soon as it began, it was over. Tresa came back through the shadows and Nyx shot through the skies and landed back by the car. "Did you get it started?" she asked.

"No keys," Roman said as he approached.

"Not a problem," Cole said. "I got this." He climbed under the dashboard, popped off the panel and started messing with the wires.

"I'm wondering how and why you know how to do that," Jeff drawled as he leaned against the door, watching Cole work.

Cole grinned over at him. "For completely honest purposes. Of course."

"How many cars have you started since the end of the world?" Kylie asked, peering around Jeff.

"My fair share. The truck is actually Nyx's. She just can't drive it."

"Wings don't fit behind the driver's seat." Nyx scowled.

There was a spark and a pop and the SUV rumbled to life. It didn't sound happy about it, more like a begrudging grumble.

But it was alive.

"Got it! Let's move!"

Chapter Thirty-Five

Nyx landed in front of them. Tresa wasn't sure she would ever get used to the fact that her sister had wings, but having her own alien DNA did make it easier to accept.

They'd been driving for hours. Further south than Tresa had ever been, and the ship was apparently nearby. She could tell because even though the blood craving had chilled out since the Pys did whatever they had to save her, it was still there. An ache in the back of her throat, and it got stronger by the mile.

"What's the plan?" Roman asked.

Tresa smiled fondly at him. "He really likes plans."

"Perfect, because I've got one," Nyx said enthusiastically. "Okay, here's the plan. We've got a bomb. It's huge, Keven-approved," she winked at Cole, "and pretty heavy. It will take two people to carry it in. Enika and I will fight off the Pys that come, and then we get out of the ship before the bomb goes off. Luckily, we just have to attach it to the core of the ship." She bent, picked up a dry stick, and drew a shape into the red sand. "Here's the ship. The door is usually right around here. Only Enika and I can open it. Since it will be after the sun comes up, no Pys will come out to fight us, but they'll be waiting when that door opens. We'll go in and engage them, try to distract them while two of you take the bomb inside."

"Why two of us?" Kylie asked, leaning forward to study the drawing.

"It's really heavy. I can lift it, but I have freakish strength," Nyx said with a lopsided grin.

"So does Tresa." Kylie grinned over at her. "She's pretty handy to have around."

Nyx glanced at her sister and gnawed on her lip. "I would rather Tresa not go in alone —"

"She won't be alone. I'll go in with her." Roman leaned his shoulder against the SUV, the look on his face clearly saying there would be no argument.

"I'll be with her, too," Cole said. "I've worked with these bombs before."

"I'll go in with Nyx," Jeff said quietly. "Can't kill them, but I can certainly hold them off." He patted the big gun in his hand.

"Dad," Nyx started but he cut her off.

"My girls aren't going in without me, Nyx."

Michelle smiled.

"Okay." Tresa bounced nervously on her toes. "We can do this."

"What do the rest of us do?" Angie asked.

"I'm glad you asked." Nyx nodded. "You'll keep the Garce at bay and help us get out of there when we're done. Then we drive like crazy away from the bomb. It's not huge, but enough to make a fire that will drive the Pys out. Any other questions?"

"Keep the Garce at bay," Kylie murmured. "Sure. No problem."

Tresa gave her an encouraging smile.

There seemed to be no more questions, nothing they hadn't discussed over and over already on the drive there.

"Okay. I think we've got about twenty minutes until the ship will be in sight. Then we'll move fast as soon as the sun has risen." She glanced worriedly at the eastern sky where the first rays were fighting their way over the horizon.

"Time for the suit," Enika said.

"Time for the suit," Nyx nodded.

"Everybody else, check weapons, make sure things are loaded that need to be loaded. Tres, Roman, come with me." Cole motioned to them while everyone else disappeared, checking their weapons and muttering about the impossibility of keeping the Garce at bay.

But they would do it. Tresa knew they would.

She followed Cole to the back of the truck, where he pulled a blue tarp back from the side. Tresa hadn't noticed it before, but that was probably because Nyx's huge wing had hidden it completely.

Her sister was sharing her riding space with several homemade, very large bombs.

"Where did you get these?" Roman breathed. His hand found hers and he squeezed her fingers.

"Keven. Tres will have to explain about him sometime. He's..."

"He was ready for the zombie apocalypse way before zombies were even a thing," Tresa finished for Cole.

Roman nodded slowly. "I see."

He didn't see. It was impossible to understand Keven without actually meeting Keven.

"So, this is where we'll light the ignition. I have a working lighter in the truck—" Cole pointed out different parts of the bomb, but Tresa cut him off.

"No need." Tresa pulled the Py blood forward and her fingers curved into fiery claws. "I got the fire part down."

"Nice," Cole said approvingly. It wasn't a reaction she'd gotten from anybody else with that little trick. Him dating her alien hybrid sister was handy.

"Let's load up," Nyx called. She was dressed in what could only be called a superhero uniform. Costume. Whatever. It was made of shimmering fabric that Tresa would guess blocked out the sun but still allowed her to fly, complete with dark tinted goggles that guarded her eyes.

"That will protect you?" Tresa asked, running her fingers over the fabric. It was like nothing she'd felt before.

"To an extent. Long enough for me to get out of the ship and into the truck before the sun kills me. Enika made it."

"I'm awesome." Enika grinned.

"You are awesome. This is incredible," Tresa agreed.

"This is version six. The first five...weren't the greatest." Enika winked and Nyx sighed.

"Let's go. I'd like to get there right after dawn." Nyx strode away and Tresa watched her go.

Her sister was a superhero.

A flying superhero.

"She's tough," Enika said quietly. "So are you. Bravest little sister ever. And I know. I am a little sister. Nyx protected our compound on her own for a long time, but she *flies* and throws her attacks. You? You fought off everything these aliens threw at you from the ground. You held your own and took theirs, too." She squeezed Tresa's shoulders. "You got this."

Tresa sucked in a breath. "Yeah. Okay. I do got this."

Enika laughed lightly and swung her ax up onto her shoulders.

"I like her," Kylie said as Tresa climbed back into the SUV. "She's feisty. And carries an ax." She twirled her daggers across her knuckles with a devilish grin.

Roman's grip was tight on the steering wheel as he followed Cole's truck through the twilight. "You okay?" she asked softly.

He looked over, one hand releasing its death grip to take hers. He brought her knuckles to his lips. "Yeah."

He was scared though. She could feel it, feel it from all of them. Even Enika and Cole, who had done this several times already, radiated fear.

Nyx did, too. Fear, worry, self-doubt. If she was still the same Phoenyx Tresa remembered, then Tresa knew the fear and worry weren't for herself, but for everyone else, and the self-doubt was because she was afraid she couldn't keep them all alive.

Tresa understood.

The ship was nestled against the desert hills, its tip towering up into the sky. The Garce ship had been as big as a motel, maybe. This was as big as a skyscraper.

She swallowed hard.

Tall, silver, huge. There were no windows, no doors that she could see. No way of getting in or out. Was their plan doomed to fail before it started?

Nyx dropped to the ground and climbed into the truck in front of them as the sun rose, tucking her wings around her. She waved at Tresa and pulled a face and if Tresa hadn't known her so well, she would have thought this whole mission was no big deal.

But it was.

They wound their way through the dirt roads, long-since abandoned and covered with baby cactus and sagebrush. It explained why Cole had a huge jacked up truck when fuel was so scarce, and why he'd wanted such a big SUV.

They stopped close, very close. Tresa could feel the Py blood already drawing her in, and the Garce weren't far off, either, drawn by the sound of their cars. It was a dangerous position for all of them.

"They can't see us coming, can they? There are no windows," Kylie whispered like her voice could possibly be louder than the roar of the engines.

"They know," Enika said. "It's okay, though. It's part of the plan."

"Should I—should I take care of some of those Garce first?" Tresa scrambled out of the SUV, eyes wide and breathing way too fast. She couldn't remember the last time she'd been so scared.

But she could do this. She was strong, like her sister. Like her dad. She could borrow their bravery if she had to.

She could do this.

"We've got them," Jessi said. "We'll hold them off until you get back."

Angie and Michelle both nodded. Kylie twirled her daggers and grinned dangerously.

Her dad, Angie, Michelle, Kylie. John, Jessi, Francheska, Cali Jewel and Chris Ann, Brittany. Amanda, Sairaika, Tracy, Kira, Shannon.

Her warriors.

They were fierce. They could keep the Garce at bay.

"Oh," Nyx said. "I'm so stupid. I almost forgot. Here," she handed Angie a large crate. "These will help."

"What is this?" Michelle cracked open the lid. The crate was full of ammo. They'd brought their own, everything they had.

"This is special," Nyx said. "These bullets are filled with Py blood. They explode on impact and kill the Garce from the inside out."

"You almost *forgot* that? That's kind of a game changer!" Francheska exclaimed.

"Yeah. Sorry. We used to use arrows but very few people can actually shoot a bow. This took a lot more work but they're also more effective."

"Tresa had that same idea when the Pys attacked, remember?" Kylie asked excitedly. "We just didn't know what to do with it!"

"Smart, little sister." Nyx patted Tresa on the head like she was small and adorable and not about to blow up an alien spaceship.

"Ready?" Cole asked as everyone else scrambled to unload weapons Cole had just told them to load a half hour ago.

"Ready," Tresa whispered. "Almost." She grabbed Roman's hand and pulled him away from the chaos. She knew they were tight on time. She knew the Garce were circling and yeah, that was a crate of ammo but it wasn't huge.

Still, this was important.

She turned toward him and wished she had time to search for the perfect words, but she'd been searching since she'd been taken from the Pys and nothing she thought up was good enough. "I love you," she said simply. "You told me you loved me, and I didn't get the chance to say it back. But I do, Roman. Your strength, your loyalty. Your kindness. And I had to tell you now because if we don't make it out of this—"

He cupped her face in his hands and kissed her, hard and long and everything she wanted to tell him was in that kiss. She wrapped her arms tight around his neck, holding him close, trying to memorize the feel of him, the smell of him, his touch and his taste.

Just in case.

"I love you, too, Tres. But we'll make it out of this. You'll have forever after this to tell me you love me as many times as you want." He winked at her and put on a brave face, somehow forgetting that she could feel what he felt. Fear, dread. And the tiniest sliver of hope.

"Let's move people," Enika yelled. "The sun's up!"

"Tresa, how strong are you, exactly?" Cole asked as she came back around the end of the truck.

She smiled.

Nyx shot out of the truck and swooped low toward the ground, rocketing for the ship.

It was time to move.

Enika went behind her, blindingly fast, and just as Nyx landed hard on the ground and her hands slid along the ship's smooth side, Cole handed Tresa the bomb.

She'd never carried a bomb before. She didn't even particularly like her dad's giant gun. But she hefted it to her chest and they ran after her sister.

The door slid open just as Tresa got close.

Behind her, the first shots fired and the Garce howled.

"What are you?" the Pys asked, voices soft and soothing even as they were laced with fear.

"I'm one of your experiments gone wrong," Nyx said, her voice just as lyrical. It drew Tresa toward it even as she struggled with the craving of the Py blood.

So close.

More shots fired, and in the space of those seconds, Nyx and Enika darted inside. Tresa heard the Pys scream, but she had no idea how many aliens were waiting inside. Cole grabbed her arm, helping her up over the lip and into the ship, yelling in her ear as Roman held her other arm, steadying her. Steadying the bomb.

Nyx and Enika fought with a vengeance, holding the three Pys off, but a blood ball still snaked through, just missing Cole. He stepped back, watched it pass, and then pulled Tresa forward. "Keep moving."

"They can't hold them off. Not alone. I have to help them," she said, straining to see her sister over her shoulder.

Kylie had come in after them.

Her daggers shot end over end, embedded in the Py's throat, and as she screamed, the one next to her did, as well. They were connected, and Tresa had no idea why.

Roman swore. "Kylie!"

She was in so much trouble if they made it out of this alive.

"Tres, we've got the bomb. Go help," Cole said, and it took both of them to carry its weight onward.

That was a big bomb.

"That's not in the plan!" Her voice was too shrill, even in her own ears.

"It's okay. We've got this. You do best when you improvise," Roman said, somehow managing to wink in the midst of the death and destruction.

"Okay. Okay."

They were gone, racing with the bomb away from her and she had to turn her back on them and try to help her sister.

It was nearly impossible.

There were very few shadows here, and they were high and not anywhere near the Pys. She'd have to free fall and hope she landed on a Py and not the hard metal floors at the bottom. And also hope she didn't get hit by an errant blood ball.

Sucking in a breath, gathering courage and telling herself she'd done this before and it was no big deal, she slid backward, into the shadows.

It took her longer now, to navigate the darkness. She guessed it was because of whatever the Pys did to save her, but she wasn't happy about it.

Well, she was happy to be alive. So there was that.

Tresa burst out of the shadow and tumbled through the air, pulling her alien DNA to the forefront, turning her hands into fiery claws as she fell. Errant blood balls blew toward her and she twisted and turned in mid-air to avoid them, toppling too fast with no shadows to grab. She heard her sister scream, and out of the corner of her eye she saw Nyx fighting to get through the Pys to her, but they were too busy trying to kill her.

Instead, Nyx fought them back, maneuvering them without their knowing she maneuvered, attack after attack until they were where she wanted them.

Right under Tresa.

She landed hard, knocking the Py out of the air. They tumbled end over end the last several feet and hit the ground hard. The breath was knocked from Tresa's lungs, but she shoved herself to her feet and attacked.

More Pys flew into the corridor, much higher than the first several. Nyx went after them, and Enika fought the one on the ground. The one who must have been connected to the Py Tresa took out because she screamed and writhed as blood bathed her throat long before Enika got to her. And finished her.

"Two down!" Enika yelled.

Outside, the sound of bullets, constant and angry, never faltered. Their warriors held the Garce at bay.

"Five more," Tresa breathed.

Two more showed up.

They didn't have to kill them all. They just had to hold them off and distract them until Cole and Roman made it back.

No problem.

No problem at all.

"Tresa! A little help up here!" Nyx yelled.

Tresa's lips turned up and she jumped into another shadow.

Chapter Thirty-Six

Cole knew his way around the ship. Apparently, the Pys weren't big on individuality, and each ship was the same layout. Same number of Pys, same sterile metal.

Roman's tired fingers slid dangerously, the bomb tipping sideways, and he fought to recover it. "Almost there," Cole breathed. "See that door up there?"

The door. Yeah, Roman could see the door. It was at least ten feet up and there was no ladder or stairs to get there. Why would there be? The Pys had wings. They had no use for stairs and ladders. Also, the 'door' was just a hole in the glass wall. No handles, no actual door to swing open and shut.

Roman saved his breath, though. Cole had done this before. He had to have a plan.

They hurried as fast as the heavy bomb would let them, groaning under the weight. Roman's hands had passed burning in pain and now seemed to be igniting with agony.

Keep going. Keep going. Don't drop that bomb.

It was Tresa's voice in his head. Always, Tresa's voice. It gave him strength, and he hefted the bomb higher and moved faster, Cole matching his steps.

"Set it here. Carefully." Cole dropped to his knees and Roman followed him, sliding the bomb out of their hands onto the floor. "Picking it up is going to suck, by the way."

Roman didn't respond as Cole dug through his bag and found a heavy chain. The bomb was already wrapped in what Roman was only now realizing were thick metal cables, presumably for attaching the chain to so they could haul it up. Cole threw the chain onto the deck above, then dodged out of the way when it slid back down and nearly hit him in the head.

"Sometimes it takes a couple tries," Cole muttered as he threw the chain again.

"What exactly are you trying to do?" Roman turned in a slow circle, watching for Pys from every direction. Surely, they had to realize what the humans were doing. What the humans had done to so many of their other ships.

"Nyx's team will keep them away from us," Cole said instead of answering his question. "There's a latch up there that the ship's mechanic hooks herself to when they fly so she doesn't get thrown all over. I'm trying to catch it on that."

"Hurry up," Roman murmured and Cole shot him an annoyed glare as he heaved the chain upward again.

Roman dove out of the way as the chain fell sideways, nearly taking his head off. Just as he did, a blood ball flew past where he'd been standing seconds before.

The Py didn't make a sound. She didn't try to talk them into giving up or whisper sweet nothings about eternal life. Her face was contorted with rage, eyes blood red and teeth long and sharp. She hurled another blood ball at them and just missed Cole as he darted out of the way.

Roman ripped his gun from the holster at his shoulder and started firing. It wouldn't kill her, but it would definitely hurt.

If he could hit her.

Trusting him too completely, Cole turned away from the Py and threw the chain again, swearing when it tumbled back down toward them. Roman kept shooting — every time she raised her hand, he shot it back down.

But he'd have to reload soon.

Once again, Cole threw the chain. Roman heard it clink and thought Cole had finally done caught it on the latch, so he focused on keeping the Py from throwing any more blood balls, and didn't see the chain coming.

It slammed into his head and he felt the skull crack, the skin tear, and for a few precious seconds, the world went black. The gun slipped from his grip and in those seconds, the Py raised a blood ball and sent it flying.

"Roman, get up!" Cole yelled. He forced his eyes open even as the world tipped sideways dangerously and heard the gun firing again. "Stay with me, Roman!"

He didn't dare touch his head. He knew how much blood he was losing—could feel it soaking his hair and the back of his neck. Instead, he pushed himself to his feet and reached for the chain, now covered in his blood.

He couldn't throw it. The motion nearly sent him toppling over and he had to catch himself on the wall. Cole monitored his progress out of the corner of his eye, yelling, "Can you shoot?"

"Yeah," Roman said, but the word slurred coming out of his mouth. "Yeah, I can shoot."

He was pretty sure he couldn't shoot.

Cole tossed him the gun and Roman traded it for the chain. "Don't hit me this time," he growled.

Cole didn't respond, throwing the chain again. It missed and slid off the deck, but Roman dodged out of the way, shooting as the Py raised her hand again. He missed, the shot was wide, but she still jerked away from him, which meant she lost her blood ball.

"Come on, Cole!" Roman yelled. Or attempted to. It wasn't very loud over the ringing in his ears.

Cole bellowed and threw it one last time. Roman braced himself, trying to watch the chain and the Py at the same time, but only half the chain slid back down.

Cole had hooked it around the latch.

Cole let out a whoop and dove for the bomb, hooking the other end of the chain to the cable. Then he jumped for the free end and threw all his weight into using the latch above like a pulley system.

It moved, inch by precious inch, while Roman kept firing, praying Cole would make it before the gun ran out of ammo. Praying he wouldn't pass out from blood loss or from the injury in his head because they would both die if he did.

Praying he would make it back to Tresa.

The Py screamed in frustration as he hit her hand, mostly by accident. She darted forward, so fast his eyes couldn't follow and he stumbled back, his head spinning.

Cole dropped the bomb and dove for the gun, pulling off shot after shot, trying to drive her away. Using precious ammo.

Kylie darted underneath her, sprinting through the rain of bullets. He wanted to yell, wanted to tell her to get out of there, but he was barely still standing. Yelling was out of the question.

"Clear!" she screamed as she made it to his side.

The bullets stopped. Cole was out of ammo.

Frantically, he started to reload, and the Py smiled evilly, revealing rows and rows of razor-sharp teeth. "All out? Too bad—"

The roar of Jeff's big gun shook the ship, the sound bouncing all over the metal walls, and she was hit by the massive bullet. It sent her flying, toppling out of the air, the wound in her side spreading dark, sparkling blood across her torso.

Kylie grabbed the chain and threw her weight backward. Cole and Roman quickly reloaded as Jeff sprinted through the hallway toward them. The Py screamed for vengeance, calling for her sisters.

"Keep your eyes up," Cole said. "They'll come from above."

Roman traded Kylie places and Cole joined him, pulling the chain hand over hand, raising the bomb inch by inch. Kylie watched the skies, watched for the Py to get up, and watched their backs.

"How do we get up there?" Roman asked between pulls. His arms and shoulders burned, his hands burned, and he had a headache like he'd never experienced, but the world had stopped spinning.

For the most part.

"Normally I have Enika with me and she jumps. You'll have to climb on my shoulders and then pull Kylie up with you. Between the two of you—"

Roman didn't wait for him to finish. They tied off the chain to a latch on the floor and with Jeff and Kylie steadying him, climbed on Cole's shoulders and pulled himself up to the deck.

That was something he never thought he'd do so easily.

"See?" Kylie crowed as she clambered up Cole's back to his shoulders like a monkey. "Humans are helpful, too!"

Jeff's gun went off and she toppled sideways to the floor. "Kylie!" Roman yelled.

Somehow, in between firing his gun and dodging the blood ball the Py had thrown, Jeff dove sideways and caught her just before she hit the ground.

The man was quickly becoming Roman's hero.

"Hurry up!" Cole yelled. "We're running out of time!"

Again, Kylie climbed, this time more cautiously. Balancing precariously, she reached for Roman. He grasped her hands and pulled her up over the edge. "Now we've gotta pull this bomb up, okay? Can you do that?"

She nodded, shoving her hair out of her face. "On three?"

"One, two—" they both grabbed the hooks, bracing their feet on the smooth metal.

Not safe. Not safe at all.

"Three!" They threw themselves backward, the bomb fighting them every inch.

Kylie's feet slid. She fought to stabilize herself, fought to keep fighting, keep pulling.

Below, the big gun sounded again and seconds later, Cole's gun, too. "Heads up!"

Another Py flew in from above, dodging their shots, moving too quickly for them to stop.

Kylie screamed. It wasn't fear or panic or pain. It was pure anger, and she threw everything she had backward. Roman pulled, lifting, felt the muscles straining and tearing, and they got the bomb over the edge.

He might never be able to use his arm again, the pain was nearly unbearable, and fresh blood seeped from his head wound, but there was no time to acknowledge any of it. "Now what?"

"Open the door," Cole yelled, fired a shot, and then continued, "Push it up tight against the core and light it up then get the hell out of there!"

"Light it up?" Horror swept over Roman's soul. "Tresa was the light!"

Below, Cole swore.

"Tresa!" Kylie screamed. Her words echoed against the metal, but between the howling Pys and the fight outside the ship, she wasn't loud enough. Not by a long shot. "Tresa! I need you!"

She pushed the bomb, her feet sliding on the metal, making little headway. "Help, Roman!"

He'd been sitting there, hopeless. Apparently, Kylie didn't do hopeless.

He scrambled to his feet, trusting Cole and Jeff to keep the Pys occupied, and he turned his back on them, pushing the bomb with all his might across the deck. Through the doorway. Grateful that Pys didn't have actual doors with handles and locks. That would have made everything so much more difficult.

"Roman, your head," Kylie whimpered. "There's so much blood..."

Which he knew. The edges of his vision were getting dark. If he passed out, there was no way he'd make it out of that ship. "We've gotta find a way to light this."

Cole and Jeff were firing constantly now, shot after shot shaking the walls of the ship and the deck they stood on. Everything echoed in Roman's head, and he fought to stay conscious.

"Tresa's coming. Just give her a second," Kylie said, tearing off her flannel shirt. She pressed it against his wound, trying to tie the sleeves around his head to hold it in place.

"Incoming!" Cole yelled and instinctively, Roman shoved Kylie back, diving the other direction.

The blood ball hit the arch above the bomb, splattering burning metal all over them. Roman scrambled toward the bomb, trying to pull the fuse into the heat.

Behind him, a Py screamed.

"I told you she'd come," Kylie said.

He risked a glance over his shoulder. The Py from above was on the ground and lifeless. Tresa had taken it by surprise. The other one was on her feet, throwing blood balls as Tresa bounced from shadow to shadow, too fast for her to catch.

Too angry.

"Dad! Cole, get out of here!" Tresa yelled.

"Got it!" Kylie squealed. "It lit!"

Roman jerked his attention back to the bomb in front of them. They'd managed to get it under the molten metal, just close enough that the heat had ignited the fuse.

"Run!" he bellowed, pushing Kylie to her feet. She didn't have to be told twice, sprinting to the deck and jumping like it wasn't a ten-foot drop off the other side.

"Get her out of here!" Tresa yelled. "I got this one!"

Cole helped Kylie to her feet. She limped, but it barely slowed her. Jeff covered them, the big gun aimed at the Py circling Tresa.

Roman stood up. The room spun and he had to grab the wall to be steady on his feet.

He'd lost too much blood.

Still, he stumbled to the edge and dropped over, clinging to the deck with his fingers so he wouldn't have so far to drop. The muscles screamed in agony and refused to cooperate and slid to the ground.

Luckily, nothing broke and he didn't fall, just sort of sank to his knees because his legs wouldn't hold him.

"Roman!" Tresa yelled. He could barely see her through the haze, darting in and out like a viper, slashing at the Py before she zipped through a shadow and back out of reach. She moved too fast. The Py couldn't catch her. Not when she was already so injured.

"You," the Py panted. "We wanted you. We wanted to see what our sister created. We wanted to see how beautiful you were. We wanted to see what you could do." Her voice was almost pleading, and if Roman didn't know better, he'd think she meant every word. "We just wanted to know you."

"Get in line," he growled, pushing himself to his feet. The world tipped dangerously again, and he stumbled forward. "We all want Tresa."

His words were slurred. It didn't sound even close to as cool as he'd hoped.

"Tresa!" High-pitched, frantic. Nyx, looking for her lost sister.

"Nyx! I'm okay!" Tresa yelled back. She wasn't okay. She was burned, bleeding, and one arm hung oddly at her side, but it didn't stop her. She moved too fast, but she was fading. He focused on her, trying to keep the darkness at bay, and he wondered how many she'd killed that night. How many she'd fought with.

"The bomb, Tres! Get out of here!"

The bomb. Oh yeah. It was going to go off soon. He should have run, but his feet weren't responding. "Tresa, go," he said weakly. "Get to safety."

She just glared at him. With one last, furious effort, she threw herself backward into a shadow and disappeared.

Seconds later, she launched herself out of the shadows above, toppled through the air and landed hard on the Py. It had been at least a thirty-foot drop, but the Py had broken her fall. Tresa slashed with her claws, too fast for Roman's blurry vision to follow, and then scrambled to her feet.

She was hurt, though. He could see her—she seemed to be standing sideways — clutching at her rib and then the wall and sinking down to one knee before she forced herself back up. "Roman, we have to— we have to go—"

The bomb went off behind them. He felt the whoosh as it sucked the air toward it, felt the heat racing toward him. Heard Tresa screaming, trying to get to him, moving like lightning despite her injuries, through sheer force of will, and then he saw wings.

Huge, sparkling wings shooting through the smoke toward them.

"Please be Nyx."

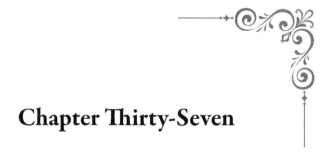

Chapter Thirty-Seven

" Tresa! Shadows, now! I've got him!"

Nyx's voice was like heaven, sliding through the smoke as Tresa's ears rang from the blast and fire enveloped everything behind them.

Behind Roman.

She could barely see him, and she knew if Nyx went into that darkness after him, she might lose them both. But she couldn't stop her. Not if there was a chance...

"Tresa! Shadows!" Nyx bellowed. "Now!"

Stumbling backward, Tresa fell into a shadow.

It was an abrupt, disconcerting change from the ship. Cool, quiet, no fire. No screaming. No Pys. Infinite darkness.

And Tresa had no idea how to find her way out.

She was exhausted. Even if she did know where she was going, she was hurt and her Garce abilities were spent. She'd used everything fighting the Pys.

Now she was lost in the dark.

She couldn't go back the way she came. It was probably incinerated by now. The blast had been roiling forward and nearly to her when she'd hid in the shadows. Going back that way would be certain death.

Maybe. She didn't even know. Maybe she could survive the blast, maybe not, but she wouldn't make it out of the ship.

She hurt. So much of her hurt, and she was lost and scared and while mere minutes ago she'd felt invincible, now she felt small and alone. She laid down on her side and curled into a ball.

"Phoenyx? I'm scared. I don't know the way out."

She knew her sister was alive. She knew she couldn't talk back to her in her head, but she didn't know what else to do. So she talked.

"Kylie, you're the best friend I could have asked for."

"Roman, I'm sorry. I'm sorry I left you with the bomb. This is all my fault. I should have stuck to the plan."

"Daddy, you're my hero. You've always been and you always will be."

Tears soaked her temple, her hair, the darkness beneath her.

"Tresa, come back to me."

It was Roman's voice, it was Nyx's voice, it was her dad's. All at once, giving her strength.

"Tresa, I need you." Kylie's voice.

"You can get back to me, Tresa. If you get lost, find your way back to me." It was Roman's voice, a memory from their training. *"Tresa, I love you."*

Slowly, almost without realizing, she made her way to her feet and stumbled through the darkness. Following the voices in her head like they could possibly lead her out.

"Tresa, I'm here. Follow my voice. Come back to me." Over and over, in each different voice, they called to her.

Later, the warriors joined them. She heard their voices, saw their faces in her mind. They were fearless. Strong. They fought their battles, they fought for her, and they didn't lose.

So many voices in her head. Nyx, pleading, scared, blaming herself for telling Tresa to hide in the shadows. She hadn't realized how they worked.

But it was the only way. She didn't have time to save them both. She had to get to Roman. Tresa would have zipped into the shadows anyway, had her mind been working properly.

Roman was angry. Angry at himself for failing her. Angry that she wasn't coming back out because anger was easier than fear.

Jeff's voice had no fear. No anger. No pain. Just perfect faith. She would find her way back to them. He believed in her with no question.

She grabbed that and held it tight. Closing her eyes, she stopped trying to find her way and just listened to the voices in her head while her feet carried her where they would.

It was the warmth that she noticed first. Her eyes flew open, but she was surrounded by darkness. Still...there was warmth. Warmth meant light and family and hope. She stumbled forward, hardly daring to breathe, and fell out of the shadow.

She was on grass. Cool, dry grass with the moon shining down on her, and absolute silence.

And then—

"Tresa?" Kylie whispered.

Tresa pushed herself up to her knees. Around her, everyone stared in shock. Nyx, dark blue eyes flooded with tears. Her dad, with that smile that said he knew it all along. Kylie, lunging for her.

But no Roman.

Within seconds, the silence erupted into chaos and Nyx and Kylie, Enika, Cole, her dad, her warriors, they enveloped her in hugs and tears and questions. "You saved me," she said over and over. "You all saved me. I was lost, and you—you saved me."

Nyx sat back, her hands on Tresa's shoulders, searching her for injuries. "We need to get you bandaged up. We need antibiotics and a wrap for her arm—I think it's broken—"

"She doesn't get infections," Jeff said. "Trust me, we'd know by now."

Nyx blinked at him and then back to Tresa. "What hurts?"

If Roman had been alive, he would have been there.

Tresa tapped her chest. "Where is he?"

Instead of more tears, instead of the pain Tresa had been expecting, Nyx smiled. "He's resting. Somebody beat the crap out of him."

"Again," Cole sighed. "I'm sorry. I thought he could fight a Py and watch for falling chain at the same time. He seemed the type."

Tresa scrambled to her feet, almost fell, was caught by many hands, and then Nyx scooped her up and flew into the air. "Wow. You're really light."

"Yeah. Bones made of shadow and stuff like that," Tresa said distractedly. How bad was it? He'd been caught in the blast. He'd pulled that bomb up onto the deck and she'd felt his pain. It was what had drawn her to them. And his head...

She couldn't breathe.

Nyx landed softly, no cracking the asphalt this time. She lowered Tresa to the ground but kept a hand around her waist, steadying her. "We need to take care of your injuries," she murmured.

Tresa nodded, but she wasn't paying attention. Her focus was the house in front of them. An old Spanish-style mansion, with a gated yard and several floors. "Where are we?"

"You came over ten miles in the shadows, Tres. That's a record, I take it? But Dad said you could do it. He said no problem. He wasn't even worried after the first three days passed."

"Three days?" Tresa gasped. "I was gone for three days?"

Nyx hesitated. "Five, actually. Ready?"

No. She wasn't ready. She didn't want to see Roman hurt. Maybe burned beyond recognition. Back before the end of the world, medical care could have saved him, but now...there was no coming back from that. He would be in so much pain. Infection would always be a threat, and there would be nothing she could do about it, and—

And it didn't matter. She had to see him.

"Yes."

Nyx pushed open the huge mahogany front door. It swung with an eerie creak straight out of a horror movie. The interior was darker still, windows boarded up, blocking out the light.

So that Nyx could live.

Tresa limped in, hugging her injured arm close. Scared of what she would find.

"How bad was it? The fight, I mean. How bad was it on our team?"

"Many were injured, Tres. But we didn't lose anyone. Your little tribe, right? Your little tribe is fierce," Nyx murmured. "This way."

She helped Tresa through the halls. It was clear their team had been staying here. Bedrolls, food, ammo, it was scattered through the rooms. Nyx half-carried her up the wide staircase and to the left, over what could only be called a bridge inside the house.

That hadn't been a thing in Utah. At least not that she'd known.

"He's in here." Nyx stopped in front of what had once been a white door and stepped back, giving Tresa an encouraging smile.

Tresa's hands shook as she turned the knob. They trembled when she pushed the door open.

"I told you to stop bothering me. I'm fine," he growled. "I need to concentrate."

Tresa froze. His room wasn't boarded up. It was bathed in moonlight. Roman stood at the window, his back toward her.

"Roman," she whispered.

He went very, very still. His hand fisted at his side, the other held against his chest in a sling, and he sucked in a breath. "Tresa?"

She swallowed and took another step. In the space of those seconds, he had whirled and crossed the room in two steps, sweeping her up against him. "Tresa! You did it! I kept calling you. You said you could hear Phoenyx so I thought—"

She hugged him, hugged him so tight her arms tingled and her heart healed. "I heard you, Roman. I heard you."

Epilogue

Roman finished loading the last of the food storage into John's truck and slammed the tailgate.

"You sure you won't come with us?" John asked. "Nyx said there's plenty of room at the compound in Utah. And that the Keven guy is really nice. You wouldn't have to yell so much."

Roman chuckled. "It sounds awesome, and I'm sure we'll come back that way eventually. But first—"

"First you're going to kill all the bad guys?" Francheska asked. Everyone else stood silently around the truck, eyes hopeful.

Their warriors.

"Tresa's not going to leave her sister, not now. And I'm not going to leave Tresa. Besides, it's kinda nice to take out Py ships. Payback." He grinned. "But you've got the crate of ammo. If the Garce come, you can kill them with Nyx's blood. Because that's not morbid at all."

"We'll miss you," Amanda said. "It won't be an apocalypse without you there yelling at it."

He laughed, remembering too well a time he'd forgotten how to do that. "I know. But they say there's a guy in the Utah compound named Blair. He yells a lot. You might like him."

"That's funny," Jessi said, "My brother's best friend's name was Blair."

"Sounds promising." Shannon grinned, "But he'll never be our Roman."

He watched as they waved and started climbing into the truck. The warriors were sticking together, going north to Utah. Some of the others had decided to go further south, and others were staying in Scottsdale. It was their home, especially since Nyx and Tresa had run the Garce out of the area.

"Wait!" A small, dark blur, made almost entirely of shadows and sparkling blue tattoos, shot out of the building and launched herself into the midst of their group. "You were going to leave without saying goodbye?"

Tresa was having a much harder time letting everyone go than he was. These people had become her family, and she loved them. She'd said she heard them calling her when she was lost in the darkness, and only love was strong enough to do that.

"She's going to miss them, huh?" Kylie asked softly, stopping next to him.

He nodded. "It's a good thing you're coming with us. Otherwise, she'd have a complete meltdown."

Kylie grinned.

Michelle and Jeff came around the side of the SUV. "We're all packed. We need to get moving before the sun comes up and Nyx is forced into the truck."

His sisters were coming with them. They had decided being alien hunters was more fun than living safely in a compound.

He was not happy about it, but what was he going to do? They were formidable.

Tresa backed away from their warriors, sniffing. "Be safe! Make good choices!"

There was a chorus of goodbyes and waving and the roar of the engine, and then they were gone.

She curled against his side and watched them go. "I'm going to miss them."

"Me too," Roman said, surprising himself. "But they'll be safe."

She nodded, leaning her head against his chest. "We're alien hunters now, huh?"

"You've always been an alien hunter, Tres. Now you just get to share it with the rest of us."

Tresa scrubbed away her tears and grinned up at him. "I suppose I can do that. It gets boring being awesome all by myself."

Roman laughed and kissed the top of her head. Because of her, he remembered how to smile.

With her, no matter what the world threw at him, he would never forget again.

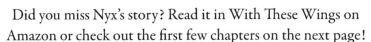

Did you miss Nyx's story? Read it in With These Wings on Amazon or check out the first few chapters on the next page!
https://goo.gl/CEc1WL

With These Wings

Prologue

A single, terrified scream tore the illusion of safety in the alley to pieces.
"Run!"

Cole jerked from the exhausted stupor he'd been in for the last several minutes. He scrambled to stand before his eyes were even fully open. "Phoenyx!" He grabbed her wrist, but she was already moving, springing from sleep to her feet.

"Enika!" They both spun toward his sister, who somehow had managed to sleep through the chaos erupting from beyond the alley where they thought would be safe. Enika stirred, her eyes fluttering, but Phoenyx had her by the hand, tugging her to her feet as they turned to escape.

Everyone in the alley screamed and ran and cried, desperate to get away. They rounded the corner, Cole in the lead, without pausing to check first.

The alien — a Garce — waited in front of him, sucking light from everything around it, drool dripping from teeth glimmering in the shadows of its mouth. Cole spun, shoving Phoenyx and Enika back into the alley. "The other way! Go, go go!"

Phoenyx was already running. Before the world had ended and the Garce had shown up, she'd been a track star. Now, her speed kept her alive.

Enika, on the other hand, did not have speed. She'd been a designer, an artist, a dreamer, but art and dreams didn't keep her alive. So Cole kept her alive instead.

He whirled away from the girls and faced the alien; although, it was more of a demon in his mind. Not solid, it seemed to be made from shadows, in the shape of a giant, evil dog. The size of a rhino, maybe, but he'd seen it swallow humans whole. Or... not swallow them. Sometimes they tore their victims apart first.

It hissed, it's red, glowing eyes the only color in an otherwise pitch-black body.

Cole swallowed hard, risking a glance over his shoulder. Phoenyx had cleared the alley. Enika was just rounding the corner.

Taking his eyes off the alien was a mistake. He could feel the shadows pulling at the light around him as he spun toward it again, but too late. It launched itself through the air, jaws open in a horrific grin. He screamed, but the scream caught in his throat, trapped behind the terror that choked him.

Phoenyx. I love you.

A thousand memories flooded through him, and time stood still while he watched them flash by. *"Cole, be nice to your sister. She's younger than you, and still learning." Cole scowled at his mom, crossing his arms over his chest. "She's only ten months younger than me. And she's a stupid girl. How come you didn't have a boy?" His mom smiled, ruffling his hair as she walked to the kitchen. "Because Heaven knew you needed a sister. You have school tomorrow. First day of second grade! Aren't you getting old?" And she'd smiled.* Birthdays, holidays, school days, all blurring together. Some memories were brighter, more vivid than others though.

"Your sister's only ten months younger than you? Dude, your sister is hot."

Cole growled, glaring at his new friend over the hood of his truck. "Step back, Keven. She's off-limits."

Keven laughed and held up his hands. "Sorry, Cole. I didn't know. Prom's next week though."

"Not a chance in h—"

His memories shifted to Phoenyx. *"Cole, right? Enika never shuts up about you. Is she here? We're supposed to work on a history project together." She tipped her head to the side, long black waves tumbling across her shoulders and down her back as she smiled at him with laughing brown eyes.* He'd fallen hard from the very first second he'd seen her, and he'd never looked back. She was the love of his life, but he'd never thought his life would be so short.

He'd lost her right after the Empyreans had landed — the aliens they'd thought were here to save them, but oh, how wrong they'd been. He'd assumed Nyx was dead. For months, he'd searched for her, almost giving up hope.

But it didn't matter, because three days ago, he'd found her. Phoenyx, his little survivor, small, sweet, and fast.

And now he was losing her again.

A lifetime of thoughts, in a mere fraction of a second.

The Garce screeched as it was jerked back, away from him. Cole's eyes flew open as a whole new horror nearly drove him to his knees.

The Empyreans. They were here.

There were two of them, light blue wings waving lazily in the darkness, beautiful faces with the ornate, sparkling tattoos twisting around their eyes. They were tall, slender, and moved with the grace of an immortal ballerina and the speed of a shooting star.

They landed on the asphalt so lightly, Cole couldn't even hear it from where he stood, but he'd seen them many times, when they were angry, land so hard they cracked the ground and sent tremors waving away from them. The Garce howled and struggled and screamed, but it couldn't escape. Where the humans had no way to fight something made of shadows, the Empyrean could grab the shadows... and suck the shadows dry.

Cole stepped back, praying they wouldn't notice him as they eagerly tore into the Garce, their delicate white fangs stretching, almost piercing the perfect lips. His feet moved silently, carrying him backward down the alley toward Phoenyx and Enika. He had to protect them. He had to get them out of here. Because the Empyreans would kill him, drain him like they did the Garce, but Phoenyx and Enika were in real danger. They would take them. The Empyreans would take them and torture them and who knew what else, because no one had ever escaped from them. He couldn't let that happen.

Once he'd made it to the shadows, he spun and sprinted around the corner of the alley, praying Phoenyx had gotten them out of there. Praying that they were safe. Praying that there weren't any more Empyreans than the two he'd left behind.

But there were.

It had Enika in its hands, long, dark blue fingernails tracing a pattern lovingly against her cheek, drawing blood. "You'll be so pretty as one of us," it purred. Already, Cole could see the tattoos forming around his sister's eyes, catching the moonlight as they sparkled like there were a thousand tiny diamonds embedded in the fine lines along her skin. Enika trembled and whimpered as she turned her face away, eyes squinched shut tight. Cole stumbled forward, looking around him for a weapon — anything. Their guns and knives did little to the Empyreans, but if he could just distract it...

"Hey! Hey, you ugly moth! Do you really want her when you could have me? She's little. And weak!" Phoenyx screamed, throwing a broken brick at the Empyrean's head. It moved so fast Cole couldn't follow; although, he would be haunted by the movement for the rest of his life. The Empyrean dropped his sister and shot across the cracked, deserted road. It snatched Phoenyx off the street and soared into the night. Enika screamed, diving for them, like her arms could possibly reach into the sky and save her best friend. And Cole was forced to turn away from Phoenyx, from his hopes and dreams and future, to save his sister. He scooped her up against his chest and ran for the safety of the rising sun.

Chapter One

Nyx scooted closer to the rocky precipice, and then just a bit further, so she could curl her toes around the edge. The wind howled, jerking at her hair and loose, black dress. She stared down, trying to estimate the drop. It was so far she couldn't see the bottom in the darkness, but then, the moon wasn't giving her much light tonight. She spread her arms wide, embracing the emptiness, and tumbled forward.

She fell so fast that the mountainside blurred around her and the scream of the wind in her ears almost, *almost,* drowned out the roar of adrenaline. The ground raced up to meet her, seemingly hungry for her blood, aching for her death.

Not today.

Her wings shot out, jerking her to a stop mid-air, her feet almost grazing the ground that had moments before been a demon about to devour her alive. She smiled to herself in the darkness, tipping her head to share her smile with the moon. She loved the moon — had always loved the moon — but even more so now because the moon didn't try to kill her like the sun did. She stretched, reaching her hands out, trying to touch the furthest edge of her wings, but they were too long. Yes, she might be a freak of nature, but she could look for silver linings with the best of them.

And wings? Definitely a silver lining.

She raised her hand in front of her face and wiggled her fingers, smiling as the fingertips turned blue and sparks of her blood — *on fire* — escaped and shot into the air. It reminded her of the Baked Alaska, when the waiters would set the alcohol on fire and pour it onto the cake. Except that her blood wasn't even remotely edible, except to the Garce. "Pretty," she murmured.

Being able to shoot blood on fire from her hands? Also a silver lining.

The blue streaks running through her black hair and the blue, sparkly tattoos that wound their way around her eyes would be pretty if they weren't so alien. So would the pale skin; although, thank everything that was good and right, her skin wasn't *blue* like the Pys'.

Another silver lining.

She stretched her wings up and down, and lifted into the sky. Faster and faster, higher and higher, until she passed the rocky mountain cliff that she'd hurled herself from minutes before. Up into the clouds, weaving in and out, feeling the condensation kiss her skin and dissolve against her cheeks, because she was hot. Always hot, apparently a side effect of having your blood on fire. Later, when she returned to the city and the tunnels, she would care that she was a freak. But right now, while she soared free through the night sky, she embraced the alien half of herself and let her wings take her places she could never have gone when she was human.

Unfortunately, she wasn't out here to soar like a bird through the salt flats of Utah. She was hunting. Or doing recon. She could never remember what the word was Keven used when he told her what to do. In a nutshell, she was looking for aliens. Because she was the only one alive who could kill them.

The Garce were like shadowy dog zombies. They weren't smart, but they were relentless and they could disappear into the shadows and out of her reach, but only if they saw her coming. They were dying out, and not just because the Empyreans — or Pys, as Nyx called them — were eating the Garce as fast as they could. No, the Garce had run out of a food supply. If Nyx had to guess, she'd estimate that there were only about 100,000 people left on the planet. She hadn't been out of what had once been the United States since before the invasion, but she remembered the news reports at the very beginning. Overpopulated cities in India, China, and Japan had been hit the hardest. Too many people with nowhere to run. And then there hadn't been enough people left to run the TV stations... or even give the cities electricity. Now, they practically lived in the dark ages.

Which suited Nyx just fine. Because if it was dark, she was very, very hard to kill.

Her eyes narrowed as she scanned the valley floor below her, running a perimeter around Ogden, what had once been one of the bigger cities in Utah. Now, as far as she knew, it was one of the few places in the state that still had human life, thanks to Keven.

And thanks to her.

There, slinking through the shadows, she finally caught sight of it. A shiver of alarm ran down her spine — while she'd been off playing chicken with the ground, the Garce had gotten within a couple miles of 25th Street, and the entrance to Keven's compound. And Garce were like mice; where there was one, there were always more coming.

Nyx tipped her wing, sliding sideways through the sky. The moon passed through her translucent blue-black wings, casting hypnotic rays of light on the ground in front of the Garce. She'd learned it from the Pys, watching them hunt while she'd been hiding from their attacks.

She shook that memory away as she almost tumbled out of the sky, forcing her mind away from the pain and the terror. The Garce froze, looking around warily before it got caught in the light. Nyx knew she had it when its red eyes dimmed in the darkness, nearly fading into its shadowy skull.

She tucked her wings in tight, a move she'd learned not from the aliens, but from watching the hawks when she'd gone camping with her dad all those years ago. She shot through the sky, and before the Garce could see her coming, she'd set her blood on fire and threw it down through the darkness, blue flames licking the air. It splashed across the Garce's skull and set the entire demon-alien on fire. When her blood hit its blood, it exploded, like always, and she had to pull up quickly to dodge the flaming bits of alien raining from the sky. Wrinkling her nose, she hung in the air, scanning the abandoned streets for more of them. And since it was still dark, she also scanned the skies, watching for the creatures that had made her the freak she was.

But the Pys had no reason to track her down. She was one of them now, so she wasn't any use to them until it was time to invade another planet. When there were too few Garce here, their master called them home, and the Pys would follow. Only then would they come after Nyx.

Or at least, that's what she hoped.

So the skies were safe. But the sun was rising, which meant she had to get back to the compound. Which meant that it had to be safe around the compound or they wouldn't survive the day. She flew down between the buildings, dodging in and out of alleys and up and down the streets. She'd almost given up when she found them — three more, hiding in the shadows, only their bright, bloodthirsty red eyes revealing them. Three blood balls, roiling with bright blue flames, shot from her hands, gathering heat as they rolled through the air. She had deadly aim, thanks to Keven, and this time she was able to get away from them without even getting alien guts in her hair.

Also a silver lining.

One last stop. She risked a look toward the east at the rising sun. Those rays could bake her within minutes, which was considerably better than the Pys, who would die an agonizing but incredibly quick death within seconds. The sun baked them alive, boiling the fire in their veins and burning them from the inside out.

She'd had it happen to her left wrist and hand. One time was all she needed to learn never to let it happen again. Because... *ouch.*

She found the house, only a few miles north of Ogden and her compound, and dropped to the ground, tucking her wings up tight and racing up the sidewalk, now reclaimed by the grass and weeds and ivy. She remembered a thousand times running up this sidewalk when it was neatly trimmed with pretty flowers and solar lights. The white vinyl fence hadn't been crushed then, and there hadn't been blood stains and deep claw marks on the neighbor's front door. Digging the spray paint out of her pocket, she risked another panicked glance at the sun and pulled the cap off. *Hurry, hurry, hurry.*

She'd done this so many times she'd lost count, and her arm could practically spray the words without her brain's help. And then she backed away, surveying her handiwork, before leaping into the sky and flying as fast as she could back to the compound. "Keven's gonna kill me," she muttered to herself as she dove under what was left of a traffic light. One last glance over her shoulder, hope nearly strangling the heart in her chest.

25th tunnels. They aren't a myth.

"DO YOU HAVE ANY IDEA what time it is?" Keven bellowed as she shoved the door to Brewskies open and raced inside, squealing in terror as the sun's rays almost caught her. The windows were boarded up to protect her because they sure as heck wouldn't have kept the Garce out. But they *did* keep the sun out. She slammed the door shut and squinted at Keven, who stood in the middle of the room with a very large gun, glaring at her.

"I'm thinking it's about sunrise?" She grinned, sliding sideways so she could get around him to the back stairs. Down into the tunnels beneath the city, where the sun couldn't get her and the Garce couldn't find them. Her wings, which were a good foot, maybe two, higher than her head, brushed the tunnel's ceiling, and she was grateful that it was fairly smooth. Once she'd tried to fly upside down in the desert, and her wings had brushed the cacti.

It hadn't ended well.

"You know that will kill you, right?" Keven asked, following her down to safety. He pulled the trap door shut above his head, ducking because he was as tall as her wings were.

"I seem to recall something about that, yes." She raised her left wrist, idly tracing the Phoenix tattoo covering the scars.

He was the only one in the tunnels, like always. There were almost 300 people in this underground city, but not one of them would be out while she was still up, wandering around. They were scared of her, because she was everything that had hurt them.

Even if she was everything that was keeping them alive.

But Keven wasn't afraid of her. He'd never told her why, but she suspected it was because they'd been friends *before.* Before the invasion, before she was taken. Before the Pys had changed her. He saw her as a weapon, but still human. Everyone else saw her as an alien, just waiting for the right time to attack.

Or something. She'd never asked, because *that* would be awkward.

"I killed four of them. One was pretty close. Three more were hiding a couple miles north of us," she said over her shoulder. The oil lamps flickered as her wings passed by them, and she instinctively shied away.

"Were there traces of any more?" Keven asked. He didn't sound particularly worried. More like... annoyed.

Nineteen going on forty. Nyx snickered to herself but straightened up when he growled from behind her. "Are you sure you can't read minds?" she asked, because this had happened before.

"Pretty sure I'd know if I could."

"Right. Of course you would. But would you *tell* me if you could?"

"Nope."

"In that case, I won't tell you if there were traces of more Garce."

She could imagine his long suffering eye roll without even turning around, and she hid a grin.

They reached the doorway with its imposing wood door and iron bars. It was at least 200 years old, but it held. She dug the key out of the little leather bag that she kept around her waist, and fitted it in the lock. Suddenly realizing how tired she was, she yawned and slumped down the stairs. "Night, Keven."

"See ya, Nyx."

She heard him lock the door behind her, not to keep her in, but to keep *them* out. The rest of the humans. Because more than once they'd tried to kill her in her sleep. Luckily for her, their guns and knives didn't do much but hurt. A lot. No, the only things that could kill her were the Garce, the sun, and being hit by a blood ball.

I really need a name for them, she mused around a yawn, tripping lightly down the stone steps. *Blood ball sounds so disgusting.*

She'd taken a little "shopping trip" to the local furniture store, dismantled a bed, and carried it all down here. Then she'd rebuilt it. More "shopping trips" to get pretty bedding and rugs and an armoire to hold all the clothes she couldn't figure out how to wear because of her wings. A vanity too, because she liked to check and make sure her skin was still white, and not blue. No lights, no lamps. She didn't need them. Now, she tugged her dress off her head and then over her wings and tossed it in the corner to wash later. Her leggings were still relatively clean, so she folded them and put them away. She pulled an oversize shirt over her head, stuffing her wings through the slits in the back, and then collapsed on her bed, breathing hard. *Changing clothes is super hard. No wonder the Pys all have magic clothes... or whatever they are. Maybe I should sneak back to their birthing pods and take another "shopping trip."* Just the thought sent her into a panic, so she struggled to her feet and found the brush sitting on the vanity. Once, her hair had been black. Maybe dark brown, depending on whether you asked her dad (who had black hair), or her mom (who had brown hair). Now, it was definitely black, except for the wide, bright blue streaks. It never got tangled, never got messy, but she brushed it anyway, then braided it because super thick, super long alien hair liked to get in her face at the worst possible moments. Finally, Nyx dug for the chain around her neck, drawing the small Phoenix charm to her lips.

Good night, Cole.

About the Author

Wendy Knight is an award-winning, USA Today Bestselling author. She was born and raised in Utah by a wonderful family who spoiled her rotten because she was the baby. Now she spends her time driving her husband crazy with her many eccentricities (no water after five, terror when faced with a live phone call...). She also enjoys chasing her three adorable kids, playing tennis, watching football, reading, and hiking. Camping is also big: her family is slowly working toward a goal of seeing all the National Parks in the U.S.

You can usually find her with at least one Pepsi nearby, wearing ridiculously high heels for whatever the occasion may be. And if everything works out just right, she will also be writing.

Find her online
Website: www.wendyknightauthor.com
Blog: www.wendyknightauthor.blogspot.com
Facebook: https://www.facebook.com/AuthorWendyKnight
Twitter: https://twitter.com/wjk8099
Instagram: http://instagram.com/wendyjo99
Wattpad: http://wattpad.com/WendyKnight

Also by Wendy Knight

———— ⌒◯⌒ ————

Fate on Fire Series
Feudlings
Feudlings in Flames
Feudlings in Sight
Feudlings in Smoke
Spark of a Feudling
Riders of Paradesos Series
Warrior Beautiful
Warrior Everlasting
Warrior Innocent
The Agents Series
The Soul's Agent
The Soul's Alliance
Toil & Trouble Series
Double Double
Cauldron Bubble
Fire Burn
Toil & Trouble
The Wings Series
Before These Wings
With These Wings
Beneath These Wings
Gates of Atlantis Series
Banshee at the Gate
Stand-Alone
Shattered Assassin
Princess of the Damned

Coming Soon
Of These Wings
Goddess Lost
The Soul's Apprentice
Cauldron's Wings

Made in the USA
Middletown, DE
03 December 2022

16834488R00215